CELESTIAL ACADEMY: ESSENCE

AFTERWORLD (BOOK ONE)

OLIVIA PHAROS

SEVENTH WONDER
PRESS

CELESTIAL
ACADEMY
ESSENCE

OLIVIA PHAROS

Copyright © 2022 by Olivia Pharos

Publisher: Seventh Wonder Press

Cover: Ninth Muse Design

Editor: Belle Manuel

Maps: Folke Mueller

ISBNs:

ebook: 978-1-949920-05-5

Paperback: 978-1-949920-18-5

Hardcover: 978-1-949920-21-5

www.oliviapharos.com

oliviapharos@gmail.com

For Sanaa, Grace, Amal and Lucy. All my love and gratitude for your support and encouragement through this—and through every other journey. Here's to being together, always.

Forthwith and henceforth, there shalt be peace on earth betwixt the Army of Heaven, and the Denizens of Hell.

So shall it be.

— THE ARMISTICE ACCORDS

CELESTIAL ACADEMY

I

The angel in the three-piece suit hurtles from the clouds like a ballistic missile. Wings tucked tight against his back, he's like a bird of prey swooping down for the kill. A couple more miles per hour and he'd break the sound barrier.

Suddenly, his wings flare a blinding light as he brakes, like a race car before a collision. His brutal deceleration ends in an abrupt hover, a hundred feet above the gathering crowd.

Then he pulls out his phone and starts texting.

His great wings beat lazily against the gloomy backdrop of the winter morning sky, their pristine whiteness a cruel contrast. They make the blanketing smog feel more noxious, and downtown L.A. seem shoddier and grimier.

Not that it's much better without the comparison. This area in specific is pimpled with tacky shops, and peppered in still-demolished buildings. And it's considered among the nicer parts of town. It's downright posh compared to where I live in the Demon Zone.

I squint up at his suspended form from my strategic location between a traffic light and a bus-stop, and curse him under my breath.

C'mon, you winged bastard, I haven't got all day.

He's still texting. Must be about the deal he's about to sign. It's an information nugget I unearthed when I researched him. He's buying the best office building on the street, with its dilapidated neighbors as an almost-free bonus.

Everyone knows he beat thirty-six, far-better bids because he has wings. He may be forbidden from coercion, but he's clearly mastered the not-so-subtle art of opportunism. Nobody wants to be on the bad side of an angel. Not when he can leverage a literal army of celestial relatives.

By the time he's done rebuilding and renovating those buildings, probably for a nominal cost, too, he stands to make a few hundred million dollars in profit. Tax-free. Designated Angels pay no taxes, and —ironically—he's one of the Virtues. While the Non-Designated ones have no earthly jobs, so are exempt, too.

Yeah. It took the Army of Heaven to beat the IRS.

Next on his agenda is another takeover of a failing family-owned bus company. Any guesses why it failed?

As I already said, bastard.

Not that his aforementioned relatives are any better. Some are far worse. We mostly see the worst kind, the designation-free angels. Those have the biggest chip on their shoulders for being generic. They're the ones who've always relished patrolling our skies, and swooping down to terrorize us since the Apocalypse.

Yeah. *That* happened. But it sort of didn't stick.

It basically fizzled out, *after* it decimated swathes of the planet—with the help of a few nukes from our side. But humanity itself wasn't even the target of this war. Just its collateral damage.

It lasted three-years and ended in three hours. Talk about anti-apocalyptic. Within an hour of the ceasefire, it was announced by some spokes-angel from the Dominions sphere, Angeldom's media arm, on global live feed. At least to the areas that still had satellite transmission. That recording is now a mandatory part of kindergarten's first-day curriculum.

Among his pontifications, said angel specified human casualties at ninety-eight million, eight-hundred and fifty-nine thousand.

That ridiculously exact number aside—and their more preposterous claim to have statistics at all an hour after hostilities ended—rumor has it that over one eighth of humanity perished, making the death toll over a billion. But that still left seven billions of us.

Long story short, the Apocalypse didn't turn out to be about the End of Days.

Days are still ongoing just fine, thank you.

Okay, so not so fine. For me, they are dreary days of drudgery and degradation—but ongoing just the same.

But the world we humans knew *did* end, if not in the way we thought it would. It's now a whole new world—Afterworld—because of one tiny difference.

We now have Hell—and Heaven—on Earth.

Instead of fighting over the planet until they destroyed it and all life with it, the enemy forces signed the Armistice Accords, ending their eternal war. That was twenty years ago. To the very day, actually.

Today marks the anniversary of when they made our home theirs.

As far back as I remember, since I was dragged out of that burning building when I was three—or four—I rarely looked up at the sky without seeing one of those celestial goons soaring high above. Reminding me of our place way, way beneath them.

Not that I need reminding. Not when I belong to the species currently at the bottom of the evolutionary ladder—and I'm at its lowest rung.

I'm basically the lowest a being can get in this Afterworld.

But I doubt even the most powerful humans need reminding of the gross imbalance of power. Not in a world swarming with the creatures who crawled out of the supernatural woodwork since that literally apocalyptic battle, and we were knocked from our pedestal as the dominant species almost overnight…

Breath clogs in my throat. The angel has finished texting—and is bomb-diving straight at me.

My mouth dries, and my heart stumbles like a three-legged horse. Even when I know he's not coming after me.

Even when I'm the one who's after him.

But seeing one of these heavenly bastards up close never fails to clang my red-alert bells.

Gulping down my involuntary response, I take inventory of his details as he approaches.

Cream handkerchief arranged in his slate-grey jacket's pocket. Turquoise tie adorned in a golden clip. Matching cufflinks glinting in the gloomy December morning light. Graphite-leather briefcase, and matching polished shoes that now point downward as he prepares to land.

As his wings emanate heavenly fire, what I consider the angelic equivalent of brake lights, I see the total disregard in his intense blue eyes. As if the people filling the street below him are ants. Less than ants.

3

I get a brutal urge to be the ant that trips him. With his momentum, he'd shovel a few pounds of sidewalk with his perfect teeth.

Some say angels are immortal unless they're killed. Others say they can be injured, but never killed, that they heal and regrow anything. The demon who told me that in his drunken melancholy, said even a heart or a head. Or a dick. He whispered that last anatomy part with a mixture of abject awe and burning envy. It was news to me. I didn't know angels *had* dicks.

But even if this angel would regrow whatever he pulverizes, it would hurt. Just the prospect of seeing him with a mangled puss, and that glowing, golden blood eating through his designer suit is almost worth the consequences. Almost.

For there would be consequences. While angels don't harm humans at their whim like the rest of the Supernaturals, they regularly throw their book, so to speak, at us. These cosmic blowhards take themselves, and acts of human "misconduct" too seriously. No sense of humor, check. Mercy? Forget it.

Still, it may actually conclude my mission faster…

Down, girl. Stick to the plan. Get what you need from this divine peacock and get out of here.

Still savoring the fantasy, I position myself as he lands with a grace that puts any bird of prey to shame. No doubt showing off.

Not that he needs to. All humans within a hundred-foot radius are rushing like paparazzi around a red-carpet. They crowd each other as they record the Designated Angel sighting. I bet a good percentage are live streaming to their social media feeds. Some will already be negotiating sales to gossip sites that overflow with Supernatural World trivia. These pay pretty well for anything that feeds human obsession with Supernaturals.

Since Designated Angels are mega celebrities now, they only interact with the highest echelons of humanity. They behave as if we, the unwashed masses, don't exist. Like this haughty bastard who's striding with his wings half-spread, forcing people to scramble out of his path. It's an unspoken law that humans are not allowed to approach any angel, let alone touch them. Even by accident.

I've broken said law many times in the past year, yet my stomach still churns like a cement mixer. It's why I make sure it's empty when I go after his kind.

Adjusting my obscuring hood, I pretend to stumble in the angel's path. Gaze not targeting me, he instinctively steadies me. As if he's stopping a sack of potatoes from spilling and littering his path.

Wait for it.

One, two…

On the count of three, he jerks back as if I've stung him. And now he *is* looking at me. Or at the part of me I left exposed. My Mark.

Low on the left side of my neck, it looks as if my jugular has been slashed with a rusty knife. Which isn't far from the truth. I barely survived the ritual that branded me like a sheep, that now proclaims me Owned. Demon Owned.

To most Regulars, what we call un-Marked humans, it looks like a weird birthmark or scar. But Supernaturals know what it is the moment they see it. It's why I'm required to display it at all times.

I never do.

I'm damned to a life of slavery, but I'm *really* damned if I go around proclaiming I'm some filthy demon's possession.

The demons claim it's how the Mark protects us. That's demonshit, like everything out of their mouths. We're targeted, sometimes fatally, *because* of the Mark. Have a beef with a demon? Send them a message by taking out their "investment."

But I discovered the Mark's real power early on. Making us useless to anyone but our "Masters."

If someone tries to "acquire" me, or if I run away, this infernal-magic brand would kill me.

The first time it almost did was during my first escape attempt.

I was five. Or six.

I was half-dead when my literally-damned owner found me, as the Mark acts like some GPS, too, or what I call, DOPS—Demon-Owned Positioning System. After he had me healed, he told me he'd always bring me back. Reasonably intact like that time, or missing pieces—or even a mutilated corpse. And he'd *still* put me to work.

The Laws of Indenture governing the Mark come with a necromancy clause included.

You're my property, alive or dead, he said.

I only told him I'd run away again, because he smells like weredog shit. He put me in a two-week coma.

Pit Demons' sense of the absurd also stinks, as much as they do. They don't take human misconduct well, either.

But floggings and electrocutions didn't stop me from running away, again and again. They actually incentivized my attempts to make the

Mark finish me. At least then I'd be dead and wouldn't mind serving him.

The last time I tried, the agony alone almost did me in. The full-body burns should have. They should have been beyond any healing spell. I still don't know how I survived. I was seven. Or eight.

Then I met Sarah, and I quit this *give me liberty or give me death* schtick. I couldn't escape, even in death, and leave her behind. Having her in my life became this prison's most inescapable bars.

Want to clip any rebel's wings? Give them someone to love.

Not that I gave up on the dream of freedom. I convinced myself I'd find another way. But for twelve hellish years, I didn't.

Then one day last year, I accidentally did. And the rest is history.

Hopefully, *I* won't be. It's always a risk when I target any angel.

They're the apex predator of the Afterworld, while the Mark plants me in the bottom of its food chain. Even if angels don't prey on us in *that* way, they're what every other creature fears.

"Begone, demon-droppings!" the angel bites off, antipathy filling his heavenly eyes.

Now *that's* a new insult. And I thought I'd heard them all.

To round up our infernal luck, us Marked are reviled for it. As if we chose this.

Okay, so some do. But most of us are straight up trafficked. I'm one of those taken and sold as children.

But this feathered prick gave me a new insight into why angels loathe us. If demons disgust them, what they consider their crap does even more.

I keep finding new reasons to hate these elitist, flying pigs, don't I? Almost as many as I find for Kondar, the worm-infested dung-heap who owns my Indenture.

Good thing the abhorrence is reciprocated. This visceral reaction is what I always count on.

It's why I block his path instead of scurrying away as I scoff. "That's harsh, dude! Aren't you the sales rep or courier of the Light or whatever? Light up my day and spare some change."

"I will spare *you*, this time. I won't be so merciful if I catch you panhandling around here again."

This up close, he's almost unbearably pretty, and he does absolutely nothing for me. He even makes bile rush up my throat. Swallowing it down along with the urge to let him walk away, I grab his jacket, almost tripping him as I wished to earlier.

"Who's panhandling? Who even *says* panhandling? I represent the Marked who clean up the streets after you celestial pigeons. You owe me a contribution comparable to the size of *your* earth-melting droppings."

He stares down in stupefaction at my grimy, calloused hands as they crush his lapels. While he's too shocked to react, I flit them all over him, patting every pocket. When I reach those on his ass, he lurches away, visibly struggling to fathom how a human can accost him, and worse, frisk him.

I tsk. "Got no change, huh? Only million-dollar credit cards from the Bank of Heaven? Figures. How about a cufflink?"

His belated rumble of affront would have brought anyone else to their knees. It makes my heart slam against my ribs. But this isn't my first rodeo with his species, and I swipe for his left cufflink. He snatches his hand away as if from a slimy tentacle.

"Not feeling that charitable? Then give me something I can sell, dude. How about a feather?"

I lunge around him, as if I'd help myself to one. His stunned expression becomes almost comical. I've seen angels lash out for far less, but my being human stymies this one.

That's why I set up this scene where I'm protected by a) my species, and b) witnesses.

Still, such protection may mean nothing if I don't manage his rising anger right. I need to push him to the edge, without tipping him over it. Any uncontrolled reaction on his side would break me in half.

"C'mon, dude, it'll only sting for a sec, and I bet you'll love it. I hear many angels have a feather-plucking fetish." I advance again, and he tears out of reach. I sigh. "Celestial baby. Okay, how about a chewed gum? A used hanky? A dirty thong? Anything smeared in your angelic secretions should fetch a pretty penny on the Supernatural black market."

He finds his voice again, an ominous rumble now. "Your reckless insolence will be the end of you, human."

I wave him off in feigned boredom. "A thong it is then. Hop to that public restroom over there." I pause, as if reconsidering. "On second thought, strip right here. That should make everyone on this street rich."

His eyes suddenly become thoughtful, as if belatedly thinking I must be deranged.

Oh, no. I don't want him cool and logical. I want him hopping mad.

"You're useless, aren't you, birdie?" I grab for his belt. "I'll get it myself."

He swings his briefcase to cover his crotch like a demure damsel. "Your end may well be today, mortal!"

"Big talk, Feather Face." I toss my head towards our enraptured audience, still keeping my voice low enough for his ears only. "You can't even risk pushing me away. Now give me that thong, or I'll tell them you didn't pay for our last feather-plucking session, and just threatened to kill me to silence me. You'll be trending all over the world in minutes."

I hold his gaze, bating my breath, adrenaline pumping in my veins in agitation.

I've made sure this looks like a minor infraction to everyone. And insolent pest or not, I'm still the species his kind claims to be here on earth to protect. But from the righteous fury in his eyes, he wants to execute me on the spot, for extorting and making a spectacle out of him. I've pushed him to the brink all right.

Now to find out if I've gauged handling him right, or if this will be the time an angel punches his fist through my skull.

I shudder with relief when he finally bites off, "I don't wear underwear."

Oh, man. This is priceless. He's actually making excuses. The Designated Angels' obsession with their public image is really their one weakness.

I huff in mock-resignation. "You're worse than useless. Fine, I'll take that hanky. Blow your pretty nose like a good boy."

Without further resistance, he does just that. The moment I snatch the handkerchief from his hand, and though he looks murderous, he settles for shoving past me.

"So long, Winged Wuss," I mutter as he strides away, dusting my mortal filth from his bespoke clothes. Angels supposedly have super-natural senses, which they tune out at will. From his stiffening, he's still tuned in to me. So I add, "Oh, and, birdbrain, thanks for the wallet."

It's delicious, the way he screeches to a halt, patting himself in alarm. I can't help laughing the moment he finds his wallet, and real-izes I set him up. I can feel him struggling not to storm back and do something reckless.

As he flounces away instead, I smirk at his winged back until he disappears inside that steel-and-glass building he's acquiring. After he does, our audience disperses, resuming their scramble to their nine-to-five jobs. Regulars. The lucky brats.

Before I get down to business, I make sure everyone has dismissed me. I also can't spot any Supernaturals. Even if many Glamor themselves to look human, I can always tell them apart. Thankfully, most play to the stereotype of nocturnal creatures. Only the angels and the Fae seem diurnal.

But the Fae, either their trickster Seelie division or monstrous Unseelie one, don't make a habit of walking mortal streets or mingling in our societies. Each prefers to lounge in their courts, gleefully plotting heartless exploitations or horrific demises.

While most angels prefer working from "home," wherever that is. It's said the internet boom in the last two decades was all their doing.

But that angel is among those who prefer a hands-on approach to business, the easiest type for me to hunt down. And thanks to this little skirmish, I got what I wanted from him.

I look up, and there it is. Time to nab that baby.

Come to Mama, my pretty.

As I get all I can, I see a bus stopping in the distance. Grr. Now I have to run to catch it. I have dirty floors to sweep and dirtier books to keep in Demonica at nine sharp.

Problem is, I never run. I can't afford the effort or the calories. But since I can't afford another flogging either, I break out in an awkward sprint. It quickly becomes a lung-busting one, and I toss my hood off my head, gasping for any oxygen left in the world.

I'm half a dozen feet from the bus when it sets off.

From the driver's taunting grin, I know. He's a Select. I'm certain even before I see his piercing.

While our Marks are different as fingerprints, the Select Sign is universal. An upper, right-ear piercing proudly displaying an angelic sign.

The Select are like us Owned, only angel owned. Granted, their slavery is implied, and not lethally binding. But they're not that much better off working below minimum wage in the angels' earthly enterprises.

But not only are they proud of the most underpaid job the angels cram them in, they fanatically share their masters' hatred of us. He would have mowed me down if we were not forbidden from inflicting bodily harm on each other that requires more than a first-level healing spell. Apart from that, making each other's lives hell has become a mandatory etiquette between us.

The Select even circulate Wild-West-Wanted-like posters of us. That's how they recognize me and make my every step in this hellish city harder, whenever I'm not disguised.

Once the traffic forces the current piece-of-shit to slow down, I bang on the bus's door. I know he won't open, just need him to look at me.

When he does, I give him the finger, and shout, "Pay you back later, Select Skunk. You'll never see it coming."

The traffic moves again, and he leaves me behind with a final hate-filled glance.

Bravado expended, I stagger back to the sidewalk among enraged honks.

Once I reach the bus-stop, I bend over, gulping down shearing breaths. It takes long minutes before I'm confident I won't die. It isn't funny how out of shape I am. Not that I was ever *in* it.

What *is* wretchedly funny, though, is this pathetic civil war of ours. Here we are, insignificant human victims of the status quo, perpetuating the prejudices of those who oppress us, and victimizing one another according to their doctrines. Classic.

I guess it was always this way. The small cogs grinding each other at their operator's whims.

The only difference is that, until the Apocalypse, it was human against human. There was always hope of changing the system, of overthrowing the despot. In this Afterworld ruled by creatures from humanity's myths and nightmares, rebellion is not even an option.

Not that I'd join one if it is. I'm no revolutionary. I only ever did whatever it took to survive our life, because I couldn't change it.

Now I finally can. *If* my plan works.

Another bus approaches, and thankfully, it's not another Select at the wheel.

Thirty seconds later, I'm out of the chilly drizzle and in the last vacant seat next to some smelly dude. It's a good thing my stomach is howling like the wind in a drafty mansion. He's wolfing down something that smells like brimstone, and picking his nose while at it. At least he exudes a dumpster-fire kind of warmth that my frozen marrow is grateful for.

Smothering my nose in my hoodie, I look down at my hand and grin.

My plan is *so* going to work.

My optimism lasts only a few moments before it dissipates.

My day is just beginning and I'm already exhausted. It takes stamina to shut off the malignant whispers of doubt and dread.

But I can't listen to them. I won't.

It *will* work. I will do *anything* so it does.

My life, and Sarah's, depend on it.

2

F ive hours of hard labor later, I am watching the lunchtime rush from the corner of Beverly Hills Avenue as I count down the seconds until the hour hits one p.m.

Four, three, two...

My burner phone rings. I tap my Bluetooth earbuds at once.

"You got the goods?"

Cheesy, I know, the mobster movie lingo I make my clients say. But in this shitty life and business, I get my fun where I can.

There's no fun to be had here. Something isn't right.

The voice was *much* higher than I expected.

In our dark-web negotiation, he said he's twenty-four. If he is, then he missed puberty. Which means he isn't.

I draw the line at dealing to minors.

Not that such considerations matter in the Afterworld. Innocence and consent are concepts of the past. The human laws that protect them are regularly circumvented and disregarded. When I needed them to protect my very freedom, they were nowhere to be found.

I was taken by demons from a human facility that probably sold me to them. And here I am, discarded in a world of immortal dictators where no human morality applies anyway.

So it beats me why I care about a Regular minor willingly buying drugs. *I've* been selling my very life unwillingly, to a literal demon, since I was a child. Why should I look out for this moron, the way nobody looked out for me when I was his age?

Hell, I was *never* his age. I had to grow up overnight since I was auctioned off at four. Or five. After over sixteen years of being Demon-Owned, I don't feel twenty, or twenty-one, but a jaded fifty.

Still, no selling drugs to kids remains one of the rules I never break.

And it isn't any drug. It's my exclusive product, the one-of-a-kind *Angelescence*.

It's so powerful, its effects so overwhelming, seasoned drug users can barely handle it. Many end up injured, maimed—or dead.

Yet, even knowing its dangers, even after suffering its side-effects, they line up for more. Beg for it. And if I asked, would kill for it.

But that's what addicts do. And I'm not in the business of rehabilitation.

"You got the goods?"

His voice is even higher this time. Sheesh. He sounds about nine.

My heat rises in frustration. I'm risking Kondar's wrath for this transaction, and now have to cancel it. If he finds me missing from my second shift, I'll end up with more scars for nothing.

At least he doesn't touch my face. Not because my looks matter to him. Kondar bought me for service, not sex—and even demons don't dare renege on the terms of the Indenture. The infernal magic that binds me binds him, too. It's the only reason I'm not finishing my work then joining the poor girls who *entertain* Demonica's scum-of-the-earth clientele.

Still, no male, Regular or Supernatural, wants Scarface serving them drinks or even bussing their tables. Kondar would have loved to maim me, if he could commission me an Unmarred Glamor for working hours. But he says I wouldn't fetch its price if he sells me. I have his cheapness to thank for having an intact face.

But my back can use a break.

Sighing heavily, I end the call and start walking.

I find my client standing where I instructed. He *is* a kid. No more than twelve.

They sure keep starting earlier and earlier.

If I thought he's an errand boy, I may have reconsidered. But from our interaction, I know he's buying for himself. I don't want to think how he got 10K in cash, yet, he didn't give me addict vibes.

So. He's heard the rumor.

It's been spreading like wildfire for months now. That beside the unique, prolonged high, *Angelescence* may give its user powers.

It's a rumor to me, too. But I know where it came from. Some of my clients must have shot sparks from their eyes and fingers like Sarah did when she took it. Also from one of my very first two clients, I know others *hallucinate* having powers.

These effects are so intense, feel so real, they fuel the rabid demand for my product. That illusion of rising above their mortality, even fleetingly, is the real draw, the irresistible addiction.

I exhale again as I pick up speed. I may still get back before Kondar discovers my absence.

Once on a bus again, I pant curses under my breath, all the way to Demonica.

Not only am I going to be flogged for nothing, but losing this transaction puts a dent in my scheduled earnings. And making up for botched deals is getting damn harder by the day.

Gone are the days when I accepted all offers and the money was pouring in. I made my first six figures in three weeks, when I was charging far less, too. But my operation gained notoriety too fast, and with it, scrutiny, then pursuit.

Everyone wants their hands on *Angelescence, and* its manufacturer.

To say exposure would be catastrophic is the understatement of the Afterworld.

To guard against that, my screening process keeps getting more convoluted, as do my actual sales. This slows me down daily, and delays reaching my target amount. That increases the probability that we could wind up dead.

Whether I play it too safe or not, I might end up killing us both anyway.

* * *

The slashes down my back throb with the ferocity of a hundred solar flares.

Kondar didn't discover my absence, but he still flogged me. Over a spilled drink. Hard enough to put me out of commission for a few days.

He said he'd have some Regulars stand in for me, even when they're even worse than I am at my job. But he enjoys flogging me so much, he's okay with letting me recuperate afterward. Only so I can withstand his next abuse session.

Not that I lie in bed writhing in agony like he hopes. I always score some kind of magical treatment, then use the time off peddling more *Angelescence*.

This time, I spiked a client's drink with a love potion for it. But that enchanted salve hasn't worked yet. If it doesn't, I'll find a way to inflict equal pain on the bastard who bartered it to me. Better yet, I'll find said client an antidote. We'd see how that elf likes being eaten—literally—by his dragon-shifter crush.

My chin trembles, and air clogs in my lungs. The burning map across my back sinks through my chest and creeps up behind my eyeballs. The broken stairs I'm climbing blur through a hot, trembling veil of moisture.

Dammit. I'm not crying over a lashing. I've had far worse.

And I *never* cry.

Early on, I realized that Kondar feeds on screams and pleas. He especially craves tears. They're a delicacy to him. Since then, I've never given any to that monster.

Yet my tears now aren't ones of pain and degradation, but of dread.

As he flogged me, Kondar informed me he's acquiring two new slaves. His money's worth, not like me. He considers he got ripped off when no one else bid for me, and he got stuck paying the two hundred bucks of his opening bid.

Now he can afford to splurge after he scored that wet job for a higher demon. His new acquisitions come at a steep price since, according to him, they're *real* house- and bookkeepers. They'll replace me at Demonica.

Then I'll become disposable.

Once I am, I'll meet a grisly fate like all decommissioned Owned. He'll barter me as a hunting prey to some Fae lord, or sell me as a ritual organ donor to some coven. If he can't find a profitable enough way to dispose of me, he'll recoup his "investment" in an even worse way. I've heard of Owned selling tickets to their own gory execution by hydra or hellhounds.

Then Sarah will be alone, and she...

She nothing. I won't let any of this happen. I *won't*.

Stopping at our flimsy door with its peeling-again blue paint, what Sarah calls lapis, I drag my hand angrily across my eyes.

Can't let Sarah see my tears. She has enough worries. And I'm already her biggest one. Can't have her think I'm vulnerable, too. My impervious act is essential to any peace of mind she manages to have.

Pinning my devil-may-care expression in place, I enter our one-bedroom apartment.

Sure, it's dilapidated, but we've made the best of it. Sarah has. She has an almost magical way with colors and arrangement, and of turning junk into amazing DIY projects. I don't have an artistic, or even organized bone in my body. I barely curb my chaotic nature to keep our shared space tidy. My only contributions are following her rules, and getting her the items she can't make.

We have an unspoken agreement that I don't tell her how I get them, and that she doesn't ask.

Not that my *acquisitions* are essential. They only complement Sarah's efforts as she creates a cozy refuge out of this criminally over-priced dump.

She's made it into the one place I've ever called home.

And right now, it smells heavenly.

Er—no. Not using angel-related adjectives to describe anything good. It smells *scrumptious*. But then everything Sarah cooks always does. Me? I specialize in bland and burned. That's why we also agreed I stay away from the stove, and keep to the sink.

"Hey, Sar, I'm back!"

Silence greets my forced cheerfulness, striking me with a bolt of foreboding.

Sarah is not here. I'm certain of it. But the stove is on. She'd never leave without turning it off, unless someone forced her to…

Before a heart attack takes hold, the door bursts open and Sarah hurtles in, chin-length blonde hair semi-dry and flapping wildly around her heart-shaped face, azure eyes wide with relief. A relief I share, so overwhelmingly, my knees weaken.

Every time we walk out that door, we both fear it will be the last time we see each other. Every time we both make it home, it feels like a stay of execution.

It's no way to live.

It's the only one we got. Unless I succeed in my plan.

No. No unless involved. I *will* succeed.

I'm already halfway to doing that.

"Where have you…?"

"At Mrs. Walters'." She cuts my anxiety short, breathlessly grabbing my hand and towing me to our cramped kitchenette. "She came banging on the door and wouldn't even let me turn off the stove before dragging me to her apartment!"

I bite back a gasp of pain as I stumble in her wake. Sarah still turns after she lowers the flame to a simmer, eyes flooding with concern as she reads my condition.

I wave it away. "Just another flogging. Got a salve for it, and it's working great."

"Wen." She makes my name that soft admonition that makes me shrivel inside.

She reserves it for calling me out when I try to bullshit her. Every time she sees through me, I say she has some kind of ESP. She insists she just knows me too well.

I shrug, freezing halfway as I feel one of my welts tearing open.

My face scrunches in a rictus of pain for a moment, before I attempt to quip. "Okay, so it isn't working yet, but it will. Nothing to see here. Move along, folks."

Her eyes redden and fill before she nods, and turns away to set the table.

We've been through this regularly since we met, and it kills her that she can do nothing for me. As if all these years, before I managed to find treatments, when she stayed up all night cleaning my wounds and holding me until I slept weren't the only thing that made me survive the abuse. As if she's not the only reason I'm still alive at all.

And I will remain alive until I get her out of here, even if it kills me.

Suppressing the pain, I start to help her, again admiring how she lacquered the table to simulate mahogany. It makes the turquoises and teals of the mismatched dining set I stole pop.

"So, what was so important Edna almost made you burn dinner and the whole building? She wanted you to see her latest knitted scarf?"

Sarah shakes her head. "She wanted me to see something on TV."

My eyebrows shoot up. "The Accords Anniversary?"

For the past fifteen years, since humanity recovered enough from the devastation of the Apocalypse, each fifteenth of December witnessed major fanfare around the globe. According to the sponsors of the celebrations on every side, that day marked the dawn of an era of unprecedented peace and prosperity.

Yeah, right.

Edna Walters, our elderly neighbor who lets us watch her streaming services in return for housework, always dragged us to

17

watch the festivities with her. That is, until a couple of years ago when I put my foot down.

I sure don't want to celebrate the day when Hell and Heaven solidified their infestation of our world.

"I thought she gave up on that."

Sarah looks up after placing the trivet. "She did. That wasn't what she wanted me to see."

"Don't tell me she came to her senses and decided to watch something else tonight!"

Her lips twist sarcastically. "As if. She was watching the celebrations all right—until they were interrupted for breaking news."

"Breaking news of what?" I scoff. "Another Apocalypse?"

"No. Not yet, at least."

My heart kicks in my chest. I know Sarah better than I know myself, can always tell when she's messing around. She isn't now.

"Uh, can I take my question back? I don't want to know."

She sighs. "Yeah. You'll hear all about it everywhere in the morning anyway. So let's eat now, huh?"

I squeeze my eyes. I should heed that suggestion, eat her drool-inducing food and not inflict more grief on myself. I have enough to worry about with what I need to do afterward.

Opening my eyes, I find her watching me. I know she knows what I'll say next.

I exhale. "Since I'm not kidding either of us, tell me."

She fiddles with the cutlery around the plates before she exhales, too. "Zinimar, the King of the Eastern Demon Kingdom, and a major sponsor of the celebrations this year, was found in his Himalayan palace—dead. With him supposedly immortal, foul play is suspected. If it turns out to be the angels' doing... Well, one anchor suggested this could lead to the Accords being broken. And if this happens, the Apocalypse might resume."

3

I gape at Sarah for a long moment before I exclaim, "If the Apocalypse resumes, I'll run to the first angel I see and report Kondar and Zeral. Once he kills them, we'll be free of our Indentures!"

Sarah gapes back at me before she bursts out laughing. "Oh, Wen, it never ceases to amaze me, the way your mind works."

I wink at her. "I'll have you know this is totally logical reasoning. I don't think we'd be worse off if the Apocalypse does resume, and we only stand to gain if angels start killing off demons again."

She breathes another chuckle. "You'd be right—if we're not among the collateral damage of their showdown, like the untold millions killed during their first one."

"I *refuse* to believe even our luck can be that bad! Anyway, the Regulars' media insinuate the Accords might be broken every day. It's good for their ratings."

She nods with a sigh. "Yeah, but they always cite far-fetched or made-up, not to mention trivial reasons for it. Zinimar's death is major. If someone murdered him—and I can't imagine how he died if someone didn't—there will be massive repercussions."

"Ugh, Sar, let me savor the fantasy. The Apocalypse resumes, angels char Kondar's and Zeral's ugly asses, and we sail away from the warzones to some Pacific island and set up a scuba diving business."

"Assuming we'll find paying customers." I roll my eyes, and she rushes to add, "But I don't want Zeral dead. Can I only make the angels force her to release me?"

Shaking my head, I sigh. "You're too good, Sar. Okay, she may live. At least until she's killed for some other reason than enslaving you."

Wincing and chuckling at once at my viciousness, she raises the lid off the casserole and my salivary glands gush so hard it hurts.

"What magic have you conjured for us tonight, milady?" I moan.

"Stew in bone stock," she mumbles around an experimental taste.

"No way *that's* what I'm smelling."

She gives me a triumphant grin. "I got *spices.*"

I goggle at her. "Whoa!"

"Yeah." She replaces the lid and dashes past me. "Nature emergency call. Make sure it doesn't burn."

"You're assigning this task to the wrong person!"

"I trust you," she calls over her shoulder.

"A grossly misplaced trust," I holler back.

As she giggles and slams the bathroom door, my heart sinks at the sight of the exotic spice jar on the countertop. It looks light years beyond our budget.

According to a bylaw of the Accords, demons are forced to pay their Owned salaries. But being evil, exploitative scumbags, they manage to get away with paying way below human minimum wages. It's actually worse than slavery, since slaves at least get food and shelter. We get neither, and all that so-called salary does is disqualify us for human financial aid and food stamps.

Bottom line is, we can only afford damaged or expired food. And very little of either. It's why I started dumpster diving years ago.

When she found out, Sarah insisted on taking turns. But I wouldn't hear of her rummaging through other people's garbage. Her mistress is a stickler for cleanliness, and I'm the one used to dealing with worse than literal shit at Demonica anyway.

Being her fair, helpful self, she still tried it once—and it was a disaster. She emerged from the dumpster a mass of contusions, and spent the night scrubbing herself clean. Which was to no avail. Next day, after one whiff, Zeral hosed her down and shaved her all over, head and privates included. She let her wear nothing but disinfecting worms for a week, insisting it was long overdue. According to her, Sarah's human reek was terrible for her allergies, and she shed worse than a werewalrus. And Sarah didn't even get anything edible out of the ordeal.

But as always, she found another way to be useful. While I lamented the loss of her gorgeous hair—what she wasn't allowed to grow back beyond her jawline—and plotted to shave off the hideous growth Zeral calls a nose in payback, Sarah concocted the only soap that has ever gotten me clean from the dumpster reek and Demonica's supernatural filth. One of its ingredients is a cleaning spell she swiped from Zeral. Since Sarah never stole anything else, the demoness still blames Kondar, her ex, for the theft.

Anyway, without my dumpster derring-dos, we would have starved, since most of our measly wages finances this roof over our heads. Homelessness, and in the Demon Zones too, trumps empty stomachs any day. Spices, even the ten-dollar store variety, were among the luxuries we couldn't afford.

Then I started making loads of money selling *Angelescence*. But we couldn't be seen spending more than our wages, or looking better-fed. We had to continue living as the malnourished paupers the Owned always were. We never indulged in even discreet one-offs. We agreed every cent spent pushed our goal back. And this we really can't afford.

So why did Sarah buy that humongous jar of spices?

The moment she's out of the bathroom, I blurt out, "How much did it cost?"

She freezes mid-step. "Nothing! You think I'd spend a cent on anything so frivolous when I know what you go through to make that money?"

"If you didn't..." I stop, moan, "Oh, no, Sar. I'm the thief in this dynamic duo!"

"I didn't steal it, either," she exclaims. "Zeral gave it to me!"

I gape at her. Zeral is as big a miser as her ex. "Sar..."

She cuts off my groan, "You think I'd steal from her, when I'm still struggling not to spill the beans about that cleaning spell—five years after the fact?"

I suddenly feel like the biggest jerk in the world. Of *course* she wouldn't do anything this irresponsible.

"Ugh, sorry, Sar," I mumble. "I'm extra jumpy today..."

My apology trails off as she pats my arm on her way to the stove. "You had every right to freak out, finding that massive beauty that costs hundreds—or more—gracing our countertop."

Feeling worse at her exoneration, I shake my head. "There's no

21

excuse for thinking you'd steal it. That's something *I'd* do. You're the Spock of this team."

She turns with an uncanny imitation of his expression and voice as she says, "Jim, I have been, and shall always be, your friend."

I wheeze a laugh, and she joins me, hers unhindered by pain. We regularly watch Star Trek at Edna's. That wonderful show from bygone times when humans thought they had to go to outer space to meet new species. As if *that* is ever a good idea.

Our references to that show, and the parallels we have with Kirk and Spock, are among the brightest pin pricks in our dark lives.

Pain forces me to sober up, and I groan. "You have to stop letting me off the hook, Sar."

She throws a towel at me as she rolls her eyes. "Stop it, will ya? Don't you want to hear the story of how Zeral, the Grand Dame of Misers, gave me a few years' supply of rare spices?"

I lower myself carefully into one of the two chairs we own. "I can't even imagine. It must be epic."

"Oh, it is. It starts when she traded that jar with a Rakshasa Demon from India for a bag of fresh teenage human teeth."

We exchange a look, and another of our unspoken rules passes between us. *Don't ask, don't want to know.*

She clears her throat as she turns off the stove. "She smothered her raw goat thigh in the spices, and wolfed it down in one mouthful. I haven't seen her stretch her mouth that wide since the—*incident* with that goblin."

I huff a chuckle. "Good thing you don't have to put up with her monstrous states on a regular basis."

"Yeah, she tries her best to look ladylike. It's such a good act, that goblin thought he could get away with killing her pet iguana."

That was Kondar's revenge when she got the magical curiosity shop in the divorce. "It was serving it to her as her favorite ostrich dish that sealed his fate."

"I never saw her as frenzied as when she realized she just ate her pet." Sarah shakes her head with a shiver. "I still didn't think she'd do something like that."

"You and him both." I snicker. "I bet he didn't believe her capable of anything he couldn't counter. He kept hitting her with spells—up to the moment she chomped off his knobby head."

Sarah shudders. "I can still hear the crunching of tissue and bone."

I smile in fond reminiscence. "Yeah, it was great." Then I frown. "Though not so great that she killed him so quickly."

"Wen! Nobody deserves such an end!"

"Oh, that serial child molester deserved far, far worse. I daydream about the much worse and far more protracted ways I would have killed him."

"I agree he deserved severe punishment..."

"I would have cut off the junk he raped all these kids with. But I wouldn't have let him bleed out. I would have kept him alive, convulsing and shitting himself in agony while I cooked it and fed it to him..."

"Wen! It's not good for *you* to think such terrible thoughts!"

"It's actually the best thing for me. Such ideas are like the comfort food we never get to have."

"I'm all for anything that gives you comfort," she mumbles as she covers the pot again, looking a little green around the edges.

Another wave of guilt drenches me. "Ugh, Sar. I'm a crude moron, bringing up cooking goblin jun..." I swallow the rest as she holds back a gag.

Before I can apologize again, she shoots me an absolving smile. "You know I love your macabre humor, even if I can't keep up. But maybe not while *I'm* cooking, hmm? I did think that goblin should die, but my stomach didn't agree with the method."

"Yeah, you threw up." I grin again, unable to stop my delight at the memory. "All over his twitching carcass!"

"While *you* whooped and hugged Zeral. *While* she was still swallowing his head!"

I laugh, no longer caring that it hurts, and she does me the courtesy of chuckling with me. "What can I say? I'm a vicious product of this shitty world." Then I hear what I said and curse under my breath. "You didn't draw a good card with me, Sar. You deserve better."

She rounds on me with a scandalized glare, ladle in mid-air. "Oh, shush, you idiot. I can't even imagine a better card. You're my wild-card, and you're everything I need."

I mumble something as I clatter the cutlery around my plate. I'm very bad at receiving her pep talks and compliments. Mainly because I'm positive I don't deserve them.

Needing to change the subject, I resume our previous one. "So how did you end up with Zeral's prized spices?"

"They gave her a fiery indigestion—literally." She gives me a conspiratorial grin and I swear it triggers the salve's effects at last.

The searing in my back eases as I grin back like a doped-out fool. Those moments after pain lifts and relief floods in to douse my tortured nerves are the only times I get loopy

"She singed off her eyebrows, then set fire to her boudoir's curtains. But it was when a burp burned the ancient Egyptian papyrus she already sold for a hundred grand to ashes that she threw a demon-phlegm-spewing tantrum." I snort along with her as she brings our sole pot to the table. "I was still cleaning up the mess when she tossed me the jar on her way out."

I inhale the symphony of aromas, gulping down my flowing saliva. "Remind me to thank your demoness, even if she used you in lieu of the trashcan."

Sarah giggles as she serves her latest concoction, and I grin ears-wide at her excitement.

After the first spoonful, I almost faint at the taste. I shove another one so fast I almost shatter my front teeth. Sarah's smile widens as she gets down to demolishing her own plate.

Then there's only the sounds of two famished girls slurping too-hot food in companionable silence.

We got good at that on days when we didn't have the energy to make accounts of our dreary days funny. It was Sarah, again, who taught me I don't have to try so hard at such times. That silence between us can be the healing balm we need to go on.

Her sudden movement, reaching back for a towel, interrupts my musings. She was eating so fast, she fed her hair. As she dabs it clean, then shoves it in what she calls a bunny-tail, before attacking her plate again, my heart clenches. She looks…so young right now.

Though at twenty-one and five months she's maybe older than I am —since I don't know my exact age—I always felt like she's the younger sister I never dreamed of having

I've had that unstoppable urge to protect her from the first day we met. That was when her family sold her to Zeral. The demoness was still married to Kondar then, before they split us in the divorce. Sarah hasn't heard from her family ever since.

While I hope this means her parents died an excruciating death, she doesn't hate them for what they did to her. Hell, she has excuses for them every time the subject belches up. It shouldn't surprise me, since she's my complete opposite in everything, not just in looks.

Like her inner goodness, she's exquisite on the outside. Fair-skinned, silky-haired, with everything about her refined and graceful. Even our chronic malnutrition hasn't erased the softness of her curves or the perfect proportions of her five-foot-five frame. While my six-inches-taller one is sallow and spindly, with the big bones of my shoulders, hips and knees jutting out awkwardly through my sparse flesh.

From my masses of indeterminate-color dark hair that always conspires to escape my braid, to my large, hooded eyes and big mouth, the latter in every way, I can pass for part desert demon. While I always thought she looks like an angel.

But unlike real angels, she's as good as those humans once believed in. She deserves far better than the lot she got.

I'm only glad Kondar got me in the divorce. If she were the one being abused regularly—I can't even bear imagining that.

Zeral, thankfully, isn't a sadist like him. Not to say that Sarah is safe with her. Zeral drinks, a lot, and what she does while drunk could have killed Sarah, many times over. It still can.

She once forgot Sarah inside the shop, sealed it with an unbreakable spell and travelled for a month. Sarah almost died of starvation, and me of desperation. Another time she mistook Sarah's bag for hers and filled it with the magical scorpions she was delivering to a client after hours. Then there was the time she accidentally infected her with a strain of demonic bacteria, and Sarah almost burned from the inside out.

I shudder at the memories, and her eyes rise to mine in concern. I pretend to be fidgeting in my chair and shove another spoonful into my mouth. Our time together is the only good thing we have, and I'll be more damned if I let the ugliness of the outside world taint it.

But no matter how ugly it gets, Sarah remains so warmhearted and generous, it hurts. It makes me fear for her even more.

You can't be this forgiving in such an unforgiving world.

But that's where I come in. I take all the hits so she can remain herself. And I'll get us out of here, and give her the life she deserves.

Midway through scarfing down the unusually large serving like a locust, my mind wanders to what this life would look like. I never let myself dwell on that, focusing only on surviving the next day, the next sale. But I suddenly can't resist speculating.

What kind of life can we build outside our prison?

All I know about the world beyond the Mark's range comes from my stolen times on Demonica's internet after I finish Kondar's work.

That is, until a year ago, when I started dedicating every second to running my operation. I could never afford a smartphone before, and now only get burner phones for my transactions. Mobile internet is useless here anyway, because of infernal magic interference.

My other sources are the summaries Sarah gives me of the books and magazines I steal for her, and the snippets I hear from Demonica's droning news or sports channels. We reserve Edna's screen-time for watching our beloved pre-Apocalypse movies and shows. The rest of my knowledge is anecdotal.

But as far as I can tell, this Afterworld looks nothing like any post-Apocalypse these shows and movies projected. Neither was the Apocalypse itself, for that matter.

Not that anyone knows what really happened. How and when and where it started before it came to earth, what exactly happened when it did, and why it ended, so abruptly. Everything remains rumors peddled in private gatherings, or conspiracy theories on the internet's back alleys. No one dares to openly discuss or investigate the war. Not when getting your social media accounts banned and losing your job are the first price you pay. Then things get serious.

I myself don't believe either side. Considering the angels are the ultimate in authoritarian bureaucracy and humans the epitome of herd mentality, who can blame me?

The fact remains that there are no dependable records of anything. The devastation made it impossible to document the war at first, then rebuilding and restoring normal life became humanity's priority.

As for the other players, demons—who are said to be the world's second largest population, with their dozens of subspecies—spread only misinformation. The Shifters, Vampires, Witches and all the other Supernatural races are far less in numbers, and they mostly live in secret societies, so we don't hear from them much. The Fae rarely bother to address the issue, or humanity itself for that matter.

So we're stuck with the angels as our only source of info. They provide the "facts." The media parrots them. Period.

By the time we're finished eating, I still can't imagine what our lives will look like on the outside. But I don't care. Anything will be better than the ones we have here.

We're almost done cleaning up when Sarah suddenly says, "Okay, out with it." My eyes widen in surprise, and she persists, "You have something serious on your mind. Tell me."

"Why don't you tell me, Sar? You can clearly read it."

She gives me a glance that can shame a demon into telling the truth.

I was going to wait until she sleeps, so I'd avoid having this confrontation. I should have known she'd read my intentions.

I sigh. "I'm going out again."

She jerks in alarm. "But you already had a—transaction today!"

It still disturbs her to even think of my drug dealing. If I could have kept her in the dark about it, I would have.

But she was my very first test-subject. Accidentally, granted, but she was there every step of the way while I figured this whole thing out, and decided to cash in on it. Being the smartest being I know, she would have figured out what I was doing anyway.

I shrug. "My client was a kid, so I walked away. But I have exactly a hundred transactions left to goal, and I not only need to keep on schedule, I must double my pace. Things are coming to a head, Sar. Good news is, I had another vetted customer lined up, so I set up the deal while I was still at Demonica."

Her hand shoots out to grab my arm. "Don't go out tonight, Wen." Her face and voice suddenly crumple. "Nothing is worth putting yourself in such danger!"

My frown deepens at her outburst. This is more than her usual anxiety. I still have one way to deal with it. Make a joke. That always works.

But when I open my mouth, I find myself saying, "Getting out of our servitude—getting *you* out of here—is worth *anything*, Sar."

I don't add, *my life included.*

Sarah gets my unspoken words, and panic creeps into her reddening eyes. "I...I feel something big is going to happen."

I wave her off. "It's all the doom and gloom news getting to you..."

"It has *nothing* to do with Zinimar's death," she speaks over me. "That's too big to touch us in our tiny lives, not for a long time. I've been feeling *this* way for a while now, that something close to home is going to happen—and soon."

This extra panic must be nerves. And who can blame her? We're living under constant threat by default, and I went and added a drug operation to our perils. The longer I do it, the more it weighs on her. She may be approaching breaking point. I can't have that.

But I can't give her reprieve either, can't slow down.

And now I can't shake the dread her fear has infected me with.

Sarah's instincts are never wrong.

"Nothing's going to happen," I say, to myself as well as to her. She shakes her head, and I add more forcefully, "I must keep doing this, Sar."

Her grip tightens on my arm. "No, you don't. You have enough money to buy out your Indenture."

I go still.

I already got us a million bucks. Five-hundred grand each. It never occurred to me to calculate it any other way.

But she came up with her own solution to the equation. That I have enough for one ticket out of this hell.

How can she even suggest this to me? How can she consider I'd leave her behind, under any circumstances?

Throat tightening with the tears I held back before, I lean down to peer into her pleading eyes, renewing the pledge she's trying to nullify. "We get free together, Sar, or not at all."

She shakes her head vigorously. "I waited until you made enough money, because I knew you wouldn't hear this before. But you must see reason, Wen. You're the one in constant danger. And things *are* coming to a head, one way or another. I can deal…"

"Together or not at all. *Period*, Sar." I tug my arm out of her spastic grasp, stride to the door before those damned tears fall, giving her more reason to cling to me, to drag this out.

I think I'll manage a clean exit when she cries, "Wen, please, don't go!"

Her tremulous entreaty lodges between my shoulder blades, inflicting more pain than Kondar's lash, making me grit out, "I'll be fine, Sar. I *always* end up fine."

Giving her no chance to say anything else, I slam the door behind me.

But as I rush down the rickety stairs, I wince as my declaration echoes in my head.

Is that what they mean by *famous last words*?

4

"**Y**ou got the goods?"

The rough rasp flows from the phone pressed to my ear, right into my brain.

It's somehow clearer than when I had earbuds. Yeah, someone stole my latest pair. I have about ten possible culprits. Each would slash my throat if I confronted them.

But even through the burner phone's inferior speaker, that voice reverberated ominously behind my sternum. That dude doesn't sound like the college frat boy he's supposed to be. From our online negotiations, I expected someone smarmy, low-life, and jittery.

That voice? None of those.

From only four words, I can tell it's like nothing I've ever heard. There are fathomless depths to it, and a trace of... an accent? And though he said the trite words I instructed him to, the way he delivered them had none of the usual entreaty. It had authority, entitlement. And that frequency of menace that made people blurt out the truth in interrogations.

What is it today with these atypical clients?

I fidget on feet going numb with cold inside my worn boots, debating what to do about this development, before I decide to dismiss it.

So I pegged him wrong. Or he's all I thought him to be, but doesn't sound like it. If I keep blowing off clients because they don't sound right, I may have to stop dealing altogether.

Just get this over with.

"You got the dough?" I counter as a gust of wind presses me harder against the side of the building, and almost jump.

The voice that emanates from my warper never fails to startle me, deep and forbidding. Nothing like my own voice. *That* Sarah once called soft and lilting.

I know she meant it as a compliment, but it was another piece of awful news, in a life littered with miscellaneous shit.

A soft, lilting voice is great for a YouTube influencer promoting beauty products, but in my world? Added to young, female, weak and Owned, it's like holding up a sign saying VICTIM or even MEAL every time I open my mouth. Many a bog demon has eyed me as the delicacy I am to them, not to mention the vampires.

I didn't end up on some monster's menu only because I know how to navigate this Afterworld, how to play devious and dirty. Sarah is so far protected by her limited movements, with Zeral's shop a block away, and by everyone's need for the demoness's arcane artifacts procuring services.

But with eBay and Etsy and other websites taking over that market, Zeral herself would soon be in danger, along with all her possessions. Another reason I have to reach my goal sum as soon as possible.

Anyway, I have to make everyone think they're dealing with a vicious thug. I'm also always disguised as a man, even though my clients never see me. The added protection in these areas is always needed.

"I got the dough, and way more. I want everything you got."

That voice again strikes something primal within my chest. And the way he said *I want everything you got.* My gut twists with an overwhelming need to hear it again, and again—and a burning urge to run.

Stop it. So the guy has a voice made for commanding orgasms in remote BDSM sessions. In a life filled with weak or revolting males, it's nice to have something so potent to fantasize about. Later.

But...he's walking around, in this part of town, with multiples of twenty grand?

Yeah. I've raised the price with each transaction, from a hundred bucks, to ten grand, until my buyers started to thin. Not many Regulars have much money, even those who steal and barter whatever they can to meet my price. And I make sure I don't deal to criminals and cartels, even if they can pay any price I set. The risk far outweighs the gain. So I only sell to individual addicts, and I stopped at ten grand. Steady transactions at a lower price are better than sporadic, more lucrative ones.

This time, with decommission hanging over my head, I asked for double the price. I would have settled for the usual one if that guy couldn't pay. I couldn't afford another failed sale.

He agreed without a second's hesitation. It made me regret I didn't push for more. I bet he would have paid anything since he has that much money on him now.

But why is that moron asking for more anyway? Everyone knows I sell 1ml per transaction. Period.

Don't get me wrong. I would *love* to sell more to anyone who can afford it. If I could, I'd sell every batch wholesale. I would have made those two mil in a month, and two more for our expenses in another.

But selling more would be fatal.

The first time I tried to sell my product, I had a 10ml vial on me. I was almost swarmed by every demon in the vicinity, before I realized they were after the *Angelescense*. Before *they* realized the scent, or whatever attracted them in it, was originating from my pocket, I smashed the vial and bolted away.

When I dared look back, I found them where the product was dissipating, writhing over each other in a frenzy.

So I experimented to determine the volume they can't detect. But not even 1ml worked. After many near-disasters, I decided to give up. But Sarah suggested I should try to find a container that masks its emanations, and got many for me to try from Zeral's shop. The plan was to get more of what worked. None did.

Then during a thieving errand for Kondar, I was almost caught. To lose my pursuers, I dove into a Supernatural flea market, only to trip over an imp, and fell face-first into his pal's smelly crotch. As I recoiled in disgust, I saw it. Hanging from a chain over his potbelly.

A breathtaking, four-inch crystal bottle, encased in engraved and filigree brass.

It mesmerized me, called to me. And I somehow knew. This was what I needed.

Needing my hands, or even info on it, but knowing how much imps despise humans, I cajoled my way into their good graces. I even paid a tribute of *fseekh*, the fermented-rotten mullet they go crazy for, and that stinks worse than they did.

Turns out the bottle was enchanted by a *Saherah*, a witch from a North-African coven, to house a Jann, a Jinn-like desert sprite. But though the imp has used up his three wishes, he insisted it was a keepsake, of that witch who sold it to him. If I wanted it, I had to give him something of equal value, to her delicious memory, and to the wishes I'd have granted.

I ended up bartering my heist for it, along with stealing two more artifacts he'd pawned off. That day Kondar flogged me until I lost consciousness. He really wanted that rare, ex-spouse pestilence curse. I didn't care. I was certain the bottle was worth the extra scars.

Once home, I released the Jann and made my first wish, a spell to mask my product's demon-magnet property. He only laughed, informing me his wish-granting was limited to minor and transient magic. A fact the witch neglected to tell the imp before selling him the bottle. But not even a full-fledged Jinn could help me. All magic deals with known elements and eternal laws, and he couldn't even guess what *Angelescence* is, or what laws governs it.

But that setback didn't worry me much, since I felt the bottle itself would work. If it could contain a magical entity, it could *Angelescence*, which is sort of a magical by-product itself.

Testing my theory needed an empty bottle, so I had to leave the Jann out, with Sarah. But I knew he could do nothing of his own will, so couldn't harm her. Not to mention that she insisted she trusted him, was already calling him Ajeeb while he called her Sar. I left them giggling their heads off as he helped her stencil and paint our nightstand.

And the bottle worked with the 10ml I first tried. I had a feeling it would work with far more.

Giddy with relief, I rushed home to make my second wish, for a spell to replicate the bottle. Surely that was limited enough magic?

But Ajeeb shot me down again. Only a witch from the same coven could make me even one more. And it would come at a cost I'd agree to, but they'd make sure I'd fail to pay. Why did I think he was enslaved unto eternity to whoever possessed the bottle? He couldn't pay the price for that coven's services, ages ago.

When I insisted I'd find a way to pay, he said they'd never deal with me, anyway. I got his prison bottle from the imp who killed the witch who made it, in lieu of paying her steep price. And when he discovered it was for what he considered a useless item, he *ate* her corpse.

Both grossed out and resigned, I looked at Sarah. As usual, she understood what I was thinking, and only nodded. So I used my third wish to set him free.

But if I expected thanks, I didn't get it. After his initial shock and disbelief, I got a lot of yelling, calling me every synonym of stupid.

He said he wanted to serve us—serve Sarah. And she could have made three more wishes, before I used my last one setting him free. He could have advised us to wish for things that could benefit us, and he could fulfill. And I wasted the once-in-our-lifetime opportunity.

Before I could say he could still help us if he wished, looking pained and scared, he disappeared.

Sarah was distraught, convinced we made another terrible mistake when we didn't consult him about the terms of his release. I only made it worse, saying we might have consigned him to a fate worse than eternal slavery, but at least he left his bottle behind.

As usual, Sarah rationalized my unfeeling sentiments, even made me seem noble that I released him, when I did because I didn't think it through. If I'd thought it to our advantage to use my last wish, and hers, I probably wouldn't have.

But though I bit my tongue on the confession, I couldn't hide my excitement. That bottle was a game-changer, and would allow me to transport *Angelescence* undetected in demon-infested areas. Then once I made a sale, I'd transfer it to a regular vial, leave it for my client and split.

That bottle did become the centerpiece of my drug operation, what made it possible to establish it at all. But using it turned out to be nothing like my initial, simple-stupid plan. I was almost caught before I developed my convoluted delivery process. And I hit a couple of fatal snags, before I established another ironclad rule. The 1ml per transaction one. No exceptions.

"No extras," I finally snap, the distorter turning it into an impressive growl. "Leave the dough where I instructed. Then I'll tell you where to pick up the goods."

For this scenario to work, after many near-lethal close calls, I obtained a spell from a solitary witch who lives in our apartment building. I pay her in monthly thieving errands, since it must be renewed every full moon. It can transport a small object across short distances, as long as I have left a "trace" of myself in both sending and receiving destinations. After many experiments of setting up my transactions, never in the same place twice, I found a drop of blood works best.

Once they put the money in the envelope I leave them, I transport it inside my backpack. Then I send the "goods" to another spot. I made an extensive map of deserted or devoid-of-demons locations across the city, so my clients can pick it before a demon finds it first. I advise taking half of it on location, so they don't get swarmed themselves walking around with it. From the stories I hear, everyone takes it all the moment they get their hands on it.

Without these elaborate precautions, I would have been caught long ago. My clients always wait around, hoping they'll see me, or whoever I send to pick up the money, so they can ambush us. Either for more product, or for far worse.

"Show me the goods first," the man rumbles.

I grit my teeth as I press the heel of my palm to the left of my sternum, the focus of disturbance his voice evokes. "I told you how this transaction will be concluded. Leave the dough and walk away."

"I'm not paying for goods I haven't seen. And I'll need to make sure it's for real."

I let out a frustrated exhalation. So that bastard is a HAC—a Hard-Ass Customer. I daily get those at Demonica, usually Regulars who try a hundred nags to get more than their money's worth.

Though the worst make me spit in their drinks, I don't blame these morons. Kondar basically offers them shit, in quality and quantity, for their money. Money that's very hard to come by in the Demon Zones, especially for humans.

But *that* moron I don't excuse. We're in a part of town with three demons to every human at this time. If he kicks up any disturbance, it would attract those chaos addicts like trash does flies.

Also, even in my enchanted bottle, any *Angelescence* in one place for too long might be a beacon to these locusts. And he's prolonging the transaction, and with it, increasing the chances of being swarmed.

I exhale loudly as I peel off the side of the building. "Your loss, pal. The deal is off."

"Eyes on target."

For a few heartbeats as I stride away, those three barked words echo in my skull like a war drum.

I don't understand why the man said them.

Or I don't want to understand.

The moment I'm forced to, everything inside me erupts. The discharge of panic is a brutal force compelling me to run.

Run for my life.

It's only after I do that I realize. If what I feel in my bones is true, by running I forfeited any possibility of claiming innocence. Running amounts to an admission of guilt.

Everyone has been trying to find the maker and peddler of *Angelescence*. My anonymity has been my one protection. All outcomes of exposure are beyond disastrous.

Stupid, stupid, stupid!

I should have walked away the second I heard that voice.

That voice. The very sound of savage compulsions and violent ends.

He kept me talking until he had "eyes on target." On me. And I ran. And it's too late to do anything about it.

No! *It can't be too late. I promised Sarah I'd be fine.*

This is the last thing I think before a gigantic angel lands before me with such force, the sidewalk explodes.

Throwing up my arms in a desperate reflex, I barely protect my face as rocky shrapnel pelts me. I dimly register the shards stabbing through my heavy clothes as the shockwave of his landing tears me off my feet. Hurls me backwards like a rootless tree in a hurricane. Slams me down like the hand of an angry god.

I lie there, paralyzed, from the spine-splintering impact, the mind-shattering terror.

My eyes bug out of their sockets as massive wings spread above me, blocking out the whole world. Twice as large as any angel's, in every shade of grey in existence. Illuminated in the darkness only by the horror stamped all over them. A tapestry of sinister, flaming runes.

My vision fades then bursts back, again and again, to the sight of lava-filled eyes crackling with mercury-laced obsidian lightning.

Then that voice that makes me quake down to my cells says, "Walter White—by the powers vested in me by the Celestial Court, I place you under arrest."

5

I stare up at the terrifying creature looming over me, and wince. Not with pain, though that's still crippling. But at what he said.

Yeah, I went there. I called myself Walter White to my clients.

So I really fangirl that show, so sue me.

But this angel will do far more than sue me. He's *arresting* me. From what I hear about those the angels arrest... Oh, wait. I never hear anything.

No one ever hears about them again.

"Get up," the angel orders, his fathomless voice a bass thrum of doom, enough to almost make my wavering consciousness blink out. "And don't try anything. Resisting arrest will only aggravate your punishment."

"I assure you, I'm in no condition to do anything—maybe ever again," I mumble as I dimly realize there's no trace of accent in his voice anymore. He's gone full-on, upper-crust British.

I also realize I'm still wearing the warper when he growls, "Shut up, Mr. White. You won't cite undue force during this arrest to weasel out of the charges being brought against you, or to garner any kind of mitigation."

"Undue force? You destroyed half the street!" I wheeze, the pain in my back and tailbone dissipating under the advance of numbness. This may be paralysis in progress. "And you may have broken my back!"

His silhouetted head tilts, his lava eyes flaring a purplish, then bluish flame, before a sound of pure viciousness makes the rubble I'm half buried in rumble. "I regretfully didn't."

Did he just give me a scan? I never heard of Designated Angels having such abilities. And I thought I knew of all levels who exist on Earth, from the Cherubim to the Powers. But this one is clearly a kind of angel no one knows about. There's no telling what he's capable of.

Yet, in a twisted way, he's managed to reassure me. About the future use of my legs.

"What now? You'll rectify that oversight?"

Yes, moron. Give that hellish angel ideas. Why don't you just lose consciousness?

His next words make me wish I already have. "There's nothing I'd enjoy more than taking you apart, Mr. White. My torture techniques are renowned for making my quarries beg for eternal damnation—and preferring it once it's granted. But we'll get to that in good time. I currently need you intact. Now, on your feet."

It's only terror that makes me try to do as ordered. But the world spins around me in a vortex of darkness and despair, and I slump back again.

This is the end for me.

But this can't be the end. I have to get back to Sarah. I can't leave her alone.

"I may need you intact, but I can inflict pain until your disgusting body empties its filth. If you don't want to experience agony you can't imagine, you'll stop stalling."

"I'm not stalling, dude—I can't get my legs to work. If you want me on my feet, you'll have to pick me up."

"I would *never* touch a human."

The way he says *human* with such loathing gives me a sudden idea. To try to convince him he has the wrong person. And if this doesn't work, to attempt getting off on a technicality. What I'm selling is an unknown drug. It isn't even a drug, per se. No one else knows what it is or how it's made. There can't be any laws against its sale.

While this is a ridiculously long shot, I have to take it. I can't give up and disappear wherever the angels send those they consider better off the streets. Or worse, becoming this monstrous angel's next torture project.

It takes everything that dread and desperation haven't eaten up inside me, but I finally sit up.

The moment I do, bile rises in my throat like magma. I barely tear the warper off before I pitch forward and throw up Sarah's spice-laden stew.

All over the angel's shiny, black boots.

The grunt of disgust that issues from him reverberates the destroyed sidewalk like an earthquake. It tells me if angels outright killed humans, I would have been street pizza underneath his sullied boot right now.

But with the churning in my stomach settling a bit, a nagging thought in the back of my shell-shocked mind crystalizes.

Isn't this angel going against the Armistice Accords rules prohibiting destruction and endangerment of mortal property and lives?

He landed like a meteor in the middle of L.A., with the equivalent destructive force of one. He decimated a hundred-foot swath of sidewalk. He could have injured or killed any Regulars in the vicinity. He might have. I can't hear emergency services or police sirens yet, but they must be on their way. Maybe even special forces, thinking there's been a terrorist attack.

Once they arrive, I may be able to use their distraction to escape him.

A frantic look around later, that hope burns to ashes. No one within sight seems to notice anything out of the ordinary. It's as if this angel is cloaking the scene of mayhem he's caused in a layer of normalcy that no being can penetrate.

How is this even possible? I never heard of a Glamor or supernatural ability of that magnitude.

"Last chance, Mr. White. On. Your. Feet."

All I want is to let the abyss of unconsciousness engulf me, but I can't afford to disregard his ultimatum. With every nerve screaming in a jumble of pain and panic, I finally drag myself up to my feet.

Swaying, I squint up at him from beneath my hood. *Way* up. When I'm well over six feet in my elevator boots. How tall is this angel? Seven feet? More?

He has knocked down the street lights, and in the deep shadows of a moonless night, all I can see is his daunting outline. A massive body against the wings he's folded high above him, making him look twelve feet tall. But now his eyes are no longer emitting this horrifying vermillion and death-laced electricity, all I can see of his face are hints of hard lines and chiseled planes. *Far* harsher and rugged than the usual angel fare.

From his "arresting" words, he's authorized by the Celestial Court, the highest authority in Angeldom. It's said to be populated by the most powerful angelic entities in existence. If anyone knows who, what they do, or where that court is, I've never heard about it. It's yet another inscrutable heavenly secret. And this here is one of its stormtroopers.

Just my luck to be arrested by the Nazi of angels.

I have to find a way out of this. Maybe if I run away screaming, his Glamor will dissipate in the diversion. Once the Regulars whip out their phones, he may be forced to let me go...

Who am I kidding? This brute Glamored away the equivalent of a meta bomb's detonation. He isn't going to drop the ball now. And this isn't even the usual visual Glamor. It messes with *all* the senses. No one heard his explosive landing, and now a couple of demons are walking over the debris without realizing it's there.

But—maybe I can pretend I don't realize what's happening myself?

Mind racing with my new, and final idea I groan. "Are you my birthday surprise?"

My voice comes out a wisp of sound. And it's like a freezing spell hits the massive angel towering over me.

I force myself to go on. "You're pretending to arrest me before you start stripping? Angels do that now? No judgement, though. No shame in making a buck. Though I shudder to think how much someone like you charges. Or maybe my friends paid with... favors? Knowing them, I bet they made it worth your while."

He still makes no reaction, nothing in him moving in the bitterly cold and humid wind, not a hair, not a feather.

I can do nothing but carry on. "Sorry for seeing through you, dude. But I'll tell them I didn't, that you scared the shit out of me. Which is actually the truth. Just don't get so carried away next time. You're supposed to entertain your targets, not hospitalize them."

Running out of things to invent, I gulp down the heart trying to squeeze out of my throat, and push the suffocating hood off my head.

Absolute silence and stillness follows. As if he created a forcefield of cessation all around us.

Then he finally rumbles, "You're female."

"Congrats on reaching that conclusion." I attempt a scoff. "Wait, you thought you were sent for a guy? Man, my friends really pranked us both, didn't they? But don't feel obliged to start stripping and gyrating now. I'll tell them you performed your whole number, so they don't ask for a refund if they paid you…"

My heart hits the base of my throat, forcing me to stop. A ray from a distant light pole struck off an unearthly emerald spark from one of his eyes. It's even more incredible, and terrifying, than the previous lava and lightning.

He's tilting his head again. Another scan, or is he considering I may be telling the truth?

Hope fizzes inside me as I fumble on, "I'll remember this incident fondly—if this pain in my tailbone isn't a fracture. So don't go all-out method again, okay? Now, I gotta get going…"

His wings snap open so hard they release a hurricane-level wind, and a sonic boom.

I dimly think I don't explode from the inside out only because he's keeping me in that stasis field of his. Very efficient silencing technique, though.

After an indeterminate period, when his celestial flap leaves me deaf, blind and breathless, my senses zoom back to him saying, "…pretense will be added to your charges. You know exactly what I am."

I almost burst out "I sure as hell don't." I never knew angels could do the things he does. But if he isn't one, what is he?

I swallow the exclamation. Who cares what he is? Only getting away from him matters.

But playing clueless has backfired. All I have left is my previous plan. Playing another kind of oblivious.

"Can you blame me for trying? You scared the hell—er…the heaven out of me. It's not every day an angel lands in front of me, destroying half the street, eyes spewing black lightning and spouting insane accusations. I had to try anything to get away from you."

"I warned you about resisting arrest. You're still doing it."

"But I have no idea why you're arresting me!"

My acting abilities are largely why I remain alive. I know I sound genuinely confused. Partially because I am. So will he buy it? Will it at least make him reconsider to any degree?

"You were using a voice warper," he murmurs, as if to himself.

His quieter timbre is more hard-hitting. It releases bat-sized butter-flies in my now empty stomach, and a molten sensation through my frozen marrow. It's far from an unpleasant sensation.

Which is weird, sick even, given the circumstances.

Definitely fuel for fantasies. The unbridled kind. When I'm a thousand miles away from him.

"You're dressed as a man. You ran when you heard I had eyes on you," he continues, as if still thinking out loud.

His voice again strikes a chord I didn't know existed within me. The brutal twang judders through me, body and soul.

I suppress a shiver as I smirk. "Last I heard, there were no laws, heavenly or otherwise, against any of that. Surely you can understand a girl needs all the protection she can get when she's out late in this part of town? And I don't understand what you mean you *had eyes on me*. You mean you saw me running? I was rushing to get home."

"Enough." His command isn't loud or angry. Like all his orders so far, I realize. It's more—weary. And if it still shakes every bone in my body, I'd hate to be around when he loses his temper. I don't think I'd be around for much longer. "You're the one who goes by the alias Walter White."

This is a statement, certain and final. My act didn't even scratch his diamond-hard conviction. I still open my mouth to object, and he raises a hand—a hand I'm sure can snap Kondar's gnarled neck like a spaghetti stick. Or bring down a building with one punch.

"Don't waste more of my time with protests of innocence. It will only—"

"Add to my charges," I finish for him, the icy calm of resignation descending on me, putting out the fires of dread and agitation.

I've tried everything, and nothing worked. Nothing can work. I'm only delaying the inevitable, and making whatever it is worse.

He gives a nod. Despair must be the only reaction he expected from me. It satisfies him that he drove me to it. "Now that we've established your guilt..."

I stumble back, hands shooting up as if to ward off another barrage of sidewalk. "Whoa! Slow down, dude! You can't go from charging me one second, to pronouncing me guilty the next! Where's your due process? Where are the stages of prosecution? What about a jury of my peers? You didn't even read me my rights, just that ridiculously theatrical arrest statement! Do you even consider I have rights?"

"No, I don't. Yet I'm still granting you the right to breathe, so don't test my forbearance. Before you slather me with more inane protestations, you're guilty beyond a shadow of doubt. You just tried to sell me the substance you call *Angelescence*. If I deem to search you, I will find the merchandise on your person."

Damn. He got me there. I didn't have time to get rid of the damning evidence. I wouldn't have, even if I did. Even to save myself, it wouldn't have crossed my mind to throw away the bottle.

I still try to extricate myself. "I'm reselling it. I know how in-demand it is, and I managed to swipe it from a coworker. I need the money…"

"What you need is to allow yourself some oxygen between the lies you breathe. We've been following your transactions, but you kept randomizing your procedure and evading us. I finally fathomed a method to your seeming madness, hacked into your latest sale, and replaced your client. We have extensive evidence on your operation, and the damage you caused."

"What about the damage *you* caused a-a human street?" I blurt, needing to lash back at him, come what may. "Or the injuries you might have caused human pedestrians? When you didn't hit your brakes to shock and awe me? Did it fill you with angelic testosterone when you struck a pose over a mere mortal like me, and basked in my pain and terror? *You* should be charged with reckless endangerment, destruction of public property and, yes, use of undue force during this arrest—and be found guilty of it all—and worse. Or do other rules apply to you? Heh, of course they do—you privileged dickwad!"

He says nothing in the aftermath of my outburst. The stillness deepens until I feel as if my very blood is stopping in my arteries.

Then he turns and strides away.

I gape after him.

He's not cuffing me? He expects me to follow him?

But what else can I do? Run? I can't outrun an angel.

Or… maybe I don't need to. If I can duck into an alley, with his ridiculous wing-span, he can't follow me in the air. With all this bulk, he can't be swift on his feet, either. Whichever, it will slow him down…

Something yanks me by the neck, hard enough to almost snap it.

I launch in the air with the violent tug, before slamming to the ground with the same force. I barely miss pulverizing my face.

The unrelenting pull drags me over the jagged debris. But I don't even feel the lacerations I'm sustaining. I have more *pressing* things to worry about.

Blood and breath clog in my head, starting to snuff out my consciousness. My life is next, if I don't obey the pull, and lessen its pressure on my windpipe.

I scramble to my feet, stumbling repeatedly with the force. Then I see it. An eerily glowing line of indeterminate material, a golden substance that—*feels* like him, connecting my neck to his hand.

That winged bastard has me on a leash!

Out of pure instinct, I claw at the noose—and scream.

It *burns*.

Jerking my hands away, finding them already blistering, panic drenches me. This thing is going to eat through my neck.

He's going to decapitate me!

6

Panic reaches a crescendo before it crashes.

My neck...the noose isn't burning through it. There's only pressure, but no heat.

How...?

The leash wrenches me forward again, scattering my thoughts.

Only the need to breathe remains, until he drags me close enough to relieve the tautness. Once blood floods my brain, it starts working again.

That burn must only activate if I try to remove the noose. A diabolic way of ensuring I don't try again. Or I should say angelic.

Not that there's much difference between angels and their infamous brother, the Devil—if he exists. Not to us humans. Especially to *this* human.

I stagger in his wake, glaring my homicidal hatred at him as he struts ahead as if he owns this earth. Which he and his kind actually do. His massive wings are gathered high above him in an arch of arrogance and disdain. If I had heat vision they'd be a pile of ash right now. He would be.

Savoring the vicious fantasy is all I can do as he leaves me just enough air to remain conscious. Even if he left me able to scream, there's no point. Not even the demons passing by can detect me.

Not that anyone would help me if they did. No one would dare intervene in his arrest. That Glamor must only be to keep the incident off the news. I'm sure his superiors wouldn't appreciate his destructive tactics tainting their public image.

After I repeatedly pass out on my feet, we approach a huge black van. It's parked in front of a junkyard a few blocks from his destruction scene.

Before I can wonder what an angel needs with a car, he flicks his wrist and I catapult forward like a kitten tossed by a cruel brat.

Landing inches from his boots, one knee gives a terrible crack on impact. But it's the pain bursting in my neck that blinds me. I bite my lip hard enough to draw blood so I don't cry out. I won't give him the satisfaction.

As he slides open the back door with a remote key, I choke, "So— am I wanted dead or alive?" I barely see that head tilt of his, skating on the edge of oblivion. I point at myself. "Human here. Breakable, no regenerative powers to speak of." His head remains at the same angle. I draw in a measured breath so I don't sound *too* strangled. "You could have snapped my neck. Twice."

He shakes his head as if in regret. "I know in detail how perishable your inferior species is. And exactly how hard I can push you before you shatter. If I had a choice, you wouldn't be still breathing your foulness near me. Regretfully, again, you're wanted alive."

I put a hand over my mouth on my next choking breath.

Holy eau de puke!

Hoping he suffocates on my stench, I smirk up at him. "Do your wings come with a mileage limit dictated by your leasing company?" I can sense rather than see his frown. I shrug. "I can't think of another reason why you'd need a van."

"I'm not transporting you. I wouldn't touch one of you. Especially you."

"Yeah, yeah, you said that already. Don't be redundant."

He does this motionless thing again. And though I don't see his eyes now they're not glowing, I feel them boring into me.

Can angels drill visual holes into someone?

I have a feeling this one can.

Next second, he flicks his wrist again, and I hurtle inside the van.

My foot barely clears the door before he slams it, manually.

Landing in a heap, my windpipe suddenly opens on a massive inhalation. I gulp desperate breaths before realizing the leash is gone. He let it dissolve now he's hauled me where he wants.

Only the adrenaline roaring in my system keeps me conscious.

That, and being inside a next-level luxury car. Though I can't see much of the interior, the seat felt like landing on a cloud. It's just my luck, to fulfill what Sarah calls my vehicular fetish, on my way to some angelic concentration camp or soul-recycling facility.

At least I get to have one wish in my miserable life answered.

Needing to experience more of the car, I claw up to a sitting position—and notice a massive man silhouetted at the wheel.

He doesn't turn or say anything. Figures. Must be a Select faithful dog, even if I can't see his piercing in the dark.

I am wondering if his master will fly over the van when he opens the passenger door. In seconds, he's inside and the car is peeling off the asphalt with a deafening screech, slamming me back hard in my seat.

My spinning head and ringing ears clear to him saying, "…clean-up team to the location." A beat of silence before he adds, "The Accords' rules are for you to follow, Caius. I use whatever level of force I see fit."

It's only then I realize he's in the middle of a conversation. Must be talking on some angelic frequency. Or is he using the human technology they seem to love so much?

There's another beat while the person on the other side says something. It earns him a calm rumble that makes me shiver. "Next time, I'll demolish the whole neighborhood." Another beat, then another hair-raising roll of menace. "And I'll rearrange your anatomy." I can only imagine the other guy's distressed reaction, as without raising his voice still, my captor adds, "Whether you meant to question me or not, you've had your first, and last warning."

As I shudder again, he taps his ear.

So it was a phone call. And he ended it the second he was done talking. Gotta admit, that was some threat. The other guy must be pissing himself now that he has a death sentence hanging over him, if he displeases dickwad again.

"What did you step into, mate?" The driver groans as he taps his own ear, and I see the earbud for the first time. So he's been listening to something all along. His voice is almost as deep as my captor's, and as posh. "You bloody stink!"

"Courtesy of the human vomitus in the back."

As if he's not the reason I puked! Sarah's precious last supper, too, and… Wait!

How is a Select so familiar with an angel? And why refer to me as human, unless this driver isn't?

But what other species can that—that *angelhole* be working with? One who dares to be so chummy with him, too?

And…wait…what the…? *Whoa!*

Where are his wings?

I can't believe this wasn't the first thing I noticed since he entered the car!

This makes no sense. Angels' wings don't disappear.

At least, the angels I know about. Which means that, among the powers I've never heard of angels having, this one has wings on demand.

Not one to hold back my curiosity, especially now I have nothing more to lose, I blurt out, "I was joking about your wings before, but are they really leased? Is that why you brought the van? Because your lessor deactivates them when you reach your flight miles limit, and you're too cheap to pay the surcharge fees?"

The driver suddenly bursts out laughing.

My captor slings him what I assume is a withering glance.

The driver bangs the steering wheel, spluttering, "Lessor, flight miles, surcharge fees—that's hilarious."

My captor sighs, the velvet harshness thrumming that spot behind my breastbone, what his every sound scrapes. "You always had the sense of humor of a ten-year-old brat, Lorcan."

"Actually, this was one piece of creative wit," this Lorcan guy retorts. "Admit it."

"I'll admit she is even more aggravating than I anticipated. But I should have expected anything from the criminal who's been leading us a merry chase for over a year."

The driver whips his head to him. "You mean *that's* the one we're here to catch in the act?"

"Why do you think I dragged her stinking arse back here?"

"I assumed she's an accessory or an errand girl, or some such." Lorcan shakes his head as he adjusts the rearview mirror to peer at me. I don't see him at all before he readjusts it. Then he suddenly whoops. "That's bloody *wicked.*"

"*Wicked?*"

"*Wicked?*"

My exclamation clashes with my cranky captor's. From the Harry Potter movies I know this means cool. But I only heard the kids using the term.

Which means Angelhole is right about this Lorcan's juvenile sense of humor. Only a cruel brat can find my current situation *wicked*.

As if to validate my thoughts, Lorcan chuckles. "It certainly is. We didn't doubt for a second that the elusive mastermind who has the human and Supernatural underground communities salivating for a taste of his product isn't a seasoned, and *male*, criminal."

I massage my semi-garroted neck as I rasp, "You do realize how chauvinistic that sounds, right?"

Lorcan flicks me another glance over his shoulder. "She can't be older than sixteen!"

I smirk at him. "*She's* right here, and is actually twenty…or twenty-one."

Lorcan hoots with laughter again. "And she doesn't even know basic maths."

"Excuse me if I don't know when I was born," I croak. "The world was busy being destroyed by your Apocalypse to issue birth certificates to human survivors."

This makes him flip the rearview mirror again, this time longer. I only see eyes, but can't figure out their shape or color. I don't know how *he* can see me in this darkness.

Then he whistles. "What a plot twist. You, my dear criminal mastermind, are one delightful development."

"Stop talking to the felon and keep your eyes on the road," Angelhole growls, and my insides quiver again. "If you total this vehicle, too, if you even scratch it, you're not laying your hands on another set of wheels for ten years."

Lorcan mock gasps. "Whoa, mate! That's even harsher than Mum and the DMV put together."

I can only see the back of my captor's head as it scrapes the massive van's roof. But I think he looks heavenwards. *If* Heaven is really up there. I guess he's in a unique position to know for sure.

Before I can ask, he grunts. "Just don't crash the car. We need this human alive. For now."

For now.

This brings *me* crashing to the concrete ground of reality, shattering my mind to a thousand pieces.

During this weirdly lighthearted exchange, I almost forgot what this—this *creature* who arrested me is. And since he can somehow retract his wings, I must assume this Lorcan guy is the same thing.

They are taking me only they know where, and it's clear my life is tied to something they need from me.

Once I provide it, my continued vital functions won't be required.

Suddenly, I hurtle forward, slam into the front seat with a sickening crunch before crumpling into the foot well

"Dammit, Lorcan! I said we need her alive." He whirls in his seat to glare down at me where I'm lying in a stunned heap. "Seatbelt. Now!"

"Keep your wings on," I groan. "Or don't, since they're retractable."

As Lorcan bangs the wheel and guffaws again, I pull myself up. My blistered hands sting so badly, I'm on the verge of another projectile vomiting bout, courtesy of this winged—now-wingless—bully. I flop back in my seat and fumble for the seatbelt.

When I fail to click the two ends together, my captor turns in his seat with a frustrated growl.

With a flick of his fingers, he flings my hands apart. So, telekinesis, too? Then as Lorcan's reckless driving continues to rock the van, he picks the ends of the belt, his hands hovering over me as if I were a venomous growth. So, no telekinesis? Or is it the…

The headlights of a car behind us illuminate his face, and my thoughts then heart stop. Before they both burst out stumbling like a horse on ice.

He—he's *gorgeous*.

No. No he's not. The adjective seems like an insult when describing something of this caliber. Divine is too on the nose, as well as inadequate.

I never knew sentient beings came with that level of magnificence.

And it isn't because he has perfect features and symmetry like other angels. Every detail of his face is forceful, noble—*singular*. A matrix of slashes and juts and chisels housing features that really had to be sculpted by gods.

Nah. Even they wouldn't have created something like him. Not when he would give any god an inferiority complex.

Yeah. Because it's appropriate to develop an arrhythmia over my captor's incomparable beauty.

My captor, future torturer—and probable executioner.

But knowing this doesn't stop me from greedily examining him.

I start with his eyes. Of course. Their exotic slant is feline—and their color? Indescribable. I can only think of one Sarah once told me about. Viridian. A green so mesmerizing, so saturated it almost hurts.

And it's not only the hue that's unique. His irises glow with rays of arcane power, seemingly on demand, too. Rounding up his eyes' brutal impact are lashes so thick, they make them look drawn in exquisite kohl.

I barely make them my mind's screensaver as he clicks the seatbelt in place. Before I can absorb more of his details, he rumbles something under his breath that sets me vibrating again, and tears back into his seat.

The headlights behind us come closer, and I sit there, staring at the angry-looking raven waves adorning his head, everything slowly sinking into me.

Every injury making my body a map of burning aches. Every realization of the depth of the shit I'm in.

There's only one light at the bottom of the spiral of despair. Knowing that Sarah has the money I made us.

The last thing I think before everything blinks out is a plea. I send it out there hoping it will reach her, and that she will listen.

Please, Sarah, give up on my return soon, and buy yourself that one ticket out of Hell. Don't let it all be in vain.

7

A bass thrum penetrates the cocoon of darkness enveloping me. A crimson glare joins its attempts to scrape me away from its embrace.

"Wake *up*, Ms. White. To be further redundant, I'm not carrying you out of here."

"I can carry her."

"No, Lorcan, you can't."

"Spoilsport."

"She has two working legs, since I saw fit not to break their every bone when she tried to escape me. She can use them."

My lids weigh a ton each, but the sheer asshattery splattering me drags them up. I swear I can hear them scraping, like boulders over silt. I see nothing but painful whiteness.

For moments, I think I'm blind. I'm too drained to feel panic, or relief when I realize it's only sunlight burning my retinas.

How long have I been out?

When my vision returns, the glorious brute materializes out of the glare. He's scowling down at me as if I were some rotting roadkill.

In the dark, I thought he was dressed in black. Now I see it's midnight blue—like the highlights in his hair. The strangely obscuring top and pants still fail to hide the magnificence below, from his neck down to his mid-calf boots. The boots that still bear the residue of my puke.

And his wings are back. Thankfully, the terrifying runes that blazed all over them are gone. Another on-demand feature. Their absence, and the sunlight, showcase those thousand-shades-of-grey miracles in aching detail. They're raised behind him, as if in anticipation of a fight.

Fight? With insignificant human me? Sure.

That must be how they react when he's revolted. That's right. His wings are puckered in disgust.

"Hey, chicken wings," I slur.

A boom of laughter issues from behind him as another stunning creature—Lorcan in my first look at him—comes into view.

"I truly hope they don't execute you, *Walter White*." Lorcan snickers. "Anyone who can call Godric the Great 'chicken wings' is too much bloody fun to die."

Godric? That's the stupendous swine's name? It actually starts with *God*?

Seems fitting, I think grudgingly.

Out loud, I mumble, "Godric, huh? Who's the pompous ass who named him? Now he probably thinks people, especially women, mean him when they gasp, 'Oh God!'"

Another bellow of laughter from Lorcan. "That's it. You should live forever."

In response to our snarky volleys at his expense, that celestial sourpuss growls, "On. Your. Feet. *Now.*"

With that, he turns and walks away, looking like—well, a god. A god of vengeance, immaculate and righteous, striding away from a battlefield he turned into a graveyard, after he slaughtered all wrongdoers and decimated all evil.

At least he doesn't do his angel-leash number on me, leaving me to struggle out of the car under my own empty-tank power.

Lorcan steadies me, stopping me from face-planting on the cobblestone ground. Seems he hasn't sworn off touching humans.

Eyes lined with sandpaper, I look up at him. Should I thank him, Angelhole's accomplice, for the assist?

Next moment, the world decides a course of action for me. It pitches and heaves a second before I lurch around and spew a gallon of vomit all over the van's pristine interior.

Sarah's serving was more generous than I realized.

Lorcan chuckles. "Now Godric will really push for capital punishment."

"Yeah, *hilarious*, right?" I wipe my hand over my mouth, grimacing at the taste and smell I feel marinated in. Nothing less than boiling will disinfect me from the reek.

Lorcan's grin only widens, and I finally register his details.

Perfection is the only adjective for his body, if on a slightly lesser scale than Godric the Great's. His otherworldly clothes are also the opposite of the latter's stealth getup. Detailed and decorated, they're Roman soldier-like at the top, but with pants instead of a tunic at the bottom. An elaborate armor molds across his massive shoulders and chest like a second skin, seeming to morph in material and color with his movements.

His super-hero arms are displayed by the deep grey short-sleeved top beneath, and his muscled forearms are wrapped in worked, holographic gauntlets that match his shin guards. His pants are the same molding material, with metal-like straps around one thigh and the opposite calf, holstering vicious-looking daggers with exquisitely worked sheaths and pommels. All that's left is a helmet and cape and he'd be some celestial centurion.

A warrior's outfit. When I thought the war was over. The one that requires uniformed soldiers, at least. No one has any illusions it was really over. It has just turned cold.

At least that's what I always thought. But maybe it isn't so cold if that's the uniform of the Celestial Court lackeys. Not that I have any idea if Lorcan is one of those, since he's still not sporting wings.

But I'm somehow certain he can sprout them at will, too. That he and GTG are the same kind of monster. He's just a nicer one.

This makes him less awe-striking than his brutal buddy. A terrible fact, I know, but a fact nonetheless. He's handsome off the charts, far above any angel, and rugged with it, but he lacks the menace, the savagery that makes GTG mind-blowing.

Noticing me documenting his assets, he smiles, as if giving me permission. Not that I need one. I openly stare into eyes that can't decide if they're brandy or amber, shining from within with a banked fire, and made to crinkle in laughter. Then I move to his shock of dark hair that glints a rich auburn in the sunlight. His grin widens, drawing my attention to the full, wide lips that don't seem to find seriousness an option.

All in all, the merry opposite of his cohort, the celestial grump.

As I step away from the van, I'm a jumble of searing aches. Not one inch of me, save my face, feels intact. When Angelhole didn't lay a finger on me. My injuries are the collateral damage of his disregard for my human frailty. Like what his kind's Apocalypse did to my race and planet.

I should be in a wheelchair. But I doubt I would have gotten one if he'd actually paralyzed me. He would have made me drag my limp body on the ground. Or towed it for me by the neck.

He can still do that if he thinks I'm stalling.

That makes me start walking. Lorcan remains a step away, and I can't help but feel grateful for his presence beside me. It makes the situation feel less dire somehow.

He disabuses me of that notion the moment it forms in my mind.

"All fun aside, Ms. White, you're in deep shi—trouble." He huffs a laugh, as if savoring my predicament. "Mariana Trench deep. What you did is—well, you'll hear all about the sheer gravity of the matter from those who are far more pompou—uh, serious than I am. I do know you're needed alive for now—"

There's that "for now" again!

"—but remember this when you're facing judgement: there are fates far worse than death."

My limping steps falter as I gape up at him. "You're saying if it comes to a choice, I should go for execution?"

He shrugs one powerful shoulder, making his uniform shape-shift. "Just giving you perspective, since from what I hear, death seems to be the worst thing to humans."

"What you hear? Seems to be? You really don't have a clue, do you?"

"About humans? I have little firsthand interaction. But it's enough to know what needs to be known about you. You are largely base creatures whose only redeeming quality is creativity, born of necessity, of course. I positively adore your arts and little inventions."

"How charming." I scoff. "Coming from a member of the species plaguing our planet, supposedly to protect us!"

My dig slides right off his nonchalant hide like water off a duck's feathers as he shrugs again. "Only stating a universal truth."

"We have an even worse opinion of you, pal."

He nods, that easy smile never leaving his gorgeous lips. "Expected, and probably merited. We can have a meaningful discussion about the fallibilities of the different species 'plaguing' this planet later—if you're still alive after your arraignment, that is."

I choke and stumble.

A light touch on my elbow supports my whole weight. Super-strength, check. More proof he's another member of that angelic breed the world knows nothing about.

"Anyway," he continues smoothly. "My earlier point was; now you've breached the world of immortals, the rules here are totally different. There are many fates that make death, even after prolonged torture, a favorable outcome."

I gulp around the spiked mass expanding in my throat. "You're talking eternal damnation, right?"

"That, too, isn't the capital punishment."

There's worse than that?

My stunned stare turns into a glower. "I guess in your warped angelic mind, you just gave me great advice and support."

He grins. "Just saying."

As he looks ahead, considering the conversation over, I tear my attention towards my surroundings. And my breath jams in my already constricted lungs.

All my life, my Mark confined me to the city limits of Los Angeles. The grandest buildings I've seen had some Greek, Roman, or Gothic architectural influences. Anything loftier I've only seen on TV or the internet. But what I see before me now? No words, not human anyway, can do it justice.

The sprawling, soaring constructions are mind-boggling. Their size and extent make it clear they were built with giants, or flying beings— or both—in mind. The architecture looks like a seamless marriage of Medieval, Renaissance and... Celestial? I guess it must be, if this is the Celestial Court.

I can't imagine what else it can be. What other place would have spires that attempt to reach Heaven? Can feel as if the very fabric of light and shadow weaved with stone to make its pillars and parapets? As if solid materials merged with mirages in its construction? As if it exists in different realms at once?

The immense grounds are no less mind-bending, their sweeping perspective arrowing away beyond the reach of my mortal vision. Within my sight's limits, dense woods spill through vast passages like sentinels, and a tapestry of parterres and pavilions wind between reflecting pools and groves. Like the building they surround, everything feels like a similar mix of the natural and supernatural.

If I have to describe everything in my own inadequate way, I'd say it's a fusion of the sensual, sublime, and sinister. That it feels like a miniature of the world's current state, an inextricable amalgam of Earth, Heaven—and even Hell.

It overwhelms me just looking at it, being near it.

Unable to take another step, I bend with hands on knees, struggling to breathe.

"Curious."

Gasping, I glare up at Lorcan. "Dude, you gotta work on your... inappropriate responses. I'm dying here...and you're finding it...interesting?"

"It is. When other humans first see the Court, they're delirious with delight. It's as if they stumbled into one of your fabled wonderlands. Like Hogwarts, only on celestial steroids." A hand on my back urges me to straighten and continue walking. "I never heard of any human being disturbed."

With my heart trying to climb up my throat, I resume limping alongside him. Secure that this weird mix of jerk and gentleman won't let me keel over, I still toss him a sour glance. "Other human 'felons' get excited when they see this place? Where they'll meet a fate far worse than death?"

"I meant other humans. Though felons also exhibit excitement—initially. But while you took my dire predictions in your stride, you're falling apart now as a reaction to the Court itself."

"Well, duh. This place is...unbearable!"

Lorcan gazes at me as if I've lost my mind. Which is a reasonable assumption. This Court *is* beyond any fantasy. It dwarfs imagination and drowns limitation. My jaw should be on the floor with awe. Which, according to Lorcan, is the unanimous human reaction. And my jaw *is* dragging on the exquisite cobblestones.

But there's something about this place that makes me quake with a crazy mixture of foreboding—and anticipation. Something pervasive. Bone deep. Cell deep.

Soul deep.

It's telling me that the moment I set foot inside this place, my world as I know it would end. Not in death. Or the worse ways Lorcan warned me about. In totally unquantifiable ways. And to me, that's the worst of all fates.

I can't handle uncertainty.

In the life that ended when Angelhole caught me, Kondar would have gloated about my fate beforehand. I would have had time to arrange for Sarah's safety. I would have gone to face death knowing how it would happen, that my purpose was fulfilled. No matter the horror or pain, I would have died content, at peace.

But this place is telling me what awaits me is something...beyond comprehension. Something no one—even those who hold my fate in their hands—knows anything about.

And *that* terrifies me.

But I must be imagining it all. I don't do premonitions. That's Sarah's domain. I can't be feeling these overpowering—transmissions. Courts, even the celestial kind, don't communicate anything, right? It must be all in my mind. And who can blame me if I'm outright hallucinating by now?

Everything I'm feeling has to be a side-effect of my ordeal at that angelic Nazi's hands. His figurative ones, since he didn't touch me, would never touch me, blah blah blah.

But his aversion may yet prove useful. Whether he's walked or flown, he has reached what looks like the central building of that endless complex. At my pace, I have minutes until we catch up to him. Enough time to bombard Lorcan with the dozen questions I...

A crack of thunder makes me swallow them and almost my tongue.

"Faster, Ms. White!"

To my ears, his command wasn't that loud. He's too far, and he didn't even shout. But I swear I *feel* his voice on different levels. To the exact intensity he intends me to feel.

If *only* I ran the moment I heard it!

If I did, I wouldn't be hurtling up this celestial crap creek. What's about to become infinitely crappier.

8

Memories of his leash force my aching, shaking legs to move faster. At least until I reach the bottom of a million steps.

They didn't seem that many from afar. But looking up now, I get inverted acrophobia.

So they're maybe a few hundred steps—reminding me of the memorials being rebuilt in Washington DC, if on a much grander scale —but they feel countless to me. And they seem carved from a single block of a faintly-glowing material that resembles marble. Probably from some "heavenly" body. And Angelhole is waiting for me at the top.

And by me, I mean just that. Lorcan is walking away, whistling a disturbing tune that can score the monster's approach in a horror movie. Seems appropriate for my situation.

Even so, I wish him back. But my captor's glare must have promised him a rearrangement of *his* anatomy, if he didn't stop fraternizing with the felon.

Peachy. It's back to being alone with him. Really alone. This place seems deserted.

But I can feel a jumble of—presences elsewhere. It's a gigantic complex, after all, could be housing thousands for all I know. Where, and who, I don't care. Only tackling the impossible task of climbing those stairs matters now.

By the time I reach the acres-wide landing, I am ready—no, *eager*, to lay down and die.

He doesn't even glance at me as I sink to the ground, gulping air like a fish thrashing out of water. He turns and strides toward the soaring portico of Ionic-like columns hundreds of feet away. It houses towering, bronze double doors embossed from top to bottom with a golden angel, clad only in loincloth, gazing heavenwards, arms and wings spread.

When I don't recover fast enough for his liking, his leash materializes around my neck again. I try to scrabble to my feet before he tugs on it. I fail, slam on my side like a lassoed calf. Then he drags me across the mirror-polished floor.

By the time we're halfway to the columns, I believe he has changed his mind about needing me alive.

I'm certain I'm choking on my last breath when he stops, and the leash disappears.

As I convulse on the cool, otherworldly marble, coughing and snatching at the air, his brilliant gaze coats me with his contempt.

Then that voice of his reverberates its searing iciness in my bones. "Had enough?"

"Not...really," I rasp. "Still...alive."

"Stall again and—"

"And...what?" I cut him off, my voice a wavering but taunting thread of sound. "You'll *almost*...strangle me...again? I've had...much worse...Angelhole."

He goes stock still, his gaze turning from ruthless yet fed-up to contemplative...and confused?

It's as if he's *really* seeing me for the first time. As if he's realizing he's underestimated me somehow, and is now recalculating his presumptions. And not liking his conclusions one bit.

I'm celebrating stymieing him when a shadow of a smile touches his spectacular lips, and my heart plummets like a bird shot down from the sky.

I've never seen anything scarier...or sexier.

And that's before he murmurs a silky, "For now."

We stare at each other for an endless moment as my flailing heart settles into a life-threatening rhythm. I realize I'm seeing him for the first time, too. I've also miscalculated.

He isn't just a more dangerous, more powerful brand of angel. He's not some officer or even executioner for that Celestial Court, either. He's something way worse.

A grim reaper.

But worst of all? He's not so grim.

With that ghost of smile, he's given me a glimpse of something I thought angels were incapable of. Pure wickedness.

He may not be grim, but his humor, what he keeps buried under that military-like facade, is. Grisly, even. The kind I appreciate most.

As if to prove it, his eyes simmer with taunting and that terrifying emerald as he materializes his leash around my neck again.

For a few beats, he gives me a last chance to back down, to lower my gaze. To give him my obedience, my defeat.

I only give him my middle finger.

He starts to strangle me, oh so slowly.

I gulp down a huge breath before he cuts off my airway, delaying the inevitable. My hatred of him soars to new heights as he stands there above me, infinitely powerful and literally blessed, and watches weak, cursed me suffocate.

As he continues to hold my gaze, his explicit with savoring my helplessness, I know he knows that I lied. Suffocation is worse than anything I've suffered before. The terror it inflicts is unendurable. Even when I know he won't kill me. Not now. Not that easily.

It takes strength I never knew I had to resist begging for my breath. When I know resistance is pointless. But it's all I have. When it's time to die, or worse, I won't go scraping and sniveling.

But this celestial bastard knows human limitations well. He'll push me to the brink of my survival instinct, and relish every second.

Midway through burning my air reserves, he raises an eyebrow. That perfect wing of cruelty and condescension repeats his earlier question.

Had enough?

My answer is both my middle fingers.

After a few frantic heartbeats, his eyebrow lowers, then both dip, and there's no goading in his expression anymore. Then his eyes shift to crimson.

This time I can see his irises, clear and aflame, like burning coals. In response, something in my mind, my body lurches violently. A rip, sharp and gaping follows, and time stops.

That something unfolds within me. It yawns wider, brighter,

louder. Something else rises—between us. Unfathomable, uncontrollable. And an unknown sensation takes over me.

In the span of two sluggish heartbeats, it intensifies—to desperation. Not for air. For a release of the need that floods me, hot and wild.

Is—is this arousal?

I don't even know what that feels like. In my lousy life, I've always avoided any level of physical intimacy, let alone sex, like the demonic plague. It was another way I could be exploited, abused, or even murdered.

Even without self-preservation as a motive, I would have abstained anyway. I've never fancied any male. Not even the kinds other females go crazy for. Not buff humans, gorgeous demons, compelling vampires, or even sex-dripping incubi.

Beyond exhausted solo efforts fueled by terribly written porn, that fizzled in anti-climactic climaxes, I've never experienced sexual arousal.

But I don't need experience to know what this clawing, molten emptiness is.

So this is what lust feels like.

No wonder—along with power and money—it makes the world go round.

Way to go, Wen. The perfect circumstances to discover your libido.

And for this hateful monster to be the one to ignite it. And to unearth a bondage/strangulation fetish while at it, it seems. When I hear angels have no use for humans in *that* way, too.

But—not according to what I see in his eyes. Those twin storms of mercilessness and destruction. They're now blazing with the things he wants to do to me.

In these suspended moments, this grim reaper of angels, who swore never to touch me, is seething with desire—the desire to take me until he finishes me. And I'm dying for him to…

No. *No.* I can't respond this way to the sadist who's taking me to the brink of death. This raging lust must be a side-effect of oxygen deprivation.

And I can't be reading *him* right. It has to be wishful thinking. So I'm not the only one suffering these depraved feelings for my enemy.

I thrash, as if this would stop them. It only makes time resume, scraping like a rusty gate that opens to my dimming vision.

A few more seconds and I will black out. I'll slip away without giving him the satisfaction of my surrender.

But with my last spark of consciousness, I tap the ground, giving it to him.

The noose immediately disappears. Air rushes into my gasping mouth under pressure, almost bursting my shriveled lungs.

As I cough and choke, I seethe. Why did I do that? I didn't want to give in. Unless…he made me?

Can he control my body? To what extent? Is that maddening ache between my legs even now his doing?

And why not? What's adding mind-control to the rest of his abuse?

The idea that he might have manipulated my responses infuriates me most of all. It's the one violation I find unforgivable.

Keeping my eyes locked with his, even when I can barely keep them open, I try to transmit my loathing and rage. He may have forced me to beg for oxygen, but I won't back down in any other way. This feud he's started between us is to the death.

Mine, regretfully.

"Angelhole," I finally rasp, reaching a trembling hand to my bruised neck. "That's my safe word for next time."

His implacable mask falls into place with a crash I feel in my bones. It's so deadpan, it makes me think I imagined the savage hunger I saw before. If he manipulated my mind, I probably did.

When he finally speaks, his voice is as expressionless. "There will be no next time."

"Give it time…Angelhole. Bullies like you…are never done compensating for their deficiencies. But, newsflash, dickwad. Abusing those weaker than you…doesn't make you dominant…it makes you pathetic."

It's clear my insults are going wide, since they're so preposterous. If a male exists who's devoid of deficiencies, that's him right there. Rather than offense, a trace of his previous weariness enters his eyes, along with something else. Hesitation? Regret?

Yeah, right.

There's nothing but pitilessness when he says, "After this day is done, you will never be a concern of mine again."

"Never say never." I scoff. "I thought this is the first thing they teach you in Immortal Kindergarten."

"On your feet, Ms. White."

He does that thing with his voice again. It sounds calm, controlled, yet cracks over my every nerve like a lash.

I'm blinded by a violence I've never experienced before, by the need to scrape my own fingers to bloody stumps clawing his invulnerable face. But I decide against defying him. I want this over. Want to meet that worse-than-death fate and be done with it.

As I stagger up to my feet, he resumes his march to the towering doors, as if he didn't interrupt it to torture me.

He retracted his wings while he did, giving me a clear view of his daunting back. The temptation to stab him in it is brutal. He didn't search me, not only because he wouldn't touch me, but because he didn't think anything I have is worth worrying about. But along with the bottle of *Angelescence*, I have a switchblade dipped in Kondar's piss.

According to demonic lore, it can poison an angel. At least, give him an agonizing infection. I'd give anything to see His Perfection covered in demonic boils.

But unlike the angel I accosted yesterday, this one *will* retaliate. Maybe by breaking every bone in my legs this time. I'm needed alive, not ambulatory.

But now I think he played with my mind, my senses, I burn to risk it. It's a struggle to bring these new self-destructive tendencies under control.

One thing helps. Deciding that I have better use for him. He can answer the questions he stopped me from asking Lorcan.

I stumble to fall into step with him. "So where is this place? Is this the Celestial Court? And you're its errand boy?"

His gaze doesn't waver from his path. "You are here to *answer* questions."

"So I don't get to make any? Are you serious?" This time, he doesn't deem to respond. "C'mon, I'm your hostage..."

"You're my prisoner."

I snort, harsher than ever with the swelling his leash caused. "Big diff. So, anyway, I'm at your mercy..."

"There will be no mercy."

"No kidding!"

Did I ever say I hated angels and demons? Hatred is nothing to what he provokes in me. He needs far stronger words than any language has. Maybe in Angelic? Surely immortals have deeper, more forceful concepts than us transient humans.

My body is still throbbing at his proximity, and his scent, now I'm this close to him. It floods me with a dozen exaggerations. If I have to pick a few, I'd say he smells like summer storms, lightning strikes and steamy nights.

Gritting my teeth against the reaction I can't blame him for anymore, I persist, "Whatever you tell me about this place is safe with me. Because…" I point to myself. "Hostage—uh, prisoner here. It'll only quench my curiosity."

"There will be no quenching of any sort. Until your sentence is passed."

"No curiosity quenching. Check. What about thirst?"

He ignores me as he flicks his hand and the massive doors swish open to the inside soundlessly, bisecting the angel.

This brute knows we humans need our hydration. I'm already dehydrated with all the sweating and vomiting, both his fault. But he will withhold even a sip of water.

A dickwad of celestial magnitude.

Seems I mutter this out loud from the way he exhales. But I forget all about him and my miserable state as soon as I step into the hangar-sized vestibule.

I've seen photos and documentaries of gigantic cathedrals, of the monuments of Ancient Egypt, Greece and China. This place combines their grandeur and painstaking detail, and takes them to an other-worldly level.

But while these monuments stood the test of time, yet still bear its ravages, this place, which feels far more ancient, is pristine. As if even time has no sway here. It probably doesn't. This is the domain of immortals. It stands to reason for it to look—eternal.

And it again bombards me with those inexplicable sensations. They almost make me prostrate myself inside that intricate symbol centering the acres of marble, and await judgement.

There's also another unstoppable need. A greed to assimilate every-thing I see.

Not that Divine Douche gives me a chance to cower or wonder. His leash is back, not tightening to a noose, but still leading me by the neck like cattle to the slaughter. Probably literally.

He's now heading directly towards a wall. When it becomes clear he won't stop, I open my mouth to object. It slams shut when the wall warps and parts at his advance.

Talk about taking a shortcut! Or in his case, making one.

As he drags me through his Moses-like passage, I struggle against his leash, tightening it myself this time. I twist barely enough to see the wall reforming behind us. Not that I should have bothered trying so hard to witness this. It happens over and over as he somehow fast-forwards us through this seemingly endless edifice.

And the deeper we wade inside, the louder it seems to be calling to me. It pulls and pushes at my every cell, until my chest feels it will cave in with the mounting dread and rapture.

My heart is all but bloodying itself against my ribs when we reach a gigantic, circular frieze. It's surrounded by a six-foot-wide frame that seems made of molten gold, and copiously engraved with runic symbols. These are arranged like the degrees of a compass, with the largest in the cardinal directions. It emanates the indifferent coldness of eternity, a chilling contrast to the vicious scene it ensconces. About two dozen massive angels engaged in bloody battle against a couple of hundred demons.

Expecting him to warp it out of our way, too, he instead goes down on one knee before it, his hand going to his opposite side, as if to draw a sword.

Next moment, he does, out of literal thin air. A broadsword with a hilt and a blade that look forged from the heart of a white-hot star.

My jaw drops as I watch him bow his majestic head and place the blazing sword below one of the angels' feet. He seems to be praying before he rises and spreads his arms, and the frieze starts to morph.

Before I can ask why all the pomp before dissolving this specific barrier, the angels start moving, as if coming to life. Then the tableau that looks made of plaster, flesh and light splits, releasing a slow-motion shockwave.

I don't know how long I stand here, blind, ceased.

It could have been hours or days before images start translating in my brain. A scene right out of a Renaissance painting and another dimension at once.

Sitting fifty feet away at a long table draped in some stark-white material that hurts to look at, with ancient scrolls and tomes opened before them, are five angels.

No. Not angels. Archangels.

Their only appearance on earth was a two-minute video on YouTube, while they signed the Accords with the demons.

It garnered over half a billion views in the minutes before it was deleted. We heard everyone involved in its recording and broadcast were executed for breaching the sanctified pact—by which side is uncertain.

Though no one was able to download it before it was taken down, someone somewhere reconstructed it, and it became one of our most dangerous contraband. That was the version I saw. It was grainy and obscure, but I still recognize them.

Gabriel.

Michael.

Raphael.

Uriel.

And Azrael.

Many humans believed that archangels aren't the top of the food chain in angelology. Those depend on popular theological sources that claim they are just a step above the generic angels. But they have been proven wrong, with the Orders we now know way below them. If there are higher beings in the angelic hierarchy, they haven't made an appearance on earth yet. Hopefully, they never will. So far, the Archangels are the big guns.

In my stunned awareness, I note that the master artists got them all wrong. Seems even humanity's prodigies couldn't imagine that level of perfection. Or these attires that seem to be made of vivid serenity, the much grander version of what Lorcan wore.

Another thing no mortal could have conveyed is the mind-numbing power radiating from their collective. I feel it can bring mountains down, can prostrate the sun and skies.

Next moment I almost am, by Godric the not-so-Great's leash.

Stupidly, I want to defy him and scramble up to my feet.

I can't. I'm too spent. Guess I should be thankful for his suppression this time. There's no telling what retribution would meet any act of defiance now.

On my knees, I stare at the heavenly quintet, and finally understand Lorcan's heartless advice.

A quick death *would* be the best outcome here.

"Good work, my son." That's Azrael. Speaking in a deep yet lyrical voice that doesn't match the chilling endings in his stare.

But—my son? As in the way a priest calls everyone in their flock my son? Or my son *my son*?

But as Godric dissolves the leash and approaches Azrael, I see them together in the same frame—and feel the answer lodge into my brain like an axe.

Godric is Azrael's actual *son!*

The resemblance, the level of power, if not its texture, are unmistakable.

I've heard of this. That the offspring of angels, the Nephilim, are not myths humanity made up, that they actually exist.

And they are the stuff of nightmares.

Hybrids worse than angels and demons combined.

But because this is my shitty life, my captor isn't any nephilim. He is the son of an *archangel*. The dragons to the other angels' eagles.

And not any archangel. Not Michael, heaven's chief general. Not Raphael, known for healing. Not Gabriel, famous for courier services. Not even Uriel—some kind of doorman of heaven. No. Azrael—the Archangel of Death.

At least, that's according to the most popular scriptures and legends. For all I know, he may be the Archangel of Worse-Than-Death, the fates Lorcan cautioned me about.

Which means Godric is *really* the grim reaper I thought him to be.

Can this possibly get any worse?

Sure it can. And it will.

Next moment I hear a mocking voice. I only realize it's mine when the words echo in the vast chamber in a wave of stunned silence.

Throwing a hand at Azrael, I just said, "So *you're* the pompous ass who named him Godric. Figures."

9

If the earth ever split and swallowed anyone, now would be a great time.

I just snarked an archangel. The most powerful being in the angeldamned universe. To his heavenly face no less. When I should be groveling at his feet—or something to that effect.

In lieu of a gaping abyss, I get Godric. He strides back toward me with a glower that could microwave an elephant in two seconds flat.

But instead of forcing me to prostrate myself in abject apology, he stops before me, giving me his back.

If I didn't know better, I would think he's putting himself between me and that mini-squadron of Armageddon.

Whatever his reason, he's giving me a *very* effective barricade to hide behind. I'll take that.

"Father, Uncles, I present you with the criminal human who calls herself Walter White."

Rubbing the itch his voice has created behind my breastbone, my mind latches onto how he addressed them. Like family, but like superiors, too. Like they're some sort of army.

Of course they are. The Army of Heaven.

And Uncles, huh? This makes sense. All the angels are supposed to be siblings of a sort. Especially the higher ups. They came into existence together or something.

It's not surprising I didn't make the connection at once. It's a wonder I can think at all. Anything lucid and logical, that is.

I *can* think plenty that's hysterical and suicidal, though. Like wanting to charge them, paw their clothes and wings and see what they're made of. The urge is almost as powerful as the pull of this place, that burning need to know what I feel should never be known.

Thankfully, Godric's blockade of muscle and feathers stops me from acting on any potentially fatal compulsion.

Of course, the moment I get comfy behind him, he moves aside.

I find out why when Raphael beckons, his gesture and voice the personification of tranquil, terrifying immortality.

"Come forward, human."

Every muscle in my body locks. I'm not afraid per se. I think. Yet everything in me rebels against approaching these beings.

Godric feels very human compared to them. They are totally—alien. Yet—familiar?

Yes. So achingly, maddeningly familiar.

It's probably some sort of racial memory, a genetic faculty that always detected the presence of angels. Maybe it's what spawned all those beliefs and religions.

I realize I always felt similar if much weaker feelings towards the other angels. They were only overshadowed by envious, impotent loathing.

But why don't they just lasso me like Godric did?

"You'll have to approach of your own free will, child." That's Gabriel, as if he heard my thoughts. Which he probably did.

I find myself scoffing. "Too late to pretend to care about free will, after Godawful yanked me all the way here on a leash."

The air sizzles at my back. Aww, I'm embarrassing him in front of his family? Tough. That name of his is a gold mine of potential insults. Ones I bet no one ever made use of.

I intend to rectify that missed opportunity while I have the chance.

The archangels stare at me, but I get the impression they're conferring mentally. They probably never had anyone talk back to them. Or talk at all in their presence, not unless ordered to.

Now would be a great time to shut up, Wen.

But whatever brakes I had left have snapped. All I can hope is that my runaway mouth doesn't deepen the hole they'll bury me in.

As if coming to a consensus, Michael addresses me, pointing to the ground ten feet away from their table. "You need to stand amidst our symbols."

Either my senses are so scrambled I didn't notice them before, or they just appeared. Five runic symbols floating two feet above the iridescent floor, each the size of a suitcase. They seem to be made of some sentient energy, each with a different hue.

Eyeing them with hot and cold currents zapping through my spine, I rasp, "Is this some kind of angelic—sorry, *arch*angelic compulsion field or something?"

"Never compulsion," Raphael says, even calmer than his brothers, but as hair-raising. "You will answer our questions of your full voli- tion. Our—field will only determine if you answer truthfully."

Only that? And what? This celestial lie detector will tase me and lengthen my nose at every untruth?

Probably something far worse.

Fine. There are ways of not telling the truth without lying.

I finally move, feet feeling like concrete blocks that will crack under me at any moment.

At the eerie, *rotating* pentacle, I stop. I don't see how I can step in their middle, especially in my sluggish state, without one bumping into me.

I don't want to know what would happen if one does. This frail human flesh can't be made for contact with archangelic runes as old as time.

Pondering my dilemma comes to an abrupt end. My feet are lifting off the ground!

Panic doesn't have time to register before I'm dumped in the center of the pentacle.

The moment my feet slam to the ground, I pitch to the side, and throw up. This time over one of those exquisite, glowing symbols. The grey one.

As the wave of nausea recedes, a guttural rumble thrums down my back, like a fed-up lion about to strike. I know it's Godric.

He's had it with me spewing my disgusting human secretions all over his angelic boots and domain? Poor monster.

Welcome to the fine art of passive aggression, asshat.

Even if mine was involuntary so far. I'm starting to feel like one of these frogs that pee when you grab them.

Let's hope sullying their sacred symbol alone isn't punishable by torment for eternity.

But a glance around tells me it's only Godric who's mad at me. And from the way I was spilled inside the circle, it was him who did it. He isn't big on free will like his dad and uncles.

In contrast to his contempt, the archangels are regarding me with an impassiveness that feels as endless as their existence. I hope they have a corresponding sense of forgiveness.

Not that I understand why they may find me worthy of punishment in the first place.

And for the first time since Godric descended on me like the Son of Death that he is, I ask myself the question: How can my small-potato business selling *Angelescence* be a crime worthy of a fate worse than death and/or damnation?

What's going on here?

"Shall we proceed, Ms. White?" This is Raphael, voice now a lulling melody.

"We shall," Mr. Grim Reaper Jr. answers for me, his abrasion blowing away Raphael's soothing effect. "Starting by having her tell us her real name."

I toss him a glare. "My name *is* White." Not a lie. Weiss is White in German. It was the name of the man who dug me out of the burning rubble. They made it mine in that orphanage. I just translated it when everyone kept misspelling or mispronouncing it.

A corner of his masterpiece lips lifts in a sneer. Strange how he's showing far more emotion in the presence of his emotionless family. "Is your name also Walter?"

"Haven't you heard that gender-specific names are a thing of the past, or are you still stuck in pre-apocalyptic times?"

"Answer the question, Ms. White," he says, his eyes promising creative punishments later.

But wanting to spite him is only a part of my reluctance to answer. I mainly loathe my name. It's the one thing I have of the mother I don't remember. The mother who abandoned me. Yet another reason to hate the damned woman.

That name was inside the antique locket with that big, iridescent gemstone I was found wearing. On the other side was an obscure picture of her holding infant me. I remember it so clearly, even when I never saw it again after that day. But I still have its shape stamped on my chest. It got so hot in the fire it gave me yet another brand. To add insult to injury, my so-called mother saddled me with the name Gwendolyn.

No one ever used that mouthful, and no two people ever called me the same thing. I was Gwen and Wendy and Winnie and Lyn and Lynnie. I was Whelp to Zeral and Wench to Kondar.

But Sarah calls me Wen, and that makes it my name.

"Wen," I finally mutter.

The imposing wings of his eyebrows rise. "When?"

"W-E-N." I barely catch back Angelass. Not advisable to mouth off —more than I already did—in the presence of those godly beings.

Strange how I can do it so easily with him, when I feel he's on the same level of power. Or weirdly, even more.

His eyebrows descend. "What kind of name is Wen?"

"Not a pompous ass one as Godric, that's for sure," I shoot back, my resolution of a second ago forgotten.

As we glare at each other, as if coming between us this time, Azrael says, "Tell us about your exploits as Walter White, Wen White."

His son doesn't leave it at that. "Don't leave out any details, no matter how insignificant. If you do so, we will resort to far more invasive—and damaging—methods to extract them."

"I thought you said free will!" I exclaim.

"*They* did," Godric growls.

So he operates with a different set of rules? He did say something to that effect to that unfortunate Caius. And he calls the archangels "they." So who are the "we" he meant? His kind? The Nephilim?

Those are supposed to be half-human. It's what makes them so terrible. Regular humans have some disturbing proclivities, making them capable of unimaginable atrocities. Add that to the power and entitlement of angels, and you have a unique, and unpredictable kind of monster.

And I continue to antagonize the apex predator of that species. The one who'll probably execute my sentence. Or execute me. Or worse.

Brilliant strategy.

I'll deal with that self-destructive streak he provokes later. If there's a later. He more or less said his gang of demi-angelic monsters can excise info from my mind, mutilating it in the process.

That perfect sadist is giving me the choice. To maim or not to maim.

Predictably, I go for keeping my mind, such as it is, intact.

Drawing a fractured breath into lungs that may never expand again, I begin, "It all started in the alley behind my apartment building…"

"We're not interested in the origin story of your descent into crime," Godric cuts me off. "Tell us how you obtain Angel Essence."

"Hang on to your feathers, will ya? It's not like I want to prolong this interrogation." Then his words sink in my scrambled mind. "Wait —it's called Angel Essence for *real*? I thought I was being clever when I came up with *Angelescence*—as a play on essence and luminescence, since it glows after I..."

"*Enough*. You will cease your rambling or I..." He stops. I'm in time to see Azrael swiping him a glance. With an almost imperceptible nod, Godric bunches his jaw muscles and repeats his question. "How do you obtain Angel Essence?"

"*As I was saying*, one night I couldn't sleep, so I stepped out onto the fire escape to get some air—such as it is in L.A.—and saw an angel and a demon fighting right below me. The angel made short work of the demon, and it was the first time I saw for myself how vicious—uh, I mean how powerful angels are, even the run-of-the-mill kind like that one was. Good thing, huh? Since you're the good guys, and we want the good guys to be stronger than the bad guys..."

Stop. Rambling.

That obsidian lightning, that almost had me peeing myself when I first saw it, is brewing in Godric's eyes. I might provoke him into striking me down even against his family's wishes, just to get rid of my aggravation.

I rush to continue, "Anyway, after the angel disposed of the demon's carcass in a dumpster, he flew off, and I saw something trailing from him, but most of it lingered below me. I wasn't getting any sleep anyway, so I went down to investigate—and it was the strangest thing. Like a hologram or some form of visible energy. It seemed at once alive, and as if it didn't exist, not in this world. Does this make any sense?"

They only continue boring into me with a focus I'm sure could denude my flesh from my bones, if they wished it to.

Forcing down another rising gulp of bile, I go on, "Though it looked intangible, I felt compelled to touch it. I reached up my hand— and it slithered to cover it. I can't even describe how it felt. The consistency, I mean. Sort of like it wasn't there, yet was the most *there* thing I ever touched. Not that I could decipher any texture or temperature, it just—was. Then suddenly, it started burning until I thought it would dissolve my hand right off. I almost fainted before the pain suddenly stopped—and my hand was intact.

"Though I was relieved it was only phantom pain, I wanted this thing off me, in the worst way. But I couldn't wipe it off on my clothes, or against the building. So I ran back up, but couldn't wash it off, or dissolve it with alcohol, and even holding my hand over the gas-burner did nothing. And I could feel this thing trying to seep into my skin. I got so frustrated, so angry, so spooked, I was willing to do anything to get it off me. Anything.

"I picked up a knife, intending to scrape my skin off if need be—but this time it started coming off, as if it didn't want me to go this far. Which can't be true, right?" No answer comes again, so I sigh. "I don't know why I didn't flush it down the drain, but the moment I scraped it into a jar, its faint bluish glow intensified, and it pooled at the bottom. Not level like a liquid, but sort of ebbing and flowing, and I had a feeling it was—upset, sulking even. Which had to be my imagination going haywire." I look at Godric. "Enough details for you?"

He gives a grave nod of his majestic head. "Proceed."

How very formal.

I bite my lip before I sneer that he sounds like some overacting character in a Victorian drama. This demi-archangel is really plucking my bitchy strings wholesale.

But how can I "proceed" without mentioning Sarah? I have to protect her, without lying. Those runes are circling me like sharks, and may strike me with angelic death rays or something if I lied. Even worse, Godric may scour my mind clean.

I inhale a shallow, bolstering breath. "Next morning, I woke up to find the roommate I had at the time high as a kite." There. The truth, with a dash of casual misdirection. "I might have thought she was trying some drug—" What Sarah would never do. "—if not for the weird energy crackling from her eyes and fingers. I freaked out at first, but she was laughing and looking at her hands in wonder.

"That sparking lasted for a couple of hours, but the high lasted way longer. She was so blissed out, I had to stand in for her at her work." And had a double-feature flogging from Kondar for missing mine. "When it was over, she told me it made her feel free, invincible—*rapturous*. Then it was beyond terrible when the heavenly experience ended. It was this comment that made me realize what happened, especially when she said she made her PB&J sandwich with the knife I scraped that stuff with.

"To make sure, I took as much—and nothing happened. A little more, then even more, and still nothing. I figured having my hand soaked in it made me resistant to its effects. So she tried it again, and the same thing happened. But now she knew what was happening, she said the euphoria was more 'out of this world.' No surprise there, right? By then I figured that energy goo was some sort of angelic secretion, so it really came straight from Heaven."

I stop, hoping this is enough to answer Godric's question.

It clearly isn't, since he commands tersely, "Continue."

I sigh heavily. "Betting people would pay good money for this heavenly high, I did a test run. But right out the gate, I hit a snag, since it was the first time I dealt drugs." I glower pointedly at Godric.

As he stares back at me, a sliver of that hungry savagery slips through his severe facade. I tear my gaze from his toward the archangels. That freezes any wayward reactions solid.

I grit my teeth as I remember that "snag."

Right after I got my enchanted bottle, my first clients were a couple of Regulars who came to Demonica to score vampire blood or any other drug, no matter how unknown or unpredictable. I was so wet behind the ears I sold each a 2ml vial. In person. And without thinking what would happen once the *Angelescence* was in their possession.

One walked out with it in his pocket, and got torn limb from limb by demons, who then killed each other for it. The other took it all in one go, got so high, he believed he could fly. He leaped off the roof, and crashed to his death. Five minutes after my first sale I ended up with a blood bath right in front of Demonica's doors.

I was so rattled, felt so guilty, I decided not to sell any more. But then I heard of a demon who was promising the Owned he'd kill our masters and free us from our Indentures, for a fee.

So I rationalized those guys' death, that as addicts, they would have overdosed sooner or later. And though I felt like crap, I decided to deal again.

But before I did, our demons ganged up on that demon. His severed head graced one of the largest squares in the Demon Zone, until birds picked his rotting flesh clean off his skull.

Not that this plan's gruesome death deterred me. The hope of getting out had taken root and I wouldn't rest until I found another way.

I thought I found it when I heard about a new coven operating out of Skid Row. They claimed they removed any curse, including Marks. But Sarah refused pointblank. Since I trust her gut instincts above anything else, I investigated further. And she was right, as usual.

From my sources deep within the sewers of the Supernatural Underworld, I found out that the ritual is either fatal, or leaves you a vegetable. The kicker was that the side-effects aren't immediate, and it works perfectly at first. That's how they built a reputation in each area they set up shop in. Desperate people flocked to them, they made a fortune, then they disappeared before the bodies started dropping.

After many dead ends, I was down to our last option. Theoretically, an Owned can buy themselves back from their Owners, at the price set during the initial ritual. That provision has never been applied in real life. What Owned could make money, let alone dare approach their demons to demand that so-called "right"?

It seemed impossible for us, too. Our Indentures were set at a million bucks a head, and I didn't even know if I could get more *Angelescence* to sell. Even if I did, and amassed that sum, I couldn't approach our demons with it. They would have forced me to make them that kind of money for the rest of my life. It would have guaranteed we'd never be free.

But as it was our only hope, I borrowed a copy of the Accords with a stolen library card. We alternated poring over the Laws of Indenture, hoping to find some loophole. After all, every law, mortal, immortal or even divine has one.

And Sarah found it. Among the endless subclauses and mind-numbing legalese, large enough to squeeze us both through. A binding provision that could guarantee our freedom.

Turns out in the event a Demon-Owned produces the *Indentura Pretium*, literally the indenture price, an Owner must accept it, and write in their own blood the *Pactum Exolvo*, or the pact of release. Any attempt to take the money and not grant it, or to renege on the *Pactum* in any way, would reverse the infernal magic fueling the Mark, resulting in the demon's agonizing death, and the stigmatization of his line.

Once I was secure all that stood between us and freedom was money, I began to deal in earnest. But to avoid more deaths on my conscience, I issued strict directions in each transaction, about the method of use, probable side effects and adverse reactions, and limited the dose I sold to 1ml.

I would have made it less after it proved too much for many clients when taken at once. But that was the least amount I could separate from the mass. And they were the ones who disregarded my warnings, and paid the price. There was nothing more I could do.

And then I figured I was no worse than those Big Pharma compa-
nies. They tell you the drug that *might* help alleviate your symptoms,
even when taken in the correct therapeutic dose, could drive you to
suicide or make you drop dead.

Not that my angelic captors need to know any of that.

But since six pairs of eyes that could turn me to Wen-flavored
powder are trained on me, I give them the abbreviated version.
"After extensive investigation, I found out there's nothing like my
product on the drug scene, or the thriving black market that deals in
anything angelic." Godric makes that sound great felines make before
pouncing again. I raise my eyebrows at him. "You didn't know this
existed?"

"We know everything."

"Not everything, since I'm here to tell you things you don't
know…" Another rumble makes my heart rev like a hummingbird.
"Aaand I'm shutting up now."

"You will keep talking," Godric grits out. "And keep to the relevant
facts."

"Yeah, right. Relevant. Where was I? Oh, yes, after realizing I had a
unique product, I raised the price, and clients still fought over it. So
after many price hikes, I sold that jar for a sum of money I never
thought I'd see if I lived a hundred lifetimes."

"When did you finish that jar?" Godric bites off.

"Within the first month…" I stop, the cold fire of dread drenching
me.

Now he'd want to know how I got more.

If I had any hope he wouldn't, his next words blast it away. "How
have you been getting Angel Essence ever since?"

I want to kick myself in the head for my slip up. Now if I don't give
him a satisfactory answer, he'd delight in extracting it out of it with
mental pliers.

I exhale in resignation. "I worked out that angels exude this
substance when they exert themselves, or when they're agitated or
angry. So I started ambulance-chasing them."

The archangels stare at me blankly. Gotta ease up on the vernacular.

From his lip twist, it's clear Godric doesn't need a translation. I still
provide one for his bosses. "I mean I began following angels, hoping
for more clashes with demons, so I could collect their—er, Essence
afterward. But since you have the Accords and all, I couldn't catch
another angel in the act. So I monitored the angels who frequent the

places I go to, then planned something that would anger them, so I could—uh, you get the picture."

Again, I get the impression the archangels are conferring mentally. But this time I can sense their reactions. They seep into my marrow like acid.

Confusion. Calculation. Disinterest. Dismay. Dread.

But how could these emotions be emanating from them? A better explanation is they're my own. I *am* at a total loss why they're treating this whole thing with such gravity.

I never considered I was doing something that bad. I wasn't even breaking any law. Even if I was, many of the human or angelic laws are messed up, and breaking them wouldn't make me a bad person. Not evil, anyway. I dealt only to adults, most already addicts.

So many got hurt or even died, but I gave them ample warnings. Also, being Indentured has a way of setting your priorities for you. And then, I was doing it only until I got us out of Hell on Earth.

So yes, what I did was morally grey—okay, *dark* grey—but what isn't in this world? Especially my world?

And who are *they* to judge morality, the beings who killed hundreds of millions of my kind?

But their involvement is a plot twist, as Lorcan said. I went to extreme lengths to avoid exposure to humans and demons. I never even considered the angels themselves.

Why would freaking archangels and their even scarier enforcer care about me gathering angelic perspiration? Or that I made money selling the stuff? A life-changing sum for me and Sarah, but not even pocket change to them?

What am I not getting here?

Next second, everything inside me, in the world, ceases.

The archangels are getting to their feet, their wings rising above them in a heart-rending sweep of unearthly menace.

Whatever they do next will dictate my fate.

In a voice as inexorable as the death he dealt, it's Azrael who delivers my sentence. "Wen White, until we determine the scope of your unprecedented offense, and discover the exact method with which you committed it, we hereby conscript you to Celestial Academy."

"*No!*"

IO

The single syllable of towering outrage practically sears through the air.

It's Godric's. When I thought he'd be delighted with any sentence I got.

He must know something I don't, since I'm not horrified. Hell—if I'm allowed to think of Hell in the presence of archangels—I can't feel anything. There's this void inside me, filled with nothing but questions.

So my sentence isn't bad enough for Angelhole? That means it's not worse-than-death, right? But what kind of sentence is conscription, anyway?

And what is that Celestial Academy?

Okay, so it sounds self-explanatory—an academy where magnificent monsters like Godric go, to— what? Study how to be the most lethal weapons in Heaven's army? With each majoring in a branch of slaughter and mayhem?

Now I know the Nephilim exist, a place like this must be a necessity. The angels who procreate with humans must need a highly specialized teaching and training establishment for their hybrid offspring. Makes sense.

At least it does, until you throw me, lowly, powerless human into the equation.

So, am I conscripted to clean their toilets? Do the Nephilim even crap? Is this going to be their version of hard labor? For how long?

Yet even if it is hard labor, and it takes years until they "determine the scope of my unprecedented offense", it isn't as bad as I feared. I came here expecting a death sentence. Or an eternity of damnation. Or Lorcan's worse fate.

But then, any time among such creatures will *feel* like forever. That's assuming I can survive at all in such a place.

And how exactly do they intend to determine the scope of my offense? What *is* that exactly? Recycling angel sweat? And what is there to discover about my "method"?

I told them I touch the stuff and it coats my hand. What more do they want from me? An explanation of the exact mechanics of the process? What would they do when I can't provide more details?

"This isn't a viable option." Godric's rumble slams the lid on my growing-again panic. "It was bad enough bringing her to the Court, but inducting her into the Academy?"

"You question our judgement, son?" Azrael is as tranquil as ever, but I sense an emotion fueling his words. It isn't affront. It's something deeper, and that much scarier for being so pervasive and unending.

There's conflict between father and son. Simmering hot as Hell.

That's good to know. Any crumb of info I pick up on these all-powerful creatures may come in handy later. However much "later" I have.

But Azrael's question, and its implied challenge, silence Godric.

So miracles do happen.

Of course you have to be the Angel of Death and his father to achieve said miracle. But at least something in the universe can check him. *Great* to know.

Even greater is that the archangels don't share his dismal view of me. Not bad having five of the most powerful entities in existence in your corner. Sorta. Sure, they drafted me to this academy, but since I expected much, *much* worse, I'm taking their sentence as clemency.

Whatever their reasons for it.

No looking a gift leviathan in the mouth, Wen. Take the stay of execution or eternal damnation. Live to fight another day.

Suddenly, all thoughts sputter. The archangels are approaching me.

With the brutal brunt of their soundless footfalls, I'm again struck by that marrow-deep familiarity.

Godric grudgingly makes way for his father as the quintet surrounds me.

They reach out their hands, each towards his symbol. The grey one I puked over is Azrael's.

Focusing on the runes for the first time, I long for a pen and paper, to sketch them all down. Though I feel they may be imprinted in my mind. That they were always there, and seeing them unearthed the memory.

This has to be another side-effect of being exposed to such a power collective. My mind must be overloading. I only hope they step away before they fry it irreversibly.

As they seem to go into a trance, eyes half-closed and looking into the depths of eternity, probably literally, I feel free to examine them.

This up close, the only things that unify them are the basic style of attire, and that mind-melting radiation of power. Apart from that, they're totally different in detail and feel.

It's Azrael who snares my focus. He looks achingly like his son— just devoid of savagery and sensuality. If I didn't know any better, I would have thought they're brothers.

But it's not how Azrael looks that mesmerizes me. It's how he feels. He's the one who's most familiar. Even—kindred? I have no other word for it. It's like we share blood, essence.

It's probably that racial memory again. For what is more familiar to mortals than the texture of Death?

Suddenly, I float in the air, my hair, my clothes lifting up, as if I'm hanging upside down. But it isn't a gravity reversal, since I don't feel blood rushing to my head. And my hair and clothes are rippling around me as if I'm underwater, undulating to the same frequency of the glowing streams rising from every symbol. They curve around and above me, enmeshing and entombing me in a cage of eternity.

For a timeless stretch, my senses are suspended within this celestial matrix. Only my heart works, emptying its beats in a frenzied rush.

Then angelic energy starts entwining through the mesh. I know because it has echoes of the waste product I collect. But the resemblance is like calling a magnificent tiger and a unicellular organism life. This stuff is the real deal. And it's skittering all over me, as if trying to seep through my pores, like the *Angelescence* always tries to.

The sensations soon become too overpowering, no matter how hard I try to suppress them, to resist. But it's no use.

I burst out in cackling shrieks.

I squirm and splutter and snort with laughter, tears running up my forehead to wet my hair. And all the time, Godric's eyes dagger me with his distaste.

What does he want me to do? It *tickles*.

Just as I think I'm going to suffocate again, this time with the forced laughter, the tickling sensations morph in texture. They become pressure, sniffing, gauging, prodding. I feel the imprint of the archangels' essences, their questions and curiosity, in every filament of my body and psyche.

Holy abduction scenario! These archdudes are giving me a full body and mind exam!

Then just as it began, it's over, and I float back to my feet outside my cage.

At least they didn't slam me down like Gordric did.

I still stagger, almost fall against those pulsing-with-indescribable-power symbols.

The archangels step back, again seeming to confer among themselves.

Then Raphael shakes his head. "Inconclusive."

What's inconclusive? What were they looking for?

"Indeed," Uriel says, his eyes tinged with an unreadable expression as they sweep over me.

"I guess it was to be expected," Michael says. "This was supremely irregular to start with."

"It was, and remains, *inconceivable*," Raphael corrects him. "It's just as impossible that I wouldn't be able to make a diagnosis."

What? What's inconceivable? What diagnosis? If they don't make sense soon, I may do something I won't live long enough to regret.

Michael nods. "This is indeed unprecedented. Yet we must fathom it, so we have no other recourse."

Raphael exhales. "Then only what we hoped to avoid remains."

What's that? Are they going to crack me open and search for what their angelic MRI couldn't find?

Before I work myself into a fiercer lather, Gabriel addresses me, "You will attend the Divining."

The what now?

Before I blurt out the question, I remember I heard about this before. Some obscure ritual from ancient times, a pact between angels and demons long before the Accords. No idea what it was for, or what it entailed, only that they picked humans for it, then they divided those who survived it. A good percentage didn't.

And they want me to attend it.

Yay me.

Validating my info, Michael adds, "It is perilous, yet unavoidable at this point."

"Perilous how?" I croak. "I can die?"

"We sincerely hope you won't," Gabriel says.

"*Not* the answer I wanted to hear, dude!"

Gabriel seems genuinely confused at the way I addressed him. "It is the only way we have left to ascertain your nature."

"My nature," I repeat sluggishly. "As in what kind of person I am?"

"What kind of being you are," Uriel corrects.

Does he mean what I think he means?

Nah. Of course not. Who knows how these detached creatures perceive other beings, anyway.

Guess it's up to me to save us all time, and me probably my life. "I can tell you that, no Perilous Divining required. I'm a garden-variety human being."

Raphael shakes his head. "You are not."

Okay. They *did* mean what I thought they meant.

"You think I'm not human?" I rasp, panic drenching me yet again. "Based on what? That I can pick up angelic BO?"

Before any of the archangels can respond, Godric pushes past his father and bears down on me.

That voice of his slides lushly over my nerves like a blade as he says, "Perceiving Angel Essence by beings other than angels should be impossible. *Is* impossible. Harnessing it in any way is something not even the Seraphim has ever done. This makes you potentially one of the most dangerous entities who ever existed."

II

Nothing has ever left me at a loss for words.

I was told I talked when they exhumed me from that burning rubble. I talked after Kondar lashed me and I was wishing to die. I even talked when confronted by this deadly nephilim and his soul-sundering family.

In a world where all creatures are more powerful than I am, what else do I have but the ability to mouth off? Shit continued to happen to me whether I did so or not. Cowering never protects anyone, and it would have only made me feel worse while enduring abuse. When I talked back, I remained in control of one thing in this messed up world.

Seems I only never got the exact amount of shock needed to silence me. Now I did. And Godric was the one who delivered it. Depriving me of my one and only power.

It's funny really, when he just said I could be one of the most dangerous entities who ever existed.

"Dude, you need to lighten up or these wings of yours, wherever you stash them when not in use, are going to molt."

Okay. Seems my auto smart-mouth function is still intact.

Thank you, mouth.

If looks could fry, and I'm certain Godric's can, I'd be crispy on the outside, gooey on the inside right now. It's only on account of the archangels' "judgement" that I'm not already.

That's the only piece of good news in this mess. In a way, he's as helpless as I am.

And boy, does this make me feel better.

In case I survive whatever that Divining is, I'm milking his impotence—the totally figurative kind I'm sure—for all it's worth.

The archangels share a final glance, before Azrael says, "Carry out our decree, son. Take Ms. White to the Divining. You will receive further guidance once you bring her back."

The storm that rages across Godric's face—even though his expression doesn't change—says exactly what he thinks of this errand.

He brought me here so the archangels would extract answers from me, before tossing me to him to roast with heavenly fire, or something. I bet he never imagined they would fail to, and his father would saddle him with babysitting me until that Divining produces the info they need.

Tough luck, big guy. If I'm spending the next years picking smelly Nephilim socks, you're putting up with a few more hours of my delightful company. They're my last chance of making you regret the moment you "made me," and I'm not wasting a second.

Azrael seems to be waiting for Godric to give his consent. These archangels are really big on free will, aren't they?

But then, how could Godric say anything but yes to his father and celestial superior? Free will doesn't feature in army hierarchy.

"Permission to soulspeak," Godric says without taking his stony gaze off me.

Azrael nods, and they face each other. As their gazes empty, as if looking beyond this existence, everything hits me all over again.

I'm really here. Standing between an archangel and his son. Beings capable of snapping me in two with a thought. Of razing the world with their army.

Now they're razing *my* world.

So it's not a world to mourn, but I shared it with Sarah…

Sarah! I can't leave her!

But they will force me to. She will be all alone.

I can't *bear* to think of her alone.

The one thing that keeps me from doing something suicidal, like scratching Azrael's eternal eyes out or kicking Godric in his celestial jewels is one hope. That they'll let me see Sarah one last time.

I have to see her. Have to instruct her in getting her ticket out of hell.

A blast of something bleak and devouring, like a void expanding, interrupts my desperation. I stumble back as I gape at the godlike beings lost in their inner dialogue.

Are they fighting in there?

If they are, I may become collateral damage any moment now.

I turn to the archangels, hoping they'll get me out of their range until they settle whatever is roiling between them and…

What the hell? The archangels are gone!

When did that happen?

Not that it matters. Only that they left me with the archangel whose diet for millennia has been human lives, and his half-human son, who has the full array of both species' vices.

Don't those archangels understand our tissue-like existence? If one of them lashes out, even mentally, I'm toast.

As I begin to think that's inevitable, Azrael looks away from whatever he's been staring into—maybe some cosmic arena where he's been spanking his son—and back to me.

"May the Light choose you, Ms. White."

Then, between one blink and the next, he's gone in a blinding flash.

"Hey! Angels can teleport? Why have wings then? Can you teleport, too? Then why the van?"

Godric turns to me, and now no one is buffering his antipathy, I almost cringe.

Thankfully, I don't. But I shake, and pretend it's with my hurrying gesture. "So—what did your dad tell you on your private channel? To bring me back in one unscathed piece, right? Not that I'm unscathed now."

"Until I deliver you back, you will not ask questions or do anything else unless I tell you to."

"How about I don't breathe, too?"

A baleful glance. "That would be preferable. Regretfully, you're still needed alive."

"Yeah, too bad for you."

He stalks away, his damn leash forming around my neck. Now that I expect it, I rush after him, to deprive him of the pleasure of jerking me around.

But as we cross that frieze gateway and exit the hall where the course of my life has changed for what remains of it, I begin spluttering for breath.

Angelhole is quickening his pace on purpose, I just know it. He's not tightening the noose per se, but he's still choking me.

Rage rising again, I pull at the string of angelic compulsion. This is still a duel, and I'm keeping up my end of it, even at the cost of more injuries.

But strangely, it doesn't burn me this time. And my tug corresponds to the slightest of jerks from Godric.

Is that a coincidence, or...?

I tug again. And again there's this almost imperceptible interruption in his perfect control.

What do you know? This thing is two-way!

There's a measure of fairness in the world, after all.

Feeling immeasurably better even in my battered condition and grim situation, I scamper to keep up with his massive strides as he compresses warping our way out into under a minute. This fast-forwarding may not be teleporting, but it's close, and far more interesting.

Feeling giddy at my latest discovery, I grin up at him as we reach the main doors, goading set on maximum. "So, if not questions, what will we talk about?"

He flicks the doors open. "We will not talk."

"Chill, dude. Can't go through eternity this wound up. Say, how old are you? You don't look that much older than I am. Twenty-six? Eight? Thirty tops!" A mature, rugged, *indescribable* thirty. "But then you might be thirty centuries!"

"Walk in silence, human."

"Don't 'human' me. You're half human yourself."

The look he gives me says how much he hates this fact. And that I'm walking on wafer-thin ice.

But since he can't act on his non-verbal threat, my grin widens as I rush down the stairs behind him, "Oh, I know something to talk about, something we have in common. We're both on a leash."

Giving me a steel-melting glance, he reaches the van waiting for us and gets inside the passenger seat next to Lorcan. I sigh as I take my place in the backseat. Gotta show him the silent treatment won't do a thing to shut me up.

Lorcan launches the car like a runaway rocket the moment I'm buckled in. After my heart slams back in my chest, I feel a pang of triumph that I managed it on my own. Then I notice it's not the same seat. We're in another car. A clean one. Too bad.

Sitting back, my tailbone reminds me with a lance of pain how I almost fractured it at the Godric Landing.

Fidgeting to a position that lessens the discomfort, I let out a long exhalation. "So, how about we compare leashes?"

Lorcan's eyes round as they meet mine in the rearview mirror. "Leashes? What did I miss?" He shoots Godric's rigid profile an eager glance. "You are going to recap that summit meeting, right?"

"Wrong."

At Godric's cutting syllable, I sigh dramatically. "His dad and uncles ordered him to chaperone me to the Divining and back. He'd rather pluck his own wings and set his feathers on fire, but he has to obey. I was just discussing with him how we're both on a leash. Though mine isn't as...suffocating. It's probably temporary, until they figure out how I gather Angel Essence and I atone for the crime of selling it. But *his* leash is genetic, so it's going to be yanking him by the neck for the rest of his life. Say...are you guys immortal like your parents? Cause that would suck, big time. Big *endless* time. Imagine an eternity on a leash. I can't imagine. Can you?"

Lorcan gapes at me before he starts laughing. Godric doesn't react outwardly, but a hair-raising shockwave emanates from him. He's incensed. But he says nothing. It feels like he *can't* say anything.

Sweet. I managed to silence him.

I can now brag I have something in common with Azrael. That's an archangel-sized win. Gotta savor it. It's probably the only win I'll have for whatever remains of my life.

I lost whatever hope I had for freedom. I may not survive that Divining, or another form of Indenture in that Academy. But for now I don't care.

Whatever happens next, I only care about two things.

That I manage to contact Sarah one last time. And that I stick the needles of my aggravation into Godric. I have nothing left but making sure she gets free, and the pleasure of seeing him strain and snap at his own leash to no avail.

Welcome to my misery, Angelhole.

12

Turns out they caught me *just* in time for the Divining.
        Quite the coincidence, if you ask me, when it's taking place for the first time in history. In a collective ceremony, that is. In New York.

And here I am—the girl who never even rode a cab—on a private jet. A flying ultra-luxury mini-mansion imbued by earthly cash and celestial magic.

My question of why we didn't teleport instead went unanswered, leaving me to come up with my own answers. That maybe teleportation is reserved for the archangels, and it's above the Nephilim's pay grade.

If so, it's one thing to my advantage. Who wants to be dissolved into only-archangels-know-what, and reformed thousands of miles away? What if they put me back wrong? Or if the angelic wi-fi blips and drops my signal?

Also if the process involves having Godric's arms of mass destruction around me—well, let's say I'm glad I revolt him.

That half-archangel, half-human, all-monster jerk dials my specific number, hard. I don't want to find out what would happen to me at his slightest touch. While he thinks mine would be a taint he can never scrub off.

So, angelic jet it is.

When we boarded an hour ago, I stood swaying on aching feet, not

89

daring to sully the pristine cream seats. I felt so filthy, I thought nothing less than an acid bath would get me clean again. Lorcan corroborated my opinion, mumbling something about needing to scrape his sinuses. Yeah, I stank that much.

Thankfully, he directed me to the shower. Even in this world where the supernatural is the daily norm, *that* felt unreal.

I now stand under the powerful spray, sobbing with relief as its temperature and pressure magically adjust to my exact preference. It feels as miraculous as archangels with a direct line to Heaven.

No. *Way* more. Who cares about pompous celestials and their inaccessible hometown? As someone who's suffered scarce, cold showers all my life, I'd take that one over Heaven any day. I swear I feel it dissolving the grime of my cruddy existence, and cleansing my very soul of the contaminations of a lifetime.

It also cossets me in ways I can only associate with two things I never experienced—a good mother, and a better masseuse.

But as the shower adds a jasmine wash to the water, I can't help but wonder. About all that decadence.

So the angels have become involved in earthly commerce and finance, taking over swathes of both. But I always believed it was about control and power, not wealth and comforts. As for the archangels, though everything on earth must be theirs for the taking, they didn't strike me as interested in worldly stuff.

So is all this in service of the Nephilim? Does their human side clamor for material gratification? And does their powers amplify their appetites?

This idea only drags my mind into a disconcerting direction. One that sweeps me along like a raging river.

Even hating the guy more than anything in a life filled with hatreds, it's impossible not to imagine Godric standing under that water jet.

My mind's eye fills with feverish images. Of his every muscle flexing, of his majestic head thrown back, and his incredible eyes closing as he lets that shower pamper and worship him.

These images segue into seeing myself joining him. I avoid imagining how I look, since I must be a starved rat next to his supremely-fed panther. I choose to see his eyes filling with that crimson-hot lust as I run my hands all over his vicious perfection.

But even in fantasy, I don't know how to inflame him. Frustrated with my pathetic inexperience, I let my mind veer into the part where he takes over.

I see him snatching me off my feet, almost feel him plastering me with all that power and virility to the caressing tile. I writhe against it, imagining him opening me wide over his hips, and clamping my neck in his ruthless hand.

The moment I imagine him pressing it, my whole body convulses.

A strangled cry tears from my depths as currents shoot down my nerves like lightning bolts. They fork from the phantom touch at my neck to my nipples, to lodge in my gushing, contracting core.

My head spins as I slide down to the floor, shaking all over in disbelief….and pleasure.

I-I just came. Without even touching myself.

And it was the best orgasm—the only *real* orgasm of my life.

And to think it was in that monster's honor.

The worst part is, now I know how it feels, I need more.

For delirious moments, I lie there shuddering with aftershocks, and want nothing but to charge out, naked, dripping and crazed, looking for him. I see myself pouncing on him, pushing him down in one of those seats, tearing him out of those obscuring pants, and…

The images stutter with my hands over his imagined bulge.

Even in the privacy of my imagination, I balk at going further. I can't even dictate his reaction, or imagine him losing control.

But if that monster ever loses control, and acts on the sensual threat I thought I saw in his eyes, he'd probably kill me. And if his leash ever loosens, he'd worse than kill me.

That thought finally tears apart the fantasy, and drenches my flaming senses in the icy, dirty water of reality.

As if sensing my upheaval, the spray becomes a cascade, soothing me, and somehow the aches of my contusions and lacerations right along.

A loud knock rattles the door. Again

"Go away, Lorcan," I wheeze. "I'm not coming—uhh, I'm not getting out until we land."

"Food," Lorcan singsongs, his deep voice permeated with teasing. "Lots of food, Wen White. Lots of amazing, heavenly food."

Another convulsion, in my empty stomach this time, forces me to sit up. As if realizing it's over, the shower stops at once.

Pulling myself to my feet, I run regretful hands down its tiles. "Oh, Shower—leaving you is almost as difficult as being forced to leave

Sarah behind. I'd *marry* you if possible. But this semi-heavenly rat just made me an offer I can't refuse."

"I left the Divining-required uniform in the dressing room," Lorcan calls out again. "Hop to it, before we big lads wipe out everything edible on board."

The unbearable idea of missing out on food makes me scamper out like a headless chicken. As I already said, semi-heavenly rat.

The only thing that slows me down again is my reluctance to see semi-heavenly brute again. My traitorous body is still tingling with that whopper of a climax. What if he can sense the pheromones blasting off of me?

I find said uniform as I come to a decision. At the first knowing, smug glance, I'll commit suicide. By attempting to murder him.

* * *

"Chew, Wen." Lorcan snickers. "Or the masses of food you've been cramming, will come back up again. I just sanitized my sinuses."

I gulp down the latest massive mouthful, and make a face at him. "I'll have you know, I'm now cleaner than any being who ever lived."

For emphasis, I sniff my armpit, and almost have another orgasm. I smell of products that must be imported from Heaven, and used as a reward for benevolent souls.

The uniform must be, too. Once I put that indeterminate-material, silver-grey jumpsuit on, it shrank down to fit me like a second skin. It would be hell to get out of, but it's more comfortable than my own.

Even better is the auto-fitting underwear. And that bra! I can't feel it on, but it somehow totally hides the enchanted bottle and piss-dipped switchblade I stuffed in my cleavage. Best of all, it provides perfect minimizing support. It's the first time I don't hate my breasts for being too large for my frame, and being damn hard to disguise. Just thinking of going back to binding them makes me cringe. If I survive the Divining, I hope they let me keep that bra.

For now, I intend to enjoy it, and as much as I humanly can of that food that has to be manna.

The only thing that initially spoiled my enjoyment was wishing Sarah could experience it all with me. My regret disappeared when I remembered this comes in a package with being a captive. And that this could be a last meal for the condemned

But even if it is, I never even dreamed of these luxuries. And my relationship with planes was to squint up at them from garbage-filled streets, while they flew lucky Regulars to places I thought I'd never see. Like New York, for instance.

It was where the Apocalypse first came to earth. It was almost fully destroyed, but is also among the most restored places on earth ever since. There was a huge celebration recently after they erected a new Lady Liberty.

When I found out we'd go there, I thought if I died in the Divining, it would at least be after seeing a place other than filthy, supernaturally-overrun L.A. I thought it would be enough to send me to my grave, if I even get one, sort of content.

But I won't even see New York. Angelhole is dragging me directly to the Divining. If I get through it in one piece, he'll yank me out to slam dunk me in that Celestial Academy, aka my new *Locus Indenturae*, or Location of Indenture.

I tried to prod him for details about said academy, but true to his decree, he hasn't uttered a word since we left the Court. So I've been talking to the more accommodating Lorcan. A. Lot. I hoped my incessant chatter would make him want to jump out of the plane.

But I couldn't even savor that imaginary scenario. Not when he has his own inbuilt glider.

On the bright side, instead of the knowing, smug looks I dreaded, he seems unaware I'm even there. That distillation of heavenly grace and earthly sins continues to sit across from me with earbuds on, and consciousness roaming better realms.

At least he has spared me from attacking him, and ending my life prematurely.

But his nearness is a constant buzz in my mind and a fizz in my blood. I can only ignore him too by constantly talking, and eating.

Up till we touch down, I'm still stuffing my face with all I can. If this is to be my last meal, I'm going out on a bursting stomach.

If not, and I end up throwing up all over Son of Death here, all the better. Win win.

As the jet stops and Godric stands up, I peer outside my window. I only see the empty tarmac of another clearly private airport.

I turn to my companions, chewing a huge lump of caviar-laden croissant open-mouthed. "So—any pointers for the Divining?"

The purified disgust that crosses Godric's majestic face as food flies out of my mouth is to be immortalized in digital painting. I can just see it. Him in wrathful demigod mode, with that flaming sword in hand, boot on my chest, glowering down at my decapitated head with that exact expression.

He, of course, doesn't answer.

Lorcan, as usual, does. "Whatever happens in the Divining, happens."

"Don't give me that cryptic crap, Lorc!" I wipe my mouth with a napkin that must cost more than all our possessions, and realize how much food I had *outside*. "The archangels want me back in one piece, so any helpful nuggets you provide will be doing your masters' bidding, really."

"The archangels are our superiors, not masters," Lorcan corrects.

"Masters, superiors—you still have to bend backwards in a bridge to see their wills done. So?"

Lorcan sighs. "No one knows what goes on in the Divining. At least, the Nephilim don't. We never had to go through it. And it's said every human's experience is different."

"So I go in blind, and hope not to explode or something. Peachy."

Lorcan chuckles. "Just don't talk—if that's even possible."

"Can't promise *that*." I unbuckle my seatbelt, again ridiculously proud of that achievement.

As I heave up, the world spins. All the blood not busy digesting the food bulging my usually concave stomach rushes to my feet.

My hands shoot out, grabbing the first thing within reach.

It's Godric.

He goes rigid, hands rising away from any contact with me. He wouldn't have displayed more aversion if he were accosted by sentient sewage.

I cling to the supple, black leather of the jacket he changed into, until the tornado uprooting my world slows down. As it does, I become aware of his scent and heat enveloping me. Though I'm sated into nausea, my stomach still growls, with a different kind of hunger— the traitor.

Once my vision clears, I look up into his spectacular scowl and mumble, "I would have grabbed Lorcan if I had a choice."

"Next time, just fall down."

"It's you who can't have me knock myself out and miss the Divining."

"So grabbing me was doing *me* a favor?"

I smirk up at him. "Sure was. Me, I'd take coma over being around you, pal. It's you who needs your daddy's gold star. You're welcome."

A crackle of lightning emits from his eyes, such a heady promise of devastation.

Before I can relish it, he steps away and strides toward the exit.

As we descend from the jet in his wake, I look up at Lorcan.

My heart stumbles as I whisper, "Will you keep your promise, or will you be a good soldier and report it to Godric?"

An hour ago, Godric left us to talk to the pilot, and I grabbed the opportunity, and the risk, of telling Lorcan about Sarah.

I made him promise that in case I don't make it out of the Divining, he'd help her buy her Indenture, and get her out of demon territory. And if I do make it, he'd let me contact her to the same end.

Lorcan gives a dramatic sigh. "Godric *is* my superior. The Nephilim take chain of command seriously. Deadly so. Literally sometimes. Doesn't help that he's also Uncle Azrael's son, and he's probably the scariest thing in all the realms."

"Who? Azrael or Godric?"

He gives an incredulous huff. "Godric, of course."

Ugh. And I'm not only fantasizing about him, I'm still antagonizing him with every word out of my mouth. But…

"Wait—uncle? Do all you Nephilim call archangels 'uncle', or what?"

Lorcan's lips quirks. "What. My old man is Gabriel. The most laid-back among the powers that make Hell and Earth weep."

"Great!" I groan. "You're another archangelspawn! And I stupidly asked you to help my friend."

"What does this have to do with anything?" He looks genuinely confused. "I said I'll help her, and I'll keep my promise."

I bite my lip as hot, painful relief pokes behind my eyes. For I believe him. I believe that if there's anyone who would help Sarah find freedom, I couldn't have lucked into better than Lorcan.

I can be wrong. But what else can I do now but cling to that belief?

"But for the record, I'd rather keep my promise in option B," Lorcan says under his breath as we reach the massive SUV awaiting us. "Don't die, all right?"

"I'll put that on my calendar," I mutter as I slide in the back. "Monday, December the sixteenth—Don't die."

He chuckles as he slams the door and hops into the driver's seat. Godric is already sitting stonily beside him, and I hear his teeth grinding as Lorcan screeches away, probably melting the tarmac.

Who thought putting that maniac behind a wheel was a good idea?

And why isn't control-freak Godric, who clearly loathes Lorcan's driving, doing it himself?

Questions. I've got nothing but questions.

Now all I have to do is live long enough to find out their answers. Even if staying alive, between the Divining, Celestial Academy, and Godawful seems very, very unlikely.

13

Thunder cracks over my nerves.

With a snort that scrapes my sinuses raw, I lurch awake.

Sand-lined eyes scratch open to the sight of my matted hair. Great. It has escaped my braid. Beyond the dark spaghetti-like mess, there are two black pillars. Powerful, jean-clad thighs.

Godric. Of course. Waking me up. Again.

Slowly, I realize I'm slumped on the backseat, face mashed into a pool of drool. In front of that paragon of perfection.

Lovely.

"Get *up*, White."

So it's White sans Ms. now. Guess I forfeited even contemptuous formality when I called him names to his family.

Good. Let the gloves come fully off. I have worse where Godawful came from.

Pushing up, I wince at the soreness of my ripening bruises and wounds. And at the missed opportunity, of sightseeing New York from the luxury and safety of this amazing vehicle.

But mainly at the big, wet patch at my jumpsuit's neckline.

I groan as I prop myself up on my elbow. "We arrived already?"

"Thankfully. You've been snoring loud enough to peel the paint off passing cars. I feared human law enforcement would issue an emergency evacuation of the highway."

He's joking? Stick-in-the-cosmic-mud Godric?

Though I did get that glimpse of his wicked humor. But I'd rather think I misread him then, and my humor centers are malfunctioning now. They must be fried if I'm finding anything he says funny.

But snoring, too? Is there no end to the indignities a girl can suffer?

Wiping my mouth on my sleeve earns me another grunt of disgust.

I glare up at him. "What? It was either that, or your pants."

His wings snap out behind him in their full glory. The wind they unleash pushes me face down in my drool again.

Struggling up with a shriek of fury, I grab his legs and furiously wipe my mouth over them. It feels like grabbing smoldering steel and mashing my lips against a lightning bolt.

My heart slams back into my spine as my gaze jerks up to collide with his. Time stutters as he broods down at me, eyes crackling like a sun-storm. And not with anger or disgust. With that vast, terrible hunger I thought I saw before.

Then his gaze slides to my lips, and how close they are to his crotch. Just like that, I see myself doing what my imagination stumbled over earlier—biting into his bulge as I frantically unzip his jeans and…

I snatch my hands away and scramble up to my knees.

With one last devastating look that has my core clenching on a rush of moist heat, he stands aside to let me get out.

Putting a shaking foot on the ground, I look beyond his barricade, and my breath backs up in my throat again.

Rising in the near distance is another mind-boggling building. It's nothing as massive as the Court, but if there is any physical representation of a Heaven and Hell amalgam, this cathedral is it.

Now their unholy collaboration would somehow determine what I am, whatever that means. If it doesn't kill me first.

Might as well get this over with.

As I step past Godric, I see the rest of the scene. It looks like one of those dystopian movies, where humans in drab uniforms trudge in despair, on their way to become processed meat for the elites or the invaders.

There's just one difference. No one is trudging. And there isn't a desperate face in sight.

Everyone around, seemingly around my age, looks nervous all right, but it's with eagerness and excitement.

They *want* to be here?

That makes three or four thousand of them. That's how many I estimate are milling around. And from everyone's demeanor, this is a hugely anticipated event.

What do they know that I don't?

Probably a lot. Since I know nothing.

As I start walking, my two demi-archangelic guards surround me, massive wings on full display, Lorcan's for the first time. They're also grey, if lighter, and streaked with an amazing pattern of subtle indigo, cobalt and emerald.

No one says anything as the duo cut the line ending at the top of another obscene amount of steps. I doubt anyone *can* say anything with their collective jaws on the ground.

It's clear they never saw a nephilim up close before. But from their awed whispers and gasps as we pass them, they know what they are. To them, the Nephilim are a long-known fact. Seems they're privy to knowledge all other humans consider rumors or myth.

Why? Why were they chosen to learn secrets kept from the rest of us?

This bodes well for the Divining not being as dangerous as I've heard. Surely angels and demons wouldn't take them into their confidence, only to harm them. Or maybe they will only if they fail whatever this is. It might then become a matter of "I-told-you-now-I-have-to-kill-you."

I look around at the eager, healthy faces, and sure hope not.

The healthy part makes me do double takes. I never saw fresh faces like these, not in real life. Even Regulars and Select in L.A. are sallow and sickly. As for the Demon-Owned, we all suffer from serious malnutrition and chronic fatigue.

But these people seem to have been brought up on a steady diet of nourishing meals and nurturing smiles. I have no doubt they've been cared for, pampered. Even groomed? For this?

That actually sounds sinister. It has the vibe of fattening sheep.

Gritting my teeth at the horrific idea, I avoid their curious gazes until we reach the towering bronze double-doors guarded by angels on one side and demons on the other.

Once we cross inside, Godric picks up the pace. As I run to keep up with him, I can't take in much detail. I only get impressions of opulent spaces and soaring ceilings where light and shadow mingle like living things.

My head is spinning as we arrive at what looks like our welcoming committee. Like those at the doors, angels and demons are equally represented. Thirteen of each.

As usual, the angels look somewhat similar. I can still tell they're from many Orders, even when they're dressed in a uniform of white, gold-trimmed robes. Also as usual, the demons are totally different from one another, each representing one of the dominant species. Three are from the handsome-devil ones, with the others sporting horns or hooves, leathery red skin or yellow eyes with serpentine pupils. But they're dressed the same, too, in black, silver-trimmed robes.

White team, black team. How literal.

As soon as we stop before them, one of the angels, a cherubim from the looks of him, comes forward. "This human is not on our list."

How does he know that? When he doesn't know who I am? Has he memorized entrants, or something?

The cherubim turns to the demons. "Is she one of yours?"

One of the scaly demons approaches, sniffs me, then pulls the top of my jumpsuit down, before looking back to the others. "She's Demon-Owned."

I feel Godric going rigid beside me. So he didn't see my Mark. And if possible, the waves of antipathy radiating from him intensify.

The prejudiced jerk.

"Then she must be yours," one of the other angels, a throne I'm sure, says.

"We will not know until the Divining decides," a gorgeous demoness with black hair to her ankles answers.

The cherubim frowns up at Godric. "Why bring her before the Tribunal at all, and ahead of the others, too, nephilim?"

Nephilim, huh? I bet my right arm everyone knows who Godric is. So the angel doesn't deem to say his name? Is there dissent within the ranks of the Army of Heaven?

Godric scowls down at the angel who dared question him. For a moment I think he might rearrange *his* anatomy.

Next moment you could have knocked me over with a feather. A hummingbird's would have done it.

Godric is looking down at me, those viridian eyes blazing with such unbridled—possession.

Before my heart remembers that it's made to beat, he releases my gaze and turns to the angel. "She's mine."

The way he says that, in that voice of his…

Heart blaring, body burning, I try not to gape at him like everyone does. Seems the idea of Godric claiming someone, let alone a human, defines the impossible to all present.

They must know him well.

Or maybe they can't imagine him wanting someone the cosmic cat dragged in like me.

So. Godric is hiding the archangels' interest in me, making it personal instead.

Clever. Not to mention almost lethal. This guy should come with all the warnings of a weapon of mass destruction.

Good thing he only looks at me in such aversion. I'll take that over that sensuality that almost singed me down to my DNA. And that's when it was totally fake.

Better pray I'm never exposed to the real thing.

Pffft. No danger of that, *ever*.

"It's most irregular," the cherubim still says, if halfheartedly.

Godric's gaze drills down into him. "Are you suggesting I'm abusing my authority?" As the angel starts to splutter a denial, Godric raises a hand that can no doubt bring this whole place down in one strike. "That's exactly what I'm doing. Don't waste any more of my time."

Wow. If I had any doubt, that blows it away. The power hierarchy is clear here. Godric is at the top, with those angels and demons, clearly big shots in their respective domains, way below him.

If he is that influential when he's that young—assuming he is as young as he looks—what kind of sway will he wield when he's a few centuries old? Or a few millennia?

Since I won't be there to witness it, what do I care?

Next moment, I no longer care about anything as Godric steps away, and the others encircle me, hands reaching out.

Before I can form a protest, the dark floor juts beneath me. From one heartbeat to the next, it becomes a pillar, shooting me up a dozen feet above everyone.

Before I hurtle off it headfirst, flaming runes well up all over my legs like molten lead. They solidify into what feels like a million scorpion stingers, hooking into my every nerve.

Thundering agony crashes in my head, my marrow. But I'm so used to withstanding pain without making a sound, keens back up in my chest.

Before I can choke on my next fractured breath, vines of lava and obsidian, what feel like scorching sin and drowning despair, emanate from the runes filleting me alive. They entwine into a cylinder of suffocation all around me.

Groping for escape, for reprieve, I look up through the one opening out of the shroud of horror entombing me. And I see it, through the tears needling my eyes. The dome two hundred feet above me, opening like a celestial camera lens, or some divine pupil.

Before I can hope it might offer a way out, a beam of blinding light, like a planet-destroying laser from one of those sci-fi movies, shoots down—and cleaves me in half.

I hear the scream.

I am the scream.

And it's unending.

I never prayed before. Never thought it was worth the wasted breath. Now I pray, plead, beg. I screech and shriek and howl. For death. For oblivion.

No one and nothing hears my prayers. The anvil of the demonic rune-cage and the hammer of the celestial laser pulverize me in between their primordial ruthlessness and greed. They dissect me, recreate me, only to unravel me again—and again—and again. And again. Each time they do, they seem to be getting more forceful. More furious.

At one point in the unending torment, I realize each is trying to pull me to its side. But I remain suspended between them, ground zero for their eternal conflict.

And through it all, I'm aware. Of every spark of suffering, every tendril of invasion, and every shred of desecration.

Just as I think this is the fate worse than eternal damnation Lorcan warned me about, something pushes between the two forces pulling me apart. It forms a barrier around me, a buffer deflecting their destruction.

But it does something else. It pushes me within its confines. Upward, toward the light.

Suddenly, it's over.

The rune talons retract from my marrow and flesh, and the beam that has been carving me to hair-thin slices buoys me up. It floats me above the seething runes until they melt back into an unblemished floor. Then, like a gentle breeze would a feather, it deposits me on my feet a second before it blinks out, and the dome above seals shut.

Breaking apart with sobs, every nerve charred, every cell shrieking, I crash to my knees, retching and heaving.

I'm not even granted the relief of throwing up this time. Everything inside me feels congealed. My tears have evaporated and no more would come, as if their glands have been seared off.

Rising up to numb feet, shaking as if in the throes of a seizure, my swollen eyes pan around.

It's as if nothing happened.

The monsters that surround me are looking at me with absolute boredom in their inhuman eyes.

Boredom!

I want to rave and rant and storm around slapping and punching their immortal faces. They put me through this mini-Hell, and don't even have the decency to look involved? Mildly interested? Entertained, even?

But I don't think I'll be able to do or say anything for a while. Lorcan's warning to hold my tongue wasn't needed after all.

"She's definitely one of ours," the cherubim who's done most of the talking intones in the same apathy dulling his eyes. "She belongs at Celestial Academy."

One of the male demons, the one almost on Godric's gorgeousness level, tuts. "Shame. A...*friend* of Godric's would be most valued at Pandemonium Academy."

Godric turns to him, and I instantly see it. The history between them. Violent, bitter, complex. "If you ask nicely, Asmodeus, I'll send her to you—when I'm done with her."

The suave devil inclines his head in dismissal. "She'd be worthless then."

Godric gives him, then me, a heart-fluttering yet terrifying semi-smile. "She is worthless now. All humans are. And they know it. Don't you, my pet?"

I nod dumbly at him, and his satisfied expression turns at once knee-melting and blood-curdling.

Man. Did I ever think I'm a good actress? Godric is on a whole new level. Academy Award worthy. *Celestial* Academy. He must be their A-lister, in every sense.

No way Asmodeus didn't buy that Godric would soon cast me aside. There'd be nothing to exploit then. I would have been thankful, if I didn't know Godric is only protecting the archangels' interest in me.

And then, he might have meant it, about sending me to that demon after they're done with me. If he even means for me to survive whatever they have in store for me.

Maybe I actually have a better chance with the demon. I survived so far among his kind. Maybe I won't among Godric's.

With that thought worming its way in my battered brain, I watch Godric turn and walk out of the hall. His leash appears in his hand and around my neck, glittering brighter than ever. So everyone can see it?

He tugs, none too gently, making me stumble in his wake.

Yeah, this is a literally heavy-handed show for their benefit.

I can't even spare any energy to dagger the acres of his back and wings with my hatred. All I can do is re-learn how to walk.

At one point, I raise my eyes to find Lorcan walking beside him. I don't know if he attended the Divining. I was busy being dissected alive at the time.

Thankfully, Godric lets his leash dissolve before we exit that unholy cathedral. The buzzing crowd stills and falls dead silent at his sight. Seems he has this effect on any sentient being. Wonder why he has the opposite effect on me.

As he descends two steps ahead of Lorcan, demonstrating his position as his superior, he parts the crowd like he did the Court's barriers. Everyone scurries out of his path, looking up at him with the same awe and dread they'd gape at a tidal wave. I don't blame them. They must know he's an equivalent force of destruction.

The moment he and Lorcan clear the crowd, it congeals again like the crashing waves of a sundered sea. Over me.

Feeling like some accused swarmed by the paparazzi, I shakily push through their rabid eagerness and curiosity.

"Who are you?" a girl yells.

Another one drowns her question. "Are you someone important? Or dangerous? Is that why you have two nephilim escorting you?"

Yeah. According to Godawful, I'm the latter. When I feel like the most endangered creature to walk the earth.

"And those nephilim, too, the superstars. Especially *Him*!"

Yeah. I heard that capitalization as loud and clear as the exclamations expanding through the crowd. Just mentioning *Him* is causing them a bout of acute hero-worship—or just plain worship. He *is* a god to these people.

The interrogation continues in an overlap of shrill voices.

"You got Celestial Academy?"

"She must have, dude. She walked out with *the* nephilim."

"She walked *in* with Him, too!"

"Oh, my Heavens, I wish I were you!"

That last exclamation chafes against the imprint of his leash. I wish I could tell the swooning girl she's welcome to change places with me at its end. That I wish I could throw him to her fellow rabid females to tear apart, so each could have a bloody piece of him.

But all I can do is keep pushing through this endless tunnel of bodies, as more breathless cries inundate me.

"How do you know Him?"

"What's He like?"

"Are all the stories true?"

"They can't be true, man. No being is that powerful!"

"They are, too. He's a level nine."

"No one is a level nine. Not even the Seraphim in the *Codex Caelestia.*"

"Well, he is. I got the info from reliable sources!"

"Reddit isn't a reliable source, moron!"

"It's not only Reddit!"

"Your gaming community isn't a reliable source either."

The two young men's debate ebbs as I'm carried away from them, and more exclamations yawn into my ringing ears.

"I so wish I get Celestial Academy, too."

"I trained all my life for this!"

"I'll die if I get Pandemonium Academy!"

"What was the test?"

"*Is* it a test?"

"How did it feel?"

"Did it hurt?"

I want to scream at them to stop being such lemmings, to run, to save themselves.

But if the angels and demons want to "conscript" them, too, there's no place on Earth they can hide.

So I put my head down and stumble in silence until I clear their lapping mass, and let them cling to their illusions. They'll face the terrible reality soon enough.

Or maybe their experience won't be as horrific as mine.

Who am I kidding? Some will not walk out of there at all.

And there's nothing I can do about it.

Still, keeping silent is one of the hardest things I ever did.

I end up not speaking at all throughout the flight. To Godric's delight, I'm sure. And it isn't only because I shredded my vocal cords screaming at that Divining. I'm just too overwhelmed, can't begin to process what happened.

I black out again during the ride back to the Court, come to only when we pull up outside, and Godric tersely orders me to get out.

As I scramble up, something finally surfaces to my lips. The question that has been revolving in my mind all through.

I shoot a hand to his shoulder before he exits the car, rasping, "What the hell happened back there?"

After a long moment when he freezes under my touch, he rounds on me, eyes bleeding black lightning, voice a deadly snarl. "Nothing happened, White. That's what you are. *Nothing*."

14

"What do you mean I'm 'Nothing?'"

In response to my croaked exclamation, Godric shoves his noise-cancelling earbuds in his ears before hauling himself out of the car.

Talk about passive aggressive.

Lucky for him, I'm in no condition to pester him.

It's like I was sliced into endless layers by that damned Divining. I now know, on a cell-deep level, how those who don't pass it perish. If not for whatever came between me and those opposing forces, I would have.

But I feel I'm still...unraveled. That I'm never going to be the way I used to be.

That Divining changed me.

How, or why, I'll only get answers if my escorts volunteer any. Godric is closed for interrogation. Some surprise there. The divine jerk. Lorcan is unusually silent. More—*serious*.

A serious Lorcan is a very worrying sight.

What's going on here?

This has to be about what happened at the Divining. Something went wrong back there. I just know it. *Massively* wrong.

Not that you'd know it from that Tribunal's reaction. They acted like a committee of bureaucrats deadened to the performance of a clerical duty, and I was another same-old case.

So what did Godric and Lorcan figure out that they didn't?

I suddenly realize we're entering the central building of the Court from another door that doesn't have a million steps leading to it. And that Godric didn't put his leash around my neck. He doesn't seem in a hurry to deliver me back to the archangels. Which is weird. I thought he couldn't wait to shake me off his hands, like some prickly pear he picked from the sewers.

This can only mean he's not eager to tell them about whatever went wrong back there.

Because he doesn't know what happened and hates to admit it? Or because it's *that* bad?

But since I have the freedom of my own pace, I fall into step with Lorcan. "Care to tell me what happened?"

"I..." He stops, shakes his head. "Godric will fill you in, if he sees fit." He stops again, then sighs. "Don't hold your breath, though. You'll only suffocate."

"Intel above your pay grade?" When he only gazes ahead, I whine, "C'mon, Lorcan. This is about me. I have a right to know."

Again, no answer.

Before I can persist, Lorcan exhales. "Consider it done, hmm?" I blink up at him. "My promise? Your friend?"

Sarah. I actually forgot about her since that Divining tore me apart and put me back together. But he remembered.

"You will let me see her?" I choke.

"If I can extricate you from Godric's grasp, and whatever our family have in store for you. If I can't, I'll go to her alone."

"Oh, Lorcan, thank you!"

"Anything for you, my dearest Godricsbane."

I would have laughed if I had the energy. "That's my name now?"

His eyes literally twinkle as he wiggles both eyebrows at Godric's legendary back. "It's the highest praise in my books, and unprecedented with it. The very concept of a Godricsbane was unknown, until you."

"Yeah, lucky me. So, about what happened..."

Lorcan speaks over me. "If they decide to conscript you still, you can do with some bullet points about the Academy, hmm?" I stare at him, the abrupt subject change throwing me off. He continues, "It's located to the southeast of the Court across the Palladium River, and is bordered by some of the nastiest landmarks in the region—so pray you never find yourself in any. The reason behind this choice of location is much debated, as the Academy was supposed to be an extension of the Court millennia ago. It ended up being separate in all ways. It even has its own Rune Gates and Palladium Wards."

"Isn't palladium some rare element?" I ask numbly.

He gives an impressed nod. "Good to see you paid attention in chemistry class. It also means safeguard or source of protection. The Gates generate the Wards that encompass the Court and the Academy. You didn't see any since you were in snore-land each time we passed through the Court's. But they're massive versions of the frame of the *Proelium Primum*—the First Battle frieze leading to the archangels' meeting chamber. The magic imbuing their runes is allegedly the most powerful in existence. No one without angel blood *and* an *Iter Tutus* can cross them or the Wards."

I smirk. "And I assume you and Godawful have matching tutus?"

His lips split wide again. I was right when I thought seriousness wasn't an option for them. Not for long. "It basically means safe passage." He chuckles at the image I conjured of him and Godric. "But our *Tutus* are anything but matching. His has way more frills."

"Yeah, figures," I huff. "So this place isn't in some other realm?" At his head-shake, I frown. "Then how can you hide it, what with satellite mapping and all? Does the Palladium Wards act like some sort of Glamor, too?"

"Glamor is what the other races call it. We call it *Operculum*, or cover."

"Uh, no thanks. I'll keep calling it Glamor."

He shrugs easily. "But, yes, the Wards have many elements. The *Operculum...*" He winks as he stresses the word. "...ensures no being, technology or magic can detect the Court and Academy. If someone somehow circumvents that, no matter how powerful they are, the *Exitium* element, which means destruction, would reduce them to ashes."

"Hey, what's with all the Latin lingo? You copying the demons?"

His lips quirk. "It's actually one of the popular angelic dialects. Angels came first, after all."

I roll my eyes at myself. "Duh. I should have thought of that. Okay, what about those who want to exit? They also need tutus?" As he nods, I groan. "So those who enter that Academy, can't leave?"

He flashes me those pearly whites. "If you were thinking you can escape, don't. The Wards treats any unauthorized attempts to cross it, in and out, with the same—finality."

"But I crossed it, when I have no tutus, and I'm human."

"*That* remains to be seen. But you're escorted by us. Even Angel-bloods need escorts or their own *Iter Tutus* to gain entry."

"By invitation only, huh? How elitist. And how paranoid. Why all these precautions?"

He chuckles. "Think about it as the ultimate in home security. None of the Supernaturals particularly like us, after all."

"Yeah, shocker. Since when do you deal in euphemisms, Lorc? They *hate* your feathery guts."

His grin only widens. "Indeed. Envy is the most powerful emotion."

"You think everyone hates you because they envy you?"

A goading eyebrow. "Don't you?"

He got me there. I do envy the hell out of angels, with their perfection and powers.

I grumble about it before something else hits me. "But—hey, when you say we, you mean the Nephilim, too? I thought no one knew you existed!"

He pouts in dismissal. "We *are* the undercover faction, the special forces. But the demons have always known about us."

"If they do, how come they never exposed your existence?"

"Oh, they do. Where do you think all these tales about us came from? But since no one believes anything they say, and we never make winged public appearances, we remain rumors and myths. But we regularly deal with individuals from the other races, mainly to kick their arses. Those don't share that fact, since power, or the perception of it, is everything in this world. Still, most do know about us."

And I thought I knew everything there is to know, living where I do...did.

I shake my head dazedly. "If they do, the Fae would want to destroy you for sure, if only because you surpass them in power and beauty. The Shifters, Vampires and other races because you'd probably seem like the ultimate threat to them. They must hate you way more than they do the angels. Man, if they ever stop their endless infighting to unite for a cause, you Nephilim would be their number one target."

"It's so hard being on top." He sighs theatrically, before he grins again. "But that's why they will never put aside their interspecies conflicts."

My inflamed eyes round with incredulity. "You mean you cause that?"

He waves that away. "We never 'cause' anything. Their blood feuds have always existed. We just don't stop them. Or we do only to the point where the balance is kept. Hell, that's the part of our job that I despise; keeping them from exterminating each other. Contrarily, that only makes them hate us all the more. So you understand why we don't let them know where we train the next generation of global enforcers."

I gape at him. "You can say hell?"

He throws his head back and guffaws. "*That's* what you gleaned from all this? But oh, yes, I can say whatever the *hell* I like. I am a quarter human, after all."

"Only a quarter, huh?"

He nods. "According to my lineage, my mother was half angel."

Was. Does this mean she's dead?

Do the Nephilim grow old and die because of their human ingredient? But if Lorcan is as young as he looks, surely his mother couldn't have been old? So did she get sick, or was she killed?

I must find out any vulnerabilities the Nephilim have. I'd love to know if it's possible to kill Godric. Hell, I'd settle for seeing him bleed. I'd even take fantasizing about it.

Before I can probe, Lorcan goes on, "But the Wards would really become a necessity if we had to keep the humans away."

I goggle at him. "You can't seriously worry about humans! What can *they* do?"

Lorcan goggles back at me. "You either don't know your species at all, or didn't think this question through. There's no end to their nuisance and damage if you give them knowledge or allow them liberties. If they ever had access to this place, their response would range from constantly accosting us for their Insta feeds, to always trying to blow us up."

"There are humans who would do *that*?"

I never heard of humans fighting the angelic occupation. No one even calls it that but fanatic stragglers on the internet. Governments, along with everyone else, treat angels as humanity's benefactors. At least, compared to the other races.

Or that's what I know. Turns out my knowledge is very deficient.

He shrugs again. "As I said, humans are capable of very creative atrocities. Better to keep them away to start with."

"But they don't know the Nephilim exist, right?"

"So far. But you saw humans today who know about us. While

they've been brought up to keep the secret, the truth will out sooner or later, and I dread the day. Can you imagine what would happen if humans knew they could procreate with angels? The best scenario is that angels and this place would be besieged by those begging for Nephilim babies. And that's when the Wards will be most needed. Out of all the races, I worry about humans the most."

Knowing my race's capacity for fanaticism and destruction, I can only agree.

After a moment of digesting this, I ask, "And the demons? You didn't mention those."

"I thought it goes without saying they are the primary reason for the Wards."

"Aren't you guys splitting the world among you in hate-filled peace and all that? Or are the Accords really in jeopardy, especially after last night?"

He suddenly sobers. "If you mean Zinimar's death, that will certainly have widespread repercussions." That was what Sarah said. She even had that exact expression when she did. Before I can push for more insights, he smiles again. "Not that we ever needed catastrophic developments to ward against them. They're demons. Need I say more?"

Knowing their viciousness and vindictiveness, I have to agree, too.

I still smirk up at him. "You're no angels yourselves, buddy. Not the way we used to think."

He huffs a pitying chuckle. "In *your* major religions, angels are the ruthless creatures who unquestioningly do their god's will. And in case you humans don't carry it out to the letter—they bring you pestilence, famine and war. They relentlessly pelt you with destruction and death. How you managed to romanticize us and make us into these kind beings of pure goodness is beyond me."

He has a point there. A major one. How *did* we ever turn this monstrously righteous army into all that romantic crap?

But I have a better question. "You keep saying we. So you consider yourself an angel?"

He frowns as if really pondering my question. "Partially, obviously. Mostly. But even one drop of human blood changes everything. We Nephilim are different—from everyone else. And then, just like any other race, we're not all the same."

"Tell me about it." I shoot daggers at Godric magnificent receding form.

Just as if he felt my antipathy riddling his back, his leash forms around my neck, and I'm again forced to run after him.

It's enough to inject me with the will to go on, whatever it takes. If for nothing else, I have to survive, so I can one day have him stumbling in *my* wake.

15

This time, I don't meet the archangels. I only meet two. My dear captors' loving dads. Gabriel and Azrael.

That Last Supper table with its ancient tomes is also missing. They're now sitting at a polished mahogany round table that can accommodate a dozen more. And they're no longer dressed like they just stepped out of a Michelangelo painting.

Gabriel is in a white shirt, black slacks and sneakers. With his auburn hair tousled, I can now see his resemblance to Lorcan.

But it's nothing like Azrael's resemblance to Godric. His midnight hair is now loose and cascading in waves to his shoulders, making me suddenly ache to see Godric's hair like that. He is dressed almost like his son, in a black leather jacket and jeans, but with a purple shirt and black tie instead of Godric's V-neck charcoal T. It makes him look more like Godric's older brother than ever. A much less dangerous one, if that can be believed.

So were they in their heavenly generals get-up before to act as judge and executioner of Walter White? Is this how they always dress? They've caught up with modern times like the other angels and Nephilim?

One thing for sure, they no longer feel alien and detached. Maybe that was another act to intimidate me into giving them the info they needed. Or this is the difference the clothes make.

I'm still debating the issue as the two archangels rise to their feet and face Godric. From the way their gazes lock but become vacant, it's clear they're "soulspeaking," a conference call this time.

Long minutes later, that trio of terror turn their attention to me.

Gabriel seems contemplative as he nears me. Azrael is impassive, but he too approaches. I really, really hope they won't probe me again. After what those angels and demons did to me, I may just attack them if they start tickling me.

Thankfully, they don't make me do something insane. But I'm dying to know if he told them what happened during the Divining.

"My son informs me you had an eventful Divining, Wen White," Azrael says, voice deep and calm.

I suddenly realize it's almost the same as said son's. But it doesn't make everything inside me jiggle like jelly on the verge of melting. His eyes, sapphire instead of viridian, and almost the same shape, don't ignite wild, wanton things I didn't know existed within me.

It's not a discovery I wanted to make. That Angelhole's effect on me has nothing to do with his looks or power.

I exhale forcibly. "You can say that again."

Azrael frowns. "I said my son informs me you had an eventful Divining, Wen White."

I scoff. "I didn't mean for you to repeat yourself. You archangels may look up-to-date today, but you certainly aren't where slang is concerned..." I stop at Godric's glare. And because it really isn't good for my life expectancy to mock a being with the power of a star.

"It's true," Azrael says, titling his head in a gracious gesture. "This is the second time you've brought this to my attention. Perhaps it's time we involved ourselves as we should in the ways of this modern world."

"You have better things to do other than learning how base humans butcher the English language," Godric growls.

"Aw." I jump as a spark of his visual lightning zaps me. "Chill, dude. Not all of us can sound like we just rolled off a BBC documentary truck." Before he electrocutes me for real, I hobble closer to his dad, hoping he'll curb him again. "But what do you mean by eventful? What really happened in that Divining?"

"You don't know?" Gabriel asks, still regarding me with this strange expression, as if he's both intrigued and unsettled. Yeah, right.

"All I know is that your Divining almost tore me apart," I grumble, unable to temper the accusation in my tone.

"It's not our Divining," Azrael says, being literal again. "We have no say in what happens in it. No one does. Once the Tribunal gathers in that hallowed spot and converges their powers, what happens is beyond anyone."

I exhale. "Yeah, I sort of got this was some kind of autonomous process, like gravity or magnetism."

Azrael nods. "That is an accurate analogy. It's the very fabric of existence that determines the nature of those undergoing the Divining."

"Yeah, it had to be something that lofty, right? But that still doesn't explain what happened in my case."

"Godric didn't tell you?" Gabriel asks, his unreadable gaze targeting his nephew.

I toss Godric a sour glance. "He told me exactly nothing. Actually, he said *I'm* Nothing. With a capital N, I'm sure."

Azrael looks at his son for a long moment, and I get the impression they're fighting again in their private astral plane.

But when he turns his attention back at me, his gaze is the personification of equanimity. "If he chose not to explain, he must have his reasons."

"Yeah, again. That's why I'm hoping *you'll* enlighten me. It's impossible to have a civil conversation with this damn son of… Uh, with him."

Just as Azrael starts to answer me, Godric's leash materializes around my neck.

Next thing I know, I'm back at the frieze.

I don't know how long I stand there until I realize what happened. Godric has fast forwarded me here and disappeared.

Shrieking in frustration, I call him every foul name I ever heard and invent a few dozen more. But of course, he doesn't come back.

I wait and wait for him to. It turns out he can maintain his leash remotely. And tie it to something other than his hand, the golden frame of the frieze this time. He also made it too short for me to sit on the floor. And he's been in there for *eons*.

Okay, so it's been less than an hour. But all through, my whole body is a throb of pain and outrage. And hunger. And a desperate urge to pee.

The last two afflictions are strange. That angelic jet cut flight times in more than half both ways. So, added to the driving time, it was about five hours since I stuffed myself beyond human limits. The Divining itself, what felt like an eternity, only lasted five minutes, according to Lorcan. And I used the bathroom right before we left the jet less than two hours ago. I shouldn't be in such an urgent condition.

But there's an even stranger thing. Or maybe not so strange, considering everything else that has happened in the last day.

All evidence of Kondar's flogging has vanished from my back. I had to struggle out of my jumpsuit's top to make sure what I was feeling was true. And it was. I may have thought that salve was *that* magical this time, if all the injuries I suffered since the Godric Landing weren't also healed. No, not healed—*gone.*

Stranger still, when I checked my older scars, they were smoother than they used to be. Apart from two that felt even more pronounced. But these don't ache and pull like all my scars used to, only itch.

Seems the Divining tearing me apart and putting me back together had a good side-effect. An incredible one. The only scars that were unaffected by it are the burn of that locket on my chest, and my Mark. Maybe because one is too old, and the other is an infernal magic injury.

But the pain it inflicted persists elsewhere. Everywhere. It's so pervasive, I can't even pinpoint its origin. It's like every cell in my body is…in flux. Straining and colliding with the cell next to it. But it goes beyond the physical. It's like having…a soul-deep toothache.

Hope it doesn't get any worse, or I may need the equivalent of a root canal for the soul. Or even worse, an extraction.

Compounding my distress is being garroted every time my legs buckle, and that maddening itch in my back.

I'm planning Godawful's gruesome death after prolonged degradation and rubbing my back against his family's likenesses like a mangy dog when the frieze at my back disappears and he finally walks out. Looking like *he* wants to murder *me.*

Now *that's* rich.

But maybe this leash is two-way in more than the physical sense, and his rage is a reflection of mine?

Nah. He hates my guts all on his own.

"Feeling's oh-so-mutual, Godforsaken," I mutter as I stumble after him.

I know he heard me.

This time, he warps us for over half an hour. But though it's mostly a blur, I'm almost certain parts of the trip was outside. I also felt as if we stepped through some threshold into another…place? State of existence? It just feels vastly different when we end up in a gigantic hall spread in mosaic-bordered floors and surrounded by soaring Greco-

Egyptian columns. The periphery appears as if it shimmers into other realms. But the central part seems rooted in this reality, and is filled with people.

This reinforces my feeling that we're no longer at the Court part of this domain. We must be in the Academy end of it. According to Lorcan, we must have crossed the Palladium river and Ward to get here…

I do a double take. There are many familiar faces from the Divining. I actually think everyone is from there!

How did they get here this fast? Even if each Divining lasted five minutes, there were too many of them. It should have taken days!

I ask this out loud, and Godric seems to take pleasure in answering me this time. "Time passes differently inside the Divining Cathedral. But it's been twelve hours since we left it."

"No way!" I exclaim. "We left the Divining thingy no more than five hours ago!"

"Twelve," is all he says.

"I would know if you left me standing outside your damn meeting with your damn family for hours!"

"Seven to be exact. And I did."

I gape up at him as my mind whirs and glitches.

Is it possible it didn't register the passage of time correctly?

It's my bladder that answers. It says it's not only possible, it's a fact.

Godawful left me standing there for seven hours!

"How about I pee on your boots this time in gratitude?"

His painstakingly sculpted lips twitch and his amazing eyes crinkle. My heart stops. Then bursts out in a mad stumble.

I just tickled his humor. In spite of all his efforts not to allow it.

No, no. I don't want to see any sign of his wickedness, no proof of his human side, no matter how fleeting. I want him to remain a snarling, humorless brute. I need only fight or flight hormones in his presence.

As if he heard my thoughts, any trace of levity vanishes as he scowls down at me. "Go relieve yourself, human. *If* you have enough intelligence to fathom the signs. Return in a timely manner, if you don't want to be dragged back on your belly."

Our gazes duel for one last moment before I bolt. Facing off with him takes a very distant second priority to committing social suicide in this elitist setting by peeing myself.

Outside the hall, I find many signs that look made of solid energy floating discreetly within ornate arches. But like that damned archangelspawn sneered, I can't decipher their angelic script. At least, I won't in time to make a difference to my pee-related crisis.

I'm beginning to think I'd go behind a column and do my thing, even if it means falling into another realm, when a symbol up ahead pulses with the iridescent bluish hue of *Angelescence.*

Before I can wonder what that means, another symbol beyond it does the same, then another.

Unable to wait anymore, I consider this is some guidance system activated in response to my urgency, and hobble along the path of the relaying pulses. If it doesn't lead to a restroom, I *will* pee myself.

Thankfully, it does. Nephilim do use bathrooms like us lowly humans, after all.

I barely make it to a stall and get out of my jumpsuit. *Barely* meaning I pee myself a little.

After cleaning up as best I can with that self-operating bidet, I rush out in search of a dryer. If I'm forced to go back looking like I *did* pee myself, I *will* commit suicide. While trying to kill that sadist.

Thankfully, I find many, powerful enough they'd dry me whole if need be. In seconds, I rush to a row of sinks right out of a lush fantasy movie. Water flows before I approach the faucet, smelling of lemongrass and lavender.

Humming at the perfect scent and temperature, I wash my sweaty hands and flaming face. My pleasure doesn't last as my hair falls into the sink. It has long escaped its braid and I have nothing to bind it with. As I attempt the futility of finger-combing it with water, I notice the drool map at my collar. Not much better than a pee stain.

Leaning closer to the mirror, I start dabbing at it, then jerk a double take at my reflection.

We only have a distorted, age-spotted mirror in our bathroom. Besides that, I never had the feminine impulse of checking myself in every reflective surface. In fact, I avoided even a glance when I passed any. I never wanted to see my lanky, semi-starved body or my hollowed-out-by-existence face.

Now I gape at myself in the pristine, gilded mirror that seems to reflect more than my face.

Is this what I really look like?

So my face is what I know it to be, all cutting cheekbones and angular jawline. My skin is sallow and my hair is a riot of darkness. It's the sum of all that's unfamiliar. And then there's my eyes.

Is this how they always were and I never noticed? A navy blue as dark and deep as a midnight sky, flecked by the simmering embers of stars? It's as if something within may ignite at any moment.

I shake my head at the ridiculous idea. That's just reflections of this sourceless lighting. And my fury at the massive monster out there.

But it's my resting face, the involuntary glare in my too-wide eyes and the permanent twist of my too-full lips that worry me. The resulting expression is an inflammatory mix of goading and insolence.

So that's what Angelhole has been responding to.

Not that it excuses that bully. *I* wouldn't treat him this way if I were infinitely powerful while his only power was a provocative face and mouth.

Problem is, this face isn't in response to him. It probably gets far worse around him, but this is how I look.

I try to soften my expression, but it only becomes sullen and sarcastic. This face isn't going to win me any friends around here. No wonder I never made any. None besides Sarah.

I'm so screwed. More than I already am. I…

A tug on my neck yanks me away from the mirror. I'm not "timely" enough for my keeper. And he can latch onto me *that* remotely.

Aaargh.

Fuming, I barely catch myself and stumble out of the bathroom. At least there were no other girls in there to witness my humiliation.

Once back at the hall, I find no sign of Godric. So he drags me where he wants without bothering to be there himself.

Struggling to breathe after running the whole way back here, I remain at the periphery, assessing the crowd.

Everyone is now thronged in groups. Forming cliques already, it seems. I'm betting I won't be invited to any. Not that I know if they're fellow conscripts or what.

But how can they be when they seem beside themselves with elation?

So Lorcan said all humans are excited when they're first brought here, and the Select are proud of the most atrocious job the angels toss them in. But these kids can't be *this* excited about cleaning Nephilim toilets, can they? And as humans, we're no good for more than that, right?

Oh, well. There's a saying among the demons that fits this situation. *If today's news costs money, get it tomorrow for free.*

The groups ebb and flow until suddenly, everything empties from my mind.

Godric. He *is* here. Right across the crowded hall.

And he's looking straight at me. Into me. As if there's no one else to see. No one else he *can* see. When there are dozens of bodies between us. The bodies I, too, no longer register.

As for *my* body, it all but combusts under his gaze, and all the things it insists it reads there.

Shutting it up is more difficult this time. It may become impossible if he keeps brooding at me like this. When he's probably thinking how he'd torture me to death once he gets the green light.

It's such a criminally cruel existence, to endow one being with all that. Did a more overpowering specimen of maleness ever exist? And to be paired with probably unlimited power, too? Yet manifest in the same package as this abhorrent personality?

But maybe the personality bit is the universe's way of balancing things. If he was nice, or at least not full-on loathsome, other beings would drop dead in his orbit like mosquitoes around a zapper.

I can't understand how the girls, and boys, are not fawning over him as he leans lazily against one of those soaring columns that seem to lead into the next realm. Unless he's Glamoring himself to avoid the nuisance of their abject admiration.

That proves to be the case when he straightens, causing a wave of bugging eyes and swooning gasps.

He just de-cloaked.

He starts cutting through the crowd as if no one else is there, and everyone scrambles to clear his path.

When he's a dozen feet away from me, and as if to stress his vileness, he makes a tranquil gesture with his hand. The leash appears in his hand in the same moment it tugs hard on my neck, making me stumble the remaining steps between us.

I come to a teetering stop, skewering him with the pokers of my fury, surreptitiously gesturing at the leash. I'd rather not be known as his pet goat right out the gate.

He only raises one masterpiece eyebrow. He isn't removing it. Big surprise.

Darting a pained glance around, I find no one staring at it. Seems no one thinks it strange for him to have me on a leash.

Fighting the bone-searing urge to pulverize my hand punching his god-like face, I smirk up at him. It gives me some measure of power knowing how infuriating my expression is. "Next time, knock before you yank, or I'll finish pooping on your boots."

The flare in his amazing viridian eyes tells me I *got* a rise from him.

When he speaks, though, he sounds like the fed-up Godric who arrested me. "Here are the ground rules, White. From now on, you shut your bleating mouth, you listen when I talk, you do as I say…"

I pretend to yawn noisily. "Yeah, yeah, when you say it, exactly the way you say it. Dude, what did I tell you about redundancy?"

"You told me many things any sane being wouldn't dare think in my presence, let alone utter." His lips slowly twist in a smirk. One far scarier and sexier than what he gave me and that Asmodeus back at the Divining. It almost makes my now-empty bladder loosen once more. "This changes now."

Refusing to back down, I raise him my most provocative grin. "No, it won't. I'm telling you the truth about your atrocious self that no one else dares to while I can, you loathsome, uppity, *insecure* bully. Since this is goodbye…"

"It's not goodbye. It will never be goodbye."

A jolt passes through me from heart to fingertips.

The way he said this, anyone listening in would think it an emotional outburst.

But since it isn't, I gape up at him until he qualifies it, and the world disappears beneath my feet.

He just said, "We will be joined at the hip, for probably the next four years—since now I'm your personal tutor."

16

Turns out we're gathered here for Orientation.

That should be a good thing. I am in dire need of anything to orient me.

Godric threw that bombshell at me, ordered me to tug on the leash once it's over, and left me scrabbling with it like a slippery bar of soap. I couldn't stop it from exploding.

Godric. Grim Reaper Jr. Son of Death. Angelhole. My personal tutor.

My. Personal. Tutor.

What does that even mean? Tutor how? Why? In what? Being a bullseye for Nephilim target practice? Surviving exposure to their semi-heavenly crap?

Not that any role I'd be assigned worries me now. Only one thing horrifies me. Being leashed to him for four more years.

Four. More. *Years.*

That takes the award of Fate Worse than Death.

Okay. So I'm exaggerating. It's *slightly* better than death.

And then, there's one thing that soothes my confusion and horror. The knowledge that I'm as much a thorn in his side as he is a leash around my neck. His volcanic frustration left me in no doubt of that.

I am the maddening pebble in his shoe. The scraping splinter in his eye. And everything else that will turn his life into a wonderland of aggravation.

Silver linings *do* exist.

Finding my lips twitching at imagining years of Godric writhing in the hell of being my dedicated jailor, I finally look beyond my turmoil.

I'm still at the periphery of the groups buzzing like human-sized bees. There are hundreds here. Maybe more. Males and females in almost a one-to-one ratio. And they're all here for said Orientation.

Unless I'm totally off base, that's an event to welcome new students and introduce them to an institution's programs and rules.

So does this mean they—*we*—are *attending* Celestial Academy?

How can this be possible? And more importantly, why?

Guess I'll find out soon enough. For now, something else worries me. The burning questions in everyone's eyes about my constant presence with Godric. At least they're not ambushing me like before. Probably afraid Godric won't like it.

Just as I hope they continue to avoid me, an abrupt, deafening hush falls over the vast space. It alarms me more than if a bomb has gone off. Then I see the reason for such jarring silence.

The archangels.

Flanked by two lines of angels, they're descending from the now-sealing, two-hundred-foot dome. It feels made of some cosmic matrix until it closes and becomes solid again, extravagantly painted with frescoes like the Sistine Chapel. I cringe with the memory of the similar dome where that celestial laser unmade me.

I realize it's only Azrael and Gabriel again. Their wingspan isn't as massive as Godric's, but they seem to have more than one pair. It has to be some illusion, but it fooled me into thinking there were more of them. And they're back to their working-hours celestial attires.

From the shockwave of profound awe and reverence that razes out from the crowd, I'm certain everyone knows who they are. And not from some obscure, forbidden video. Another proof that these people know far more about the angelic world than I do. My only advantage here is that I already had a personal audience with these dudes. Twice.

Everyone drops to their knees in a thunderclap of human joints meeting marble, reverberating the ground beneath me. I don't realize I'm the only one left standing until I get death glares from those around me.

Don't literally *stand out, moron.*

Just as I start to kneel, the leash slams me down on my knees.

Oh, I'm so going to enjoy introducing this archangelspawn to my own brand of hell.

But even with the leash pressing me down, I'm still the only one to look up as the archangels and their companions land before us. A platform blossoms from the ground to meet them, as if it were alive. It probably is.

"Rise, my children."

Gabriel's deep voice cascades over us in a sweep of power and tranquility, seeming to come from everywhere. Weird. His voice didn't have that surround quality when he talked to me before. Everyone gets up in a synchronized wave, as if compelled. I know they're not, free will, and all. But his demand is compulsion enough on its own.

After both archangels fold their wings, I notice that Azrael is sporting his soul-reaping scythe today.

A shudder runs through me at its sight. To my shock, it's one of pleasure. As if something inside me delights at the scythe's proximity. At its macabre power. Other sensations follow, those familiar, almost kindred feelings.

That Divining did a number on me. Combined with exposure to this place, and those beings, my senses must be scrambled by now.

Just as I wonder if Azrael is here to reap some young, unwitting lives, Gabriel spreads his arms, encompassing everyone in the gesture.

"My children, you are here today because you were chosen during the Divining. It has ascertained that you are all Angel-Graced."

Angel what now?

"Each of you has been singled out," Gabriel continues. "Whether from childhood or more recently, and groomed to attend the Divining. But you only knew its verdict might bestow the honor of training alongside the angels' offspring—or of joining the demons' elite forces. But no knew which fate awaited you—like you know not what it means to be Angel-Graced."

Wait! Does this mean I'm Angel-Graced whatever that means?

Is that what that angel at the Divining meant, when he so wearily said I am definitely one of theirs?

Bating my breath for the archangel to elaborate, I feel everyone else doing the same.

Gabriel doesn't let us suffocate with anticipation. "It means that our presence on earth has altered you, whether in the womb, or later in your lives, imbuing you with a measure of our Grace. You, of all humanity, will develop angelic powers."

I don't know if the gasp that quakes through me is mine, or a reverberation of the collective one. I feel like a guitar cord that was strummed mercilessly, and left to twang so violently it might snap.

"The others who attended the Divining with you have been deemed Demon-Blighted. Those have been affected by the demonic presence on earth, and will manifest demonic traits or powers. They will attend Pandemonium Academy in the Infernal Court, as you will attend Celestial Academy in our Court."

Gabriel stops, as if to give us a chance to digest the mind-blowing info he just dropped on us.

In the ragged silence, I hear people whimpering, some outright weeping.

I can't blame them. This is *momentous*. Fate-changing.

My heart slows down to deafening thuds, as if curbing its beats waiting for Gabriel to continue.

He does when he deems his words have sunk far enough in our minds. "All Graces or Blights remain dormant until a certain age, even in the Nephilim and most demons, historically around twenty-one. And yes, there have always been Angel-Graced and Demon-Blighted on earth, since both angels and demons were always present.

"But for ages, there was no way to tell which side the Altered belonged to before their powers manifested, and then it was too late. Without guidance, the humans usually went mad. This necessitated the creation of the Divining ritual with the demons, as both sides have a vested interest not to let those humans go rogue.

"The Altered have long been found, deciphered individually, before being trained and placed in strategic positions to serve the cause of Heaven, or the purposes of Hell.

"But after the Apocalypse, with our pervasive presence on earth for the first time since creation, we detected a sharp increase in the numbers of the Altered. So we had to add a collective Divining clause to the Armistice Accords. You are the first to have reached the age of Manifestation since the Apocalypse."

The Apocalypse ended twenty-two years ago, and Heaven and Hell's denizens have been here in force since. Since everyone here seems around twenty-one, it all computes.

"Being Altered has signs, some from infancy," Gabriel continues. "When your individual signs showed themselves, that was when you were approached, and groomed. This was why you were selected, and summoned to the Divining. This is why you are here, and will be the first collective class of Angel-Graced to be inducted into Celestial

Academy. To nurture that kernel within you, to make it grow, so you can come into your full powers, and join the Army of Heaven."

Someone bursts out clapping.

He or she falters when they realize no one else is doing it. Then another one joins in, hesitantly. Then another, and another. And suddenly the hall is shaking with the thunder of frenzied applause.

These guys are *really* happy to be here. I'm the only one around not clapping my hands off.

Maybe I should be happy too, what with those latest revelations. But apart from the—irregular circumstances of my presence here, this sounds too good to be true. I have trouble believing in anything good at all happening to me. Anything *that* good?

Forget it.

But that would mean Gabriel isn't telling the truth. And I feel he is. So do we really have Angel Grace inside us? *I* do? That's why the light pulled me up, forcing the dark to relinquish its hold on me?

Only one problem with this theory. The light *didn't* pull me up. I was *pushed* by that thing that enveloped me.

So maybe this *was* the test. Since as a human being, I have both within me, and that's why they almost tore me apart in their stalemate. Until that shrapnel of angelic fallout inside me rose, and pushed me to the light.

Does that mean I had Angel Grace all my life?

But I never felt a thing. I still don't. And then, this isn't why the archangels sent me to the Divining. They wanted to find out what I *am*, not what I *have*. They said that Angel Essence collecting ability is unprecedented, and that I can't be entirely human.

So if neither the light or dark chose me, what does that make me? Humanoid? Human-lite? Nothing, like Godric said?

What is really going on here?

I'm brutally tempted to ask when Azrael steps forward, and the simple step makes everyone fall to their knees again. Some drop in a dead faint.

As he again gestures for us to rise, everyone struggles to brace themselves in the face of such inexorable power. I sure wasn't anywhere near that affected when I first met him.

Then Azrael's voice inundates us, and I think everyone is no longer breathing. "Today, on your first day of enrollment in Celestial Academy, you enter a new world beyond anything you ever imagined. Your enthusiasm for what comes next gladdens me, but you must also heed that you are enlisting in our army, and that it will be anything but predictable, or safe. You will face challenges and trials, few of which we have control over, and all of you will be changed forever, in every way. Some of you might not survive."

I can almost feel hearts stopping wholesale. I bet they're not that happy to be here anymore. It's not that exciting having the Archangel of Death telling you now you enlisted in his army, he might be reaping your souls soon. And of course, he's not offering the choice of backing out.

"But you have been prepared for this all your life. And from now on, you will experience what few other mortals ever did. You will have a purpose far greater than your own lives, lives that will be what your fellow humans could not even dream of. Rest assured that whatever comes next, it will be glorious."

Okay, gotta admit, that's a great sales pitch. And I can already feel its magic working, the crowd once more seething with eagerness.

Well, I'm not buying it. They can keep their glory. I want nothing but my own lousy life back.

Problem is, I'm even more trapped than any of my fellow conscripts. My conscription is a penalty, not a privilege.

Azrael, that inexorable force of entropy, goes on. "Today, we welcome you to your new distinguished lives and our sublime purpose, and I am certain each and every one of you will do us proud. In the coming days, your professors will introduce themselves and their classes, will apprise you of your schedule, and of the upcoming Imperium Trials."

More trials? And I bet they're the kind we might not survive, too.

"Once we depart, your welcome packages with everything you need to know about the Academy will be distributed. Afterward, you will each seek out your accommodations. Apart from that, there's one thing you need to know, and always remember."

Azrael pauses and the whimpers are back, as if human components are creaking under the pressure of his presence and power.

Then, as if judging it would break his new recruits if he remained silent a second longer, he carries on, "While we value free will above all else, and we do understand the demands of your youth, discipline and commitment to the Academy's laws are paramount. Any serious disruptions and conflicts within the student body will be dealt with by *Pax Vis*, our peace force. They are authorized to assess and deal with infractions as they see fit." Another pause that freezes everyone's blood in their veins. Then he adds, "We sincerely hope you will keep them getting paid for being idle."

He makes a gesture with his free hand, as if allowing us to react. Generalized choking and splutters ensue. Everyone clearly can't believe the Archangel of Death just made a joke. And that they are actually allowed to breathe, even laugh in his presence, and at something he said, too.

I should tell them I called him a pompous ass.

As I snicker under my breath at the memory, I elicit more horrified glares. Then Azrael's gaze finds me. Everyone scrambles away in a wide circle, leaving me exposed like a lone zebra in a lion's crosshairs.

If he makes an example of me for my "disruption" or even addresses me by my full name as he always does, I would be "marked" for ignominy all over again.

But he says nothing as he holds my gaze. And again this searing kinship expands between us.

As my mouth dries with an inexplicable, unbearable—longing, he's the one who looks away first and focuses back to the crowd.

I rock on my feet, not knowing how much of that they noticed, and how much was between Azrael and me on a private channel, like the one he has with Godric.

My senses come back online to him saying, "…but before I let you explore the Academy and find your living quarters, it's time to meet with your fellow cadets."

The doors open as if to obey his intention, and in walks Godric spearheading twelve others in formation like a squadron of fighter jets. Lorcan is behind him on his right hand side. All the others are way above angels in looks, exude way more power. It makes me conclude they're all archangel offspring.

And four of them are female!

In their wake, about five hundred other Nephilim walk in.

I never even imagined such an enthralling sight.

While not on the level of the archangelspawn, the Nephilim are still above angels in caliber when it comes to looks and overall effect. There's always something about hybrids that makes them surpass their parents. They usually amalgamate their traits into something new and mesmerizing.

Their collective as they march in, in their semi-celestial uniforms, a sea of breathtaking wings and superiority, is something else, too. I always admired the sheer synchrony of human soldiers in those parades I saw in documentaries. But when it's the Nephilim, that inhuman quality to their carriage and precision is—above. Beyond anything humans captured even in fantasy.

And to think they're only first years, too.

So what does that make Godric? A personal tutor was always a student in school. But he looks too old to be even a senior. Assuming he's as old as he seems, and not a thousand years old. And Lorcan said he's his superior, not senior. He's also in possession of all his powers— and how. One of those Angel-Graced guys called him a level nine. An unheard of level of power. And his reputation seems to precede him. So, long established, too.

No, not a student. Of course.

So is he a professor? Sometimes those can be tutors. But he has the vibe of a seasoned warrior. Unless he's both, I'd go with soldier—*and* secret agent—since Lorcan said they're the undercover faction.

So did he drill the others in that entrance? But how, if this is their first day in the Academy, too? Or were they here already, the presence I felt yesterday? And they were here long enough for him to drill them in that immaculate parade? Why would they be here that long before the start of the academic year? Summer school?

Questions, questions. The more answers I get, the more questions crop up like mushrooms.

For now, I step aside like everyone at the Nephilim's advance. I bet most of the deference is for Godric. Although they're all imposing, they're still the kittens to his sabertooth. The other archangelspawn range from bobcats to mountain lions.

As the squadron of hybrids follow him towards the platform, to pay homage to the archangels, their expressions are coated in severity and disdain. I can tell he is their role model in arrogance and ruthlessness. And like him, they hate having us here.

Great. A whole regiment of mini-Godawfuls.

I sure hope being Angel-Graced will somehow even the playing field with those superior beings.

Soon, the archangels fly off, leaving us to meet our "colleagues." Not that any nephilim deems to look our way. I wonder if they'll keep that up until graduation. They probably will.

Suddenly, I realize why Godric specified four years. That's how long academies last.

I can't imagine being here this long, or being here at all.

What am I supposed to be doing here again?

Yeah, I'm here to be probed and punished. They sure have the punishment down pat. Having Godric as my "personal tutor" goes under the cruel and unusual variety.

But how will sticking me in this place achieve the archangels' other purpose? Finding out how I gather Angel Essence and produce *Angelescence*?

Yep. More questions. Ones I don't expect answers to any time soon.

For the next hour, or seven, since I no longer trust my inner chronometer, I phase in and out of focus as I recede to the periphery, watching, and not really registering anything.

That is, until I see a set of horns.

A double take later, they're still there.

A nephilim with horns?

Unless this isn't a...

"What are you looking at, human?"

The hiss entwined in a rumble scrapes down my raw nerves.

A demon! There's a demon at Celestial Academy!

17

I blink at the stunningly beautiful creature who just snarled at me.
The curvy bombshell in a tight black sweater and pleated,
checkered red-and-black mini skirt seems to have stepped out of
an anime. She has golden eyes, blazing-red hair, light mocha complexion, and of course, those elegantly-ridged, glistening-onyx horns.

And no one else seems to notice her sauntering about as if she owns
the place.

There are two explanations. I was put back wrong after the Divining, and now I'm seeing things. Or I was put back in a way that only I
can see through that demon's Glamor. Maybe an extension of the way
only I can see Angel Essence?

Either way, I must keep my cool. If I'm seeing a demon who isn't
there, I can't alert anyone to the fact. If she's really here, and I already
stared, I can't let her know I'm seeing her for what she is.

"I asked you a question, Mortal Slime."

Without the least volition, I find myself snarling back, "I'm looking
at the horns, Bog Breath."

My heart stops with horror. Way to go misdirecting her.

Now, according to her response, I'll find out which explanation is
true. Whether she is a hallucination—or my probable murderer.

From the way she slinks closer, like a boa constrictor approaching a
guinea pig, I'd go with the second option.

She leaves me in no doubt when she says, "Didn't whatever shit you into the world covered in slimy secretions teach you those who stare get their eyes gouged—and eaten?"

My mouth takes over again as I toss back, "Didn't whatever hatch your putrid egg teach you talking goats aren't entitled to an attitude?"

I'm busy shrieking *shut up* inwardly when she whistles and growls at the same time, the polyphonic sound hair-raising. "Ah, you're one of those."

I want to grab one of those blithely walking around, unaware of the enemy in their midst. I want to yell for help, to run away. But I do none of that.

Compulsion? Some demons have that power. Or is it knowing that if I attempt anything, these long, red nails can slash my throat in a second?

Whatever it is, I only ask, "One of what?"

"Demon snacks."

"And you're one of those," I shoot back. "Demon brats."

As I groan that I said that, and worse, that I didn't come up with something better, she draws in a spectacular snort, purses her crimson-painted lips and spits—*spits*—up in my face.

A copious glob splotches in my right eye. As I squeeze both shut, a dozen dreads explode in my mind. That her saliva will eat through my eye and into my brain. That it will spread a demonic infection that will consume me from the outside in.

In a literally blind panic, I rub my eye in a frenzy. I open the other in time to see the glob, frothy and pristinely-white, landing over my drool stain with a wet smack.

As it slides off my jumpsuit to land on the ground without eating through either, I let out a whimpering breath.

It's just regular phlegm. Thank Hell.

Shuddering in disgust, I wipe my eye vigorously on my sleeve, glaring down at her with the other one. "You're also a gross asshole."

Her lipstick un-smudged, she shrugs in ladylike elegance. As if she hasn't just snorted and spat like a tobacco-chewing, black-toothed sailor. "What do you expect? I'm a demon."

She's admitting it out loud for anyone to hear, and those closest to us do look at her. I can swear they notice her horns. But no one seems to care. What's going on here?

"What's your excuse, human?"

Since I can do nothing else, I go with the flow of this weird encounter, come what may.

I spit back at her.

I only end up spraying my own chin with pitiful droplets. And she's actually tapping her foot waiting for an answer.

"How about spending sixteen years and eight months as a Demon-Owned?" I snarl. "And having the day from Hell *and* Heaven, *while* PMSing?"

Her puffy lips quirk in a mischievous smile. She's *really* one of those heartbreakingly gorgeous hellspawn. "So you're demon droppings, too, huh?"

Demon droppings *again*? That's a thing now, it seems. And both sides used it. We Demon-Owned can't catch a break, can we?

I sigh. "I was also recently told I'm a Nothing."

She throws her head back and lets out a cacophonous yet delightfully melodic laugh. "Well, that's new."

"That's me. Brand new here."

"We're all brand new here, Maggot Brain. It's everyone's first day at the Academy."

"I'm brand new to it all, Fly Magnet." I'm really not coming up with adequate insults to do her creative ones justice. So I pull myself to my full height, my only advantage over her, with maybe four or five inches. "Till yesterday, I didn't know this place existed…" Her words suddenly hit me like a mallet in a cartoon. "Hey! Are you saying *you're* attending the Academy?"

She flashes me two rows of dazzlingly-white teeth with too-sharp canines. "It's called diversity, Junk Genes."

I swear I hear that comic blinking sound effect as my lashes flutter.

Then I blurt, "You're really a student here? And everyone can see you?"

She gapes at me, before bursting out in snorting snickers. "You thought you're the only one who can? Wow. How do you even walk and talk? Creatures with your IQ sit around and drip slime."

"Excuse me if the only thing anyone told me is that demons are off-limits here," I mumble.

This wipes off her merriment, and her face literally darkens with a frown. "Yeah, if they're not invited, like I am. Lucky them. But this damned Academy is required to accept a five to ten-percent quota of all Supernatural races and Demon-Blighted. The same percentage of

Angels, Angel-Graced and Nephilim also attend Pandemonium Academy."

I stare at her as the whole situation gets rewritten in my mind.

So everyone sees her, and no one cares because they already know about this. A demon student among the angelic brood.

Wow.

At least that means she won't kill me to silence me. That's a win for sure.

As the fear of decapitation deflates, I realize this demoness told me more than anyone did so far. And she can tell me more. If I manage to ask nicely.

I attempt a grin and hope it doesn't look sour or provocative. "So you're not the only one? Other demons and Demon-Blighted go here?"

"I can demand your firstborn as a price for answers." She inspects her long, perfectly manicured nails. "But I wouldn't feed your squalling offspring to my pit buzzard and spoil her healthy diet of roadkill. So yes, Blighted go here, as students and teachers. I don't know about other demon students this year, but they have demon teachers."

I whistle, genuinely stunned. I never thought angels and demons could collaborate, let alone in something like this. "How progressive of them."

She waves my comment away. "The blowhards on both sides are the definition of stuck in the rotting past. One that stretches back unto eternity. But this little exchange arrangement was in the fine-print of the Armistice Accords. Both sides loathe it, but the agreement was forged in one of the most powerful alchemies in Hell and Heaven—a consenting mixing of an archangel's and an archdemon's blood."

Wow. Just wow.

I stash the new info for later examination, and rush to ask my next question before she decides to stop answering. Or take my head off.

"I know about the 'By Invitation Only' part. But how do they know you won't expose the Academy's location?"

Vermillion flames invade her golden eyes, swirling around the pupils as she sneers, "A Bog Golem is smarter than you, when all it does is fart methane and wait for its next prey to stumble in its open maw. What do you think? They rely on my good character or earnest word?"

I snort, but it doesn't come out as effective as hers. "As if. But how can I possibly know how they stop you from spilling the beans?"

I get the feeling I'm not the target of her flaming fury as she grits, "The provision for that is in the Accords, too. Part of the admission process is binding the applicants. We'd burst into eternal flames if we attempted to reveal anything about this angel-infested dump or what we learn here."

"Whoa. That's some cool—or should I say blazing hot—security system."

I sense her mind leaving me and wandering into some bottomless hellpit. Of resentment. Wisps of crimson smoke start billowing from her nostrils.

Anyone else would walk away now. Smoke means fire means her next exhalation might grill me.

But she's providing me with vital info among the verbal abuse and not-so-implied menace. If I can stroke her ego, she may be amenable to answering more questions. The beautiful demons are as vain as the Fae. They love talking about themselves.

Risking a burst of flames in my face, I draw her attention back to me. "So, you're gorgeous." Just the truth. "What kind of demon are you?"

She blinks, as if coming back to the moment. Then she flings her ponytail back like a model in a photoshoot, striking a pose as sultry as her croon. "An archdemon."

I'm congratulating myself that my ploy worked when I almost choke.

Archdemons are *way* up there, on par with the archangels. They're an exclusive echelon right below the heaviest hitter of all evil, if *he* really exists. As far as I know, there are very few archdemons in existence. I never heard of a female one, since they also go by Princes and Kings of Hell.

And here I am, standing with that rare creature, a *Princess* of Hell, having what amounts to a water-cooler chat. If one full of scorn and threats of mutilation.

"My father is one of the original Princes of Hell, which makes Beelzebub and the rest my uncles."

She said that like a girl trying to impress. This makes me wonder if she is as young as she looks. She did sound young right now—and insecure with it.

If she is, at least in demon terms, that may explain why someone as powerful as her has been sent here.

But someone like that would throw around her father's name. Which means she doesn't know who he is.

Refraining from making a comment that may separate my head from my body, I whistle again. "That's some big guns you have in your family."

She huffs, and tongues of flame issue from her red lips. "It's why I'm here. Hell invented nepotism, after all."

"But I get the impression you don't like being here."

Her golden eyes turn full-on obsidian, glittering and fathomless. "I hate it!"

I'm numbed to seeing all kinds of horror-show demons. But that impossibly gorgeous creature still spooks me. There's something deeply horrifying within her, and I just got a glimpse of it.

Knowing it's bad for my vital functions to show demons that they rattle me, since they feed on weakness, I twist my lips in the nonchalance I've long perfected. "So why didn't your family use their influence to spare you the ordeal?"

Eyes back to that hypnotic gold, she shakes her head pityingly. "Do you even think before you open your chow chute, Imbecile?"

"That was a legitimate question, Asshat!"

I really need to lay off the name-calling. With the imbalance of power here, it should be a one-way thing.

Thankfully, she only rolls eyes gone blood-red this time, at my lameness, no doubt. "My family are demons."

"So?"

"*Imbecile* was the wrong adjective, since it assumes some sort of IQ. You do have 'Nothing' between your ears."

"Got *nothing* better than century-old jabs? Or was that the last time you were let out of your cage?" Lava begins to bubble in her irises, and I rush to add, "Consider me a moron all you like, but with the most powerful demons in existence for a family, you should be getting exactly what you want. I don't get why you're here against your will."

"I'm here because they, more than any hellhole-variety demon, show you they care by torturing you."

Huh. She was right. That *was* stupid of me. I should have worked that out after being around demons' reverse logic all my life. I just never considered what they do to each other could sometimes be a demonstration of twisted love.

I cough a laugh. "Talk about tough love."

"Lethal. My mother told me to either pass with honors, or die. A couple of cousins took bets in their festering gaming community that I won't survive the first semester. They must be trying to arrange my death now, so they'd win that bet."

I goggle at her. "You're being melodramatic, right?" When her exhalation singes me, I yelp, "Hey, you demons breathe lies as easily as fire and brimstone."

"You know, Nothing, you're so pathetic, I may give you a primer of how this world really works, so you don't get splattered on your first day. Or, better still, I can just kill you and spare you the suspense."

As she advances on me, Godric reappears. Between one breath and the next he's looming over us like a skyscraper of overriding maleness and aggravation.

He tersely nods at my demonic companion. "Demoness."

Her nod is as curt and hate-filled. "Nephilim."

The certainty hits me, that they know each other, and not as members of the eternal enemy species. There seems to be an abyss filled with mountains of corpses and rivers of charred blood between them.

Interesting.

The way her eyes simmer with animosity rather than the derision she's been slinging at me—*or* the swooning every female has been fluttering at him—makes me warm to her. Enemy of my enemy and all that.

All newfound fuzzy feelings splinter into a million shards when she walks away *through* me, a steel shoulder ramming into my arm.

Before the burst of pain and fury makes me tackle her to the ground, and get disemboweled by those lovely horns, she tosses cheerily over one elegant shoulder, "Catch and fry you, later, Nothing."

Fearing she may have broken mine, I gingerly examine it as she prowls away like a lioness deciding which prey to shred next. Her ponytail flits behind her as if with a life of its own, making it clear who she is. Future resident mean girl.

And I managed to attract her attention, even while trying to blend into the background. Then I proceeded to make myself her primary target.

Another jerk on the leash reminds me there's always worse.

And as I stumble after Earth's and Heaven's Ultimate Angelthug, I wonder.

Between these two monsters, the archangels' finite interest in me, and my punchable expressions and runaway mouth, how long can I possibly last around here?

By now, I only hope I last long enough to make certain Sarah is safe.

18

"I'm done letting you drag me around like a lamb to the slaughter."

I glare up at Godric, welcome packet clutched to my chest, refusing to budge.

He's towed me out of the Academy's central buildings—or Raziel Complex as I've found out—in front of everyone. It took me a long while of regulating my breathing while keeping up with his pace before I could afford acting on my fury. The moment I stopped around one of its buildings' corners, I expected him to drag me on the ground and choke me, in a repeat of our first encounter.

For some reason, that doesn't come to pass.

He only turns, dissolves the leash and exhales. "It's more to pasture. I don't intend to kill you. Yet. Now move your scrawny arse, White."

"Oh, shut up, Godawful. You can do zip. Not for four more years, remember?"

His eyes sweep me in a swathe of lazy malice before resting on my neck. "I can spend those years dragging you on your belly for all your fellow cadets to see. Up to you."

"You don't have to be such a jerk *all* the time, y'know," I grit out.

"I don't see refraining from being one bearing any fruit. I removed the leash, yet I don't see you walking."

I almost blurt something snide, but manage to swallow it. I really need to pick my battles with this bastard. Right now, I need him to give me some leeway.

"Look, I just want to find this Jeremiel Domus Feminae on my own. You know they gave me this cool interactive magic map, so I won't get lost. And it really doesn't become Godric the Great to be reduced to the role of my escort—or shepherd."

He says nothing to that, keeps his gaze locked with mine. The moment lengthens, warps, and I almost moan under the brunt of his sheer charisma and gorgeousness.

Something expands in the depths of his incredible eyes. I vaguely think it should scare me out of my mind. It only intrigues me, exhilarates me. And is that hesitation, too?

Before I can make sure, another wave of students gallop closer, raucously yelling and laughing, fracturing the moment. Then they turn the corner and see Godric.

They all fall silent as if someone hit a mute button. All but scraping and bowing, they pick up speed as soon as they pass him, almost running away.

His eyes remains fixed on me all through. But anything I thought I saw there is now gone as he drawls, deliciously posh and haughty, "The moment I leave you to your own devices, you'll cause or get into trouble. You'll either try to run, probably tripping the Palladium Wards and getting barbecued. Or you'll find some other monster to piss off, like you inexplicably found that demoness, but without me around, they won't hesitate to turn you into human shish kebab."

It doesn't make me hate him any less that I want to close my eyes and listen to him forever. Or that he's right. About most of the above.

Suddenly, his eyes blaze with a fire I haven't seen before, black and consuming, and it's—terrifying. "She could have maimed or killed you."

Heart pounding like it would outrace itself, I wave him off. "She wouldn't have done anything with all these people around."

"You underestimate her viciousness. And your provocation." He says this last word as if it stymies him.

Yeah, sure.

Yet, he's right again. I'm probably in one piece only because he showed up. I hate owing him anything.

But then he wasn't protecting *me*. He was preserving the test subject he has to keep alive until they get whatever they want from me. As for seeming to negotiate his treatment of me now, he must have gotten further orders not to rough me up—too much. Also for his bosses' purposes.

I finally exhale. "Okay, fine. Lead the way. Just no leash."

"No leash, if you keep up. You're already late as it is."

"Late for what? My afternoon nap?"

His gaze rests on me for one last knee and panty-melting moment before he turns and continues walking. He doesn't say anything again.

As I walk behind him, I wonder what it would take not to feel my every nerve discharging every time I look at him. Intensifying loathing or impending doom are doing nothing to lessen my appreciation of his assets. This guy is something else. In the most literal sense.

What was the universe thinking when it made him?

I mean, *really*? No mercy at all for XX chromosome carriers?

For the rest of the trek to the dorms as he walks at my pace, I ponder those weighty questions, and ogle his splendiferous behind.

All too soon, we reach our destination, and the building housing the girls' dorm looms above us. The boys', or Jeremiel Domus Hominae, is in the far distance, its towers barely apparent over dense woods, and a massive complex of buildings called Regulus Host. They sure take segregation of the sexes seriously.

From the welcome packet Godric let me explore for a while before dragging me behind him, one of the strict rules around here is separation in living quarters. Males are not allowed in the female dorm at *any* time, and vice versa.

Suits me fine. If the dorms have shared rooms and showers, I'd rather not see morning wood or stumble on dangling bits.

Taking a deep breath, I cross the threshold after Godric, feeling I'm entering a different kind of unknown.

I actually feel more anxious now than when I faced the archangels, the Tribunal, or that demoness. Or even when I first faced Godric. I haven't been among that many girls my age since I left school at thirteen. School life was hell then, when they were just stupid human kids.

I better be careful how I set the tone of my presence here. Best thing is to shut up and keep my head down, attract no one's attention.

This resolution comforts me, for the seconds before I remember it's already too late for that. And that every decision I've taken in recent memory has backfired. Case in point is that beautiful monster three paces ahead.

Thankfully, the interior soon takes my mind off worst-case-scenarios.

Like every inch of this fantasyland, everything is exquisite, if far less prodigious than the Court section of the domain, or even the central complex of the Academy. Which makes me prefer it. Instead of some celestial mausoleum, this place feels lived in. As if it has accommodated cadets for decades or centuries—or more. I sense the emotions and experiences permeating these halls. There's also solid evidence all around. Banners hanging from arches, vitrines full of trophies, and portraits of smiling young women in uniforms on the walls.

Maybe that's why, more than ever, those sentient vibes assail me. The ground seems to breathe, and the walls to whisper. I swear the friezes and paintings watch me, meet my eyes, and when they're in the periphery of my vision, beckon.

I would have given anything to stop and examine each detail, to see if what I glimpse of movement, what I feel of awareness, is real.

If only Godawful left me to find my own way.

I need to get the lay of the land. It's the first thing I do at a new place. I always did that when Kondar regularly sent me on thieving errands. It was vital to concoct an escape plan in advance, scoping possible exits, places to hide, things to destroy as a diversion...and so on.

Promising myself I'll make that reconnaissance tour the moment I get rid of him, I brace myself for the four-story climb.

This time he waits for me to catch my breath at every landing. Though I guess I'm lucky they have stairs at all in a place built for winged residents, I grumble about the lack of elevators all the way to the door marked on that magical floor plan as my dorm room.

It's at the end of an endless corridor with twelve more before it. The far-apart doors indicate the massive sizes of the rooms inside. The archangels are generous with their cadets, huh? No wonder the students were fluttering at being here. Me, give me my dump with Sarah any day.

As I fumble with one hand for the spelled key that can be wielded by only me, to open only my dorm room, Godric flicks the door open. I'm in time to see how he did it, with a rune that flamed for seconds in his palm.

"How is this allowed?" He scowls at my blurted question. I elaborate. "For you to be here, when you're a male?" *The* male. "And what was that? Some kind of angelic master key? How come you're allowed to open my dorm room?"

The massive pain quirks a mocking grimace. Mean and vicious, but still so hot it singes me down to my core. "What do you think I'll do? Slip in and watch you sleep? Or bathe? I assure you, unlike you, I like food to stay in my stomach."

As in he'd barf if he saw me naked. I have to admit he's probably right about *that*, too.

Before I can lob something insulting back, somberness descends over him, causing my heart to hiccup in my chest.

He sounds even bleaker as he says, "I can be here, and can open your door, because you're my charge. My responsibility. When I'd rather demons harvest my organs alive."

Just what I thought earlier. He's as trapped as I am, and hating it as I do.

And it makes me feel *infinitely* better about this new form of Indenture. About even my upcoming demise.

I smile brightly up at him. "Thanks for seeing me to my door, Godawful." I stand on tiptoes, raising my face with a duck-lipped pout. When his frown only deepens, I quip, "Aren't you standing there expecting a kiss for your trouble?"

The very air starts to vibrate as he gazes down at me. Every hair on my body stands on end with the charge of his frustration.

Man, I can really get addicted to pulling his strings.

Suddenly, he severs our visual duel, turns to the towering window at the blind end of the corridor. He reaches it in two strides, then as if by levitation, he's on the sill.

Before another thought fires in my mind, he drops.

My heart almost kicks me flat on my face as I bolt with a strangled cry to the window—in time to see him coming up in a steep climb.

I forgot for a moment there that he can fly.

Heart still in my ash-dry mouth, I watch as his masterpiece wings blaze with those runes, and beat the air in a symphony of ferocity and grace. It's no longer than a minute before his soaring ascent takes him to the clouds.

Such absolute, overpowering, *cruel* beauty really shouldn't exist.

Once he pierces the billowing cumulus overhead and disappears, it takes a while for my heartbeats to calm down.

The thought that I aggravated him into trying to fling himself off the planet to avoid me helps. A lot.

As I turn to my prison cell for maybe the next four years, I wonder how many inmates I'll share it with. And if I'll *ever* see his wings unfold.

I really, really want to see that.

I push the door he left ajar, only to drop the cluttered items in my aching arms over the threshold. A cry breaks over me as I swoop down for them.

Going numb all over, I raise my eyes from my crouch.

For moments, I can't credit what I see.

This—this can't be happening. I have to be hallucinating.

She can't really be here. Not her. Not…

Sarah!

19

"**W**en!"

I remain crouching on the ground, staring at Sarah.

She's real. And really here. Flying to me with tears streaming down her face.

Shock beats down on me with her every bounding step across the expansive room, almost making me keel over.

No. No, no, *no*. She can't be here.

How is she here?

Lorcan. It has to be him. The *traitor*.

And to think I trusted him.

But that's all my fault. He's a nephilim. He laughed at how we humans once romanticized angels, told me what remorseless monsters they are. What was I *thinking* when I exposed her identity to him, her importance to me, after they sentenced me to another form of slavery?

But I had no other way of reaching her, ever again. And I needed her to get free!

I only managed to trap her here with me.

I barely get up to teetering feet when she throws herself at me, crashing me into the closed side of the double door. Head barely clearing my chin, she clings to me and weeps into my chest.

Heart exploding against my ribs, fingers feeling like exposed wires, I push away enough so I can look down at her.

"Sarah..." My voice comes out a cracked croak. "Stop crying —please."

Drowned, frantic eyes zip up to meet mine as a harsh hiccup tears out of her. "You're okay...you're okay!"

That's why she's crying? Not because she was abducted by a terrifying nephilim? Or because she was hurled into this otherworldly place filled with beings who can turn her inside out with a thought? She was worried about *me*?

"Oh, Sar, I'm so sorry." I drag her back for a tight hug before stumbling away, unable to bear feeling her close, here, sharing my fate. "I should have listened to you. If I didn't ignore your premonition, none of this would have happened."

She shakes her head vigorously. "No, no—if you stayed put every time I had a premonition, you would have never left the apartment. I didn't know what I was sensing that night, and it could have turned out to be paranoia."

She's always so quick to absolve me, and I can't bear it this time. "But it didn't. It was a set-up. And they caught me. But I only care that they caught you with me." It's me who grabs her now, unable to contain my fury and anxiety anymore. "Tell me what happened. What did he do to you? If he laid a finger on you, I'll pluck and boil him!"

She blinks, looking taken aback. "You mean Lorcan? He assured me you are okay, and was really nice!"

"Nice?" After I bark, I remember that he *is* as nice as you can hope a nephilim to be. But if he told her I was okay... "Then why were you crying so hard?"

She points a shaking finger across the room. "Because she told me she ate your eyes!"

Said eyes snap across the room, and I see her. A girl lounging on a queen bed draped in black sheets and red satin comforter, one shapely leg dangling off the side, exposed to her panties by a too-short skirt. Some glossy fashion magazine is hiding her face.

I know who it is at once.

The Demoness.

My blood rising to my skin in a wave of lava, I stalk toward her, kick the foot of the bed with all I have. Those boots are really sturdy and the impact shakes the bed enough, the magazine flops from her red-nailed hands over her face.

"Get out of here, you freak!" I shriek.

Lightning-fast, she sits up and flings that magazine at me. It clips me like a glancing dagger over my right eyebrow.

I yelp as the flare of pain is immediately followed by a gush of blood dripping into my eye. The eye she was aiming at. If I didn't jerk at the last second, it would have been its contents dripping down my face instead. She *meant* to blind me.

Literally seeing red, I launch myself at her.

I land on top of her, take her down to the bed. I have no move beyond that, don't even know what this one can achieve except vent my rage, at her, at everything since Godric crash-landed in my path. Except get me maimed or killed, as he said.

But there's no rationality left in me. Knowing she terrorized Sarah is the last straw my mind snaps under.

Before I can grab that ponytail or head-butt her, I find myself beneath her, spread-eagled, and her soft, manicured hand is around my throat.

She squeezes my windpipe with steady, inexorable strength as the burning stench of brimstone suddenly envelops me. If I could breathe, I would have gagged.

Her nails lengthen and sharpen as they dig into my neck, as do her perfect, white teeth as she grins maliciously down at me.

"It was a choice between educating you and killing you," she purrs. "Thanks for making the decision for me. Option B it is."

"Stop, please," Sarah begs as she tries to pull the demon off me.

No, Sarah! Get away from her. Get out of here. Out of this immortal monsterland, any way you can.

But Sarah would never give up on me like I would die before I give up on her. She isn't considering her own survival as she claws at the demon's arm and shrieks, "Let her go!"

But that demon won't, will only turn on Sarah. I have to keep her focus on me.

From my helpless position thrashing beneath her, I choke, "That all you got...Death Breath? Or is this how...you plan to kill me? Make me...*puke* myself to death...on your stench?"

Just as the brimstone started, it disappears, a scent of ozone and hyacinth replacing it. Then the demon presses the claw-like nail of her other hand into the wound she inflicted, deepening it.

As the pain darkens the world already teetering on the verge of blinking out, the smell of burning skin and barbecue assails me. A smell I never forgot since that day Kondar marked me.

She's branding me again!

I can barely draw enough oxygen to keep from passing out. But thanks to Godric's—*conditioning*, suffocation no longer incapacitates me, and I wheeze, "Brand me now...and I'll come back to haunt you... until you lose your mind. They'll have to...put you down...like the rabid Grunge Demon...that you are!"

She only grins, increasing the pressure on my neck until I stop struggling. And as Sarah sobs and begs frantically in the background, she continues whatever she's doing to my wound.

Just as I think she'll punch her claw through my skull and into my brain, she's off me in one fluid motion.

"You're lucky you're entertaining," she says breezily as she adjusts her clothes and fluffs her ponytail. "Inferno knows I'll need all the entertainment I can get in this dump filled with angel prigs, nephilim pricks and angel-graced doormats. You may live."

Struggling to draw breath through my bruised, swelling throat, I lurch to a sitting position as Sarah rushes to help me. She strokes a shaking, soothing hand down my back as I grab the demoness's pillow and wipe the blood from my eye.

Gritting my teeth at the idea of a facial brand, I check the damage. I feel nothing. She must have given me a third-degree burn and killed my nerve endings.

As I get off the bed on quivering legs, I push Sarah behind me, needing to hide her from that monster. I contemplate every way I know how to kill a demon as she puts the finger she dipped in my blood into her mouth with a wicked wink.

Suddenly, she frowns and goes still. Her gaze sharpens on me as she approaches me again. I really, *really* want to cringe.

I somehow don't. Still wheezing noisily, I glare at her, holding an adamant hand back to Sarah, warning her against interfering again.

When the demoness stops in front of me, I don't let her see I'm ready to crumple at her feet. And I'm tall enough that she has to look up at me, some sort of edge in this vicious game of power. False as it is, it steadies me. Somewhat.

Then she issues those simultaneous sounds that make my hairs almost pull out of their roots. A hiss and a moan, like the scrape of rock on gravel, and the whistle of wind in a desolate desert.

"What are you?"

"You have the attention span of a fruit fly," I grunt. "And the disgust factor of a demon-sized one. I thought we established I'm Nothing."

Her eyes goes black again, and my mind races with possible counterattacks if she decides to continue her torture. But nothing I do would be effective. Not when I can't reach for my switchblade before she finishes me off. And not with Sarah within collateral damage range.

I hate being so helpless. Even in a life of Indenture, I always had some plan, some way out of trouble. But if this gorgeous monster changes her mind and decides to snuff my life, I'd be helpless to stop her. Then she'd turn on Sarah.

I doubt she'd even get into trouble for killing us. Godric believed she could have maimed or killed me in front of everyone. He must know there would have been no serious repercussions for her. After all, she's basically demonic royalty, and we're two worthless humans.

Her irises heat, like a coal set on fire, and I feel something slithering through my mind. It feels like the cold, slippery tentacles of an octopus made of evil.

That monster is mentally probing me!

Rage and revulsion fill me with violent images, of Azrael's lovely scythe chopping off those defiling probes in one vicious slash.

The demon cries out and stumbles back, pressing her fists to her temples. I stare at her as her face scrunches in pain, trying to understand what just happened.

Did I do this to her? But how?

If I have Angel Grace inside me, did it flare at her demonic intrusion? Or maybe that was my Mark acting up?

I thought it's only made to kill us, rather than let us be taken over by another demon. Maybe this time it actually lashed out to stop the takeover attempt?

Whatever happened, it hurt her. Badly. And it feels *fantastic*.

Maybe I'm not so helpless after all.

Satisfaction burgeons in my chest. "Did that hurt, you poor, unfortunate, soulless fiend?"

Opening eyes flashing between glowing embers and magical ambers, and though I can tell she's still in severe pain, she *grins*. Not a grin of bravado, but of glee.

She had to extinguish any sense of victory I felt, didn't she?

Argh! Those demons and their perverse sense of humor!

"You might replace my hellcat in entertaining me while I serve my sentence here." She chuckles, the laugh ending with a sound like a rattlesnake's. "It's going to be fun having you around, Nothing. "

I strike my best challenging pose. "Which will be never. Now take your gnarly horns, and that pointy tail you must have coiled under this mini-skirt, and scram."

Her smile only grows serene as she pushes past me, and jumps back on the bed.

The last trace of any triumph evaporates as I watch her fluffing the pillow I just smeared with my blood, before settling back on it and picking up another magazine from the bedside table.

"I said get out!" I shriek so loudly, I feel my already damaged vocal cords tearing.

A touch on my arm makes me jump and whirl around, nerves jangling in anticipation of another attack.

It's only Sarah, and she's mirroring my grimace. "She's not going anywhere, no matter how much you yell at her."

"Oh, I know she's a demon, and has all these powers, but did you see what just happened? Maybe I can…"

Sarah shakes her head, the apology in her eyes silencing me as she says, "She's going nowhere because she's our roommate."

20

Before I can process this horrifying piece of news, an explosive bang shakes the whole room.

I stumble in front of Sarah, shielding her as I sway around to face the new danger. I only see a statuesque blonde walking in.

Blinking at her, I realize what happened. She flung the already-open door so hard, it slammed against the wall—and cracked it. A jagged fissure has traveled up to the thirty-foot high ceiling.

I remember her at once. One of the four female archangelspawn from Godric's parade. The tallest, most stunning one.

As she passes us, her gaze sweeps us and the demon with no attempt to meet our eyes. Her expression says it all. She considers she's fallen into sewers. Sewers filled with maggots. She wouldn't acknowledge those, would she?

"Don't tell me—you're our roommate, too!" I moan.

Her disgruntled haughtiness as she stalks toward the bed at the far end of the room says it all. She puts down her suitcase, opens and starts emptying it. Her precise movements remind me of an assassin methodically disassembling her weapon.

Roommate, check. Hating that fact and us with an abhorrence the breadth of Heaven, check. Another supernatural monster and potential future murderer in residence, double check.

I can only minimize the chances of ending up dead if I move out. Surely the Academy's room assignment office or whatever can find us

—find *me*—some nice human girls with manageable levels of the supernatural to room with.

My thoughts stutter as the nephilim walks back toward us.

I put myself fully in front of Sarah as she stops midway between us and the demon's bed.

"Here are the ground rules. I will only state them once."

Her voice is like strumming a lyre from Heaven—melodic, mesmerizing. Her accent is the same as Godric's, and like him, her enunciation has the cultured cadence of a higher being. Which she is.

But unlike his voice's effect on me, hers only strikes icicles deep within my bones. Whether of dread or distaste, I can't tell. Probably both.

"The ground rules are one rule," she continues. "That I don't feel you around. To elaborate, so you never claim miscommunication: You do not come near me, my space or my belongings. You do not sully my senses with your sight, voice, noise, scent and mess. We are prohibited from harming humans—or demons—on the premises. Unless they transgress against us. I consider all of the above transgressions. Commit any of them, and there will be no second chances. I *will* harm you."

The demoness only snickers, goes back to reading her magazine. The pervert who seemed to enjoy the pain I caused her is probably delighted at the promise of future mayhem. *Of course*, she is.

"Whoa, Godawful's Twin!"

The nephilim focuses on me for the first time, and I get the urge to cower and to punch her in her perfect face all at once. I stand straighter, but she's regretfully taller than me. She must be at least six feet without the spiky heels she's wearing. With them, she towers inches over me.

I can't even have that advantage?

I inject my voice with all the venom flowing in my heart for her and her kind. "I'd rather not see you or even know you exist. I'm requesting a transfer right now." I toss a gesture between her and the demon. "You two can play Heaven and Hell together to your non-existent hearts' content."

The nephilim gives a tranquil tilt of her head that belies the aversion and frustration roiling in her pure-violet eyes. "You're not transferring anywhere."

"Watch me, archangelspawn," I spit out as I start herding Sarah to the door. "I'd rather sleep in a coffin than in a room with you two."

"That can be arranged," the nephilim drawls. "However, the assignment of roommates is immutable."

I turn to gape at her. "Immu—what?'

"It means it cannot be changed," Sarah whispers at my back.

I toss her a chagrined glance. "I know what immutable means, Sar."

I'm nowhere as book-smart as she is, but I'm not illiterate! But that nephilim *has* to be messing with me.

Yet one look at her inhumanly gorgeous face tells me she's not. She's probably incapable of it. If she is, and can turn on her sense of humor at will like that cousin of hers, she wouldn't do so now. She's as upset about this as I am.

I throw my hands up. "This can't be! We're totally incompatible. Why stick us together? *Who* stuck us together? Your dad and uncles?"

She folds her arms over perfect breasts snug in her otherworldly pseudo-military outfit, the condescension in her amazing eyes deepening. "The Choosing is akin to the Divining. No one has any control over it. And no one can contest it."

I gape at her. "You telling me the forces of Light and Darkness themselves chose us to be roomies? Don't they have better things to do?"

She shrugs her majestic shoulders. "It is what it is. Now, I advise that you curb your self-destructive human impulses, and obey my ground rules. This is our status quo for the foreseeable future, and it's up to you to survive it."

I'm almost tempted to tell her that her family needs me alive, badly. But I'd also be telling her their need has an expiration date.

Clamping my lips over a hundred inadvisable things, I grumble, "Whatever. Now if you'll excuse me, I have to see my friend off."

Grabbing Sarah's arm, I stride away, dragging her behind me.

We're almost at the door when the nephilim's serene words hit me between the shoulder blades. "Your friend is going nowhere. She's one of the five chosen for this dorm room."

Don't listen to her, Wen. Keep walking.

But I somehow know this archangelspawn knows something I don't.

Heart twisting with foreboding, I turn to her. "How can she be chosen by whatever that

Choosing is? Her presence here is totally incidental."

She tucks a swathe of gleaming, gold silk behind her ear as she exhales. "Nothing is incidental in existence. She's here because she has to be here."

"Don't give me that fate crap!" I cry out. "She has to be free, and away from all of you monsters. That's where she has to be."

The nephilim raises one dense, perfectly-plucked eyebrow at me. "Why are you bleating at me? Tell that to the universe."

I stomp my foot, head about to explode with frustration. "Universe shmooniverse! My friend is human, and humans have no place here. The universe made a mistake this time."

She gives a disdainful nod. "It's true mortal cattle do not belong here, unless they're Angel-Graced mortal cattle, like those wretches we're being forced to train with."

"See? We finally agree on something! Regular mortal cattle and hybrid celestial vipers don't mix."

She frowns, as if wrestling with the urge to "harm" me, before she shrugs. "But that's the reason she's been chosen. Your mortal cattle friend is also angel-graced."

21

"**N**o!"

Without even acknowledging my outburst, the She-Godric turns and walks back to her bed.

I stare at her as she puts her stuff away in her walk-in closet with that same psychopathic neatness, a storm of implications battering me.

Sarah's presence here *is* a total coincidence. A terrible mistake. One I was responsible for.

But what if—what if I'm also the reason they think she's angel-graced?

She ingested *Angelescence* once by accident, and again to ascertain its effects, when it didn't work on me.

What if a second dose, so closely after the first one, left a residue in her system, and it's making them think she's angel-graced?

Sarah's gentle touch brings me out of the tornado of dread and guilt. I turn to her urgently. "Did they take you to the Divining?"

She shakes her head dazedly. "What's that?"

So she didn't suffer through that horrific test. How did they decide she's angel-graced then?

Lorcan. He must know what's going on.

Grabbing Sarah's hand, I resume our interrupted escape, and hurtle out of the room in search of him.

He's going to answer my questions. *Then* I'll brain him.

It's only after I reach the building's entrance that I stop. Basically because I'm dying.

As distressed, Sarah bends over, hands on knees as she wheezes. "Tell me...you're not thinking of...escaping."

"There's no escaping...these monsters," I gasp as I fold almost in two, feeling like a hot poker is embedded in my side. "I need...to find Lorcan."

"You know where he is?" She straightens, recovering faster than me.

I didn't even think how I'd find him before hurtling out of that room as if I had a demon snapping at my heels.

Oh, wait. I *did* have one. I'll have an archangelspawn, too, if I ever breathe near her again.

I force myself to straighten. "I'll figure it out. C'mon, we gotta clear this misunderstanding up and get you the hell out of here."

This time, when I try to drag her after me, I only slide her over the mirror-polished floor.

Frowning down at her, I find that expression I so dread gripping her face as she raises her dainty chin. "I'm going nowhere without you."

"*I'm* going nowhere, Sar. They arrested me for peddling *Angelescence*, which seems to be an unforgivable offense to them."

"Yeah, Lorcan told me. He also said it's a huge problem no one else must know about, but they're inducting you into the Academy until they figure out how you do it. Now I have the chance to be with you for however long they'll keep you, you think I'd leave?"

I start to blurt something, before clamping my lips over it.

Arguing with Sarah would be an exercise in futility. She's the personification of accommodation—until it comes to my wellbeing. Then there's no budging her. Not to mention that she always had this crazy conviction that my life is somehow worth more than hers.

Once I know I can make Lorcan fix this disaster, *then* I'll argue.

From the brief look at my schedule in that welcome-to-prison packet, there's another part of Orientation that's required attendance for all Angel-Graced.

Was it *Afterworld: Introduction to the Post-Apocalypse* or *Angel Grace 101*? Neither?

Whatever, we're supposed to meet some professors.

Not that I care. But if everyone is heading there, Lorcan could be, too. As a tutor or guard, or whatever the hell he is.

Taking the magical map out, I watch it orient itself. A glowing path snakes across it, with the angelic language I couldn't read before morphing into English. At least I see the meaning in my mind in English. It indicates that my destination building is Jophiel Hall. As I hover my hand over it, the map provides the extra info that it's named after the archangel of learning and education.

This map either knows my schedule and is pointing me where I should be, or it reads my intention and is taking me to Lorcan. Either way, I can only follow its directions.

Sarah falls into step with me, looking disapprovingly up at me. "I know what you're doing. You're postponing our argument until you know for sure you can get me out of here."

Ugh. She knows me *too* well.

"I made a mistake ignoring your premonition, Sar, and fell into their trap. You have nothing to do with it, and you can and must get out of your Indenture." She starts to protest vehemently, but I drown her voice. "It's only going to be four years max. I'll serve my time, then catch up with you wherever you end up. Easy, peasy."

After a stretch of silence, I'm starting to hope she might be seeing reason when she whispers, her voice shaky, "When you didn't return that night, and I feared y-you died, I wanted to die, too. You're the only reason I want to live, Wen. And I *can't* live in this world without you."

"You *can*, in the real world outside our prison. When you're free…"

"I don't want to be free without you!" she cries. "We get free together, or not at all, remember?"

Ugh, I should have known this would come back to bite me in my "scrawny arse."

"When Lorcan showed up and told me you were okay…"

I cut her off, boiling blood hurtling in my veins. "This isn't why I sent that traitorous hunk of muscle and feather to you! I sent him to help you get free, not to imprison you with me."

"*When* he told me you're okay—" She continues as if I didn't rant anything. "—it felt like a stay of execution." What *I* always thought every time I knew she was okay. "I wanted *nothing* but to come be with you."

I gape at her. "You mean you *asked* him to bring you here?"

She throws her hands up in exasperation. "Of course, I did. You think I'd do anything else?"

"If this is why he brought you here, you've seen me, and now you can go!"

She twists her lips. "I said I want to *be* with you, not just see for myself you're okay and go back to Zeral."

"That's the whole point. You *won't* go back to her."

"I won't, because I'm staying here."

"Listen, Sar, if Lorcan took you because you asked..."

She shakes her head, stopping me again. "I didn't ask, I *begged*. He kept saying it's impossible. I was almost groveling when he suddenly fell silent, but kept staring at me as if in a trance. When he came out of it, he said he's sorry he can no longer help me with my Indenture, and has to take me with him."

"So he *did* break his word! He did take you against your will!"

She rolls her eyes. "Didn't you hear anything I said? I was sure it wasn't my pleas that changed his mind, but I didn't care what did. I practically jumped in his arms!"

"Oh, hell no, Sar!" I moan, feeling my skull tightening over my brain. "But no—he would have taken you anyway. That you wanted him to doesn't make him less of a treacherous bastard." I hold up a hand to stop her objection. "But that's okay, because I'll make him take you back, and fulfill his promise. You'll get out of L.A. and your Mark will be deactivated..."

Everything comes to a jarring halt.

The Mark! I can't *believe* I didn't think of this before. That it hasn't activated all this time, when I traveled as far as New York!

As always, Sarah answers my unspoken confusion. "Lorcan thinks the Mark's infernal magic was neutralized by such proximity to their angelic magic. It's why he felt confident he can take me away without my own Mark activating. And he was right. Though he thinks this effect won't last. But he said they'll deal with it."

"Deal with it how?"

She shrugs. "He'll tell us when they figure it out. Just think of it, Wen—when they deactivate the Mark for good, we'll be free from our Indenture in a way we never dreamed of."

I shake my head. "This isn't how it works, Sar. Deactivating the Marks will mean we reneged on its rules, and we'd be considered fugitives."

"Who cares? The demons won't be able to do anything as long as we're here."

"As if here is any better!" I exclaim.

"Of course, it's better. We're both safe…"

"We're not safe! This place is filled with Supernatural monsters…"

"If it is, you even think I'd leave you among them alone?"

"You can't do anything for me here, Sar! But you can get free, forever. No other being can enslave you again. This is the best thing you can do for me!"

"And the best thing for *me* is to be with you. And this is where I'm staying. Whatever the reason Lorcan brought me here, it's the best thing he could have done."

I stare at her, tongue going numb with frustration. I want to shake sense into her. I want to knock her out until I get her out of here. I want to hurl myself to the ground and throw a fit.

She holds my gaze, letting me know I can do whatever the hell I want. She said she's going nowhere without me, and that's that.

Feeling like I'm about to have a heart attack, but knowing we've reached the end of this argument—for now—I turn and continue walking.

We say nothing more all the way to Jophiel Hall. On the way, we pass by Raphael Sanatorium, and Jegudiel House, where all professors live. Or have offices. Or both.

Apart from sharing the opulence and timelessness that stamps every inch of the Academy, this building isn't a maze like Raziel Complex. Its layout is intuitive, and I only need the map for a few nudges in the right direction.

Finally something that follows logic. Or maybe I'm getting the hang of this place? Or is it getting the hang of me? But if this place, or this map are guiding me on auto now, maybe they will pinpoint Lorcan?

Neither do, and before I come up with a search strategy, cadets pour in from outside.

At Sarah's insistence, I let the crowd sweep us into the Roman theater-like auditorium. It's only going to be an hour-long lecture, and maybe I'll spot Lorcan lurking around somewhere.

As we take our seats in the sloping rows, I'm stunned to sense that Sarah is excited. It's confusing, even disconcerting, until I think about this situation from another angle. Then it makes some sort of sense.

We were both forced to leave school after sixth grade. I myself was glad to be rid of school. But Sarah would have loved to continue her education, into high school and beyond if possible.

Now, in this total mess of circumstances, she finds herself attending an insanely exclusive college-level Academy. With the Nephilim, of all beings.

As I ponder the implications of this realization, a massive angel walks in with a smaller man in tow. Half a dozen other angels, all in solid dark grey uniforms adorned by a single emblem over their hearts enter the stage behind them, and stand at the back like guards.

The angel seems at least a decade older than the usual late-twenties-to-early-thirties appearance all angels sport. Which is very strange. Do angels age?

Also unlike all the dressed-to-kill Designated Angels I've seen, he's wearing a faded t-shirt that's stretched to bursting over his muscular torso and arms. Only the contrast with his stark-white wings tells me it was once black. It has seen better days—years ago. Even at its prime, it would have been something *I* can afford.

Even more casual are the knee-length khakis and toe-ring sandals, not to mention his drab-gold hair. A far departure from the precise stylings of other angels, it hangs lankily in haphazard waves to his shoulders. It doesn't seem he's washed it or used a cleaning spell on it in a while. And he has a scruffy, five-day blondish beard.

Without the wings, he'd pass for some sun-bleached, fitness-freak uncle back from a camping trip. Or, considering his striking looks, some Hollywood A-lister taking a break from a Wild West set, and out for a stroll on the beach.

I never even imagined angels could look this human. This *approachable*. I can feel the same reaction from all around me as he takes the podium, and a hush of anticipation falls over the hall.

But my optimism starts to dim when, instead of addressing us, he eyeballs us. For what feels like an hour.

Everyone starts to shuffle uneasily under his unnerving focus, what I'm certain each feels directed towards them in specific.

I'm starting to wonder if he's mute or something, when he finally says, "How new and shiny you all look."

His voice, like the archangels', comes from all around. But while theirs felt like a sensory surround system, his bears down on me, burrowing in my very marrow.

Then he adds, "I *loathe* new and shiny."

Well, that's about the last thing I expected an angel to say.

Shaking his head, he gives an exasperated sigh.

Wind explodes across the auditorium, smashing us all back in our seats.

Everything slows down as my mind fast forwards, as it always does in response to danger.

I see and hear everything at once.

The shockwave sending anything not nailed down shooting through the air. Cries and yells bursting around the hall in a cacophonous chorus of shock and fright—and pain. The angel who caused that hurricane-level wind, and the man he came with, not a feather or a hair on them moving. The angel starting to smile. Missiles hurtling straight at us.

Act. Now.

I ram into Sarah, taking her down. A fraction of a second before we get hit by welcome packets at near the speed of sound. Those paper cuts would have been fatal.

After ten seconds or minutes, the wind dies down as abruptly as it detonated. I'm still holding Sarah down, arms spastic around her, breath still bated, screams still splintering inside my head. And now stampeding feet are reverberating like an earthquake in my bones.

This is why I hate being in a crowd. They're in my way to the exit, to escape. But I must find a clear path out of this deathtrap.

I raise my head enough to scope the situation. The scene of mayhem that assails me is what I expected.

Many weren't as quick in dodging the flying debris. The screams and sobs continue, intensifying as the injured try to run out of the auditorium, or others try to drag them out. I see a girl with something sticking out of her chest and blood drenching her whole front. Another boy is shrieking as he holds up an arm, spurting blood from his half-missing hand. Another has his face almost torn off, his flesh dangling off his skull.

All this because that angel sighed.

What would happen if he blew out his breath for real?

As macabre images of human body parts flying around in an angel's exhalation flood my mind, I duck down to pull at Sarah. "We have to get out of here. We'll crawl below…"

Thuds reverberate the ground, cutting off my frantic words. My heart convulses as I realize what the sound was. Doors slamming shut. That monster angel has locked us in.

"Sit."

His voice again bombards the whole space from every direction. It makes my every cell vibrate with rejection, defiance. It has the opposite effect on everyone else.

It's like a compulsion comes over the crowd. I can hear them stumbling to obey him, see the group cowering in the row behind us scrambling up.

I exchange a look with Sarah. She doesn't seem compelled either, but she nods. We have to sit up. We can't afford to find out what would happen if we're the only two who don't.

As we clamber up to our seats, I keep Sarah's hand clutched in mine, keep my eyes on the source of danger, while stealing glances all around, assessing the situation and escape plans. None of them is viable.

We are trapped.

With the rows full again, the auditorium looks back to normal. If you discount the gored cadets, the smashed objects, and the blood on almost every surface, like a post-massacre scene.

The angel sighs again, and whimpers shear through the hall as we all brace for another onslaught. This time, with him forcing everyone to remain seated, that body parts maelstrom may still happen.

But—nothing happens. There's no wind, no projectiles this time. The whole hall exchange still panicked if confused glances.

I'm not confused. I was exposed to gratuitous violence all my life. I know his type. They live to inflict damage on others. They feed off their pain and terror. He caused that first hurricane on purpose. The sick bastard.

"That's more like it," the angel says, accent a cross between American and Irish, voice now filled with satisfaction. "You may still be disgustingly new, but you're no longer shiny."

We certainly aren't. Apart from those with severe injuries, the rest are either bloodied or disheveled.

"You must be wondering, why? Simple. Because I am Azazel. Yeah, hurry, get out your phones, fire up your search engines and look me up —and shake in your new, shiny, Academy-issue boots."

Everyone frantically whips out their phones. As their thumbs fly over their screens, I burn with envy that they have the latest models, with working, and clearly lightning-fast internet. I have to get us phones like these before Sarah leaves, so we can stay in touch.

I'm busy planning the acquisitions, when the cadets put down their phones, every face pale and terrified.

Azazel laughs, and the sound is the most hair-raising thing I ever heard. Not because it's hideous like Kondar's belching cackles, on the contrary. His voice is as darkly smooth and sweet as molasses.

But it sends something like an ominous memory burrowing into my spine.

Azazel spreads his arms and makes a small bow, as if receiving applause. "Yep, boys and girls, I'm *that* Azazel. Fallen and very, *very* averse to all that's Light and Good."

Fallen? As in a Fallen angel?

I never heard about his kind outside of religious stories. Even Lucifer is talked about as if he's just a myth. In the version of the Apocalypse we heard about, he wasn't leading the armies of Hell against those of his estranged family.

But since Azazel exists, then Lucifer probably does, too.

Just the idea zaps through me with dread and—delight?

Yeah, right. After all I've been through in the past couple of days, my brain must be a jumble of misfiring neurons.

But what else don't we know about the angels? About the Supernatural World? What more have we been misled about?

Though I shouldn't say "we." From the reactions of the Angel-Graced, I'm certain they knew the Fallen existed before meeting Azazel. They just didn't expect to see one here, let alone for him to be their professor. But they were "groomed" as Azrael said, receiving intel that is kept from humanity at large.

It reinforces my belief that neither I nor Sarah are Graced. If we were, we would have been sought out long ago, and told truths reserved only for those with angelic potential.

Not that knowing could have made any difference. Knowledge is certainly not power when its imbalance is that unimaginable.

As if to demonstrate that imbalance, I can feel Azazel pinning everyone in their seats, as with a pleasant smile and conversational tone he says, "I will be teaching you two subjects—the academic Fallen History, and the applied Fallen Magic. Both are mandatory requirements for every Angel-Graced student. A passing grade is an A. A failing grade is punishable by dismemberment."

22

The silence suffocating the hall thickens until it congeals.

Minutes ago, everyone would have considered Azazel's dismemberment statement a tasteless joke. But after he gratuitously maimed many of us as an introduction, everyone must believe he means it.

I have no doubt he does.

The buzz of panic mushrooms all around like a high-voltage current. But though I feel he has lifted his compulsion, no one can move. Not even to save themselves or others from bleeding to death. No one will risk being singled out by this monster.

This is the reaction he meant to provoke. That was his purpose for that opening act of wanton violence.

This guy is a lunatic!

Or maybe this is just what it means to be Fallen.

He feels on par with the archangels in power, but while they felt somewhat detached from the world, this guy is very…present, very… fleshly, what I mistook for having human qualities.

But then again, he does. He radiates the cruel cunning of a sadist, and the insectoid energy of a serial killer.

And they made him our teacher!

Those archangels are more out of touch than I thought.

Even if this place were the best place on earth, this Azazel guy is enough reason to get Sarah out of here, at any cost.

Azazel suddenly cackles. "Kidding!"

Tension becomes stifling as I feel everyone's confusion rising. They don't know what to believe, must be hoping against all hope that he didn't mean the havoc he caused, or for it to go this far, that he isn't as monstrous as the bleeding evidence proves.

He shatters any wishful thinking when he grins. "You'll die in one piece."

As gasps tear around the auditorium, Azazel's smile widens. "My tests are designed with only two possible outcomes. Pass—live. Fail—die. You're training to become soldiers of Heaven, and in war there is no place for weak mediocrities and foolish failures. The archangels want only the best, even if they are inane cowards who can't announce their terms in such clarity. And no, not them, not anyone else has any say in my curriculum, nor have they approved my tests. I have full autonomy, according to my personal clause in the Armistice Accords. So don't think you can run to them complaining. My only concession to their idiotic qualifications is making everything fair. As if anything in this cosmos is 'fair.'"

He frowns, his angelic-blue eyes darkening, and with it the auditorium, and my mind.

The horrors I can suddenly see, the curdling blood and burning flesh I can taste, almost make me hurl once more.

I'm somehow seeing the contents of his mind, his memory. Being forced to exercise fairness in an unfair existence bothers him so much, he's bleeding horror and siphoning light and hope from his surroundings. Involuntarily, it feels. I can't imagine the brunt of his darkness if he cast it out on purpose, and in full force.

But the most disturbing thing is something else I feel. That not all the terrible appetites I'm sensing are issuing from him…

Sarah squeezes my hand tighter, bringing me back to the moment.

I find myself still staring at his eyes, now clearing to their vivid blueness, as if at another thought that pleases him.

Choking sounds echo all around as light floods the auditorium again.

Azazel grins. "In observance of said fairness, you'll be given the knowledge and tools you need to pass. And this ain't no lie, since we Fallen only tell the brutally ugly truth. If you fail, your gruesome death is on you."

With that final cruelty, Azazel turns from the podium, extending an arm to the man two steps behind him. The man who's actually a demon. I can always tell.

Failing *that* one's classes probably comes at a worse penalty than dismemberment. Maybe he'll sell us an organ at a time—while keeping us alive till the day he auctions our hearts.

This really keeps getting better and better.

Azazel leans in over the podium, as if speaking confidentially, and being louder than ever. "Now I turn you over to one of your many useless professors—the lackluster Astaroth. Look him up, too, and yes, he's *that* Astaroth. Though, a word of warning—the online information on him comes from your asinine human 'sources,' and they make him sound impressive and important. Since he's neither, he's going to be teaching you the supreme snooze fests of Preworld: Basics of the Pre-Apocalypse, and Afterworld: Introduction to the Post-Apocalypse. Also since he's a weakling, his classes don't come with death attached to failure. I expect many of you will flunk them, for lack of motivation. But inattentive, truant brats are the least he deserves. While *you* will get what you deserve in my classes."

Really? The demon offers a kinder fate? Where's the catch?

Azazel smacks Astaroth on the back, in that way obnoxious bullies belittle and have fun at weaker men's expense. The crack of his palm is an explosion that has us all jumping in our seats. If Astaroth were human, the front rows would be splattered in his body parts and fluids.

With that last put down, Azazel walks through Astaroth, slamming him in the shoulder and head. Just like that demoness did to me what feels like a week ago.

As soon as Azazel clears the podium, giving us his back for the first time, I see the red engulfing the bottom of his icy-white wings. At first glance, I think his wings are turning red, maybe as a consequence of being Fallen. Then I realize it's blood. And it's still dripping.

I feel my shudder echoing in Sarah, and throughout the auditorium.

The demon takes the podium, but no one pays him any attention. After being freed from Azazel's threat, the auditorium explodes in the panicked efforts he suppressed, to save themselves and others.

The demon clears his throat.

The sound isn't as loud and encompassing as Azazel's voice, but it still snaps everyone's attention to him, in anticipation of another nightmare.

"Cadets, please remain seated," Astaroth says, his voice the very sound of calm authority. "Those of you who are injured, or trying to help the injured, please refrain from further action."

So the angel cuts us up, and the demon stops us from helping ourselves? This is that unlikely duo's evil plan?

As panicked objections rise, Astaroth raises a hand. "I have alerted the Sanatorium, and a team of healers are on their way. Please don't compound your injuries by any ill-advised efforts."

Silence descends on the hall. This is also the last thing I expected a demon to say.

But true to his word, in under a minute, the locked doors are thrown open, and six angels and six nephilim enter the auditorium.

They descend on the scene, dealing with all injuries in mouth-dropping efficiency, no doubt aided by healing magic. They bundle those with severe injuries for transfer and take them away, leaving the others bandaged and obviously high on pain-relieving meds or incantations.

Meanwhile, another team who look human, probably Angel-Graced, has swept in to tackle Azazel's bloody disaster scene. In under ten minutes, everything is restored to its previous pristine condition.

Man, I would have loved those cleaning/clearing spells during my years in Demonica.

Once everyone is gone, the cadets whip out their phones again to research Astaroth.

For once, I'm not feeling left out without internet. I already know Astaroth. Of him.

Living in demon territory, you hear a lot about the higher ups in the hierarchy. And this demon isn't any higher up. He's supposedly the Great Duke of Hell, in the first hierarchy with Beelzebub and Lucifer, a part of *the* trinity of evil.

His appearance suggests none of these things. Contrary to the outdoorsy, Wild-West-outlaw look of Azazel, this guy appears cultured and suave, a perfectly put-together, outstanding late-thirties/early-forties. When not standing next to the massive Azazel, he's a very tall, *very* handsome man who fills his three-piece suit exceptionally well. With his slicked back thick black hair and monocle he resembles some aristocrat or inventor from the early nineteen hundreds.

When everyone raises their eyes from their screens, disturbed, but also confused after he helped us, Astaroth clears his throat again.

"Now that the—disruption has been dealt with, let me at last welcome you to Celestial Academy." Astaroth flicks a graceful gesture to encompass us, and a calm descends. Not over me, but clearly over the others. I didn't know demons could do that. "I hoped I'd be the first to address you, but my—colleague 'called dibs' on giving you your introductory speech. I hope it hasn't disheartened you—too much. I urge you not to dwell on it. In previous years those who didn't heed that advice, suffered greatly. Some with breakdowns that ended in suicide."

As that generalized gasp I'm getting used sweeps around the hall, he sighs in regret as he takes off his monocle. He wipes it for moments, before rearranging the crisp white handkerchief in his breast pocket with utmost care. It's as if he's pondering what to say next.

Once the monocle is wedged back into his eye socket, Astaroth sighs again. "I hope you'll prove Professor Azazel wrong, and excel in my classes without needing lethal incentives. Now, let me take your minds off all that unpleasantness, by applying them to practical matters you can control. I will start by outlining your coursework for your first semester."

For the next hour, I'm sorry to say, I prove Azazel right.

Without the threat of execution hanging over my head, my attention soon wanders away from Astaroth, before it blinks out completely.

23

I'm standing in the middle of a demolition site.

The official story of my life says I was found in a burning, collapsed apartment building after a gas line explosion. The man who found me estimated my age at two, but since I was talking the orphanage said I was at least four. They ended up settling on three. That's why I don't know how old I am.

But when I once tried to investigate my origins, I found online photos of the demolished building.

This destruction scene looks nothing like it.

This wreckage is on a far grander scale, of a totally different place. It has the vibe of ancient ruins. Every pulverized wall and shattered column seems imbued with time and fables.

But the rubble all around me is still flaming, the very ground burning, melting. And the hacked corpses strewn all over are fresh.

Then I realize I'm covered in still-warm blood. None of it my own. The stench of charred skin and scorched flesh choke me up to my very pores, fill me with an uncontrollable revulsion — and hunger.

Hunger like I've never known, like I never imagined exists.

Then I see Godric soaring through the towering inferno besieging me. His heavenly broadsword blazes a swathe that cleaves the billowing barrier of fire and smoke between us.

Crying out, I reach desperate hands up to him. A ring of another kind of fire, as if from the heart of a white-hot star, forms around him. It starts to *shrink, to darken, until it's like the slit-pupil of a serpent. And I hear its eagerness, feel its yearning, its endless loneliness—and bottomless greed. It wants to gobble him up whole.*

I cry out again, weeping with fright, and delight. His incredible wings, now sooty black among the flaming runes, snap wide with the force of solar storm, shattering the ring—and the rest of the world.

Then he dives towards me.

My mind fills with pleas.

Godric, yes, please. Come to me, my love.

As he swoops closer, I see his face, his savage beauty stamped with agitation and voracity.

In the last breath separating us, his eyes burst into emerald flames, before he plunges his sword into my heart.

"Wen, please!"

The world rocks urgently, and I wake up with a violent lurch.

My eyes don't open. They're already open. My vision was just turned—somewhere else. It now bursts back, filling with Sarah's anxious face. She's shaking me with all her strength.

"Oh, Angels Above, Wen, do you hear me?"

I try to nod. But *I'm* shaking. So hard, I couldn't feel hers until she put her back into it and snatched me from the depths of this—this dream?

"Wen!"

Her eyes fill with tears and I finally find my voice. "I hear you—I'm fine…"

"You're not fine! Your eyes were open, but you couldn't see me, then your face twisted in such pain. You're still trembling like a leaf!"

I force deep breaths to bring my quaking under control. But it's so hard to leave that dream behind when it's still trying to pull me back.

Shaking myself on purpose, I try to break its insidious influence, and stop the involuntary shudders. "I'm okay Sar…"

Her tears spill. "You're clutching at your heart, Wen. You could have been injured during Azazel's attack!"

My hands *are* clawed over my heart. The memory of Godric's sword plunging through my ribs and piercing it is still slicing through me. Hell, it felt so real.

There's no pain, though, and I'm scaring Sarah. She's had enough upheavals for one day.

I force my hands down. "I'm not injured, just had a disturbing dream."

"You always have pretty gruesome dreams and never react that way." She heaves to her feet, yanking me up with her. "Let's go to that Sanatorium, get you checked out!"

Rising unsteadily, I resist her pull. "Sar, I'm really okay. After everything that happened since I left home, followed by this Azazel dude scaring the crap out of us, and Astaroth putting me to sleep, I just zonked out."

"Are you being a pain as usual and bottling it all up so you won't upset me?"

I take her by the shoulders. "You can read me better than I read myself. What do you think?"

Suspicious eyes search my face before she exhales. "You're telling the truth. This time." She clutches my hand and drags me behind her. "Let's get out of here anyway. Azazel may have another punishment for those who leave the auditorium last!"

Looking around, I find Astaroth gone, and the cadets crowding each other on their way to the exits.

I trudge after Sarah as we join their shuffling progress, still feeling that sword embedded in my chest. My stomach churns at the phantom sensations, at the vividness of the dream.

But it felt more than a dream. More like a—premonition?

But I'm not the one who has premonitions. If I did, I wouldn't be here.

Another thing tells me it's not one. What I called Godric. *My love.*

Hah. As if I'd ever call him that in this lifetime, or the next, if any exists.

Also if—or is it when?—Godric kills me, it won't be in such a dramatic setting or fashion. The moment his dad and uncles tell him he can, he'll probably vaporize me with a final glare of disgust.

So, not a premonition. Therefore no need, or use, worrying about it.

Yet it feels branded in my mind in high-definition detail. It's still replaying like a video on a loop. One that involves all my senses.

Suddenly, nothing remains in my mind but seething fury.

The demoness, my so-called roommate, is standing at one of the exits, as if searching the departing crowd. Adding insult to the injury she inflicted on me, the moment she spots me, she waves enthusiastically. I snarl at her as my hand shoots to said injury.

I didn't check it since we fled that dorm room, just dragged my bangs over it before we reached Jophiel Hall. I didn't want anyone to stare at yet another brand by a demon.

Grimacing in advance at what I'll feel, I frown. It doesn't feel as bad as I imagined. So that healing side-effect of the Divining is still ongoing?

As I wonder if it may be permanent, and how incredible that would be, I'm compelled to look back. It's then I see Lorcan. And Godric.

They're in the deep shadows of the stage, seemingly having some serious discussion. Deadly serious, from Godric's stance.

I don't know what made me look that way, or how I can distinguish them from that far. Maybe it's the MGS of this place, or the Magical Guidance System as I'm calling it, nudging me toward my target.

Not that I care how it happened. No looking a gift archangelspawn in the wings.

I pull at Sarah's arm. "I'm going to talk to Lorcan, but I need to do it alone. Wait for me outside—please!"

Before she can protest, the exiting crowd sweeps her away. Thankful for their existence for the first time, I push against their current.

As I near the stage, I realize it's higher than I am, with no steps. Seems there was no thought of diversity when it was built, or catering to the limitations of mere bipeds like me.

Oh well. At least they installed stairs where it really matters. I'll just have a difficult, not to mention undignified climb…

Godric's voice fills my head. I stumble to a halt, dismayed that he saw me prematurely—and is yelling at me.

But—he isn't even looking my way. And his voice is actually a low, deadly purr.

Disoriented at feeling his voice inside my skull, entwining with my deepest dreads and urges, an abrasion and a caress, I resume walking unsteadily, working out theories.

Is it the acoustics? The others' voices did come from all around.

Nah. I'm only hearing him. There are stretches of silence when I assume Lorcan answers. Acoustics would carry both men's voices to me.

The other possibility is that his leash is working on auto, even without manifesting, letting me hear him remotely and…

My mind feels like it crashed into a wall. That of Godric's last words.

He just said, "No one can know what happened in the Divining. I would gladly kill, *anyone,* to keep this contained forever."

24

hat happened in the Divining?"

"W The two nephilim swing around at my gritted demand.

I'm disheveled and out of breath from my struggle to climb the stage. I'm furious, mainly at myself for throwing away my plan to ambush Lorcan alone, after Godawful left. But I couldn't stop myself. I need to know what happened in that Divining.

My only gratification is that I shocked them both. Especially Godric. He can't believe I creeped up on them. I don't, either. Even without engaging their super senses, they should have heard me stampeding closer.

Somehow, they didn't. And as their singular faces crease in frowns of dismay and displeasure respectively, I see them for what they really are. Beyond the facade of impossible beauty and magnificence.

Monsters. Capable of unimaginable cruelty and carnage.

Lorcan alluded to that fact before. I just heard Godric saying he would gladly kill. Anyone. I have no doubt he would—and has. And far, far worse. And is remorseless about it all.

I'm standing in the presence of demi-gods, a hybrid that's probably the most powerful, most ruthless of the Supernaturals, and I'm provoking the monster inside to lash out.

But in these suspended moments as we stare at each other—as *Godric and I* stare at each other—I feel no awe, no fear. None at all.

Instead, something as feral and ferocious, as harrowing and horrendous as the power staring back at me, expands inside me. It tears aside the human tissue barely wrapping it—and roars in challenge.

Mercury-laced obsidian lightning bursts from Godric's eyes in response. That thing inside me only shrieks in exhilaration, and burgeons to encompass us both in its inferno.

His power, jagged lines of pure, elemental destruction shatters its siege. Raging against his counteroffensive, that thing implodes around us, as if to crush him. His hands only cut the air in some magical ritual or celestial martial art.

The force within me erupts like a solar flare. But it's still no match for him. With one final swipe of his hands, the surreal sensations raging through me fizzle out.

Crashing back into my frail human body, I find I'm still squaring off with the two nephilim, like a beetle interrogating two great felines. It's like nothing happened.

Yes, moron, because nothing did.

Lorcan's unchanged expression says so. I blink up at Godric, looking for some kind of confirmation either way. He's glaring at me with even more intensity.

That doesn't mean he experienced what I just did. Of course, he didn't. He's just furious I committed the unprecedented offense of ambushing him. He must be on the verge of vaporizing me for that alone.

I must have fallen into that dream state again. This time filled with delusions of having a power that rivals Godric's. *While* wide awake.

This means I might start spacing out in public. As if I need another kind of brand to make me more of an outcast. Fantastic.

It might not be strange, though. This might be another side-effect of the Divining, like that accelerated healing.

But no. It's not that. Or not only that. Every time I'm around this guy, I feel weird, overriding things. Everything about him, from his voice to his vibe, acts like a mind-altering drug. It's like the effect of *Angelescence* on others. Though I haven't heard of an aphrodisiac side to the drug.

So he's even more potent where I'm concerned. His proximity might now be producing hallucinogenic effects.

Yet another reason to despise this spectacular bully.

It's also a reason to get this over with quickly. I can't afford to keep getting lost in Mind Warp Land while Sarah is still here. I'll figure this out *after* she leaves.

Sticking my fists at my sides as I stalk closer, I channel my scary once-headmistress, Mrs. Potts. "Well? What *did* happen? I have a right to know."

"You have no rights here, human." Godric straightens, making the world shrink. "You only have orders. And if I catch you eavesdropping again..."

I wave him off. "Yeah, yeah, dire consequences ensue. You gotta up your game, pal. Today Azazel made me a much better offer of fail-and-die, so I bumped him to the top of my priority list of Do Not Cross. You and your threats just tumbled down to the bottom."

Before Godric can retort, I turn on Lorcan. I'll have this showdown with him here and now before he flies off again, and Godric be damned. As I'm sure he already is.

I poke Lorcan in his ridiculously broad chest, and almost bend my finger out of shape. "How could you! Is that how much a promise is worth to a nephilim? Less than nothing?"

Lorcan raises placating hands. "It's not what you think."

My snort is impressive for a change. "You mean you didn't use privileged info about my best friend's identity, not to help her as you promised, but to drag her here into this Sinister Academy?"

"I did intend to carry out my promise." Lorcan grimaces at Godric, who's clearly hearing about this for the first time. "Then I sensed—something I had to report. My father himself decreed that she belongs at the Academy."

"She doesn't!" I cry out, stomping my foot. "You just sensed the residue of *Angelescence* in her system!"

Lorcan's gaze tinges with pity. "I know what that residue feels like, from those we examined while we tracked you. That's not what I sensed."

"But you all said only the Divining can determine if a human is angel-graced! Now *you* can suddenly tell?"

"I didn't say she's angel-graced, but my father agreed that what I sensed about her is cause for induction into the Academy."

I don't pulverize my fist against his perfect teeth, only because I'm uncertain if that healing factor would heal them. "So what did you sense?"

He shrugs uneasily. "It's inconclusive."

"That's the favorite diagnosis around here, isn't it?" I scoff. "Well, I think you're lying. You took her to hold her safety over my head!"

"Why should we do that?" Godric interjects, back to being an arctic son of an archangel. "We don't need any more power over you."

"Yes, you do. By now you know threats to my own life don't give you total control over me." I jab another intact finger into Lorcan's chest. "*You* knew her life means far more to me than my own!"

Lorcan looks almost pained at my accusations, but it's Godric who answers again, "Your overestimation of yourself is indeed prodigious. We already have total control over you." Before I can blast him, his lips quirk in one of those chilling semi-smiles that can liquefy lady bits at a hundred paces. "Now we have that over your best friend."

He holds my gaze, and I again tumble into that battlefield raging between us, deeper and vaster than existence. When I'm fully awake and aware this time.

Then those images flare again, of him plunging his sword into my heart.

I flinch. But he does, too. He did first.

Lorcan doesn't seem to notice anything. This was totally between us.

Or I imagined it all again. Exposure to Godric might be scrambling my mind irrevocably.

Yet—that uncertain flicker in his eyes makes me think he experienced something. And he, too, has no idea what it was. So the scrambling is involuntary on his side?

Great. I might be getting Godric Poisoning, and I can't even hate him—even more—for it.

Next second, I doubt my senses all over again. Whatever confusion I sensed in him is gone as his drawl abrades every single one. "If you're petitioning for your friend's release, don't hold your breath. And if you care about her that much, you'll behave."

"Or what? You're not allowed to 'harm' us. Or was that another lie?"

He shrugs one power-laden shoulder lazily. "No harm will come to you or your friend, not on account of your insolence or pathetic attempts at insubordination. But there are other ways life here can be very difficult for both of you, if you persist in instigating conflict."

"*If you persist in instigating conflict.*" I mimic a nasal parody of his elegant delivery. "Why don't you do us all a favor, and return to the eighteen hundreds, pal? They've been asking for their source of pompous assery back."

But even as I lambast him, my shoulders slump. My fury and bravado are expended. I lost. Worse, I fought this battle in the worst possible way.

Not that any other way could have gotten me a different result.

For some undisclosed reason, they dragged Sarah here. And, like me, she's going nowhere until they decide to let her go. If they ever do.

Dismissing that bully who roasts my mind with the blaze of his very existence, I turn to Lorcan, trying one last time. "Please, Lorcan, she doesn't belong here. She deserves to be free."

Lorcan's gaze becomes apologetic, only intensifying my despair. "You think I betrayed your trust, but think about it, Wen. Getting her out of the Demon Zones wouldn't have assured her freedom or safety. As a lone, inexperienced girl in the world outside, she would have been exposed to more dangers. I would have provided for her financially, but I wouldn't have been able to guard her 24/7. I did consider not reporting what I sensed about her, and fulfilling your wishes. But I do believe she's better off here."

"If she survives, that is," I mumble over the lump of shards filling my throat.

Lorcan sighs. "Mortal danger would have been ever-present in any life she could have had on her own. At least now she's with you. And that's all she wants."

I stare at him, my anger and urgencies collapsing like scaffolding struck at the foundations.

Lorcan's words, and the heart-wrenching truth behind them, cleave into me, tear a sob from my depths. And I burst out crying.

Tears, sudden and copious, stream down my face as my lips tremble out of control, and my breath scrapes like claws in my chest.

Feeling Godric's gaze intensifying over me, I whip my head up, finding his eyes almost obscured by his deepest frown yet.

"What are you looking at?" I hiccup among shearing sobs, flinging my hand at Lorcan sympathetic expression. "Why don't you look at *that*, Godawful? *That's* a nice guy!"

Godric's jaw muscles bunch, but he doesn't lob something back at me. Almost as if he's lost for words.

Ha. As if.

When he does answer, as always, he makes it a lethal blow. "Let's hope it doesn't get him killed—too soon."

His gaze sweeps to Lorcan as he turns away, and a lot passes between them. Things I can't hope to fathom.

As he walks to the stage, he tosses over his shoulder. "Get on with the rest of your day, White. And try not to make your roommates incinerate you. I need you alive and in the Lycurgus Arena at five a.m."

"*Five* a.m.!" I croak a shout at his unfeeling back as he floats to the auditorium floor.

"Sharp."

His voice echoes back to me as he passes Sarah who came back inside, not even looking at her before exiting the auditorium.

Lorcan takes my arm when I remain gaping after Godric, frustration fizzing in my blood.

As he leads me back to Sarah, I wipe at my tears and look up at him. "Is it only me, or does he make everyone want to kill him?"

Lorcan huffs a chuckle. "Sort of an acquired taste, is our Godric. Or an atrocious medicine you must endure."

"Endure to what end? Anyone recovers from exposure to him?"

"No one recovers from Godric. But everyone comes out of the ordeal—transformed."

Curiosity reviving, I probe, "Speaking from personal experience?"

He only grins. "From what I gather, he intends to transform *you*."

"Transform me into what? A compliant prisoner? Save us both time and aggravation and tell him that's never happening."

Lorcan's grin widens. "Why do you think he wants you at the Lycurgus Arena before the crack of dawn?"

"To torture me, of course."

He sighs. "That's what he does. But if you have what it takes, he'll hone you into a lethal weapon."

"Yeah, right." I scoff before realizing Lorcan is no longer grinning. "Okay, quit fooling around. After the stunt you pulled with Sarah, you owe me. If you know what he wants to do with me, you tell me right now."

"I already told you."

"But you can't be serious!"

"He is. Deadly so."

"But...how can he hone me into a lethal weapon? Weapon how? And lethal to who?"

"To anyone."

Sure now that he is joking, just with a straight face, I go along with it. "Even to you archangelspawn?"

He nods. "Knowing his overachieving arse, maybe even to him."

I start to scoff again, before Lorcan's expression makes me swallow it. He *is* serious!

My eyebrows almost shoot off my face. "Why would he even want to do that?"

Lorcan's gaze grows conspiratorial. "Why care about his reasons? If he can turn you into a weapon capable of killing even him, maybe you'll get the chance to act on your burning desire after all. All you have to do is survive him."

That's *all* I have to do?

Easy peasy.

25

I survived. My first day at Celestial Academy, that is. *And* somehow, my first night with Ms. Brimstone and Ms. Archangelspawn.

Now all I have to do is survive Mr. Death Jr. himself.

That's what Lorcan said I have to do. And he wasn't even joking.

I was premature calling him a nice guy.

Those Nephilim, being presumably immortal like their dads, have a seriously warped perspective of life and death. Especially when it comes to their significance to us mortals.

Even *that* nephilim, with his rare compassion-like sensibility that made him take pity on Sarah and me, didn't see anything wrong in what he said. In his world of eternal conflicts between immortals, human lives being snuffed in the crossfire is a matter of fact. Nothing to worry about too much. Or at all.

Humans frail, humans die.

They're probably concerned about our continuation as a species only for their sacred balance, or whatever. Individual lives are not even on their radar.

Based on that rationale, Lorcan probably meant "All you have to do is survive him" as a pep talk. Something along the lines of "You can do it, girl!"

So he knows Godric won't kill me on purpose, as ordered by their family. But he thinks it a possibility I might not survive his "honing" anyway. Maybe Godric would then go to them and say *oops*.

Contrarily, that's why I didn't hide in bed until Godric dragged me out by the toe—or neck. If there's even a possibility he can hone me into a weapon capable of killing even him, I'm there for it. The idea made me crawl from the toasty cocoon of my magical dorm bed, to suffer temperatures unknown this side of Pluto. And *that's* less of an exaggeration than the possibility of me becoming such a weapon. Or a weapon at all.

But if Godric intends to somehow "transform" me, so I can maybe one day knock him on his legendary ass, *that's* something I'd wake up this early for any day. Every day.

Not that I'm really awake now. My body is barely erect, and I feel as if I'm wading in some alternate reality. What Celestial Academy certainly is.

It's more so among the serpentine trails of the spooky Oriphiel Woods, what the map insisted is a shortcut. I'd hate to see what it considers the long way around.

When I first consulted it for the best path to the Lycurgus Arena, it kept freezing, like those internet searches when the signal drops. Then it sent me down the wrong path twice before recalibrating, like a malfunctioning GPS. That made me wonder if angelic magic is on the glitch, especially after what happened to me in the dorm building yesterday afternoon.

I left Sarah in a class safe among a crowd, and rushed back there for that reconnaissance tour. But no matter what path I took, I got diverted to the corridor leading to our dorm room.

I thought the map was stuck, until I realized the building itself was casting illusions. It made me think I was going someplace new, when all the time I was circling back to that damned corridor. But I couldn't linger to figure out how or why, had to rush back to Sarah.

Then this thing with the map happened, and I started wondering if it's me this place isn't responding to anymore? Or if it keeps herding me back where it thinks I should be? Or if it's a generalized problem with magic?

Whatever it is, here I am, trudging through these woods, sneakered feet shuffling on that semi-paved path that echoes with sentience. Dawn is a distant glimmer in another time zone, and only that faint, sourceless light illuminates my way. But it's so cold and humid, my breath is thick enough to almost blind me. And I'm only wearing those flimsy gym clothes Godawful specified. I'm so frozen and stiff I swear I hear my bones whine, and my joints creak.

All my external and internal noises are probably why I didn't hear them at first. But now they suddenly blare in my head. The crunching sounds behind me.

Someone is following me!

The certainty swamps me, booming in my heart and head.

Being followed anywhere always meant trouble. But here? It could spell disaster.

What was Godawful thinking making me walk alone at this hour across this principality-sized supernatural territory? Which randomly turns into a ghost town even during the day?

But maybe it's him behind me? I thought he'd be at the Lycurgus Arena, hoping I'd be a minute late so he'd drag me inside by the neck. But maybe he's running late? If he is, he's what? Trying to spook me? Or is he hanging back because he won't suffer my company unless absolutely necessary?

Who am I kidding? That's not Godric. I'd know this guy's vibes in my sleep now. I would never mistake his presence.

And then that presence closing in on me feels—malevolent. Yeah, shocking, but this isn't how Godric feels to me. His aura is intimidating, savage, but also intoxicating, spine-tingling. And I'm not even talking about its overwhelming sensual component.

But whoever it is behind me, they could have been following me long before I felt it. So if they haven't caught up with me, maybe they don't mean to? Maybe this is someone walking through the woods unrelated to me?

No. I'm being followed, no doubt about it. My sense of danger is too honed to question it now. The only time it failed me was with Godric. That guy scrambled my senses even then. I'm positive I will never be exposed to anything like him ever again.

A simple—and great—explanation is that it's some guard I attracted trudging about like a zombie at this infernal hour. The malevolence I felt could be my jumpy imagination.

But since great things don't happen to me, this someone is trailing me with ill intent.

It could be the demoness. She could have felt me sneaking out, and this errand could be providing her with the perfect opportunity to torture me some more, or even kill me with no witnesses around. It could also be that other roommate who came in after I went to sleep.

She shook me awake to demand why I was always with Godric. That seemed like a cardinal sin in her book. Hell, it could even be Ms. Archangelspawn, deciding to put me in my place after I mouthed off to her.

But the crunching noise is much closer now, drenching me in fiercer waves of dread, and telling me more about my pursuer.

It's not the vile demoness. Or the pissy roommate. Or even the self-important, substantial archangelspawn. It's someone much bigger, heavier. So is it Godric after all?

No. I'm certain it's not him. So who else could know I'd be here at this time? Someone he sent after me? Why? A test? Or something worse?

What if he decided to cut off my tutorship short before it begins? But since the archangels already know he wants to get rid of me, he's sending someone else to do it, while having an alibi himself?

But if so, why tell Lorcan he intends to transform me and hone me and all that crap? More misdirection?

No. That doesn't sound like him. Godric is many horrible things, but he wouldn't let anyone do his dirty work for him. Especially when it comes to me. I just know that whatever fate awaits me, he wants to be the one to dole it out.

This leaves the last possibility. Since I've eliminated everyone who would target me specifically, this has to be random. I'm in the wrong place at the wrong time. Thanks to Godawful.

Unable to resist any longer, I look over my shoulder. There's nothing in the winding path behind me. My pursuer is stalking me from the comfort of the dense tree cover. It's a classic stalker location, after all. Again, thanks to Angelhole.

I'm striding now, as fast as I can without running, but the heavy footfalls crunching dead foliage wholesale are gaining on me. As they come closer, another certainty pummels me.

It's not someone, but some*thing*.

As my heart attempts to beat its way out of my throat, I try to calm myself with one last hope. That it's some creature that patrols the domain, coming to herd me back where I should be.

That hope fractures with my next heartbeat. The putrid evil emanating from that thing is all but suffocating me now. And from the increasing speed of its shuffling, it has decided to attack.

I never run from danger. The one time I ran, I landed in this mess.

I'm a lousy runner, anyway. Cool-headed retreats, no matter how terrified I am, have kept me alive so far.

But there's no retreat here. The dorm is two miles behind, and I can't turn around anyway. There's no escape either, as the Arena is two more miles ahead, at least. I'd lose steam long before I reached it.

Still, if I ran, I'd have the advantage of initial speed. That should keep a distance between us until I do. That thing sounds so heavy, it can't possibly run...

A thud shakes the ground beneath me, then another and another.

It's running.

I explode in a run, blindly, desperately. Terror, and the hefty packaged dinner they distributed last night lending my feet speed.

But I'm no match for the stampeding creature. It's closing in on me, too fast. And I already feel my lungs tearing apart with the frigid air. My nerves feel like searing cables shooting up legs. Legs that are starting to cramp up, and would buckle soon, too soon. There's no way I can outrun it.

Suddenly, I'm no longer terrified. I'm *incensed*.

I envisioned my death a million times. In a gladiator arena, between the claws of a hellhound, with thousands paying a premium to see me struggle to my last breath. In an arcane ritual, carved up by enchanted daggers, my organs a conduit for high mages' unbreakable curses. And since I came here, I added elaborate scenarios to my morbid fantasies, of dying slowly, creatively at the hands of that beautiful monster.

But this, dying as an unintentional prey to some mindless beast out looking for dinner? This is too pointless a way to die.

How could you have expected a grand end to your insignificant life, moron? A snide voice sniggers inside me.

No, dammit. I'm *not* insignificant. Godric, that demigod with unlimited powers, said I may be the most dangerous thing to have ever existed. I'm so significant to him and the archangels, he's been forced to become my personal tutor, for Hell's sake.

Yet my significance is only a potential, and he did turn around and told me I'm Nothing. And if I die here, I will have lived and died as a Nothing. I will have done nothing, too, if I leave Sarah alone in this immortal monster land. That's what's most driving me out of my mind with fury.

But if this is it, there's only one thing left to do. What I always do.

I refuse to cower. In life, or in death.

Bringing my limping run to an end, I stagger around to face my hunter.

I won't die like some harebrained, forgettable victim from a B-rated horror movie. Not when I felt something within me capable of taking on even Godric.

Even if that was a hallucination, I *do* have the unique ability to capture and transform Angel Essence. I don't know how this ability makes me dangerous, but maybe I can do more with it. Far more. I can't become a meal for some beast and let it go to waste. I *won't*.

My heartbeats are detonations and my skin is magma as I plant shaking feet to that almost-sentient earth beneath me, and fist my burning hands. I feel the air shimmer around me with the heat of my anger and aggression.

The thudding footfalls come nearer, nearer. But I still can't tell where they're coming from. That damn place with its illusions and misdirection.

"Bring it, bitch!" I scream. "I'm going to rip out your essence and shove it up your ass!"

Next moment, everything goes silent.

For endless moments, the only movement in that ominous forest are my violent shudders, the only sounds my wheezing breaths.

Where did my hunter go? Could I have scared it off? If I did, I should have heard its retreat. So could it be hiding, waiting for me to give it my back again? It can't be afraid to face me, can it?

What the hell is going on here?

When nothing moves or makes a sound again, I'm forced to conclude whatever was after me somehow transported away.

That still doesn't make sense. If it can do that, why all the stalking? Why not materialize on top of me, take me to the ground and gouge my neck? It wanted the hunt? If it did, why did it leave? It understood my threat, and believed it? And it's gone to look for an easier meal? Or is the answer something more complicated and malicious?

Knowing my luck, it sure is. Maybe I have another enemy out there already, and it's not only Godric and my roommates that I have to survive.

Welcome to Sinister Academy, Wen.

26

With a combination of agitation, exhaustion, and sleep deprivation, I finally drag myself inside Lycurgus Arena.

Lycurgus, as I found out yesterday, is an angel who taught humanity competitive sports, and is responsible for the creation of the Olympic Games. He was elevated to archangel status for his dedication to pushing the boundaries of human physical prowess, and the peaceful tournaments that supplied humanity with the best of internationalism.

Not that I give a fig about him or any of that. I sure didn't research that info. The article appeared on the Magitech tablet issued by the Academy to every cadet. It kept beeping loudly until I finished reading it, and taking a quiz. *And* answering all questions right. Courtesy of Godawful, of course. He's going in hot in his role as my personal tutor.

The Arena is *much* larger than the stadiums where lucky Regulars attend the frivolous sports that droned nonstop on some of Demonica's TV screens. In the underbelly of the demon world, I only witnessed blood sports, where I expected to end my life.

While this makes my current situation seem like an upgrade, as Sarah said, I'll probably have a worse ending here eventually. I just got another sample of the dangers I'll be facing.

Just what was missing from the crap vortex that is my life. A mystery.

Focusing back on this Arena, I realize it's enclosed, but the ceiling is so high it fools you about the fact. Another facility made for beings with wings.

Unbidden, the image of Godric soaring with those unique shades-of-grey, rune-encrypted wings flares in my mind. I have to shake my head like a wet dog to dislodge it.

That image is only replaced by an even worse one. The actual Godric, standing in the middle of the space, somehow undiminished by its vastness. Wingless now, he's in black trainers and a matching sweatshirt.

He looks world-tilting.

But it doesn't matter how supremely edible he physically is. I hate his guts with a numbing intensity.

Thankfully, as I approach him, any numbness doesn't reach my tongue. "Thanks so much for waking me up at a time as atrocious as you are, Godawful."

He raises a superb arch of haughtiness, a corner of his lethal lips lifting, as if against his will. "Anything for you, Nothing." A beat, then he drawls, "You're late."

"Thank your lucky feathers I'm here at all."

"I did wonder if you'd defy me. I'm almost surprised you didn't."

All the way as I trudged here, I debated telling him about my close encounter of the unknown kind. I decided against it. I don't know if it was something after me in specific, if it decided to make a meal of me —or if I hallucinated the whole incident. From the way it disappeared, and the other hyper-real experiences I had, there's a big chance I did.

Whatever, I'm not giving him more ammo in this duel of ours.

"I was about to come drag you from bed by that copious hair of yours."

To my chagrin, I find myself grinning like a lunatic at the image of him as a caveman. "I thought you would—by my toe. Or neck."

"Both would have been counterproductive to my purposes. I need your appendages and breathing intact from now on."

"Yeah? What are these purposes? And what does it mean, you being my personal tutor? What are you going to tutor me in? And why?"

"What did I say about questions?"

"You're getting nothing but from me, chum. I got nothing else on my mind. So why don't you save yourself the hassle of dealing with a spaced out cadet, and answer them?"

His gaze lengthens, and heats. At first it's nice, thawing me, then I feel I may start melting like a snow cone on a stove.

Before I buckle, he finally exhales. "One question."

Is that a concession? Godric actually knows how to do that?

"Three questions," I shoot back before he reconsiders this momentous precedent. "I have more than three thousand, so I'm being too considerate of your severe allergy to being questioned." He starts to say something, and I drown his voice. "Don't say two!"

"Two. Final offer. Take it or leave it."

Gotcha.

I look down as I doodle a half-circle with my sneakered toe. Can't have him see triumph in my eyes. He'd cancel the deal, and leash-slam me to the ground. "Any two?"

"Don't ask about the Divining," he grits.

Son of an archangel. That's my most important question.

Still, I can work with this, if... "I can ask anything else?"

"Yes."

"And you will answer? Cause you can be playing with words, allowing me to ask, but not committing to answer."

"I will answer."

Whoa. This is huge. Major. Gargantuan.

Now I gotta be very, very careful what I ask. This is a once-in-my-mortal-lifetime opportunity.

"Why do you hate me so much?"

My heart splotches in my empty stomach like a rock dropped in slime.

Who said that? It can't be the Wen White I had the misfortune of being all my life!

But I did say it. I wasted an unrepeatable chance to find out the things that matter.

Retract it, idiot. Now!

"Wait, wait—don't answer that! I'll ask another one!"

The vicious, pseudo-smile he gives me makes me shiver all over as he shakes his head, triumph in *his* incredible eyes. "Too late. I pledged an answer, and you'll get one. To *this* question."

My shoulders slump in frustration, with myself mainly.

But maybe all isn't lost yet. Maybe I'll glean some info when he explains why he hates me.

"I don't hate you."

What?

"Oh, no!" I blurt. "I will not accept this answer. You *do* hate me, and it has nothing to do with me peddling *Angelescence.* There's something else. And you said—*pledged*—you'd say why."

He's the very image of long-suffering as he exhales. "I wanted you here at five am so we'd have a solid two hours before you have to go prepare for your first day of real attendance at the Academy. You came fifteen minutes late, and I'm giving you fifteen more to answer your two questions. Will I get the chance to answer, or will you waste your allotted time blabbering?"

Clamping my lips, cheeks flaming, I gesture for him to go ahead.

He gives a mock-grateful nod. "As I said, I don't hate you. Hate implies emotional involvement."

"Heh, yeah. And everyone knows you're an emotionless bastard, Godawful. My bad." I shake my head, still not convinced, and to dispel the heaviness settling in my chest. "But you do feel something very fierce and specific to me."

His gaze all but shreds me to ribbons. "I do. You're a conundrum I have to fathom, a misshapen piece of clay I have to mold, and I resent that only I can achieve these onerous tasks. I'm now forced to devote my focus and time and expertise to you, when you…" He stops, as if looking for the right word, and finding none. "You *aggravate* me. You…" He stops again, before gritting, "You vex and provoke and exasperate and frustrate me."

"Whoa, easy on the synonyms, pal! I get it."

"I doubt that you do. I myself don't get it. You—*stymie* me. When no other being ever has."

When he stops this time, I know he's said his piece. He cocks his magnificent head at me, waiting for a response, something brazen and crass, I'm sure. I shake my own head.

I can't talk. My jaw is on the floor and I may never be able to pick it up again. My heart is battering my ribs with—exhilaration.

I'm as unprecedented to him as he's unprecedented to me!

It's a way bigger deal because he's older—no idea by how much—and, well, he's "Him." Godric the Great must have dealt with everything this universe, and any other, has to offer. But no friend or foe, even the eternal kind, ever yanked those responses from him. They're all negative, sure, but explosive—and they're mine.

All mine.

I have power over him that no one ever had.

Take that, *you Semi-Celestial Bastard!*

He raises one eyebrow. "Is that a comprehensive enough answer for you?"

That makes me find my voice. "No, it's not. There's more. I know there is."

And it has, in part, something to do with the Divining.

If he says more, I might get a clue about what happened there. What he'd kill to keep secret, forever. And forever isn't a figure of speech to his kind. Which means it was something that important. That dangerous.

I shudder to think what *he* considers dangerous.

His words, what feels like a lifetime ago, echo in my head all over again.

This makes you potentially one of the most dangerous entities who ever existed.

"Yes, there is more. You're..." He stops, eyes raking my face, a searing emotion setting them on passionate fire. It's even more hard-hitting than when he pretended I was his. Then he grinds out the rest, "...an abomination."

Whoa. *Whoa.*

That sure came right out of left field. And it...hurts.

Why anything he says would is beyond me. But it does.

So. He has power over me in *this* way, too.

He now has a perfect score in all kinds of power over me.

Will I ever run out of reasons to hate that half-heavenly lout?

But there is something to be learned here. If he's willing to elaborate.

I have to get it out of him without making it a question, or I'm certain he'll consider it my second one.

I smirk up at him, struggling to feign nonchalance. "First I'm a Nothing, now I'm an Abomination. All this because I can see and collect Angel Essence."

"I at first thought this ability terrible enough on its own. Now I suspect it's a symptom of an even worse underlying disease."

"Disease!" I dread illness way more than death. Forgetting my resolve, my exclamation comes out a question. "I'm sick?"

"I don't *know*." His wings tear out behind him, causing a mini gale that almost blows me off my feet.

As I catch myself, eyes watering, I seethe that I *still* didn't see his wings sprouting from his back. And how they don't tear his clothes.

Yeah, I'm known for such conveniently-timed musings.

Another one is about Azazel's destructive demonstration. Since I feel Godric is more powerful, he could have destroyed half of L.A. when he crash landed that night, and blown my flesh off my bones. Which means he held back.

He held back just now. When he is agitated this time. Maybe I'm messing with his mind like he's messing with mine. And if I ever make him lose control—I doubt Earth is ready for an out-of-control Godric.

Suddenly having power over him isn't that exciting anymore.

He folds his wings, then in a flash, they're gone.

I blink up at him in chagrin as his gaze sweeps over me from head to toe broodingly before he exhales. "That's why you're my shadow until I find out. It's imperative that I discover how you do what you do. Right now, you do it instinctively, have no method, no under-standing of what you do, or how to control or expand it."

The last two words clang in my head. He said them in the same tone, but they rang differently somehow.

This might be the point of this whole thing.

"That's what you're going to train me to do," I say, careful to make it a statement, not a question. "To control and expand my Angel Essence collection feature."

"Yes."

I know he's done answering my first question. Along with all the non-questions I managed to slip in.

If I want to know more, I have to use my second question.

He raises one masterpiece eyebrow and looks pointedly down at his wrist.

I drool a little at the abundance of muscle and sinew in the forearm exposed by a pushed up sleeve, before I notice he's wearing a watch. It resembles the activity trackers used by those who exercise for fun and want to lose weight voluntarily. Would a nephilim's measure flight miles instead of steps? Those before he has to retract his wings?

What the hell am I thinking? My "allotted time" is running out.

He says as much, that voice of his a sweep of inflammation. "Ask your second question right this second, White, or forfeit it."

Oh, who am I kidding. There's only one question I *have* to ask.

"Why? Why do you want me to do what I do on a larger scale?"

His eyes flare emerald. And I know. I asked the right question. What he wished I wouldn't ask.

I also know he'll answer it. Because *I* just found the answer to something as important. His one weakness.

It's his own commitment, his own word.

He finally exhales. "Because if I can understand how you gather and transform Angel Essence, and make you do it on a 'larger scale,' it might be the weapon to end the eternal battle."

27

I try to swallow, but my mouth is as dry as L.A.'s demon-tainted dirt.

Thankfully, desiccated or not, it still functions on auto, and I croak, "*The* Eternal Battle?"

Both his eyebrows rise. "There's *another* one and no one told me?"

I thought his humor deals only in viciousness and violence. But that was an actual—quip? Or is my brain so fried I can no longer understand sarcasm?

Sarcasm? I can't understand a damn thing anymore!

I raise both hands. "Rewind and replay, please. Assume I know nothing. Yeah, yeah, to go with your lovely name for me. Along with Burden, Abomination, Conundrum, and Misshapen Piece of Clay." His eyebrows descend, and I rush to my point. "You can't think I can possibly become a weapon in that battle, let alone the one with the ability to end it!"

For an answer, he only turns and strides away to a sleek assortment of exercise equipment and padded surfaces, each as big as our apartment...

Our apartment!

I rush after him, head feeling waterlogged. "I never got the chance to ask—what will happen to our apartment? Our lease and stuff? And the money we stash there? What about our demons? What if they issue a warrant for our arrest? Can you angelic bigshots deal with that?" My hand shoots to my Mark in belated dread. "Lorcan told Sarah the Marks didn't activate because of your angelic magic. But he didn't sound all that reassuring when he said you'll deal with them. Deal with them how? What if they activate again before you do? Will you let us go back within our allowed range? Or, since I don't know where this Academy is, are we still in it? Or are we in another realm or...?"

"No. More. Questions." He tosses me exercise gloves. "Put these on, White—or should I say, Weiss? Any reason you kept that name?"

I catch the gloves before they hit me in the face, and glower at him. So he found out more about me. Probably everything. Now he wants the context of personal explanations so he can—what? Have more insights into my character? So he can better use me for his "purposes"?

Good luck with that. He only gave me incomplete answers that only spawned a hundred more questions. And he already has the upper-hand in every way. I'm not handing him any more advantages.

If he wants more answers, he can investigate his gorgeous butt off for them. And when he only comes up with assumptions, he can live in uncertainty like the rest of us. Like me.

I give him my best taunting smile. "No. More. Questions. Yourself."

Feeling mighty pleased with the crackle of lightning that escapes his control, I turn my attention to the gloves.

It's harder than I thought it would be. I keep pushing two fingers in one slot, then the wrong finger in the wrong slot. He watches me struggle with them, and the gym darkens.

"Hey, that doesn't help!"

"I expected you to be a difficult student, but I thought I had to start training you before you tested my patience."

"So I never put on gloves—sue me."

"If I didn't have use for you, I'd far more than sue you."

I tsk. "Don't just stand there imagining all the torture you have in store for me, and writhe in impotence. Do something useful for once in your life, and come help." I snort a laugh. "Oh, you can't, can you? By now I know you can't break your word. Maybe you'd go up in hellfire or something. Too bad you swore never to touch me, huh?"

"I didn't swear."

My eyes shoot up, and so does my heart. "What...?" He stares back at me as what he said sinks in. It comes back up in a coughed scoff. "You did, too!"

Eyes filling with malicious enjoyment, like that time he suffocated me, he shakes his head. "I said I'd never touch a human, especially you. That's a preference, not a pledge."

"Are you saying you—can touch me if you want?"

The look in his eyes almost gives me a heart attack.

Then he makes it far worse when he murmurs, deep and devastating, "If I want."

It's then I make a terrible discovery. That I felt secure, thinking I had his pledge. Not from physical harm, since he doesn't need to touch me for that. Secure in having that last dignity. Of not being in danger of melting at my enemy's touch.

Now I know I don't have his pledge, I can rely on his—what? Will? Whim? Revulsion for humans, especially me? The one who aggravates and stymies him? What if that makes him decide to touch me instead, to tame me, to break me? So I'd be easier to use?

I'm suffocating without the aid of his leash before he adds, "But I won't."

I shove my hands into the gloves to hide their tremors. The random move slots them right.

His lips twitch. "I see that incentivized you to finish your task. Now…"

He beckons, once. A tranquil flex of these fingers of power and perfection. I bet it would make any female dash to hurl herself at his feet. It only makes me want to "defy" him. But though he hasn't leashed me since yesterday in public, he will in private, if I waste more time.

Not wanting to be garroted this early in the morning, I approach him.

He instructs me to sit on some exercise machine that must be made by aliens. Which the Nephilim are to me. It also looks made for Nephilim-level muscles.

I toss him a sullen glance as I sit down. "What do you expect me to do here?"

He goes still, returning my glare. "I'm beginning to suspect you can't utter anything *not* in the form of a question." Before I can retort he holds up a hand. "I'm testing your fitness level."

"What for?"

Ugh. Seems I *can't* say anything not in question form.

Wonder of wonders, he chooses to answer this one. "The extent of powers any being possesses is linked to many factors. Genetics, mental discipline, correct application and consistent practice. But physical resilience and stamina, which depend largely on nutrition and exercise, remain vital to unlocking and sustaining the expression of such powers."

I look him up and down. "Is that why you're in such disgusting shape?"

"My body *is* a weapon."

Tell me about it. One of mass destruction, especially of ovaries.

His lips quirk, all but gloating at my obvious, and fully expected, appreciation of his assets. "Keeping it locked and loaded, as you American humans say, is a duty, and a privilege."

I exhale, flapping my lips like a horse in annoyance. "What a good little soldier you are."

"It's my birthright, and my destiny."

That sounded—solemn. Wow. A solemn Godric is yet another level of yum.

But he let the "little" dig go. Of course. A secure male would see such taunts for what they are, standard bitchiness to get a rise from him. And this guy has to be the most secure male to ever exist.

"Now, enough. Pump those bars."

I try. I really do. And I raise the handles above my head. My arms shake like a tightrope beneath a bouncing acrobat, before they give out, and the bars crash down.

But at least I raised them!

Godric dispels any pride before it fully twinges in my chest. "It's even worse than I thought. I put no weights, so those bars are not even set on minimum. Your muscular development seems to be in the minus."

I scowl at him as I point a shaking finger to myself. "Human, Demon-Owned, semi-starved for life. What else did you expect?"

He shrugs one prodigious shoulder, the superhuman image of sleek muscular development himself. "The worst, obviously. But that's also good news, since I can work with this. I'm stipulating that such a poor physical condition is limiting your access to your power."

"So we're calling it a power now?"

He exhales forcibly at yet another question, fluttering his lips like I did a minute ago—and looking fan-nephilim-tastic doing it. When it's ridiculous on me and anyone else. "Now to test your lower body strength. Set the machine to the first slot and push the footplate."

It takes me moments to understand his order, then many more trying to figure out how to implement it.

His impatience bombards me until I raise frustrated eyes. "Keep your shirt on, Featherboy…"

The rest vaporizes in a blast of heat.

He's taking his sweatshirt off!

28

"W-what the...?"

Nothing else comes out of my mouth as it slackens, hangs open, gathering drool.

My brain feels tasered, convulsing uselessly inside my skull. Time itself seems to spasm and decelerate. Either this or Godric is taking off that sweatshirt in slow motion.

Gazing straight into my very essence, he raises the dark material, exposing his body inch by maddening inch. By the time it clears four of his endless packs, I'm almost moaning in suspense.

C'mon, you sadistic tease, show it all to me already.

As if he heard my mental shout, his movements slow down more. Or maybe it's my mind. Or time. Who knows what his powers are, or what he's capable of.

One power for sure is turning taking off a nondescript sweatshirt into an act of torture.

To thwart him, I close my eyes.

When I open them again, he's moving at a normal speed, as if time has resumed its pace. He whips the sweatshirt over his head, and makes me sorry for mentally yelling at him.

Fully-dressed, and in his celestial-assassin/death-incarnate obscuring clothes, I thought the universe insane to have created him. Half-dressed, I think it has an annihilation agenda—for mortal and immortal females alike.

His body *is* a weapon, in every sense. A cruelly beautiful, sublimely lethal weapon.

It's his uncanny proportions, of bulk to definition to height to breadth. It's the mesmerizing shape and movement and girth and length of every line and muscle. It's the golden tinge to his tan skin, the polish of its smoothness, the dusting of silky hair where it should be and no more. It's the power, combining with elegance, entwining with savagery that composes what he is.

Sheer cosmic poetry. An ode to infinite blessing and destruction.

Then I focus on his tattoos. Because, of course, he had to compound it all by having tattoos.

They all stem from a circular mark stamping his left pectoral, which resembles that frieze's frame in design, but not in details. I'm certain the runes encircling it are different. And within it, a vortex seems to swirl away into endlessness. Chains of entwined runes emanate from its cardinal directions to cascade over his chest and side, and down his left arm, each as if following a vital artery, or a line of power that runs through him. Under my dazed eyes, they change from a dark blue-green to a simmering emerald glinting with sparks of fire.

Godric throws down his sweatshirt and continues to watch me watch him. Gobble everything about him up, like a starving woman. One who knows she may never see food again.

Before I make his semi-nakedness my mind's permanent screen-saver, the question belatedly hits me.

Why did he take off his sweatshirt? And will he take off something else? ·

Yes, please!

No, not *please. Have some self-preservation, moron.*

But what if he does? What if he touches me? He said he can, but won't. Was *that* a pledge or did he only mean, *It's a hard pass on your scrawny arse, White?*

What if he has changed his mind, and decided it's the best way to break in the Aggravating Abomination he failed to subdue with shock and awe? And what if he leaves me no choice? Free will isn't something he considers.

Not that he'd force me. If he touches me, he'd probably need to scrape me off him afterward.

All these debates race in my mind as he walks back to me. I swear the ground moans under his footsteps. It, too?

I sit like a flightless duck, staring up at him. Storm clouds gather in his eyes, and it's right there. The resentment he talked about, the frustration. But there's something else I can't fathom. Something ancient. Endless. Just how old is he? How powerful?

But one thing wipes every thought away. This time I know I'm not imagining it. The hunger I see, in his igniting eyes, his parting lips. His evident arousal.

My gaze snags on the massive bulge in his pants. I doubt I'd survive *that*.

But something inside me screams at me and my mortal fears, roars it *must* have him.

It's this crazed voice that makes me snap out of it.

But it doesn't seem he has. He's still staring at me, yet I feel as if he doesn't see me, or not just my face. He sees more. And it—inflames him.

I can see it in the sparks of power crackling through his lethal tattoos, the flecks of ruin slithering within his glowing eyes. This is how he looked in my dream, before he drove his sword in my heart.

Oh, hell.

My mouth fills with ashes, my chest with lava. And that's before I see them. The runes. Or *a* rune. Appearing within a vortex appearing inside his tattoo, right over his heart. As if some invisible hand is chiseling them with molten iron and eternity into his skin.

It's only when the smell of burning flesh, his flesh, fills the air that he frowns down at it.

Before I can read his expression, he clutches it, as if in pain—no, as if he would tear it and the flesh it branded out.

I choke in alarm, and his gaze snaps to mine. He looks like himself, yet different. And I know why.

He's allowing me to see the real monster inside at last. And it's harrowing. Incredible. Irresistible.

Next moment, I think I imagined it. Imagined it all.

The monster is gone. And he's not towering over me as I thought.

He's not even looking at me as he growls, "About time."

His bass notes strum in my marrow as I gape up at him. I can no longer comprehend English, it seems.

Then Lorcan enters my field of vision, and I crash back to reality.

Godric was addressing him.

The first thing I check after that realization is Godric's new rune within that vortex. It's absent.

Did he mess with my head and I imagined it, or is he Glamoring himself now?

I bet I'll never know.

After waving at me, Lorcan also starts taking off his sweatshirt.

He is many levels above human perfection himself, yet not of Godric's caliber. Not to my eyes. And not to the rest of my senses. As for my hormones, he doesn't even register.

Seems that celestial sadist is a species of one where I'm concerned.

I hope he molts!

I wish it even harder now I know I wasn't the target of his semi-striptease. How did I think I was? I must have had a meltdown at my first glimpse of an expanse of his flesh.

"Last chance to change your mind," Lorcan says, facing off with Godric, fists bunching.

What's going on here?

Godric gives a curt headshake. "It's the only way to observe her power at work firsthand. Also a must as a frame of reference for its future development, if any. I have to chart it from the baseline of her current fitness level, through the curve of improvement as I whip her into shape."

It's still as if he's talking in Nephilim, if they even have a language of their own…

My mind blinks out as the two nephilim explode towards each other.

My cry of alarm is cut off as I launch in the air and slam on my back on a mat a dozen feet away. I was thrown there by the shockwave of their clash.

They're fighting.

State the obvious, won't you, moron.

Seems the slam restarted my intelligence as I suddenly get what they're doing. Then my mind empties again as the spectacle of those colliding forces of nature unfolds.

Soon, I realize it's no random brawl. It's some highly-evolved martial art, far more complex and vicious than any human form I ever saw. One created and practiced by celestial beings.

Their movements are a breathtaking choreography that no human body can achieve, an intricate dance of grace, precision—and savagery.

Then there is the power. Each blow they land releases a thunderbolt that reverberates the super-stadium-sized space, and shakes me down to my cells. Any would have pulverized any lesser being.

Mesmerized by the sheer beauty and brutality of their duel, I lie there, watching them, distantly realizing they're both now winged, have taken their fight to the air. And I didn't see the moment their wings emerged. Again.

Among the many bone-crushing blows Lorcan lands, one to Godric's jaw sprays blood from his mouth.

Enthralled, I watch the crimson yet glowing fluid arcing towards my face. I don't try to evade it. It doesn't even occur to me.

It hits my right cheek like a shower of embers. But when I flinch and shudder, it isn't with pain. Or not only pain. Then it trickles down to the seam of my lips.

Instead of wiping its still-warm moistness in disgust, my tongue snakes out and laps at it. A moan of intense pleasure reverberates through me, arrowing straight to my core. I bolt up when I realize it's mine.

I swallowed his blood. As if it was vital water when I was dying of thirst. And I loved—*love* the taste. If ambrosia exists, this would make it taste like dust. I also delight in the effect. It's like—like getting a lick of a star.

I never had any mood-altering drugs, could barely afford caffeine. But this—I just know this surpasses any high I ever heard about. Even that of *Angelescence*.

The best, and maybe worst part, is it's not affecting my awareness. It's actually making me clearer than ever. Present. Connected. As if I have a direct line into the power of the universe. The fount of *his* powers.

All this from a drop of his blood?

But why, when the Angel Essence had no effect on me whatsoever?

A theory flares into my streaking mind. I wait until it's Lorcan's turn to bleed to test it.

Hoping they don't see me scrambling like a lizard where his blood lands, I smear my hand in it, and stick my fingers into my mouth.

This time, I only taste blood. Not like human blood, from my experiences with tasting mine during beatings. Its metallic overtones are more pleasant tasting, have a zing of something fresh and heady, and a depth that flares images in my mind, of the vastness of open space studded with millions of stars.

But nothing like the overwhelming power, the brilliant clarity and sheer *bliss* a drop of Godric's blood caused me. Is still causing me.

So only Godric's blood has that effect on me? Is that why he's the only one who can "fathom and mold" me? We're compatible somehow?

Weirder and weirder.

I'm so engrossed in my musings, I don't notice the fight is over until the two nephilim land. Lorcan like a graceful bird of prey, Godric in his preferred landing method when I'm around, like a rogue asteroid.

At least he must have curbed the shockwave this time, since it doesn't swat me away. Or destroy half the gym. Though it's probably built to take an archangelspawn's punishment.

I find both ruining crisp-white towels with their silvered red blood. Not sure when they got them, I focus on the proof of that vicious fight all over Godric's face. I'll treasure the sight of him bruised and bleed-ing. Even if his injuries are gone by tomorrow.

As if the universe won't even give me that petty pleasure, I find the damage Lorcan inflicted on him healing before my dismayed eyes. Between each blink and the next, his face is returning to its unblem-ished, chiseled ruggedness.

Aargh! Not even computer graphics are that fast!

Unlimited power. Check. Impossible beauty. Double check. Instan-taneous healing. All the checks remaining in the box.

As I call the universe every filthy name I can think of, Godric, the personification of its injustice, looms over me.

"On your feet, White. Get to work."

I consider playing dumb, but my neck won't thank me if he hauls me up by it. Scrambling up before he does it anyway, I know exactly what he meant. He wants me to collect the Angel Essence resulting from their little staged conflict.

Not that I can accommodate him.

"I don't see a thing." As his scowl darkens, I rush to add, "Maybe because you were only pretending to fight?"

Lorcan grins wryly as he rubs his blackened eye, which is also resolving, if slower than Godric's. "I assure you, there was no pretense involved."

I look around again and shrug. "There's nothing. Maybe because you're only half-angel?" An ominous grunt issues from Godric, and I cover my mouth. "Oops, excuse me—half-archangel?"

Godric closes in on me, and it takes all I have not to stumble back. Or worse, to grab him, climb him and lick all remnants of blood from his mouth in a frenzy.

As I pray he won't come too close or I'd succumb to the urge, he grits, "Describe exactly what you saw when you collected Angel Essence."

I roll my eyes. "I already told you in painstaking..." I stop, shooting a finger at what must be a hundred feet above us. "It's up there!"

Both nephilim snap their gazes to where I'm pointing. They see nothing, of course, and Godric looks back at me. "We didn't get into the real fight until we were airborne. So the Essence is expended where true conflict occurs."

I nod at his summation. "It probably took some real damage to get you pissed at each other, and work up an angelic lather."

He exchanges a glance with Lorcan, making the other guy sigh, and advance on me, his wings snapping back out.

"I hope you're not afraid of heights," is all Lorcan says before he wraps an arm around my waist, and shoots in the air.

Gulping down a shriek, one of my fantasies becomes an instant casualty of this take-off.

Flying in someone's arms *isn't* an incredible experience. It's a recipe for seeing your mortality with your own eyes. Eyes that might fall out as I watch the ground—and Godric—recede.

But his sight exasperates me enough to overcome the fright and vertigo. He's saddling his cousin with the dirty work of touching me. When I'm apparently doing him and his kind a huge favor, too.

"Tell me where," Lorcan says, interrupting my murderous thoughts, adjusting his hold with his other arm beneath my knees.

Needing this appalling experience over with, I mutely point to the largest mass of Angel Essence.

"Stop," I croak as he almost overshoots it.

He brings us to a brain-jarring standstill. I would have head-butted him if I didn't already feel like I've flown through a windshield. I settle for pinching his underarm. Or trying to. Hard to pinch satin-covered steel.

He chuckles. "You said stop."

"I should have known you fly like you drive. I left my stomach, and brain, a dozen feet back!"

"I've had no complaints from previous passengers. Every single one even insisted on repeat...rides."

"Ew, Lorcan. You didn't just brag about your sexual conquests!"

"More like contestants. And no bragging involved, or needed."

I glare at his impossibly handsome face with its disarming smile, and exhale. "Yeah, tell me about it. You probably need a forcefield to zap supplicants away."

"I'm not in the habit of rebuffing my fans."

"No kidding. Your backlog must be as long as the Great Wall of China."

"I do what I can to fulfill requests."

"On a first come, first served basis?"

He grins at my chagrin when I realize what I said. I'm more concerned that it was unmeant. This is the one area where I'm too inexperienced to live!

But in my shitty life, I had the best reasons to abstain from anything sex-related. Even innuendos would have been asking for major trouble. I think it would be here, too. But I feel I don't need a filter around Lorcan. He makes it easy to say anything to him.

"It's the other way around." It takes me a moment to get it, then I slap his chest. His smile widens. "But I'm not a stickler for rules in that arena. I'm easy."

This forces a chuckle out of me. What I just thought. He's not only a nice monster, he's a drama-free one.

Suddenly, I realize something else. "Hey, you can hover without flapping your wings! I've never seen angels do that."

He winks at me. "I can do lots of things. And I'm certainly no angel."

"Yeah, I'm discovering that." And it actually surprises me. I wouldn't have pegged him for a playboy. "If I didn't know better, I'd think you're flirting with me."

"Oh, no, I'm *never* going there. I'm fond of my organs where they are." He tips his head down toward the glowering up Godric. "You've been claimed."

Claimed. That word shoots through me with something ferocious, primeval.

It makes me see red. "You're out of your flipping birdbrain, big guy. I'm no such thing, especially where this colossal angelhole is concerned!"

"He said you're his in the Divining."

"That was an act for the Tribunal!"

He pouts dismissively. "He said it. That's enough for me."

"That's it? He says something, and it's law?"

"Pretty much. I told you before how deadly serious the Nephilim are about chain-of-command."

Yeah. And I didn't take him seriously because he's always half-joking.

So what's really going on in this messed-up world of those Nephilim? What kind of rules govern their society, their hierarchy? And what does Godric do exactly to wield that kind of power over Lorcan? Or is it over his whole kind?

Unable to wrap my mind over the implications, I turn to the energy only I can see.

This up close, I realize it's nothing like the Angle Essence I'm used to. Not only that, but there are two forms. Like distinct signatures. Godric's and Lorcan's. And I know which is which.

Lorcan's is the one with faint echoes of the usual angel fare. But it has deeper dimensions, mysterious corners where unsettling things I can't fathom lurk. It's far more complex and way darker than I would have expected.

Yet another surprise about the one I thought the open, easygoing good cop. This nephilim isn't at all what he appears to be.

But Godric's Essence is something else completely. It resembles neither other angels' nor his cousin's. Like him, it's in a class of its own.

If it reminds me of anything, it's what he exhibited during that dream battle. A whirlpool of power that transcends Light and Darkness. Maybe existence itself.

That same uncontainable hunger I felt then, prods me to reach for it, bathe in it. But I pull back. Saving the best for last, I guess.

I reach for Lorcan's Essence, but it doesn't turn into the usual ecto-plasm-like material when I touch it. It pulses around my hand, as if investigating what I am. This never happened before. The energy always seemed to have reactions, but never a will of its own. This one does.

Then, as if approving whatever it sensed in me, It coats my hand.

I snatch a look at Lorcan. From his expectant expression I know he still can't see or sense it. No one ever does at this stage. That's why I moved around with it, without demons tearing me apart. The frenzy only occurred once I turn it into *Angelescence*.

Secure in his obliviousness at this stage, I admire his Essence. It's not the bluish glow of Angel Essence, but an iridescent pulse that reflects the range of cobalt, emerald and indigo. Much like the highlights in his wings. It's absolutely stunning. I wonder if it will retain these magical hues once I scrape it off.

Then I do what I'm dying to, reach out my other hand to Godric's Essence. I'm literally shaking with anticipation as I touch it—only to lurch back.

It *zapped* me. With a thousand volts of roiling sensations.

Like its owner, it doesn't want me near it.

Even so, I know I can contain it, tame it.

A voice inside me yells, *Don't. Not now.*

For some reason, I consider this good advice. Probably from the violent rejection, what never happened before. But this contradicts the compatibility theory. Which means I no longer have a valid one.

"You okay?" Lorcan asks, something close to concern in his whisky-amber eyes.

"Yeah, it's just your Essence isn't what I'm used to." Not a lie, in case he can tell. "Now put me down, please."

From a standstill, he explodes into a nosedive. I leave my shriek, organs and blood behind.

Once he sets me back on my feet in front of Godric, I promptly throw up all over that chest I've been salivating over.

29

I t's not the most flattering thing in the world when the guy you're hate-crushing on associates you with vomit.

Not that Godric is a "guy." Or that I'm hate-crushing on him. Or I am, in a literal sense. I hate him, and I want to crush him.

I still wish the ground would drag me into my eventual tomb already as he strides back from cleaning up, wings tucked away. He's regretfully dressed again, in grey this time, with a backpack thrown over one shoulder.

I preempt whatever disgust he would splatter me with. "Every projectile vomiting instance was totally your fault! Hope you've learned the consequences of tossing me about."

He only bores brooding holes into me. "I assume you collected the Angel Essence?" I nod dumbly, strangely deflated that he didn't engage me in a nastiness fest. He produces a lab jar and blunt knife from the backpack. "Show me how you transform it into your *Angelescence*."

"I told you how," I mumble as I take the knife and start scraping into the jar he holds open. I see the moment the stuff becomes visible to them in the way Lorcan's eyes widens, and Godric's narrows. "See? I just scrape, and voila!"

I gesture for the jar once he closes it, and strangely, he gives it to me. The swirling mass is still the same colors, vivid and mesmerizing, if in a different consistency. But its tidal motion is different from the usual measured rhythm, pulsing like some kind of Morse code. It also changes direction as Lorcan moves. It's following him, like a compass pointing towards its north.

Would other *Angelescence* do that within its owners' vicinity, or is this something special to the Nephilim? Or to Lorcan in specific?

Guess I'll make comparisons when I get more Essence from others of his kind. As I intend to. This is my so-called "power" after all. I may have use for it soon enough.

For future comparison and utilization, I have the un-scraped portion of Lorcan's Essence, which will soon make its way into the bottle I keep tucked away in my magical bra. And neither of them is any the wiser. It feels *great* pulling the wool over Godric's for-once-unseeing eyes.

But what would have *his* essence done? Would it have followed him, too, as if longing to reunite with him? Or would it have roiled and raged against its confines demanding a way out? Would it have shattered its prison, and tried to square off with me? What would it have done when it discovered I can subdue it, as I'm sure I can?

I'm getting sorrier by the second that I didn't capture it. I would have loved to leash that ornery extension of him into submission.

As if reading my mind, Godric's eyes harden, looking between me and the jar in suspicion. "Is that all you saw?"

"It's not all I saw."

Not a lie. I didn't get all of Lorcan's Essence. And I'm not mentioning I got none of his. Not until I understand why it reacted to me that ferociously. Maybe not even then.

No, no maybes. Most *definitely* not then, or ever.

I'm keeping any knowledge about his Essence to myself. I need any trump card for leverage against him.

I hand him back the jar. "I only take as much as what sticks to my hand. I never thought I could actually get it all."

Also not a lie, just not the whole truth in this situation. I felt I could have taken *his* Essence—all of it.

He pouts in contemplation, and I again want to drag him down and lick those lips, even when no trace of blood is left.

I'm fighting the urge when his eyes sharpen in assessment. "You're so unfit your body instinctively takes only as much as it can handle. But by the time I'm done with you, not only will you be as tough as a Pit Demon's hide, but your old instincts will be wiped out and replaced by the ones I install."

I mock-salute. "Sir, yes, sir."

After he inflicts one of those singeing glances on me, he flicks his head at Lorcan. "You can leave now. I still have an hour with White."

Lorcan pulls on his sweatshirt, smirking at Godric. "As long as you know it won't take that long to 'whip her into shape,' mate. Don't go breaking your new toy, eh?"

We both glare at Lorcan's nonchalant back as he strolls away. Me because I can't figure out his percentage of unfeeling Nephilim. And Godric probably on account of his irreverence, in front of me of all beings.

Then Godric turns to me. "Drop and give me twenty."

Gaping up at him, I scoff. "I hope you mean twenty bucks. Though I still can't give you those. Give me a year or so, and I can save up."

A baleful glance. "Pushups—now, White."

I shake my head. "Never done a single one. Twenty would need a miracle, if you Nephilim are into such things."

"I know you attended mandatory school."

"And you think they taught us PE? How sweet. As Owned slaves whose lives revolved around serving our masters, they let us attend school for only four hours, all focused on making sure we didn't 'graduate' at the ripe old age of twelve or thirteen illiterate."

His frown deepens. "So you *never* had any kind of physical exercise?"

"Apart from being on my feet fourteen hours a day at my demon's dive—and doing everything else he ordered me to do, the moment he said it, the exact way he said it…" I shoot him a pointed, visual dagger between his eyes. "…no. I had to conserve the meager energy and calories I had for continuing to do so. You know, in an effort to reduce floggings to a bi-weekly basis."

"No wonder you're so weak." But there's something besides contempt and exasperation in his eyes now.

Realization? He never realized how the Demon-Owned live? How deprived and abused we are? How stunted? And what? He's starting to sympathize?

What am I thinking? Sympathy? From Godric? Ha.

As if to validate my thoughts, he lifts his superhero chin and says, "That changes now."

Backing away, I raise my hands. "Now *now*? Remember what Lorcan said! This toy is mucho breakable."

"You're no toy, White. You're a weed that only grows stronger under adversity."

"All those names you have for me. You're so inventive, Goddamn."

He makes up for the step I put between us, and his heat drenches me in delicious currents. "One more word and I'll make them forty."

"Go ahead. Make them forty thousand." I push my sweatshirt up my arms and hold them up horizontally. "See these? Not happening. Not even one."

He starts to open his mouth, only to shut it when his gaze flits to my spindly limbs.

Gotcha.

Poor nephilim. He wants to expedite my "transformation" so much, to get me out of his gorgeous hair faster, he's trying to ignore his own assessment of my non-existent fitness.

Almost taking pity on him, I say, "I can try a few, from the knees."

He grunts something I assume is assent, so I drop to the mat and attempt the move. I manage the lift off, my arms wobbling and aching. During the descent, they give out and I plunk face down.

As I flop on my back, he crouches beside me. "I thought I would have to start from scratch with you. It'll take some strategizing to decide how to start below even that."

"Yeah, *waaay* below." I struggle to sit up, heart and body pounding with the exertion and his nearness. "I'm *really* looking forward to it."

His eyes narrow with his signature fed-up expression, before he realizes I'm not being sarcastic, and they widen. "You are?"

I nod. "I'm even weaker than I thought. It's really pathetic, and I hate it. I hate being helpless. So if you want to make me stronger, whatever your self-serving reasons are, count me in. *All* in."

I extend my hand for a deal-sealing handshake, remembering his never-touching-me "preference" only when he ignores it.

As I kick myself for giving him another chance to treat me worse than dirt, he heaves up to his feet and stands like a monolith, smoldering down at me.

I can swear his voice has that reverb of momentous moments in movies as he says, "Then prepare to become stronger than you ever imagined possible."

212

30

After I told Godric I'm all in for his transformation—*something* changed. Between us. Subtle, yet almost tangible.

Under its effect, I felt his harshness lessening, his exasperation starting to dissipate. I even felt my excitement almost echoing within him.

Everything was going better than I could have hoped as he tested my aerobic fitness—which doesn't exist—until he brought up diet.

When he quizzed me about my eating habits, he didn't bother to hide his horror, equating them with a dumpster critter. I told him it wasn't far from the truth, and proceeded to relate some of my dumpster-diving adventures.

He looked murderous as he said he'll quintuple my caloric intake. I was thrilled, even if I didn't understand what infuriated him this much. I didn't eat that badly out of choice, and I was always starving. I didn't know what being full felt like until that jet ride.

Then I said his caloric requirements are no problem since I'll be stuffing myself with every sugar-laden, carb-rich comfort food this Academy has to offer. I swear he grew a foot taller as he bit my head off.

According to him, I'm not having *any* empty calories.

When I whined, he lectured me on substituting one kind of malnutrition for another, and decreed he's adding Mortal and Immortal

Nutrition to my curriculum. I *will* learn how to fuel the lethal weapon he's turning my body into.

I haggled all the way to Ariel Hall, the commons named after the archangel of the spirit of nature and nourishment. He only stopped at the door to tell me *exactly* what to eat for breakfast. A list for every meal—for the *whole semester*—would follow.

And what took the cake I'm not allowed to eat? He's assigning people to watch me, to make sure I stick to his regimen.

Talk about the personal tutor from Heaven!

It was beyond me not to provoke him. It really, really was.

I told him that whomever he put on my tail, good luck having them catch me sneaking in junk. If the Academy has it, it's finding its way into my belly. I was raised in the next-worst thing to Hell, and if I want to get away with anything, I will.

Whatever improved between us during that gym stint, when we parted, it was on the old hateful footing.

In reality, I don't mind his menu at all. I either love everything on it, or always yearned to try them. But could I have told him that?

Of course not!

Entering Ariel Hall, I'm taken aback to find it packed with what looks like thousands. It seems every cadet in the Academy is here. Breakfast must be the one meal everyone gets at the same time.

Then I start picking out the Angel-Graced from my year, and I'm stunned to see everyone looking as good as new. Those healers must be really something. Unless the seriously injured are not here, though I doubt it. The number of smiling faces among them also surprises me. Seems they're heeding Astaroth's advice, putting Azazel's terrorist attack behind them, and bent on enjoying every moment they have away from him.

The next thing I notice is the uniforms, the simplified version of Lorcan's. Our freshmen version is in dark blue with silvery, holographic accessories. Everyone is wearing theirs. Everyone but me, that is. Godric didn't tell me to bring mine, and I assumed I'd have time to change. He probably meant for me to walk in here disheveled and in sweaty gym clothes, and stick out like more of a sore thumb.

Thanks, Angelhole. More pain that I owe you.

Avoiding appalled glances from the Angel-Graced and condescending ones from the Nephilim, I rush around, looking for Sarah.

We agreed to meet here if Godric was done with me in time for breakfast. I'm on time only thanks to my dismal physical condition. I bet he would have kept me longer, if he found reason to. But there was nothing more he could do with me today. Not before he devised that way-below-scratch training program.

And true to his joined-at-the-hip remark, I'm meeting him —*reporting to* him—after classes for another kind of training. The mental discipline and stamina kind. No idea what *that* entails.

When I finally see Sarah, I do a double take. She's smiling. Grinning, actually.

At the demoness!

Blood shooting to my head, I streak to their table.

Skidding to a stop, legs like jelly, I grab Sarah's arm and pull.

She looks up at me, smile brightening. "Oh, you're done! How was it? Tell us all about it as you eat. And boy, will you eat! The food here is, well, heavenly."

As she giggles, I gape at her, then sweep the rest of the large, round table.

The demoness is sitting next to the roommate I haven't registered beyond her furious interrogation when I was half-asleep.

Next to her is our resident archangelspawn. Five more—two nephilim, two angel-graced—and is that ethereal beauty Fae?—sit on the other side of the table, no doubt the denizens of another dorm room. Only one seat is empty, clearly for me.

Does the Choosing thingy require we stick with our roommates for meals, too? Whatever it is, one thing seems to unite everyone at the table: how they look at me. As if I'm something the cat refused to drag in.

I pull Sarah's arm again, and it's like pulling on a sack of wet cement.

She *doesn't* want to leave this table?

There has to be some kind of mental manipulation going on here.

I glare around the table again. "Let her go!"

Everyone exchanges disgruntled glances at my tone, some actually baffled. The archangelspawn goes back to eating. The demoness smiles slyly. She gets my vote for the one compelling Sarah.

Sarah pulls me down for an urgent whisper in my ear. "No one's keeping me here, Wen."

"You think the monster who almost punched a claw into my brain wouldn't mess with yours?"

Sarah winces as she gazes at my now-intact forehead. "She said she put something in your wound to make it heal quickly. I guess it was her way of apologizing."

"She's a damn liar. I healed on my own. I'll tell you about it, after I get you the hell away from her influence."

"I know demonic mind-control well, Wen. She isn't doing anything to mine."

"Whatever she is or isn't doing, it's enough we have to sleep in the same room. I'm not eating with her, too! Now let's go, please."

A slap on my back makes me stumble and almost sprawl over the table. It's the damned demoness.

"Oh, stop being so melodramatic, and go get your breakfast. Get me pineapple juice and another croissant." Her gaze sweeps around the table. "Anyone want something else?"

Struggling to straighten up, I snarl at her, "I'm not your waitress here!"

"But you were one, in some base demon's brothel, too." She wiggles her perfectly-contoured brows at me. "Among other lowly things."

Incredulous, I gape down at Sarah. I can't *believe* she told them.

Paling, Sarah bites her lip. "Each of us said what we did before coming here. Since you weren't here, I…"

She stops, slumping in apology, and I pat her shoulder. It's not her fault these monsters manipulated her.

Apart from the five years we attended school together, Sarah mostly interacted with me and her demoness. With near social isolation and her forgiving nature, she never developed the skills needed to play the vicious power games of the Natural and Supernatural worlds. It's why I always shielded her from the cruelties of those with no morals and far more power. And I'll do so here, whatever it costs me.

I smirk at the demoness, provocation set on maximum. I need to keep her focused on me, so she'd leave Sarah alone. "Whatever I did, none of it was lowly. I worked for a living, something I bet you can't do to save your pointy-tailed ass. But here, I'm a cadet just like you." Until Godric succeeds—or fails—in making me his experimental weapon. But she doesn't need to know that. "Whatever I was before, I'm your equal here. Chew on that, along with this disgusting demon-mess you're gobbling, Brimstone Breath."

With that, I flounce around, only to stumble. It's the demoness who stops me from face-planting on the ground.

As her uncanny strength plops me back on my feet, she grins at my chagrin. "Name's Jinny. Pleased to make your acquaintance, Gwendolyn White."

Sarah told her my full name, too? What else did she tell her? And was it of her own free will as she believes?

And why is this "Jinny" suddenly being nice to me?

Smelling a demon-sized rat, I look around. It's only when I see the angels dressed like Azazel's escorts spread at the periphery that it makes sense. These must be *Pax Vis*, the oxymoronic peace force, who are mostly Designated Angels of the Dominions order.

Feeling more brazen at their presence, I scoff. "Jinny? What kind of wimpy ass name is that for a demon?"

Her face falls, and she grumbles almost inaudibly, "The demonic joke kind."

"She believes she may have Jinn in her ancestry on her father's side," Sarah whispers so only the three of us can hear. "But she tells everyone Jinny is short for Jinnifer."

I blink at Sarah, to stop my eyes from bugging out. The demoness—Jinny—took her into her confidence?

What on this messed up Earth happened since I was forced to leave her alone four hours ago?

Sarah's face blazes crimson as she winces at Jinny. "I hope you don't think I'll blurt out any secret you tell me, Jinny. I just tell Wen everything, and she's the world's best secret keeper!"

Jinny slams me with a death glare. *Me*, the one who received the secret, not Sarah, the one who spilled it. But it's clear Sarah already enjoys a special status with the demoness. How that happened, I can't begin to tell.

It should make me feel better, since that means Sarah is maybe safe from her. But it doesn't. Why, I can't begin to tell, either.

My stomach grumbles so loud Sarah giggles. "Oh, go get your breakfast. And try not to heap everything on your plate like I did."

"It all ended up in a 'demon-mess' as you can see." Jinny points to the jumble on Sarah's plate. The exact thing on hers.

So did Sarah emulate Jinny, or the other way around?

What on this monster-infested Afterworld is going on here?

Head spinning with the implications, I walk to the food station at the end of the gigantic hall.

As I approach, the smells of delicious food hit me so hard, my legs tremble. Then I see the details of the open buffet and I almost faint.

To think this spread that far surpasses any royal feast I've ever seen is available for free. And around here, it's only breakfast. If I didn't dread my and Sarah's fate in this place, I would have been ecstatic to stay for the food alone.

And if I weren't afraid of committing another form of social suicide, I would have fallen on the serving plates in a frenzy, cramming my mouth and hoarding everything. I could easily become a glutton if I'm not careful.

Not that Godric is leaving it up to my willpower. I just "made" one of the people he has watching me. The Select chef at the omelet station.

As soon as I approach him, he starts making one. He's done by the time I reach him, according to Godric's exact recipe. I give him a baleful glance instead of thanks, and move on to gather the rest of today's supremely-healthy, calorie-dense breakfast menu. It amounts to the quantity of food I ate in a week. Let's not even mention quality.

After I load my tray, and with all the liquids sloshing in their glasses, I start my wobbling trek back to the table Sarah won't leave. She seems oblivious to how precarious our position here is, how dangerous these she's treating as newfound BFFs are.

Engrossed in fuming, I don't notice the barricade of muscle until I bump into it, tray-first. I don't even have time to cry out before the tray is magically caught undisturbed in large, male hands.

Raising my eyes, expecting Godric to be checking on me, I find myself looking into the literally glittering turquoise eyes of another celestial stunner. I know at once what he is, and where I saw him. In Godric's parade.

His incredible eyes crinkle at the corners as he holds the tray away from my groping hands, his accent that posh one of his cousins' as he says, "Uh-uh. Get your bearings first."

"Sure, as soon as *your* bulk stops blocking the horizon." I reach for the tray again, and he only keeps it out of reach. "Give it back!"

"How about I give you an escort back to your table?"

"How about you give me the damn tray and go block some major highway?"

He only grins at my surliness. "Accept the offer of steady hands, angel-graced. You don't want to add crashing that ridiculously crowded tray to your pathetic resumé of sweaty gym clothes and leash."

Argh. He got that right. I have too much against me already. All thanks to Godric. And to think I stupidly started to mellow towards him because he promised to torture me into shape.

I still narrow my eyes at his relative. "What does my disastrous standing in Sinister Academy matter to you, archangelspawn?"

He barks a laugh, deep and nerve-tingling. "Is this what you call Godric?"

"Nah, him I call Angelhole and Godawful, among other things."

Another boom of laughter, and if possible, it makes him even more gorgeous. This guy is really way up there in looks. I'd even say Godric-level, just all golds and bronzes, the sunset god to Godric's midnight one.

"I've *got* to be there when you call him any of that. I never thought the day would come when someone, let alone a human, called that bastard out on his shite, and to his face, too."

"Not a member of Angelhole's fan club, huh?" I say, marginally warming to him.

He rolls those jeweled eyes. "Bloody hell, no! It's enough of a bane being secondborn."

"Yeah, tell me about it..." I stop, blink up at him. "Wait...second-born? Does this mean you're...?"

He gives a mock-bow. "Gideon, Godric's half-brother, at your service."

31

"Holy shit—another Death Jr.," I exclaim. "Are there more of you, or are you dusk and night versions all the wild oats Azrael sowed?"

Gideon's shoulders shake with laughter, but even the tray's liquid contents remain unmoving. Must be some stasis field. "Do you ever say anything that's not arch, Wen White?"

"Is arch your posh way of saying funny?"

He nods. "In a saucy, mischievous way."

"I don't know about that, but whatever I say, people usually punch or flog—or leash—me for it," I mumble, still suspicious. "No one ever laughs. So what's your deal, Giddy?"

"Gid…" He cracks another laugh, before holding one hand out, the other still balancing the tray perfectly. "Please, stop. I have an image to uphold as Death Jr. The Second, after all."

"Can't have the new recruits seeing one of their slave drivers giggling, huh?"

"Well, not *that* much." He winks before schooling his face into a more serious expression. It reminds me of Godric so much, my heart misfires. "But it's not true that no one laughs. Lorcan told me he's been laughing his head off from the first words he heard you say."

"Oh, Lorcan doesn't count. He would find a dung beetle rolling its dung ball funny."

His face splits on another megawatt smile, dripping with blinding white teeth and charisma. "That he would. But I almost pity Godric. The bloody bastard's anti-humor Grace must be killing him with you around."

Yeah. *Really* not a fan of Godawful. Another string of familial strife to maybe wrap around his neck one day.

Gideon starts walking, forcing me to scramble behind him. "Now I saved you from making an even worse spectacle of yourself, repay my kindness with the origin story of that leash."

"You block my way to cause the accident, then demand payment for preventing it. You're Godawful's all-bastard semi-sibling, all right."

As he guffaws again, I reach a conclusion. This guy is almost as dangerous as his half-brother. He only blinds his prey to the fact by the camouflage of friendliness.

But how much does he know about me? Is he in Lorcan's—and Azrael's—confidence, and knows about the Angel Essence situation?

I doubt it. From the way he called me angel-graced he doesn't know the circumstances of my presence here. But Godric's inexplicable involvement with me inflamed his curiosity. And I don't want more beautiful monsters' interest. That would only lead to more disasters.

Also this one seems viciously intelligent, and if he works out any of the secrets Godric would kill to keep hidden, I don't wish him to die at his brother's hands. Even if it would land said brother in Hell and get him off my back. Too Cain and Abel, even for me.

But the more I evade him, the more he bombards me with questions. Snarking the living hell out of him only seems to delight him.

"Got anything, Deon, or were you too busy laughing?"

The lyrical, feminine voice comes from behind me. I turn to find another archangelspawn from that parade looking me up and down. Up close, she's on par with my roommate. A statuesque grey-eyed brunette with the most striking bone-structure I've ever seen. She would make a perfect Artemis, the Greek goddess of the hunt.

Gideon gives a sighing headshake. "This one is as slippery as my accursed sibling, Tory. But at least she's entertaining, not infuriating like him. I haven't laughed that much in the past decade."

Tory falls into step with us, sandwiching me in their celestial perfection. "Shouldn't she be blabbering her heart out by now, Deon? Or are your charms failing? You said it would take you two minutes to find out why Godric is leashed to her."

"*She's* here." I scoff. "And sure, *he's* leashed to me. Gotta ask that Angelhole if my neck yanks too hard on his hand."

"See what's been keeping me?" Gideon grins at her over my head. "This Wen White is delightful."

Tory looks at me as if I'm some kind of exotic lizard. "Did she just call Godric Angelhole?"

I smirk at her. "And *she* sees angelholeness runs in the family."

Tory's feline eyes widen. "Bloody heavens, she *is* a find."

I roll my eyes at her. "Listen, Giddy's cousin or sister, or whoever you are—tell him to give *her* back *her* tray, then show *her* your 'bloody' backs."

Gideon chuckles. "Where are my manners? Let me introduce my cousin, Ashtoreth, daughter of Michael."

I twist my lips at both of them. "I would say charmed, but I'm too hungry to lie. Tell you what? You keep my tray. I'll load up another one."

As I turn around, a steel hand clamps my arm. Tory's. I blink up at her, wondering if she'll break it, if it would heal, and find her smiling at me—maliciously or not, I can't figure out. I'm too hangry to care.

"Listen, Ashtrays, I'm telling neither of you squat..."

I almost swallow my tongue at the—presence that flares at my back. The knowledge is instantaneous. Godric.

So *can* he teleport, or did he just sneak up on us?

The three of us turn to him, and that first moment says everything about where they stand with him. Gideon in a brutal sibling rivalry. Tory in a mixture of desire, deference and defiance.

I fling a hand at him. "Here's your Angelhole relative himself. Ask *him* if you're so curious."

As Godric levels a lethal gaze at them both, Tory turns to me, resuming her smile. "*I'm* not lying when I say I'm charmed, Wen White. I will most definitely catch you later."

Uncertain if this is a threat or what, I watch her streak away.

Gideon meets his brother's displeasure with a bedeviling grin. Seeing them in the same frame is almost too much for my mortal female mind.

Without taking his eyes off his brother, Godric grits, "Take your breakfast and go eat, White. Finish everything."

"I would, but your semi-sibling's hands seem welded to my tray."

Gideon starts walking again. "I told you I'm escorting you back to your table."

I huff. "Do you do room service, too?"

His gaze slides over me suggestively. "I can be convinced to..."

He stops abruptly, as if something caught him by the neck, and squeezed.

An invisible leash this time? Or another of Godric's undisclosed powers?

Gideon swings a pee-your-pants scary glance at his brother. Yep. I was right. Another devil-in-disguise.

Just as I think he'd ram into Godric, and they'd destroy this hall and half its occupants in a clash-of-the-gods-style brawl, Gideon turns to me. His face seamlessly switches back to that knee-melting smile. "Say the word and I'll deliver the tray right to your seat."

He's tossing the ball in my court. He'd defy Godric if I chose his side.

I *want* to defy Godric, of course, but I also don't want to give that ruthless charmer what he wants. I won't be a pawn in their probably eternal familial war.

What decides for me is seeing everyone at my table watching us openly. I don't want to rejoin them with those two hulking nephilim fighting over me like a bone.

I hold out my hands for the tray, and with a sigh of resignation, Gideon gives it to me. "It was an honor to be of service, for as long as it lasted, Wen White."

"Dude, quit Wen Whiting me," I groan.

"I'll be happy to dispense with formalities. Can I call you Witty? A play on both your names, and character?" His smile widens, heats, as if we're sharing an intimate joke. "It also goes with Giddy."

Godric's rising fury flays me, so I grin up at Gideon. "No one called me that before. I guess it can be yours."

"It will be my privilege to have a special name for you. And Witty, I *am* definitely charmed." He swings a baleful glance at his brother. "Till we meet again, don't let this boor get away with anything."

I glare up at the volcanic Godric, before I wink at Gideon. "Oh, don't worry, Giddy, I never will. See ya."

With that, I walk away from these paragons, hoping I won't stumble and fall into my tray.

Back at the table, the blatant expressions coating every face make me wince. They run the full gamut from incredulity to envy to fury.

As soon as I sit across from Sarah in the only seat left vacant, she blinks at my tray, before grinning. "Now that's a healthy—*and* orderly —selection!"

"She sure makes us look like pigs, Sar," Jinny drawls.

Sar? *Sar?* Sarah told her my pet name for her, too? And she *dares* call her by it?

"It's such an inferior selection, if you ask me." That sullen room-mate—who I now notice is a glorious auburn-head—is looking straight at me, not my tray. Her green eyes have been skewering me since I first showed up.

I toss her a visual lance of my own. "It's a good thing nobody did."

The glance Sara gives me is pleading. She doesn't want me to "instigate conflict" with these girls. Can't she see *I* didn't start this?

"Cara Vanderbilt is angel-graced and our fifth roommate, Wen," Sarah says.

I actually thought she was a nephilim, since she's almost on par with Ms. Archangelspawn in looks. But from that last name, seems she comes from old money. That would explain the disdain and enti-tlement.

When neither of us acknowledges Sarah's introduction, she fills the awkward silence with a winning smile at Cara. Weirdly, it erases that harpy's scowl.

Okay. It's official. It's only me everyone hated on sight.

Am I even surprised? Apart from my epiphany in front of that angelic mirror, it has always been that way.

But before, I thought it was by design. Mine. I always placed myself in front of Sarah, an obnoxious target for abuse. Now I wonder if I would have been one anyway. That like my unique ability to collect Angel Essence, I also squeeze Bitch and Bastard Essence out of everyone.

If so, it always made me a more effective barrier between Sarah and the rest of the world. Others never bothered or even noticed her

But others notice her now. Others who are magical monsters to boot —and they are *nice* to her. *If* this doesn't turn out to be some sort of cruel game.

"What was the hold up with Gideon? And Tory?" That's Ms. Archangelspawn, addressing me for the first time. She looks confused that one of her kind would spend a second voluntarily around me. "Did you bump into him on purpose?"

I have a dozen "arch" answers to that. But I have to sleep in the same room as this supernatural predator. So I shrug. "He's the one who intercepted me. Your cousins had this little plan to investigate what I've been doing with Godric."

"What *have* you been doing with Godric?" It's Cara again, voice dripping in venom.

That's also official. Why I'm at the top of her Skewer-And-Barbecue list. Her antipathy has a name: Godric.

I ignore her, mouth already filled with that buttery, aromatic omelet.

"We saw you cut the line with him at the Divining," Cara persists. "Then he dragged you after him at Orientation, then he brought you to Ariel Hall himself."

"You sure have been keeping tabs on me," I mumble around my crammed mouth, spraying bits of omelet all over my tray.

Cara's aristocratic features twist in disgust. "Anyone will notice a turd if it's stuck to Godric's boot."

Now I'm a turd. The names never stop coming.

I only grunt in response, swallowing as I cram more into my mouth.

"Are you a special-needs recruit he has to cart around? I heard the Academy has to take a quota of those, too, as well as from the inferior Supernatural races, the dregs of Hell and the cursed Blighted." Cara flicks a disdainful hand towards the fae, Jinny and one of the others, seemingly a blighted not an angel-graced as I assumed.

The platinum-blonde fae isn't even glancing our way as she tucks into her massive breakfast. The blighted looks crestfallen. But the moment crimson smoke rolls out of Jinny's nostrils, I cough a laugh that catapults almost everything out of my mouth.

A big lump of half-chewed omelet hurtles across the table, wetly slapping Cara in her right leaf-hued eye.

Cara cries out in outrage and revulsion, rubbing frantically at her eye with a napkin, smearing her exquisite kohl and mascara. I only continue shoveling in food.

I have expected and noticed the unhealthy interest, with Godric dragging me around. But I have to wonder, what *is* his going story? Or is he leaving everyone stewing in their curiosity and forming outlandish theories?

After retouching her eye—she actually has a mirror, makeup remover and makeup in her backpack, in a supernatural military academy of all places—Cara spears me with pure hostility. "What's your special-need, *Wen*? The inability to eat with your mouth closed?"

Nodding, I shove in another mouthful. "And the tendency to spit food with absolute precision across long distances."

Jinny snorts, Sarah winces, and the graced and blighted pretend we aren't there. But now the nephilim, and the fae, are watching us like people watched fighting lizards, when Kondar once sent me to steal a rare one from the zoo's reptile house.

Can't say I blame them. We must be pathetically entertaining to them, two human females, apparently fighting over the supreme nephilim, who considers us both less than lizards.

Before Cara prods for more answers that would cool her laughably misplaced jealousy, a line of professors stream in, heading for the stage. They are led by Astaroth, and Azazel is nowhere in sight. I almost cough another food-laden laugh at the wave of whimpering relief.

After a hush falls, Astaroth's voice again comes from all around. "Good morning, cadets. I apologize for interrupting your breakfast, but we needed to have all the first-years in one place for this announcement."

All around me, the Angel-Graced exchange wary glances that all but groan, "What now?"

After escaping becoming some beast's breakfast earlier, I can't bring myself to worry. And then, whatever it is, it can't be worse than Azazel's possible death row.

"Yesterday, you perused your first semester schedule," Astaroth says. "Which is divided between Academic Fundamentals, and Cadet Basic Training. But there will be other classes and training, based on your individual areas of affinity."

Okay, that's bad in a way I haven't expected. I can't handle more on my plate!

A buzz of dismay shatters the silence. Seems everyone thinks the schedule is packed enough as is, even without my added Godric-sized workload.

Astaroth raises an elegant hand and the droning dies down.

"The additions to your curriculum will commence only after the subject of this announcement takes place. But before making it, I need to give you some background first." He pauses until everyone is bating their breath before he carries on, "Grace-given powers, whether in the Angel-Graced or the Nephilim, are divided into the broad categories of psychogenic, transmogrifying, corporal and elemental—with thirteen main subdivisions. By your age, most Nephilim have basic powers like heightened strength and senses, as well as flight. Some of them, along with rare Angel-Graced, have an idea what their core powers lean towards. But none can know for sure, or access the majority of those powers, until they undergo Activation."

Activation? That sounds sinister somehow. But what else is new around here? It's what I dubbed this Academy, after all.

"After your specific Graces and core powers are unveiled and assessed, you will be assigned to one of the four Hosts of Celestial Academy. *Regulus,* named after the fixed star of Archangel Raphael, the watcher of the North, *Fomalhaut,* Archangel Gabriel's, the watcher of the South, *Aldebaran,* Archangel Michael's, the watcher of the East, and *Antares,* Archangel Uriel's, the watcher of the West.

"After your assignment, the extra classes and targeted training of Grace Development will commence. In our experience that benefits best from a blend of individualized assignments and continuously optimized practice."

He looks around, as if waiting for anyone to ask anything.

When no one makes a peep, he continues, "Activation will take place midway through the semester, which is eight weeks from now, in the Imperium Trials."

Okay, that's another thing I don't like the sound of. The word "Trials" brings to mind impossible tests, mortal danger—and a thinning herd.

I can almost swear Astaroth looks straight at me as he concludes, "While there's no specific way to prepare for the Trials, your very destiny will hinge on your performance."

32

"What exactly are the Imperium Trials?"

Godric doesn't look up from placing what he called Seraphic Crystals around me.

I start to ask again when a massive yawn interrupts me, almost dislocating my jaws. It's not yet evening and I'm ready to drop into a coma. No wonder, after the night, and day, I had.

Sore, physically and mentally, I basically slept through every class. At the end of the last one, his summons woke me up.

Okay, so it was his tug on the leash. He removed it as soon as I saw him at the main doors, but I still wished I could strangle him with it.

And the pathetically funny thing? Cara's glare was explicit with her wish to strangle *me*. For the privilege of being literally jerked around by him. I wanted to tell her I'd serve him to her if I could. Sliced and sizzling like a fajita.

I was the one who fumed as I followed him for what felt like miles across campus, to the far end of Jegudiel House.

According to the articles he kept sending me—that pinged and made me more of a spectacle until I read them and got a hundred percent on their quizzes—Jegudiel is the archangel patron of those in positions of responsibility.

My Nephilim Nemesis, the one "responsible" for me, led me below the imposing edifice, to an underground cave right out of an evil cult movie.

As we descended down, down, *down* to a vault that brought to mind human sacrificial rituals, I really wished I had powers. If I did, I would have singed his celestial butt and escaped.

But since I knew I was safe with him as long as I was valuable, and I'm powerless anyway, here I am. In the middle of the heptagon he drew around me in what I can only describe as angelic lasers.

When he finally speaks, it's not to answer me, as usual. "This Mindscape session will test your psychic affinities."

"Isn't that what the Imperium Trials are for?"

"This has nothing in common with the Trials."

"So are the Trials more like the Divining?"

"No."

"So what do they entail? How can we prepare for them? Why did Astaroth say we can't? Where are they going to be? In the Imperium Maze I saw on the map?"

"Maybe I should change your name to What, How, Why, and Where, along with Wen."

"Hardy-har-har." But I do grin at him. There's progress here. He's no longer glacially or volcanically exasperated at my constant questions, is almost resigned. I am the drip of water on his rock.

Before that image leads to more involving wetness, hardness, me and him, I pelt him with another barrage. "What happens if I don't have any affinities? Like I didn't have any muscles or aerobic fitness? What if I don't have any 'core power' or 'specific Grace' like Astaroth said? Am I even actually Angel-Graced? Is that where my Angel Essence recycling ability comes from?"

For answer, he stalks towards me, cutting through the lasers with his body. I have a feeling anyone else would have passed through them as the aforementioned fajita.

"Hold out your hands, palms up."

This close, his aura is like a cascade of sultry night, sifting with that dark velvet voice of his through every nook and cranny of my nervous system.

Sighing in pleasure in spite of myself, I comply.

He starts gesturing over my open palms, and more of this angelic tapestry starts to form over them in a sphere of hypnosis.

Watching the forming patterns intently, I continue throwing questions at him, hoping one will strike off an answer. "If you find I have no psychic affinities, you can't strengthen them like you promised to hone my non-existent physical abilities, right? An affinity can't be strengthened if it doesn't exist, can it...?"

The world falls out beneath me. Disappears around me.

It never existed. And I—I never was.

Nothing exists but him. His eyes. His breath. The prod of his mind. The pulse of his power. The pleasure of his being. He's everywhere. Everything.

Then, among the infinite cosmos of Godric, another presence begins to twinkle, like a distant, almost invisible star. It blinks faintly, dazedly, before it flares in alarm, retreats, disoriented, daunted.

But his compulsion is patient, drawing it out of hiding, coaxing it closer. It floats nearer, shy and uncertain at first. But it gets bolder with every realm it traverses in answer to his temptation, growing bigger, brighter, bolder.

And all the time, it remembers. That it hungers. For everything. But most of all, it craves the vastness of his burning darkness, the inevitability of his endless endings.

The moment it touches them, it howls in reality-sundering rapture, expanding into a white-hot ring of infinity. Eternal tentacles of greed explode out of its nonexistent core, seeking to consume everything in its path. Nothing would ever stop it again. Nothing.

But him—him it won't devour. Him it wants. Wants to assimilate.

It besieges him, beseeches him. Come to me, it cajoles and coos. It swells in triumph and exultation as he reaches back.

Then it hesitates. There's something else here, witnessing its need, learning its secrets.

Before it can decipher it, he sinks his power in its fabric, and it shrieks in realms-razing fury.

It's another betrayal! He only means to subdue it, to starve it!

It convulses around him, attempting to contain him, to incapacitate him. But it has been buried in eons of suspension, eons when he had free rein.

His power is unbound and boundless as it surrounds the ring of its being, suffocates it, compacting it into a pinpoint. A pinpoint that shudders with the force of a dying galaxy for an eternity, for a breath, before it blinks out.

* * *

Snapshots spark in the darkness as I fade back into consciousness.

They're of Godric holding that orb of angelic energy over my palms, as I bombarded him with questions.

I remember nothing afterward. I feel nothing, too. It's as if my every inch, my every *cell* is bound by intangible, enervating threads.

I lie at the bottom of sensory deprivation, no longer even sure I have a body.

Is this part of the assessment he's conducting? Is this how being in this Mindscape he mentioned feels? Or did something go wrong?

Did—did he paralyze me?

The suspicion detonates inside me and I try desperately to move.

"Don't struggle."

How does he know I'm struggling, when I can't even twitch the muscles I no longer feel?

But hearing his voice somehow soothes me. Between one heartbeat and the next, I'm no longer afraid.

Then slowly, curiosity replaces everything else.

What's he doing? Is he doing something? Or is he waiting? Waiting for what?

Suddenly, something streaks through my nerves, like a blaze eating gasoline towards the tank. Once it hits it, my senses reignite in a wildfire.

As the conflagrations dies down, I remain still until I'm sure I can feel every part of my body again, and that nothing is missing.

Then I open my eyes.

Godric is looming over me, and I'm lying on some altar.

Where did this come from? Are we still in the crypt? What exactly did he do while I was out?

Should I be more worried that I'm spread before him like a sacrifice, or because I'm not worried about it?

"What happened?" I croak as I struggle up to my elbows.

"I tested you."

When no elaboration comes, I prod, "And? What are my affinities?" Again, nothing. "Do I have any?"

His eyes flare emerald in the dimness. "No."

I exhale. "So I'm really Nothing like you said."

"Nothing wasn't an insult."

"Heh. Could have fooled me. But it's what makes me an Abomination in your opinion, isn't it?"

"Neither was *that* an insult."

I blink up at the leashed intensity in his voice, and my gaze unwillingly snags over his tense body and face. Unbidden, images of him half-naked, bearing down on me and pushing my legs further apart with his, cascade like a honeyed wave over my nerves, pooling hot and wet between…

Focus, moron. Find out more.

I exhale again, purging the hypnotic, erotic images. "What were they, then?"

"They were the only way I could describe you. But I now realize neither description was accurate. I..." He pauses, as if words elude him, then his frown darkens. "I think you shouldn't exist."

I lurch to a sitting position, feeling as if he backhanded me. "Whoa, dude! Now this has to be an insult. Or is it a threat? Even a decision?"

"It's none of those things."

"That you're being this serious means it's something even worse." His grimness only deepens, sending my heartbeats stampeding. "Actually, give me back Nothing and Abomination. Shouldn't Exist is far more disturbing."

"And this when you have no idea of the possible implications."

"And you do?"

"I can only hazard guesses at this time."

"That's still about that ridiculous idea that I might be one of the most dangerous things to ever exist?"

"Actually, that was only on account of your ability to see and collect Angel Essence, and depended on the potential to weaponize it. Which remains to be seen." He grips his nape, the movement laden with frustration. "Now I believe I was being overdramatic."

I toss my hands at him. "Yes! Thank you! About time you admitted what a drama queen you are!"

"I'm not being one now. This..." He tosses back a gesture, one that encompasses me. "...is something else entirely. But it's connected. Maybe even the root of your impossible ability. Maybe..."

He stops, shakes his head.

What did he see during that test that disturbed him so much?

Something *is* flitting at the edge of my memory. Reminding me of that wide-awake trance, when I hallucinated there was something inside me that could take him on. It ended up losing, because even in wish-fulfillment, I didn't know how to wield power.

These images and sensations that elude me feel similar. Like it involves him and another conflict we had. But it feels different at the same time, because of some other presence that...that what?

I don't know. Can't remember.

But he does, and it disturbs him that he doesn't know what it was, either.

So is it something new within me? Or only newly "activated"? By the Divining? I *did* feel it changed me. Even if that fast-healing side effect is already gone. And I feel the same as I always did. Weak, achy, limited. A.k.a. puny human.

I look down at the deep paper cut I got during our first Angel Grace 101 class—and find it gone. What the…?

So the healing activated again? Like this thing that I—and now he —sensed? Can these changes within me only be detected under specific conditions, all involving him? Is he some sort of catalyst to me? Is that another effect of the compatibility I suspected before? If it really exists? And if it does, why, and what would it lead to?

I have to stop this, or really change my name to Questions. Ones I won't get any answers to. Not from him. The one time he isn't being an angelhole, he has none.

My luck really sucks.

I let out a shuddering exhalation. "Man—I'd rather be in mortal danger in demon-infested territory. I knew what to expect there, had a plan, a way out. Now I'm trapped among you magnificent monsters, and every time you come near me something worse happens. None of this would have happened, and you wouldn't have such an Abomination That Shouldn't Exist on your hands, if you just left me alone."

His eyes grow heavy-lidded and ten times more hard-hitting. If he wanted to, I bet this guy can make me climax just by looking at me.

Even now, with him dismayed, and me agitated, my core flutters as he rumbles quietly, "Believe me, I wish I could have. But neither of us had a choice in this matter. The moment you collected your first batch of Angel Essence, this course we're on was set. And there's no escape for either of us."

"Sound a bit more ominous, why don't you?"

He gives a mirthless huff, his gaze growing even more troubled.

That I'm the reason he is at such a loss stuns me. But it also excites me, I must admit. Stupid, I know, but there it is. It's a thrill that I continue to make Godric the Great feel things nothing and no one ever did. Terrible things all, granted, but still.

I'm a pioneer here.

I sigh. "The archangels know about this Nothing/Abomination/Shouldn't Exist business, right?"

He shakes his head. "They only know what I told them. About what happened at the Divining."

"Will you tell *me* what happened? You told me this much. Just tell me the rest."

As I think he'll ignore me again, he exhales. "I told them you were going to be pulled to the Darkness."

"But this isn't what happened! I—"

"I *know* what happened," he cuts off my objection harshly. "Neither the Light nor the Darkness could claim you."

"You mean they tried to pull me apart. That must be how people die in that Divining!"

He shakes his head again. "Those who die are not pulled apart, they're swatted by each side until they expire."

"And you monsters just stand there and let them die!"

"The Angel-Graced or Demon-Blighted who don't attend the Divining die anyway, only after much suffering, to themselves and everyone they come in contact with."

"So you consider watching them die in that ritual a mercy, huh?"

"If you're talking about me, I never personally attended a Divining. But, yes, it is a mercy of sorts. Anyway, those who die do so because they're *rejected* by both Light and Darkness. But you..." He pauses again as his eyes sweep me, glowing with yet another brand of heat, one that ignites something new inside me. "They *fought* over you. That was another unprecedented occurrence. I had to keep it a secret from everyone, including Lorcan and the archangels, until I figured out how or why it happened myself."

"How could you keep it a secret when everyone saw it happen?"

A shrug of one prodigious shoulder. "Everyone only saw the usual vacillating between Light and Darkness, until a side chose you."

Another use of his Glamor powers, no doubt. That's why the Tribunal looked so bored. They didn't see anything out of the ordinary.

"Not that you made it easy covering it up. Your cacophony was so loud, even I couldn't mute you. Bloody hell, I could barely lower your volume." He shakes a finger in his ear with a grimace. "You probably gave me hearing damage—when I thought that was another impossibility."

"Oh, did my screaming in the agony I thought would last forever hurt your pretty immortal ears, you poor Death Spawn?" We all but bare our teeth at each other before I mutter, "So, when you told Lorcan no one could know about what happened, you..."

"Wasn't talking about what *really* happened," he finishes for me. "He already suspected something, so I told him one truth. I told the archangels the same thing to—neutralize them...for now."

I so want to know what he means by that. But I go for the more urgent question. "And what *is* that truth you told them?"

"That since we need you, and I had to claim you for Celestial Academy, I intervened, and pushed you to the Light."

"So it *was* you!" I exclaim. "And that's what you'd kill anyone to keep hidden forever? Why is that such a big deal?"

His scowl seems directed at himself more than me for a change as he bites off, "Because I tampered with the Divining, and falsified its results for you. If anyone else even suspects what I did, it would be a matter of time before it gets back to the Tribunal."

"And? I got the impression that you have more power than they do."

"I do. But that's not the issue. What I did was a massive violation of the very balance of this reality. Not to mention the Armistice Accords. With tolerance between the Celestial and Infernal Courts at its most precarious since their signing after Zinimar's murder, exposure of such a breach could lead to their severance. And if this happens, the Apocalypse will resume."

33

I burst out giggling uncontrollably. Almost as hard as when the archangels tickled me.

Godric towers over me, viridian eyes darkening to brooding emerald, watching me splutter and snort, until oxygen depletion brings my fit to a wheezing end.

"It's always something on a cosmic level with you," I pant. "Isn't it, Ricky Boy?"

His lips twitch at my latest nickname. I swear he's fighting the urge to laugh. Which is a mind-boggling concept. That his sense of humor isn't only macabre, and that I can set it off.

He purses his lips as if to show me I can't. "You think anything less would make me put up with you?"

But I already saw his unwilling mirth, so I stick my tongue out at him as I rub away tears. "So you risked messing with the laws of the universe, or restarting the stalled End of Days, just to claim me for the Academy? Wow."

His scowl returns as he watches me wiping wet hands down my uniform. "I had to. I regretfully have use for you."

Of course. It isn't as if he cared if I lived. Actually, he'd rather I died.

But no matter his motive, he still saved me. I wonder if this means I owe him a life debt? Or did putting me in danger in the first place cancel it?

Deciding it did, I raise my chin. "And you also stopped them from realizing I was ground-zero for a supernatural tug-of-war. Not that I understand why *that's* such a big deal, either."

"I already told you, you have nothing to mark you for either side."

"Like *I* already told you, that's called being a human. But I see why you consider that stalemate unprecedented. The Divining is always attended by the Angel-Graced and Demon-Blighted, so you only know the results they get. Now you've found out what happens with a garden-variety human."

"You're no such thing."

I roll my eyes. "Listen, if this is about this last test, this 'Shouldn't Exist' business, here's a thought. Maybe in this weird hypnosis ritual you did, we shared some hallucination? I've been having my fair share of those since we met, and maybe this time you entered one with me? I sure feel very human."

His nod is terse. "You are. But the archangels were right. You are also something else."

"What? And don't say 'Inconclusive'!"

"How about 'Indeterminate'?" As I start to growl, he exhales. "At least to me. To the archangels, they now think you lean towards Darkness."

"If they think I'm Demon-Blighted now, how did you explain intervening to push me towards the Light? You could have still claimed me, since every kind of creature attends this Academy."

"This isn't how it works. Once you're 'Divined,' you're carted off to the Academy of your affinity."

"That's still not the end of the world, no pun intended. You could have gotten me back from Pandemonium Academy."

He gives an exasperated huff. "The Demon-Blighted who come here are like exchange students, and it's Pandemonium who chooses them, like we choose the Nephilim or Angel-Graced we send."

"Couldn't you have asked for me as one of the exchange students?"

"Asking for someone in specific is also unprecedented. I could get away with the personal interest angle in the Divining, because I just cut the line, not actually assigned you where I want. There are non-negotiable laws about nepotism."

I cough a laugh. "That demoness told me she's here *because* of nepotism."

"That's on Pandemonium's side. Here, the angelic free-will laws extend to a plethora of moronic, self-sabotaging mandates."

"You really are no angel, are you? You're all for every sort of intimidation and subterfuge. And I used to think angels were all bad. Turns out they have their good sides, compared to you Nephilim."

He inclines his majestic head, as if I paid him a compliment. "Anyway, if I broke our Academy's rules for you, they would have realized there's something significant about you. They would have turned you inside out, and scoured your mind and soul of every secret you ever harbored, to find out what it is."

"You mean exactly what you threatened to do to me?"

He ignores the dig. "Once they found out what you can do, losing you to them would have been only the first in a chain reaction of disasters. That's why the archangels condoned my intervention."

I gape at him. "You thought of this whole convoluted scenario on the fly? And now you're straight up lying to your dad and uncles and best friend, huh?"

Raising his haughty chin, he looks at me down his patrician nose. "I never lie. I only don't tell the whole truth. I'm now keeping a potentially catastrophic part of that specific truth a secret. If you value your life, you'll keep it, too."

"Hey, now this *has* to be a threat…"

His rumble bulldozes over my exclamation. "The archangels sent you to the Divining almost certain you're not Demon-Blighted. They're nowhere as accurate as the Divining, but they would have felt *something* when they scanned you. Especially Raphael, who would have sensed a kernel of the demonic disorder, and also Uriel, as the archangel of seers. It's why I had to make them think you're a kind of human they haven't come across before instead, one Darkness favors, probably because of your yet-unexplained ability."

"I still don't get why you won't tell them the whole truth," I persist. "They're archangels, and your family."

"That's exactly why I know I can't tell them. If they find out Light and Darkness fought over you, you would become their most important research project, with all the ensuing attention and danger of exposure. As it is, my own involvement with you is causing enough unhealthy curiosity."

"How *are* you explaining that, by the way? Why don't you tell me, so the next time Gideon interrogates me, I have our stories straight?"

His scowl literally darkens the cavern. "You will tell him nothing, because you will not talk to him again."

"How about no? I'll talk to anyone I want."

Viridian-laced obsidian lightning begins to seethe. "See this? This is the only reason I told *you*. I couldn't risk you relating your experience to anyone, but I also couldn't order you to refrain from doing so. I knew it would only make you defy me. Like you just did, again. But now you know the stakes, and the danger to your own life—and your friend's by association—you'll keep your mouth shut."

That does shut me up. The leash of Sarah's safety would always be the most vicious power he could exercise over me.

Not that I would have blabbed without a threat to her. I wouldn't tell Gideon, or anyone else, anything. I never spilled any beans, not even under torture. I just wanted to pull his strings. And Gideon is a massive one. A Nephilim-grade steel cable and fishing line in one. And boy, will I enjoy sinking the hook of that sibling antipathy and watch him thrash on its end.

He exhales and the lightning and darkness recede. "Which brings me back to the Mindscape session. There was no hallucination. It was real, and so are its results."

I throw my hands up. "But you don't even know what they mean!"

"What I know is that any human, any *being*, has more of an affinity for either Light or Darkness, if only by enough for a stalemate to *never* occur. And it never did. Being indeterminate has never been an option. Which made me make the Nothing/Abomination diagnosis. But I am more right than I feared. After this test..."

As he falls into that stumped silence again, the implications crash in on me.

Until this test, I thought there was something weird about me, but not *that* big a deal. All of the archangels' and his cryptic verdicts haven't really sunk in.

But what if I'm really changing? Because of the Angel Essence, the Divining, exposure to Godric—or all of the above? Or something else completely? Would I start manifesting some power beyond that lame Angel Essence collection? Like the Angel-Graced or Demon-Blighted do, even when I'm neither?

That would be *awesome*.

I'll take anything to level the playing field in this land of the supernaturally blessed.

With this thought buoying my spirits, I grin up at him, making his frown darken once more. "Bottom line is, you don't know what I am, or what I'm turning into. I can't be categorized. No wonder you hate wasting your time on me."

He takes a sudden step towards me, as if he's going to take me by the shoulders.

My whole body surges in anticipation, but he stops a foot away. His struggle, to keep his hands off me, reverberates inside me. And against all reason and self-preservation I find myself begging inwardly.

Touch me. Let me know how it feels.

Visibly struggling not to, he fists his hands at his sides. "I've changed my mind. It won't be a waste. It will be anything but a waste —if I can harness this—thing inside you."

This thing. Inside me. He's certain it exists, but can't even find a name for it. And more than anything, *that's* terrifying.

All lightheartedness draining, I gulp. "So you think it's what makes me potentially dangerous? And potentially useful?"

"I am not sure. How it all connects. I can't tell what I felt inside you yet. This is unknown territory, so I only have theories. Until I am certain, you already heard me say I'd gladly kill anyone to keep this whole thing contained. And I will."

I believe him, of course. Anyone but either of us knows about this, and they're dead. Which means I can never tell Sarah.

This, more than anything else, makes me feel truly alone, for the first time since I met her.

Alone with *him*.

He blows out a forcible breath, letting me see he isn't feeling any better about it. "Since no one else can suspect your power, and even more, whatever you have inside you, I'm wary about you entering the Imperium Trials. I have no way of knowing what they'll expose. That means I need to find a way to exempt you." That sounds like great news to me. Or it would have if he didn't add, "If I can't..."

It's there in his eyes, the alternative. Something drastic. Like going against the archangels' directives.

Ending my life would surely solve all his problems.

For suspended moments, I'm lost in him, reading his conflict as if it were my own. And he's as lost in me. I have no doubt this time.

It's how I know the moment he reaches a decision.

A decision not to act on what he considers the best course of action. And it isn't only out of duty, or on account of my potential use.

For some reason that is up for debate, Godric no longer wants to kill me.

34

"**C**an't you give it a rest for one damn day? Would it make your paint peal to stop being so damn shifty and slippery?"

I hear how rude and grumpy my hiss sounds and wince. I can't afford to be my offensive, provocative self right now. I'm a beggar here. I gotta lighten up if I have any hope of smooth talking her.

Yeah, her. Cause I always considered her female, even before I learned enough Latin/Angelic to realize that Jeremiel Domus Feminae means Jeremiel's House for Women.

Yeah again. I am talking to my damn dorm building.

For the past two weeks, every time I could, I skipped out on a class to get back here, for that reconnaissance tour I never completed. Hell, I haven't been able to start. Because of her. She continued to lead me around like a blind mouse, and herd me where she wanted—without me even realizing it.

Right now, I got so frustrated after she again led me to our corridor, I decided to have a word with her. I am convinced she's been diverting me on purpose, not according to some spell or programming, and that she had sentience. And moods. Some days she just leads me on for a few minutes then I'd find myself outside. Today she seems more— playful, seems to want to keep me around. She had me pacing that corridor for thirty minutes before she let me see where I was.

But that also meant I might be able to reason with her. Now if I can just curb my temper and coax her, I'd stand a chance.

I just hope no one witnesses this, or on top of all the strikes against me, I'd be known as the cadet who talks to walls. With the way I've berated her, and now would cajole her, they might even spread that I have a wall for a boyfriend.

Oh, well. It isn't like I haven't had worse. What's important now is that I have a heart-to-heart with Fem, as I now call her. I think my best bet is to flatter her, while endearing myself to her by taking her into my confidence. Both strategies would sound sincere. Because they are.

Drawing in a calming breath, I inject as much sweetness in my demeanor and voice as I can. At least enough to soften my insolent and inflammatory edges. Can't have my expression and tone undermine the truths I'd tell her.

"Sorry for the outburst, but you really had me chasing my own tail long enough, don't you think? Gotta admit, though, I admire a fellow persistent lady." I stop, focus. I can swear she's listening to me. So I go on, "Since we're talking at last, let me just tell you how I've been feeling since I first stepped inside you. How every moment of history permeating your spaces resonates within me, and how every fixture and ornament and painting beckons to me. Your every inch just calls to me on so many levels. Living inside you is the only thing ameliorating my—uh, unjust sentence, and the enforced company of my roommates."

Somehow sensing she accepts my declarations, I venture further. "Can I call you Fem?" When I again feel she approves, I grin in relief. "Great. I really hope we can be friends—and that you will let me explore you, experience you without herding me back to my room or outside." I again feel that she's agreeable, so I take it another step. "I was wondering if you can help me? Anything I can do for you is yours to ask, too, of course!" I wait until I feel a sense of curiosity emanating from her before I ask, "Would you show me where we can hide within you, or better still how to escape in case of an attack? The Academy itself, if need be? Do you harbor secret tunnels or magical gateways that could lead out of this domain, without trip-ping the Palladium Wards?" I feel a dimming, a disapproval, so I rush to add, "I assure you I'm not trying to escape my sentence! I only need a way out in case of emergency, or a contingency plan if

Sarah is in danger. You like Sarah, don't you? This is all to protect her."

Nothing happens, for ten more minutes. I'm again forced to consider that my mind could be irreversibly fried, convincing me the building can understand me, and would respond, too.

Finally giving up, I begin shuffling on my way out, and something flashes at the top of my field of vision. I snap my head up, and see those pulses of energy relaying within her soaring arches.

She *is* responding, guiding me somewhere!

Shrieking in gratitude and excitement, I rush to follow them.

This time, I feel the difference, between following her illusions, and actually going somewhere else. The farther away from our dorm she leads me, for real this time, the more hopeful I become she is answering my plea, and showing me a secret way out.

I don't know how long it is before the pulses stop. When they do, I'm in a deserted area. One that doesn't exist anywhere on the Academy map. I know because I consulted it, and the usual "You're Here" glowing blue dot is nowhere to be found.

But then again, what kind of secret way out would be marked on the map?

With that thought erasing my initial discomfort, I finally look around.

It's nothing like the rest of Fem's pristine areas. The ruthless hand of time is evident in every inch. But that does nothing to hide it was once on par with the Court's level of magnificence. Actually, even more, and in even more prodigious proportions. When Fem or any other building in the Academy aren't large enough to house these dimensions.

I find only two explanations for that. Either I didn't realize it when she led me out of her and the Academy altogether, and to a part of the Court I haven't seen—which is almost all of it. Or she took me some-where even further within the Celestial Region.

Whichever, this place isn't only untouched by the timelessness that permeates every place I've seen in this domain, it feels—abandoned, by eternity. This formerly extravagant-even-by-celestial-measures construction feels like the court of a deposed dictator, or the temple of a forsaken god.

I hope this means it's un-warded, and it's where a way out of this prison can be accessed.

But before I can explore as I feel compelled to, the pulses resume, flaring within the walls themselves this time. Walls I'm sure can tell me many forbidding, forbidden stories. I actually feel they *are* trying to transmit something urgent to me.

But I can't stop to listen. The pulses are leading away too fast, leaving me behind.

Forced to curb my burning curiosity, I rush to follow the signals.

This time, when they die down, they've lead me to a dead-end passage.

"Uh, Fem?" I prod, staring at the peeling wall. "Are you going to recalibrate, or what?"

Minutes pass with nothing happening, until I'm forced to start thinking Fem's magic *is* designed to misdirect anyone trying to poke their noses where they don't belong. Or she's decided to take stymieing me to new levels.

But neither thought holds water, not after she showed me that place. What I feel certain is a massive and long-hidden secret. So why stop now?

Finding no answer as usual, I start turning back—and the wall warps, as if under the brunt of Godric's power.

Oh, no. He must have felt I'm not where I should be through the leash.

I brace myself for another harangue, and probably a reinstatement of its constant use.

But moments pass and he doesn't appear on the other side of that dissolved wall. By now I know he won't. He isn't the type to hold back for suspense value.

And now everything in me isn't primed for facing off with him, I notice the eerie, reddish light flickering beyond the door-sized opening. Spooky.

Leaning forward gingerly, I try to peep through without stepping in. But the ground ripples beneath me, like a freaking wave, tossing me through the opening, and crashing me inside.

Heart thundering, hands and knees throbbing with pain, I scramble up to my feet, gaping around. I'm somewhere so vast, so dimension-defying, my mind and senses glitch. I can no longer tell if I am above or below ground. If I am still in the same realm at all.

The scare, the daze disappear under the impact of something even greater. That soul-deep ache of familiarity, only a hundred-fold in intensity this time. It emanates from what occupies the center of the endless cavern, the source of the unearthly, fluctuating light.

A statue of an angel.

He's much larger than the massive one embossed on the Court's main doors, but looks larger still in statue form. Even from a distance that seems like a mile, I feel like an ant in comparison. And not only because of his size. It's his—presence.

If the statue has such an overpowering aura, what would the real thing be like?

His arms are raised against the backdrop of his folded wings, his fingers spread with his palms facing him as if rousing crowds. His head is bent in a way that reminds me of a maestro engrossed in the music he's conducting. But I can't tell his expression or what he's wearing. It's hard to fathom much detail because of the light swathing him. No. Not light. Flames.

He's burning. Blazing.

Without volition, I find myself walking toward him as if in a trance. Even when I know the flames are real. More than real. I somehow realize that's heavenly fire, far more devastating than any earthly or even hellish one.

I still approach, and the heat sears higher through me, echoing the memories branded on my psyche. My earliest ones, of that day I was dragged out of the burning rubble.

Then I'm close enough to make out the details of the massive pedestal he's standing on. And I realize what it's made of.

Bones. Heaps and heaps of them. A veritable hill of remains.

The horror of that sight finally fractures my stupor

I explode around, run back where I came from—but the opening I've been spilled through is gone. Nothing remains but seamless walls. Walls I can now see are made of razor-sharp crystals. Endless, deadly facets reflecting scorching darkness and suffering.

Horror still sinking in, taking root, I turn back, unable to resist examining the angel's macabre pedestal.

The bones are in gradual stages of disintegration. At his feet, they've burned to ashes. The piles lower down are still flaming, but feel ancient. Further down still, they look newer, until at the very bottom they are—*fresh*.

Heartbeats almost burst my head as a dozen dreads inundate me. That I've been beyond stupid trusting that capricious edifice, when it must be as disregarding of human life as those who built her. That she's punishing me for attempting to probe her secrets, like she has thousands before me, trapping them here until they died. That I'm looking at her handiwork throughout the ages, and until recently. The newest bones still have decaying flesh coating them.

But even in my panicking mind, it still doesn't make sense.

If those people died of starvation, they should be lying around in complete skeletal forms—in their clothes. The bones wouldn't be separated and piled like this.

There's only two possible explanations. Either the place itself magically took the skeletons apart, and gathered them beneath the statue, or someone has been doing it.

I lean toward the second explanation.

If I thought the cavern where Godric takes me looks out of a cult movie, that one feels like the real deal. It must be the largest sacrificial chamber in existence. Fem could have been leading gullible and greedy humans here—and other creatures by the look of many bones— for millennia. To become sacrifices at that statue's literal feet, to burn at the pyre his heavenly fire fed.

Suddenly, the blaze of my panic is doused. And like the time when that thing pursued me in the woods, I'm incensed.

One second I'm about to beg Fem to let me go, the next, I'm screaming at the top of my lungs. "I'm not letting you use my bones to decorate this grisly pedestal, you treacherous bitch! I'm calling Godric and he will put out your precious idol's fire with one flap, and level the whole place with one blow. Then I will suck the sentience out of you and this whole place, until you collapse into so much inanimate rubble. Do you hear me, you evil heap of bricks?"

But even as I rave and rant, I know my threats are just that, fury with nothing to back it up. I can't reach Godric, through the leash or any other way. And my Essence gathering ability is nowhere that powerful, and I may never be able to use it that way anyway.

I'm running out of threats and shrieks, when something at the closest wall to my left moves.

Heart already booming beyond its capacity, I stare at it, knowing that if someone comes in to kill and fillet me, I won't be able to stop them.

But I won't go down without a fight. Godric hasn't taught me much yet, since he's been focused on building my strength and stamina from the ground up. But I will use every dirty trick I know. As for my "power" I will give it all I got, one last time. I owe it to myself, to Sarah, to strike back at this shitty existence and the monsters who populate it, to do as much damage as I can on my way out.

Aggression and rage boil my blood as I reach deep within me to that thing that takes Godric on in the Mindscape. I'm trying to draw it to the surface, to with it while conscious, when I realize the movement isn't someone coming in. It's another wall warping open.

Without a second's hesitation, I streak towards the forming exit, even as more dreads swamp me. That Fem may be leading me someplace worse. Or may actually be showing me the way out of this domain. Instead of only knowing about it, I'd have to get out, and be unable to return. Once Godric catches me again, my four-year sentence might become forty.

But worrying about anything but becoming sacrificial tinder is a luxury I don't have.

I throw myself through the opening without trying to look where it leads—and fall.

I plummet in blinding nothingness, forever.

I have no idea how long it is before I finally land, slamming on solid ground on my back.

Lying there stunned, I find myself staring at the cloud-laden sky. I drag myself to my elbows and realize I'm outside Fem, just at her back, where I've never been before.

The moment I can use my legs again, I explode up and into a run.

Thanks to Godric's conditioning for the past two weeks, I last almost a mile before I am forced to slow down. Then as I drag my feet all the way back to Jophiel Hall, questions inundate my still-spinning head.

Why did Fem take me to that place, and show me that burning angel? And why did she let me go? Did she believe my threats? Or did she mean to scare me before letting me go all along?

Whatever the answers, this is it between me and her. I'll zoom to and from our room with my gaze glued to my feet, so no part of her would catch it. I'll fill my thoughts with mind-worm songs, so she couldn't read them. And I'll certainly never try to explore that crazy building again, or say another word to her. Not even if I'm dying to know what this was all about.

But since dying is an actual possibility here, I'll just have to live with another mystery. What's one more to add to my growing collection of potentially lethal ones?

I just have to wonder, will I ever find answers to any, before one finally kills me?

35

K ill. Kill. Kill.

The word echoes in my mind like a grisly mantra.

At first, I thought it's my own subconscious chanting the word. I did have lots of reasons for the vicious desire. Especially since that schedule amendment separated me from Sarah.

Two weeks ago, the faculty decided we were too many, and divided us into groups of three hundred for the applied subjects. I wasn't allowed to be in Sarah's, so many of our classes aren't at the same time. It's been particularly nerve-wracking leaving her alone in Azazel's. Even if, to my stupefaction, she enjoys them the most. According to her, he's the best teacher around so far.

But I soon discovered the droning word wasn't originating from me.

Strangely enough, after four weeks at Celestial Academy, I no longer want to kill anyone. Including Godric.

Okay, okay, especially him.

Only because it's no longer in my best interests to kill him, I always assure myself.

This guy is a cosmic-level slave driver, but boy, is he effective. I live for our three-hour daily training, and I'm boggled by the progress I keep making every single day.

I leave the Lycurgus Arena he empties for our sessions feeling like I've been stretched through a pasta machine, and battered inside and out with a meat tenderizer—when he still hasn't laid a hand on me. Yet I also feel so alive, so transformed, I'm on fire to do it again, and again. The one time he had to cancel our training four days ago, I felt I'd combust. I went running to discharge the unspent blaze licking through my blood. Yeah, I run willingly now. And I don't feel I'm dying after two miles, when before I did after two hundred feet.

He wasn't exaggerating when he said he'll make me stronger than I ever imagined. I'm already ten times as strong in that short period.

It's been making me wonder if there are other elements to my too-rapid progress beside his virtuoso coaching and my all-consuming commitment. Whether it's exposure to him, or that thing inside me that might have been activated by the Divining. Not that it's been showing itself beyond our Mindscape escapades. And we're both still in the dark about what it is, or what it can do. *If* it can do anything beyond giving us psychogenic shows and exercises. Ones I barely remember after I exit said Mindscape.

Anyway, my rocketing physical progress is probably a mix of everything, each element boosting the other. And like he predicted, it's all strengthening my ability where Angel Essence is concerned.

I no longer only see it when an angelic entity is angry or agitated. Other reasonably strong emotions will do. Also I can now harvest more of what I see, not just what clings to my hand. Lately, I've been able to yank and wrap it around up almost my whole arm. It's a major pain scraping that much off, especially when I no longer keep any of it to myself.

Though I made sure my bottle can indeed compress and conceal far more than 10ml, I room with an archdemon, and can't risk her sensing it on me. After I had a nightmare of her tearing my breasts apart and scooping my heart out with those talons to get to the bottle, I got rid of most of my stash, keeping only Lorcan's portion of it. Losing that potential weapon because of her is yet another reason to hate lava-filled guts.

What really galls me, though, is that I still didn't get any of Godric's Essence. With the way he's been hanging on my every move and counting my every breath, I'm certain I wouldn't have been able to pull any wool over his mesmerizing eyes. Especially if his Essence lashed out at me again when I tried to capture it.

So I continue to gather more and more of other angelic entities Essence for him. To say he's been increasingly elated—in that swoon-

249

ingly scary way of his—at my progress, would be an understatement as massive as he is.

He's been stockpiling it all, which confuses the hell out of me about what he really wants. Does he want to make *me* a weapon, or am I supposed to make *him* one? And how would *Angelescence,* even if I make him gallons of it, be a weapon anyway?

I constantly prod and probe him for an answer. I get none, of course.

At first, I kept hoping he'd tell me it's the latter possibility. That if I can provide him with enough *Angelescence* to make that weapon of his, he might let me and Sarah go.

Not that I think Sarah would *want* to go. And maybe, just maybe, I'm starting to think sticking around isn't so bad either.

To my shock, things have been sort of good on the Academy front.

For instance, Azazel hasn't killed any of us yet. Injured most, and hospitalized some, but apart from the kid who lost half his hand during his initial incursion, and the one who now has a diagonal scar where his face was put back together, we're all more or less intact. So far.

A good thing since my own healing factor is unreliable. Seems it depends on how soon I can be around Godric after my injury, and how bad it is. If I'm with him within an hour or two, something like contusions, floggings or Jinny's wound would heal completely. I'd rather not pit my Godric-activated healing ability against the test of a worse injury. Not to mention that I hate depending on him for something like that. *And* I'm sick of running to the Sanatorium with every injury so everyone would think all my healing is their doing.

He thinks it's the Divining activating the latent Angel Essence in my system because of constant exposure. I keep him thinking that. It's as good a theory as any, after all.

Other than Azazel's ever-present threat, most of our professors, even the severe or outright cruel ones, have been great. I've grown to dote on Astaroth's classes most. That guy is an artist at delivering complex information and making it stick. But I also enjoy most other classes and appreciate each professor's methods. It's been astonishing to discover the thrill of applying all my faculties in the uptake and practice of new knowledge and skills. Who knew?

On the social level, though, nothing has changed with my roommates.

When our schedules don't separate us, we're bound together in grudging coexistence, during meals, and during the Combat and Weaponry classes of our Cadet Basic Training. Thankfully, we're not required to pair up or anything yet. Otherwise, my visits to the Sanatorium would have been all-too-real. In our dorm, cohabiting with three girls who despise my very existence, especially when needing to use our shared bathroom, isn't fun.

Even in the presence of the demoness, I'm still the most unpopular one, the outcast no one tolerates. Except for Sarah of course. Sarah, who's become the only binding agent of our ragtag team, the one who somehow keeps the peace.

Weirdly, outside of my *Unitas*—as each quintet in a dorm is called, ironically meaning unity—I've been making friends. Okay, okay, not friends, or even companions. But many of the archangelspawn and nephilim have been pawing and sniffing me, some literally, trying to figure out my deal with Godric. Tory has been treating me like a prized pet. Lorcan, well, he's Lorcan, so I can't tell if liking me is specific to me, or part of his open-for-business-with-anyone personality. But where I'm concerned, he's my only other friend around here.

As for Gideon, I can't figure this one out yet. He seems to actually enjoy my company, and he's been seeking it whenever possible, but I can never discount his omnipresent motive of spiting and sabotaging Godric.

Not that I care about that, really. He's fun to have around, and he thinks I'm hilarious, and keeps making all those jaunty advances and posh insinuations. It's become a game between us, especially when Godric is around. We're both united in our love of pissing him off.

All in all, everything has been going far, far better than I expected.

Only three things have been bothering me. Okay, driving me up the wall. More so because I haven't been able to tell either Sarah or Godric about them.

Sarah, so I wouldn't worry her and spoil her excitement at being here, and Godric...I don't really know why I can't tell him. Probably because he has enough worries, too, where I'm concerned. And because I don't know what's going on myself.

The first thing is that voice in my head, that isn't a voice at all. It's more—an emotion I'm picking up on. An obsession. It could be originating from anyone in the Academy.

So I guess I *can* cross out a few names apart from Sarah. Lorcan, Godric, and the archangels. Probably the archangelspawn, too. I don't see any of them having the capacity and/or the need to obsess in secret about anyone. Strangely, Jinny, too, since she's the impulsive not obsessive kind. Cara, and everyone else in the Academy I don't know or don't know enough to judge, can be a possible suspect.

Suspect of what, I have no idea. I don't know what this word means. Is it an order to kill? Who? Or is it a threat? To me? To someone else, and I'm picking up on it? Or is it just a wish?

And why am I the only one hearing it? *Am* I the only one hearing it?

Again, I have nothing but questions where this insidious fixation is concerned.

The second thing is this—presence I've been feeling. An inhuman one. And not in the way the Academy denizens are, or like that putrid thing that followed me in the woods. It feels—primordial. That's the best way I can describe it.

At first I thought it's whatever Godric says is inside me rearing its head in my conscious mind. I had to discount this quickly, since it feels totally different. Yet, it's familiar. In that maddening way so many things have been since I set foot here. Actually, way more.

It's also almost always there. Sometimes like a white noise buzzing in my very cells, but mostly it's that unnerving silence of someone listening in on you.

Apart from creeping the hell out of me, it really bugs me to feel I'm being bugged by some ancient entity.

To what end, from my record in resolving mysteries, I'll probably never find out.

I still can't dismiss the possibility that it *could* be all in my mind. All the inexplicable things I've been feeling could be misfiring neurons in my brain. After all, the poor thing has been through the supernatural wringer in the past weeks.

But I *definitely* didn't imagine the missing things.

Initially, I wanted to think I was misplacing stuff. But even I am not *that* sloppy. During the past three weeks, I had over a dozen disappearances, from my brush to my map to my tablet.

Though I was furious, I didn't want to kick up a fuss, especially since the Academy replaces anything we lose or destroy without question. But when I got a new tablet, I realized it was useless without a specific Magitech setup. In my case, only Godric can do it. Before I could bring myself to ask him, he was breathing down my neck because I stopped solving his incessant quizzes.

Once he realized why, he immediately thought it was another of my slobbish incidents. Lots of obsidian lightning ensued.

When the storm abated, I reminded him I wouldn't deny it if I lost the tablet. Since when did I care about looking bad, or about his opinion? It was stolen, and it had to be one of my roommates.

After brooding down at me with enough heat to ignite a star, he said it wasn't.

From the thousands of crimes he studied during his training, and the hundreds he'd solved in his Praefectus Praesidium role—which literally means Chief Protection—it was never the too-obvious suspects.

Yeah, I *finally* found out what he does around here.

He's the Praetor, or commander of the Praetorian Guard, a unit of the Army of Heaven serving as the guardians of Celestial Academy, and the secret service agents—and assassins—of the Celestial Court. He has more subtitles under that lofty Designation than the Mother of Dragons.

As if he needs to be more impressive.

But his assertion made it even worse. I have someone *else* who hates me enough to steal my stuff, and has such access to me?

Then he traced the missing tablet, and found it in the woods, in a conflagration. The fire has already spread to dozens of trees, and might have raged into a full-blown forest fire if Godric didn't find the tablet then. It was spectacular the way he used his elemental Graces to put out the raging blaze. Spec. Ta. Cu. Lar.

In the aftermath, we found an almost-burned backpack containing all my missing articles. But since I didn't tell him they were all mine, Godric had no reason to think I was singled out. He assumed the thief was a prankster or a kleptomaniac, since none of the things were valuable, and every cadet had them anyway.

He reasoned the perpetrator must have worried someone would report a theft eventually, and the *Pax Vis* would be involved. The thief must have panicked and decided to get rid of the incriminating evidence.

Only I knew this wasn't the case. From the echoes I felt around the bonfire site, this was no desperate act. This was premeditated. Ritualistic even. I don't know how I knew that, but I did.

What made it even more disturbing is that the thefts stopped. It means that whatever the thief wanted, it's been accomplished. What that was, I can't begin to imagine.

The questions only keep piling up. And there's no answer to any of them in sight.

"Penny for your thoughts, Wen."

Sarah swings our clasped hands, drawing my attention back to her.

I look down into her eyes with a grin. "Just a penny, huh? How the mighty have fallen, when we have a million dollars."

She clears her throat, making a serious face. "The acquisition of wealth is no longer the driving force in our lives." She laughs, and I do, too, at her perfect British accent, *so* much like Godric's. "And isn't it wonderful we don't need money anymore?"

"Yeah, but I still want *our* money, Spock."

"What will we do with it, Jim?" She elbows me affectionately. "Though that was a Picard quote."

"Gah! I can't believe I mixed them up," I groan. "But it's our money, and I toiled over a year for it, and we should have it. And that damn archangelspawn won't let us get it."

Sarah, as always, looks uneasy when I call Godric, and all who deserve it, names. It's not like I owe anyone politeness when I'm a glorified hostage here!

But I know she wishes I was nicer to everyone. I *have* been trying. But they *really* provoke me, and I was never a Miss Congeniality candidate to start with. Still I wince a silent apology as I promise myself I'll try to be better at holding my tongue. I hate making her uncomfortable.

Never one to make me feel bad either, she smiles encouragingly at me. "At least no one will find it when they re-rent the apartment."

That's the only reason I'm not going batshit crazy worrying about our hard-earned mil. Sarah hid it in the wall and painted over it, and made an undetectable opening in the baseboard where we added more. No one will find it, unless they tear the whole place down. So I guess the money is safe until I can find a way to retrieve it.

Sarah suddenly jumps, squealing in excitement, swinging my hand harder. "I still can't believe Jophiel herself is teaching us a class!"

I skip with her as I laugh. "Tell me about it. It's amazing there's a female archangel at all. I always thought it strictly a Boy's Club."

"She's literally one-of-a-kind," Sarah gushes, azure eyes glittering in the afternoon light of that permanently overcast sky. We've come to realize the sun never shines over the Celestial Region. "I was blown away when I read about her history in educating and inspiring humanity in arts and philosophy. And that's from the internet. I bet when they finally let us into the Metatron Library and we get our hands on his Codex, we'll find out way more accomplishments."

"Maybe we can get the definitive rundown right out of the archangel's mouth, now we have her as a teacher."

"Yes, we do! At least for as long as she remains here." She leans into me, voice lowering. "I heard Aela telling Tory that she never met her aunt, as she hasn't been on earth since long before the Apocalypse."

Aela, as in Ms. Archangelspawn. Yeah, you guessed it. Raphaela, Raphael's daughter.

This seems to validate she's as young as she looks. But still, every time Sarah even mentions her, her voice hushes and she seems to shrink. I hate seeing her intimidated.

Though I guess it isn't Aela's fault, since she treats Sarah the best of us all.

That isn't saying much, since when she deems to interact with us at all, she treats me like an animated curse, Jinny like a nasty growth, and Cara like a pitiful upstart. Yet it's Sarah she gazes at in bewilderment, as if she's never seen a warmhearted innocent before. Which she no doubt hasn't. But she does reserve softened tones and expressions for her.

That might only be because Sarah abides by her rules of non-encroachment to the letter. I don't think Sarah ever addressed her or even talked in her presence. She's too awed by her.

I don't really blame her. I avoid that paragon as much as possible. There's something—unsettling about her. And not in the way of all the other archangelspawn.

Shaking my untimely musings away, I engage Sarah in her current subject of wonder. "Did you also hear why Jophiel dropped planetside now?"

Sarah nods excitedly, "Cara says she heard It's because of the numbers of Angel-Graced this year. Celestial Academy never had more than a couple dozen per year. It's the first time in history they have almost fifteen hundred. Seems it's a momentous enough occasion to warrant her presence."

The hairs on the back of my neck bristle seconds before *she* barges between us, disengaging our hands

"And since she's teaching Angel Grace 101," Jinny says as she grabs Sarah's hand, the one she forced me to drop, her flaming red ponytail undulating like a contented cat's tail. "It seems she doesn't want those inept professors leading you fledgling pseudo-angels astray, and wants to set you on the right track from the get go."

"*That's* why I smelled brimstone!" I exclaim as she drags Sarah ahead. "You're really Jinny the Jinni, aren't you? You popped out of nowhere, you…"

Sarah looks back with that plea in her eyes, and I bite my tongue on the rest of the invective. Not that I needed to bother. Jinny pretends she didn't hear me as she tows Sarah in a half-run, chattering a-mile-a-minute. I swear she does something demony to keep me from catching up with them all the way to Jophiel Hall.

I forget all my renewed plans to murder Jinny as soon as we enter the auditorium. It's a shock to see it overflowing. Not only is every Angel-Graced here, but all the Nephilim, too. None of them was present in the previous Angel Grace 101 lectures when they were delivered by the Academy's Senior angel-graced, Professor Zachary Caine.

It figures, though. The Nephilim all run at any archangel sighting, since they revere them. But it must be an extra draw with Jophiel being the unicorn of archangels.

But it's not only First Years crowding every square inch of the auditorium from stage to exits. There are thousands here today. It's probably everyone in the Academy, professors, administrators and all. The only ones visibly missing are the archangels, and Azazel.

Seems this Jophiel is a rockstar to everyone.

Something flares at my back, only to trickle like a lava stream of sensations down my spine.

I know what it is even before I turn my head around.

Godric. Standing at one of the exits, in his full Praetor regalia.

I almost have a heart attack. One worse than the first time I saw him in it.

He showed up for our Mindscape session a week ago, in that celestial super hero/otherworldly Roman emperor getup. He informed me he was leading a team escorting Michael on a diplomatic mission later. They were still trying to contain the fallout from Zinimar's death, and conducting their own investigations. I was busy marveling at how he now told me stuff of his own accord, and drooling too copiously, to focus on the details he related.

Seems Jophiel's presence is on par with such a weighty undertaking, warranting the pomp and ceremony of him donning his formal threads. They make him look more of a god of ruthless justice than ever, with or without his wings.

To make it worse, he's looking straight at me. In his patented way of making me feel he sees no one else in existence.

As always, my heart hiccups violently in response. It's always the same when I first lay eyes on him, when our gazes clash, and his delves into me.

This man is driving me crazy, with his nonstop jumble of signals.

When he's training me, he's my detached drill sergeant, and I'm a sexless subordinate he has to mercilessly rehabilitate and reshape.

But the moment our "official" time is over, whenever he sees me, he looks at me like that first day, or like that first time in the Arena. Even more, as if he's slowly losing his prodigious control, his razor-sharp mind. As if he's warning me that when they finally snap, there would be no stopping him from taking everything I have, everything I am. It both exhilarates and scares me out of my own messed-up mind.

I'm so engrossed in our hot, sweaty visual tussle, I don't notice the hush that falls over the crowd, until I hear the blood hurtling in my ears.

It still takes Godric tearing his gaze away to make me crash back to reality, and snap mine ahead. It's only then I see her.

Jophiel. The one female archangel. Walking onto the stage, alone, no accompanying entourage like the archangels' Sentry, Azazel's Cadre or Godric's Praetorian Guard.

Oh. My. Archangel.

36

Every superlative thing I thought when I first saw the archangels turns to ash at the sight of their supposed sister. If a star can take humanoid form, that's how it would look. Jophiel certainly shines like one.

But though her light fills the auditorium with such intensity it whitewashes everyone, it isn't blinding. It seems to be reflecting from within our bodies, our beings. It certainly doesn't feel like anything on the spectrum of regular light.

So, heavenly light? The illumination of knowledge and imagination?

Whatever it is, it's an entrance to end all entrances.

As her light dims, more of her details come into focus.

Almost as tall as her brothers, she has blue-black hair that falls to her ankles, contrasting starkly with the pure white of her wings and Roman-like toga. But maybe I should call the flowing, gold-trimmed garment Angelic, since as Lorcan said, they came first.

Adding to the compelling simplicity of her outfit is a lone adornment; a medallion that rests on her ample chest, hanging there without a chain. It strobes like a beacon, as if absorbing her light, storing it until she unleashes it again. Once its brightness dies down, and even from that distance, I can see its intricate etchings and filigree. Those look like a cross between the angelic runes of Godric's tattoo and the patterns on my bottle.

As she stops at the podium, I can hear and feel the sighs of delight emptying everyone's chest. I can't blame them. From the stunning bone structure of her face, to the masterful strokes of her features to that power and grace of her figure, she's the epitome of femininity and finesse.

But it's those glowing lilac eyes that mesmerize me. I can see them inspiring humanity to explore the best of their collective existence with a glance. A glance like the one she's bestowing on the crowd now. I feel its effect permeating me with urges I never felt before; the drive to shatter limitations, to covet knowledge and aspire to greatness.

"This is exactly what I always hoped for."

Jophiel's voice blankets the space like all the supernatural bigshots who addressed us here. But unlike them, the awe it inspires has no intimidating components. That's a voice people would follow through fire willingly.

"This congregation of the unlike," Jophiel elaborates, sweeping one graceful arm to encompass the auditorium. "This integration of the disparate."

I can swear she sprinkled angel dust or something, and that it has settled on everyone, as I again feel the generalized sigh of rapt content-ment. And that's before she floats down from the stage and heads towards us. Exclamations overlap in a crescendo as everyone realizes what she means to do. They die abruptly as she starts ascending one passage separating the rows of seats.

"I always believed learning can bring all beings together," she says, taking her lecture to her audience. "Learning about oneself, about the other, and about shared histories. We cannot hope to coexist without learning about what brings us together, and what keeps us apart. The only other alternative is constant conflict, and unending war."

She stops a dozen rows below us, and I feel all in her proximity fidgeting, as if with the need to kneel or maybe throw themselves at her feet. This lady is radiating something more powerful than Azazel's compulsion. It's all the stronger because her spell is devoid of dread, of coercion, generating voluntary, no—eager obedience. I think even the demons around are as smitten.

Jophiel inclines her head as her gaze sweeps the presence in tran-quility and empathy. "Everyone present today thinks that this current integration happened under enforced injunctions. That left to their own devices, none of the races would choose this practice of diversifying the student body, of training side by side with those they've historically considered other, even enemy."

Uh, yeah? That's exactly what everyone on any side thinks. They believe that clause in the Accords is as ridiculous and loathsome as it is binding. Is she going to provide a different perspective? And would even her influence make a difference to the entrenched sentiments?

"You may also think it is hypocritical to preach integration, then practice the counterproductive regulations that negate it. Like binding students from other races so they would never share any of the secrets and methods they learn here, and vice versa at the corresponding Academies of the Infernal, Fae, Elven and Vampire Courts, and the various Shifter Domains, Mage Guilds and Sorcerers' Cabals."

Wait, what? There are more academies apart from Pandemonium? Every race has them, and they've all been exchanging students since the Apocalypse?

I can see a thousand new questions hurtling Godric's way. Strange how it doesn't occur to me to ask the more amenable Lorcan or Gideon. It never does. I relish poking him too much. And when he eventually caves, ah, the joy!

Jophiel resumes her slow progress among the sections, drawing more swooning gasps from those she passes. "But I, more than anyone, know that acquiring knowledge is tortuously slow and inescapably cumulative, and that the acceptance of its lessons is even slower and harder. That's why it was imperative to start the process even in the most unfavorable conditions, at the very nascence of the Accords, to accept its imperfections so it *can* start, to disregard the obstacles and the setbacks, and to persist in going forwards no matter the disappointments. There's a very wise adage I learned many of you use, and it's indeed what we're doing here. We're faking it until we make it."

A beat of absolute silence follows, before the crowd bursts out laughing. I laugh too, even if nowhere as unbridled as Sarah or anyone else. But I can really understand their intensifying delight in her. She is an incredible orator, with a spot-on sense of timing—and comedy. A unicorn among archangels indeed.

Then she nears our row and I feel Sarah shivering, as if she might pop like a corn kernel. Before I can take her hand, she grabs mine, and squeezes—hard. She too has been getting stronger than I ever imagined.

Jophiel pauses, and her gaze stills. On Sarah. When I've been the target of everyone's curiosity so far. Sarah's grip on my hand starts to hurt, her color and breathing rising. I squeeze her hand tighter, trying to vent her agitation at being in an archangel's focus, before she hyperventilates.

"But all the faking in the world couldn't amount to anything, if the intention of making it didn't exist. And this is why I'm here now," Jophiel says, her voice softening, her gaze unwavering from Sarah's trembling face. "Because this year I felt a shift in the balance that had remained in a stalemate for too long. This shift brings with it the chance for real and positive change—and this shift is you."

I almost think she means Sarah in specific before her gaze finally, mercifully moves away, blanketing the crowd, leaving Sarah a mess of tearful tremors.

Jophiel walks on, taking her enthrallment elsewhere. "This shift is every Angel-Graced and Demon-Blighted here today, and in every other Supernatural Academy. For the first time in history the representation of humans reflects their importance to the scales of existence. And that's why I am here. As the one archangel who had the most interaction with humanity, I know firsthand what greatness they're capable of. I've overseen the best of them as they brightened this realm with their aspirations for a better world, and their burning desire to leave a legacy before mortality reclaimed their essences. I know how they maintained the balance for the rest of us.

"And here you are at last, not only enough of the best of your race to make a difference within our ranks, but imbued by our powers and burdens, and therefore, uniquely positioned and qualified to provide a vital input and make a critical impact. I am here to shepherd that input, to nurture that impact, to regulate everyone else's interactions…" She pauses and sweeps her gaze towards the side where the Nephilim separated themselves. "And to check their egos."

I laugh heartily at that, tossing a taunting glance back at Godric. I'm so thrilled to find him already brooding at me, I don't realize I'm the only one who laughed—until a few thousand eyes' worth of disapproval and disgust bombard me from all sides.

Hey, she made a joke! And she paused after delivering it, waiting for them to laugh at her dig. It's not my fault they're stuck-up freaks on one side, and cowering cowards on the other!

I almost die of mortification nonetheless. Then I almost die, period.

Godric winked at me.

He *winked*. At *me*. A slow sweep of sensuality. Premeditated. Targeted. Devastating.

With every inch of me combusting, I know he knows exactly what it did to me. Vengeance scenarios crowd my mind as he serenely turns his gaze away, as if he didn't just give me a heart attack.

That tormenting, confounding bastard.

As Jophiel continues her wandering, I can no longer hear her above the roar of blood in my head. Even when the upheaval he caused with that momentous little blink starts to subside, I can't understand a word she says anymore, until thunder rocks me out of my daze.

It takes me heart-pounding moments to realize it's applause.

Everyone is on their feet, giving Jophiel a standing ovation.

Not knowing if she said something new to warrant the storm of adulation, I rise at Sarah's trembling prodding, and clap too.

With a final tranquil bow of her head to acknowledge our homage, Jophiel's light intensifies until it washes out everything in the hall. When it dies down, she's gone.

As if freed from another brand of compulsion, excited voices rise like a roaring sea as everyone move towards the exits. The humans fall back, making way for the faculty and the Nephilim.

I look around for Godric. I *need* to follow up on that wink!

But my Dr. Jekyll and Mr. Hyde mentor and tormentor is gone.

That semi-celestial tease!

So I know he didn't disappear on purpose. As Praetor, he always has world-shaking-and-shaping things to do. I, and continuing to mess with my head and hormones, don't even feature on the totem pole of his priorities. I also know he gives me his priceless time and attention only because he's forced to. Anything he does around me is under duress, and against his will, his very nature. So it's nothing to celebrate about if I mess with his head and hormones, too. If I do, it must be a side effect of his constant exposure to me, and maybe to my mysterious power. And it probably doesn't bode well for my life expectancy.

I should abstain from provoking the monster he keeps in check, shouldn't even fantasize about breaking its shackles. Then once our forced proximity is over, we'll both be free of each other's maddening and unwanted effect.

That all sounds good on paper. In practice, I'm helpless to do anything but the very opposite. From that very first day, every second with him has been the same. Prudence flies out the window, and self-preservation is nowhere to be found. And it's been getting worse every day of the past month.

It's still impossible to believe it's only been that long since he descended on me like the darkest fate. It feels like a lifetime ago when he shattered my plans, and confiscated my choice. I hated him and being leashed to him then.

I still do, but it's getting harder to imagine a day that doesn't revolve around our sessions together. And it's only in part about my delight in my physical transformation. Most of it is about being with him, and being embroiled in our intensifying war of wits and wills.

Which is ridiculous, since I should be counting the days until I'm free of him. *He* must be counting the *seconds* until he's rid of me.

Knowing that doesn't stop me from being dejected whenever he's forced to even cut short our training. Now, I feel deflated at his absence, especially after that damn wink!

Wanting to kick myself in the head for being so stupid and contrary, I focus back on Sarah and the others—only to realize something unprecedented is happening.

All my roommates are talking. Together. Or I should say exclaiming and tittering over one another. Over Jophiel and her every detail and word. Even Aela, when I didn't think this paragon is capable of admiring anyone, even the archangel who's supposed to be her aunt. But just like the others, she's gushing like a starstruck groupie.

I have to agree with my fangirling companions, though. Jophiel is the ultimate in girl-power goals. Mind-boggling beauty, authority, intellect and accomplishments. And boy, can she give a speech.

After we exit the auditorium, Sarah loiters at the doors, as if hoping to catch another glimpse of her. I grin at her hero-worshipping expression. Sarah has found her ultimate role model. Gotta admit, she has impeccable taste. That lady archangel is something else, in every literal sense.

To my chagrin, Jinny says just that, if more colorfully and effectively than I would have.

"Okay, gotta admit, this Jophiel chick can give you angelic blowhards a good name." Jinny smirks mainly at Aela. "The first non-pompous Heavenly entity I've ever seen. And the first interesting and intelligent one, too. If you had a brain among you, you'd make her your spokeswoman—or your empress. But since you don't, we all miss out on having a worthy frontlady for your snooze-fest collective."

"I assure you, cadet, I *am* their frontlady—when and where it counts."

I freeze, and so do all the others. That voice is unmistakable.

I'm the first one who turns to face her. This up close, with those wings arched above her, Jophiel looks ten feet tall. The others turn one after the other, each sporting some awed or agitated expression. Sarah staggers around last, leaning on me.

As I support almost her full weight, Jophiel smiles. "Who do you think conceived and mostly established the Accords? And added the mandatory integration clauses of the Academies?"

The first one to recover is Jinny, who smirks up at that goddess. "That's more like it. I wondered for years how these testosterone-addled bastards on either side could have come up with something that comprehensive." Then she frowns. "Though now I know who to blame for being carted off to this angelically-plagued academy."

As Aela's gaze impales Jinny with murderous disgust, Jophiel only inclines her majestic head graciously. "I can see how a high-ranking demon would find being steeped in angelic company less than savory. But this is exactly why I'm here. It's time the intended integration went from a nominal and forced situation to an applied and mutually bene-ficial one. It *is* in everyone's best interests to lay our eternal conflicts to rest."

Jinny shrugs. "I'd say dream on, but hey, if you managed to teach some humans to rise above their base natures, I don't put anything beyond you. It'll be fun to see you try."

Aela practically shoves Jinny behind her, clearly not realizing she's going against Jophiel's wishes as she nods solemnly at her. "It's an honor to finally meet you, Archangel Jophiel."

Jophiel's gaze lengthens, at the crimson smoke bleeding from Jinny's nostrils, but more at Aela's scornful action and snooty expres-sion. Yep. She isn't impressed with Aela missing the whole point of her presence here.

Just as I feel everyone start to buckle under her focus, she waves an elegant hand that can probably swat away an army. "Please, Raphaela, don't stand on ceremony. True respect only suffers under pretensions, but flourishes with sincerity. It's my brothers who are enlisting you in their army, and chain of command works for them as your generals. But I am only your teacher, and I've always been Jophiel to my students. Since we're family, too, Aunt will also do."

Aela's spectacular face blazes with color, and she looks flustered for the first time as she nods again. "Aunt."

It's strange hearing this Aunt bit, when Jophiel looks at most a few years older than Aela. But I do feel the vast difference in age between them, far more than I do between Azrael and Godric. Especially when Aela feels as young as she looks, when that's not the case with Godric.

But I also feel that Jophiel is not as old as Azrael. Which makes sense. Death must be as old as life itself. Still, I have no doubt Jophiel is untold millennia old. The endlessness of her history is like a silent storm engulfing us all into the stillness of its eye.

The sheer weight of her wisdom permeates the air as she reaches out to touch Aela's chiseled cheekbone, so much like hers. "I've heard so much about you, Raphaela, and about your successes. I look forward to learning more about you and about your earthly endeavors. Come see me anytime."

Aela nods jerkily, struck dumb. Seems only archangels can silence these archangelspawn pains.

Jophiel lowers her hand and turns her gaze toward us. "Sarah Conrad, Wen White, walk with me."

37

I gape at the archangel as one thing fills my mind.

How does she know our names?

And just *what* am I thinking? This is the freaking archangel of knowledge, basically. She probably knows everything there is to know in the universe. What matters here is this "walk with me" part.

What can she possibly want with us in specific?

Did her "brothers" tell her about me? And she's—what? Curious? If so, why include Sarah in her curiosity? Why do I feel she's its main target?

My own curiosity has to wait as I catch Sarah before she collapses beside me. Jinny rushes to support her on the other side, trying to pull her away from me. It's really getting old, her fighting me for my spot as Sarah's best friend.

I bare my teeth at her over Sarah's head, then almost smack hers when she simpers up at Jophiel, "Can I come with?"

Jophiel gives her a courteous nod. "I'll be happy to walk with you, Jinny, at a later date. Now, I would like to have a private word with your friends."

"She's no friend of mine…"

"I'm only Sarah's friend…"

My and Jinny's objections falter under Jophiel's tranquil gaze. Her expression hasn't changed, but I bet Jinny felt her disapproval smack her over the mouth, too. As for the others, the gaze she transfers to them seems like a dismissal of archangelic proportions. This celestial lady might be benevolent, but she just let us know it's not wise to test her forbearance. Rather than fear, it's the threat of losing her regard that motivates us to obey her wishes.

Aela and Cara slink away without a moment's delay. Jinny relinquishes Sarah's support to me, but her visual skewer blames me for Jophiel's exclusion. Of course. Though she does glower at Jophiel, too. That's one demon who isn't afraid to cross any angelic entity.

Must be nice being an archdemon that even archangels consider an equal.

But Jophiel doesn't acknowledge her this time. It's as if she no longer registers anything on the mortal plane as she walks away. Sarah stumbles after her, almost tearing out of my hold, as if with the pull of an invisible leash.

I rush to resume supporting her, glancing at Jophiel sourly. "Take it easy on Sarah, will you?"

Jophiel slows her stride, looking back in surprise. "I apologize. I didn't realize I was going too fast."

"You're not. You're just..." I toss my free hand to encompass her. "...*you.*" Then I nod down at Sarah who's still blinking mutely up at Jophiel. It's as if she's no longer aware I'm there. "I've never seen anything hit Sarah harder."

Jophiel's incredible lilac gaze grows thoughtful as she looks down into Sarah's dazed eyes, before she raises them to me. "But I'm not having the same effect on you, hmm?"

I shrug. "I've seen enough archangels up close, I guess. It's no longer a novelty."

Her gaze becomes knowing. "But you weren't affected from your first exposure to my kin."

Heat rushes to my cheeks. "Ugh. I hope your brothers didn't go into too much detail about that—incident."

"You mean when you called them names?"

"I only called Azrael a...." I stop, almost swallowing my tongue.

"...a pompous ass," Jophiel completes for me.

"Holy shi—I mean—ugh," I groan. "I can't believe they told you that! I can't believe I said that."

"But you said it, and to Azrael of all archangels. Not even we have ever dreamed of disputing him, let alone disrespecting him."

Sarah's dazed gaze transfers to me. It dismays her when I insult lesser angelic entities. Now Jophiel shared this little gem from my first meeting with Death Himself. Yep, there's always worse with me.

I wince into her shocked eyes as I mumble, "Yeah, I got the impression I set a precedent there. But he was very—uh, lenient. Probably because he didn't realize I was disrespecting him. He doesn't seem versed in modern lingo."

Jophiel's amazing eyes flare a more intense violet before she murmurs, "Azrael knows far more than he lets on."

My eyebrows shoot up. "How do you know that if he doesn't let on? From the experience of millennia as his sister?"

"It has nothing to do with experience. I don't believe my other brothers, who had much closer interactions with him throughout the eons, know that about him."

"So it's female intuition? Yours must be a superpower in its own right, after said eons of being the only female in such a family of all-powerful males."

She gives a slow blink that multiples her allure and forces me to sigh, before she looks away. "I suppose."

"So you mean he got my insults, and let them go?"

Her unfathomable gaze returns to me. "Probably because they *were* unprecedented. When you've existed for as long as we have, unprecedented is an unimaginable concept. We've witnessed and experienced everything, too many times."

"So you're saying he found my insolence—what? A refreshing jolt in a desensitized eternity?"

She nods. "In our world, anything novel, or inexplicable, warrants as unique a response."

Inexplicable, huh? So she knows why her "kin" dragged me here?

I somehow doubt that. There must have been a reason only five archangels attended my arraignment. Telling her I pompous-assed Azrael doesn't mean they told her everything.

But whatever they told her, one thing's for sure. *I'm* not telling her anything. If she already knows what they do, more info and her fathomless insight can work out what they *don't* know. The secrets Godric would kill to keep hidden. The archangels must be exempt from that threat, but exposure would instigate conflict with his folks. And it's not in my best interests to be in the middle of a celestial family feud.

Jophiel regards me as if she's following my every thought. Which

268

must be all in my guilty imagination, since archangels have this free-will clause tattooed on their frontal lobes.

But I'm not taking my chances. I need to lower the volume of my thoughts, so they don't trip her mental wires. Especially since she's taking this walk with us, clearly for answers she can't get anywhere else.

A serene smile touches her lips, as if acknowledging my worry, and assuring me I can let it go.

I'm debating if I can trust her when she says, "Not that Azrael would have punished or even berated you, regardless. It's not his temper or his ego that make him the force all beings fear."

"Who needs temper or ego when you're Death incarnate?" I scoff.

"He's not exactly that."

I blink at the quieter timber of Jophiel's voice. It's as if what he truly is disturbs her.

Does she *fear* Azrael? Can even immortal beings be afraid of the Archangel of Death? Why?

And if he disturbs his supposed sibling, how come I had such kindred feelings toward him?

My rationalization, that Death's texture is familiar to me on a genetic level, no longer holds water. Not after I saw how other mortals were terrified of him, down to those very genes.

So why doesn't he terrify me like he does everyone else, even her?

I would have asked if I thought it prudent to. But that might be among the info she needs to work out the stuff I don't want exposed. I'll have to rely on Godric, and my own investigations, to work out my Abomination status.

Out loud, I ask different questions. "So what is he? Come to think of it, I never gave much thought to his job description. I mean, how does he reap a hundred thousand souls a day? You know, those who die of different causes every day globally? What's the logistics of that? Where does he send or keep them?"

Jophiel doesn't say anything for long moments. Just as I think she won't comment, she says, "Valid questions all. No one but him knows their answers for certain."

Wow. So even the archangels don't know such fundamental stuff about Azrael?

This validates my idea that he came first. And he's been keeping his cards so close to his chest, his so-called siblings only have theories about what he is and what he does.

But what about Godric? Does he know more about his father?

She inclines her head at me. "Maybe when you see him next, and can refrain from disrespecting him, directly or through disparaging his firstborn, you can ask him for all of us."

"Can't promise that..." My laugh chokes in my chest at Sarah's whimper.

But what really stuns me into silence is realizing Jophiel means it.

She wants to know, and seemingly can't ask. Yet she thinks I can, and that Azrael might answer me, about something so ultimate as how Death actually works.

Whoa.

We walk in silence as I try to digest this, until I decide to resume our earlier subject. "I do get that Azrael is above the petty reactions to be expected from any other being. But if he got my insults, and they were the first in his history, I don't get why he was actually courteous. He must really be the opposite of his Godawful son..." Sarah's fingers dig in my supporting forearm, and I grimace at Jophiel. "Why don't you talk and I'll shut up? The more I say the worse I make it."

Jophiel waves my chagrin away. "Like I told Raphaela, I appreciate candor and sincerity above all else."

She lets my gaze go as she turns a corner. I realize we're in a place I've never seen, since I've only been where I have classes. But this area seems so extensive, I feel I can walk for a day and not cover it all. I don't even know if we're still in her namesake building.

But as we enter another section, I just know we are. Maybe even her private wing. It resonates with her presence, as if its building materials were mixed with it. They probably were.

She leads us into a corridor that makes the one leading to our dorm room look tiny. The whole left side is a floor-to-ceiling worked-silver vitrine. It's teeming with artworks and artifacts that gleam and luminesce as if with some internal light.

Midway, Jophiel stops before a panel centered by a life-size statue of an angel. It's emitting that same sourceless glow, but it intensifies as I approach with Sarah, until it's almost as bright as that blazing angel.

But while that statue had brutal feet planted on the remains of his sacrifices, and was overpoweringly male, this one is floating in place, and androgynous. Or it is, until its form starts morphing. When it stops, it has become voluptuously female.

So is it responding to Jophiel's proximity, and would turn male in the presence of one of her brothers? Why?

Not that this is important. Only one thing is. Jophiel. And the way she's looking at Sarah. It fills me with the urge to push Sarah behind me, to insulate her against the unsettling interest in the archangel's eyes.

But since I can't do that, I resort to recapturing the archangel's focus with my own super power, the ability to ask endless questions.

"So, Jophiel, what else did your brothers tell you about me?"

Yeah, I know I said I'm not telling her anything. But I have to keep her away from Sarah, even at the cost of possible exposure.

But this lady has interacted with humans for millennia, and must know all their tricks. Without the need to read my mind, I feel certain she sees through my pathetic efforts to distract her.

"They told me enough," she finally says.

If that isn't a conversation ender, I don't know what is.

Before I can think of something else to say, she reaches out a hand to Sarah. "May I?"

Sarah's arm jerks out of my grip as, like a marionette yanked by its string. I don't let go of her as she places her shaking hand in Jophiel's palm, more worried now.

The moment their hands touch, that pervasive light that emanated from Jophiel during her lecture flares. It merges with that of the statue behind her, the combination blanking out everything.

It's not only the world that seems to disappear. I can no longer feel Sarah's arm under my hand, or my hand itself. Or my whole body.

For suspended moments that could be a couple of heartbeats or a short eternity, I transcend my physical form. It's different from the way it happens in the Mindscape. Yet both experiences have something in common. They gnaw at me with- clusiveness. With so many things I can't fathom. Things I feel I should know. Should remember.

When the celestial flare dies down, I find myself alone, facing the now-dimming angel statue.

The moment I can move, I whirl around, heart in my throat. My gaze first slams into Jophiel, who's standing two feet away, staring down. Then I follow her focus, and find Sarah.

She's on the ground, convulsing!

Crying out in fright, I crash to my knees beside her. But before I reach for her, something barrels into me, knocking me aside.

Jinny!

My first impulse is to pounce on her, come what may. But in the last wisps of my fleeing rationality, I realize she's turning Sarah to her side, opening her mouth gently and shoving a crimson handkerchief there. So Sarah won't swallow her tongue or bite it off, or choke if she vomits.

Vaguely wondering why a demon would know mortal first-aid, I still want to pummel her away, take care of Sarah myself. But I know I won't be able to budge her, and I grudgingly admit she's doing a perfect job. While I have something as important to do. Stopping whatever is happening to Sarah at the source.

Heaving up to my feet, I yell at the archangel, "Whatever the hell you're doing to her, stop it—*now!*"

Seemingly unaware of me, Jophiel continues to stare down at Sarah, a rapt expression coating her heavenly face. I'm about to blast her again when I register what I'm seeing. Her Angel Essence, swarming all around her like a solar storm.

It's on a whole different level from the usual fare. The dragon to the angels' falcon like I once thought. Nowhere as amazing to me as Godric's, but it *is* stunning.

More stunning is that I'm seeing it at all. I thought archangels didn't experience any strong emotions. But there's no doubt here. Jophiel is experiencing a potent one as she gazes down at my convulsing friend.

And it incenses me.

Self-preservation and every other caution disintegrating, I launch myself at her, grabbing her by the arms. It's like sinking my fingers into supple steel. *Electrified* supple steel. But the jolt only makes me angrier. Hungrier.

And it happens again. Hurtling into that out-of-body state while fully aware. But this time it's not that sudden expansion that engulfs me, it's more like an explosion.

Caught in the shockwave, I no longer see the entranced archangel, just her Essence. My mind empties of everything but need. To take it all. To *hurt* her…

"Wen, stop!"

Sarah.

Her plea blows away the vicious haze, and tears my hands off the archangel. I swing around so hard, I almost trip over my legs when I see her sitting up with Jinny's help.

Crashing down beside her, my hands flit over her head. She might have hit it when she fell. This might be why she had this seizure. She might have a concussion—or a cranial bleed!

But I find no bumps. And her stricken expression is fading as she gazes up at Jophiel, a blissed-out one replacing it.

I exchange a worried glance with Jinny of all demons.

"Are you okay, Sar?" I ask, shivering with unspent fright and aggression.

"I'm more than okay." She continues staring up at Jophiel, lips spreading in an exquisite smile. "Thank you."

"What the hell are you thanking her for?" I exclaim.

Jinny frowns up at Jophiel. "I hate to agree with anything Wen says, but she's right here. Your archangel lady crush just gave you a seizure!"

Sarah pulls away from both of us and gets up to her feet, reprimanding gaze pinning both of us. "What's wrong with you, guys? Of course she didn't do anything to me!"

I jump to my feet, too, already discounting her objection. Sarah has been under the archangel's influence even before she laid eyes on her. "Why else did you have an epileptic fit? Right after she took your hand, and put on that light show? Too much of a coincidence if you ask me."

Jinny rises, too, glower deepening. "Yeah, and I don't believe in coincidences. Put your heroine-worship aside for a sec, Sar. None of us knows what happened after she started glowing. She somehow blanked even my senses. And while we were all out of commission, she did something to you!"

Hating to agree with Jinny again, I add, "And it was premeditated."

"You bet it was," Jinny growls in that hair-raising polyphonic way of hers. "That must be why she insisted on leaving me behind. It's a good thing I followed you!" She glares up at Jophiel, her eyes starting to glow like hot coals. "Out with it, archangel. Why did you single Sarah out, and lure her to this deserted mausoleum? And what did you do to her? "

I square off with Jophiel, too. "And we'll need proof you didn't damage her, and she won't drop into a seizure out of the blue again."

Sarah steps between us and Jophiel, wincing up at her. "I'm sorry they're being this way. I don't remember having a seizure, but it must have rattled them." She looks back at us, eyes filling with a warning to let this go.

Jinny raises a defiant chin, unwilling to back down. Just like I wouldn't, with Sarah's wellbeing at stake. Damn her.

"If you don't remember," Jinny drawls, still glaring at Jophiel. "How are you so sure she didn't do something to you?"

Sarah bites her lip. "Nobody who has a seizure ever remembers it. But I do remember how Jophiel's light felt, and it was anything but damaging! It was as if it illuminated every dark corner in my mind."

I swing my gaze back to Jophiel. "So that was you flooding her with the light of—what? Insight? Inspiration? Why? Why her? What for? And did you overload her brain, and that's why she convulsed?"

Jinny sticks her fists at her sides. "Yeah, what she said."

But I'm not done, continue my bombardment of the archangel. "Shouldn't you know the limits of the human mind after millennia of poking and prodding our collective consciousness? If you don't know when to stop before you drive one of us to convulsions, maybe instead of presuming to teach us about each other, you should be updating your own knowledge!"

Jophiel blinks at me as if unable to credit that anyone would dare question her, let alone this insolently. It must be that unimaginable concept she mentioned earlier. I've gone and given her a disrespectful anecdote she can share with her deadly brother.

She's welcome.

Instead of answering me, she looks at Sarah, a troubled tinge entering her eyes. "I didn't intend for my light to affect you this way, and indeed, that effect was another unprecedented occurrence. I was the one seeking enlightenment."

"What the hell do you mean by that?" I exclaim. "Isn't that your gig? Aren't you the archangel of enlightenment itself? And what does anything you seek have anything to do with Sarah?"

"Yeah, all that again," Jinny hisses. "Stop stalling and answer us!"

Jophiel inclines her head in our direction, as if really registering us again. I think I see the tiniest crack in her composure when she finally says, "It was an effort to accommodate Gabriel's request. He enlisted my help in determining Sarah's nature, what he's uncertain of, but which necessitated inducting her into the Academy."

I snatch a worried glance at Jinny. Jophiel more or less said Sarah isn't Angel-Graced, that there's another reason she's here, one big and baffling enough to stump an archangel.

But if anything, Jinny looks worried, too. Seems that's one area where I don't need to fear her. She's not only rivaling me for the position of Sarah's best friend, but of her protector as well.

I grit my teeth as I resume interrogating Jophiel. "So you probed her? Without her consent? What happened to absolute free will?"

Jophiel seems genuinely taken aback. "I did obtain her consent."

"You mean when you said, 'May I?'" I scoff. "You consider that asking for consent? And when she gave you her hand—because what else could a human do when an archangel asks for it—you considered she granted it? I must have missed the part where you said, 'May I flood your brain with archangelic radiation that may fry it?'"

Jinny takes another aggression-laden step into Jophiel's personal space. "I bet you omitted mentioning any of that on purpose, so don't play dumb, archangel."

I nod. "I also bet you realized she'd give you far more than her hand if you asked for it, without asking why. You manipulated her, put her at risk, and now we don't know…"

"That's *enough*, both of you!"

Jinny and I jerk at the sharpness in Sarah's voice. We turn to find her usually soft expression harsh enough to give us abrasions.

She divides her frown between us equally. "I am right here, and I can speak for myself. You both make me sound like some helpless lemming."

We both grumble defenses, and Sarah raises an adamant hand. "But what I don't accept is you accusing Jophiel of being callous and devious, when she was actually doing me a favor. I've been worrying about what Lorcan saw in me, that made him bring me here. If she said she'd attempt to find out, I would have jumped at the offer. She probably sensed that. I fully believe she didn't expect or can explain that seizure, but I am perfectly fine now. Better than fine. I know it must have been scary for both of you, but that's no excuse for being so rude, and to Jophiel of all beings! So drop it—and apologize!"

Sarah's displeasure is so unknown, it's mortifying. It clearly has the same effect on Jinny since she fidgets on her high-heeled feet and mumbles a sheepish apology to the archangel. Before I can manage one. It makes me hate her even more.

But after I issue the required apology, I have another question for the archangel. "So, was that scan worth the seizure? Did your brand of archangelic MRI reveal any answers?"

After a moment too long, Jophiel says, "It was inconclusive."

"What do you mean inconclusive?" Jinny growls, the spiked collar of Sarah's disapproval forgotten. "You gave her a seizure mucking about her brain for nothing?"

I huff. "Don't bother. It's their favorite answer around here."

But Jophiel seems to have considered the episode over, and is already walking back where we came from. Before we can pursue her with more questions, Sarah's glance of disappointment is enough to deter us both.

On the way back, I find myself walking beside Jophiel, with Jinny keeping Sarah beside her. Blood boiling at her petty tactics, I still consider this an opportunity to ask one more thing of Jophiel. It isn't the best idea, but I really want to know.

Not knowing how to draw her attention when she's gazing into infinity, probably for real, I pipe up, "If you wanted to scan Sarah, why have me along? What did you want with me?"

She doesn't answer until we're back to the main auditorium building, then she gazes down at me. "Why do you assume I wanted anything? I could have asked you to come as Sarah's best friend, so that your company would make her more comfortable."

"You could have, but you didn't. So why?"

Her eyes simmer purple, until I feel I might tumble into the depths of their endless history.

Then they fill with something I can only describe as melancholy. "Evil wasn't created, Wen White, it was chosen. With the most solid of convictions. While good stands on shakier ground, is made of more friable fabric. And as they feud, the victor has never been either, but what lurks in the end, and at the beginning."

Huh? Where did that come from? And why does it squeeze my heart dry even when I don't understand any of it?

I shake my head, as if to tear down the creepy cobwebs her words spun inside it. "Is this your way of getting out of answering, or did you scramble your own brains back there?"

Her gaze grows grim even as a mystifying smile touches her exquisite lips. "Remember that, Wen White, when the time comes. Convictions can reverse, when existence stretches long enough. Good and evil no longer exist, only choice. Choice, and chaos."

Before I can say anything to that lofty-sounding word-salad, her light intensifies again, then she's gone.

I gape after her, before realizing that Jinny has overtaken me by a hundred feet, dragging Sarah with her toward our dorm. This time I don't rush to catch up, weighed down by a thousand new questions.

By now, I'm getting good at waiting for answers, or not expecting any at all. Okay, okay, so I'm being forced into both virtues.

This world of immortals will only give up its secrets when it wishes. Or not at all.

There's nothing I can do about it but go with the flow of its tempestuous current. And hope it will eventually satisfy my curiosity.

At least, before it kills me.

38

"You're going to kill me!"

My gasp shears through lungs filled with glass shards as I curl on my side, every muscle spasming uselessly.

Ominous and lethal, Godric towers over me where he threw me to the ground. Without touching me, of course.

Flopping onto my back, I look up into the face I've grown addicted to, in spite of all my efforts not to, and pant, "I see…your plan now. You tried to…get me exempted…and failed. You're now down to… your last option. Killing me…to make me miss…the Imperium Trials."

The Imperium Trials which are today.

I still can't believe it has been two months since he first loomed over me like this. Sixty-three days to be exact. A crammed-full-of-events blur that feels like a year, a whole new life. Where he's concerned, it's been an exacting, exhausting blur that has taken me to the edge of human endurance and way, way beyond.

And I am *only* human no matter what that magnificent monster says.

"Get. Up."

I can't even shake my head as I croak, "No. Can. Do."

Next moment, I feel the world tilting beneath me when his expression suddenly brightens.

I go blind for seconds. From the blast of mind-scrambling male

278

beauty and charisma. A brooding or bedeviling Godric is devastation incarnate. A beaming one? Wholesale annihilation.

"You're over three hours."

This shocks me enough, I lurch up on my elbows. "No way!"

"Way." He tosses me a towel, his lips pursing, as if catching himself about to smile is a capital offense.

Yeah, he still has me on that rollercoaster.

It's a given he remains Death Jr., my drill sergeant. But he keeps having those bouts when he watches me as if nothing else exists, when he forgets to be Angelhole around me. *Then* he catches himself in the act. Tension builds until he reverts to full Godawful mode, and the leash is back in public.

But his slip-ups have been increasing, until that other Godric who wants to devour me breaks through. I thought I was getting better at withstanding the savagery of his lust-igniting glances, until those progressed to almost-touches. Those leave me scrambled for days.

Rinse and repeat.

If it wasn't for Sarah, and fearing to leave her alone in this world, I would have climbed and begged him to give in, to take me until he finishes me already.

I sigh as I wipe off the sweat pouring into my eyes. "You're trying to motivate me for today, right?"

He rumbles a pseudo-chuckle deep in his chest, and I almost faint. With arousal this time. Making it worse, he bends to stick his face closer to mine, letting his mouth-watering scent flood my laboring lungs. Adding another dose of inflammation, he waves a hand in my face. A hand I want to grab, suckle and bite into. A hand I need all over me.

"Do you see me? Do you know who I am? You think I'd exaggerate to make you feel better? I would think that's a concussion talking if you didn't execute that last landing perfectly."

Rubbing my legs together, trying to subdue the molten pounding between them, I glare up at him. "Then you're being your Angelhole self, giving me false hope so I'd get up, only so you can toss me around some more."

His gaze follows my movements—against his prodigious will, as I suspect—skittering mini-bolts over my thighs, and cascading magma inside my core. And that's before I glimpse the daunting bulge that conquers the tightness of his pants, and the camouflage of his Glamor.

Knowing I affect him like he affects me was a delight—at first. Now it only pours gasoline on the fire of my frustration.

Not only because he won't act on those potentially-catastrophic sensual threats, since I have serious doubts I'd survive *that*, but because I'm rooming with so many girls. I can't relieve myself in his honor anymore, except in hurried and literal anti-climaxes. My own inexperience and hang-ups have also been thwarting me. I still balk at visualizing his fully naked body, let alone having it all over and inside mine, doing to me all the wild, wanton things I'm disintegrating for. The unspent desire keeps accumulating, and my condition keeps worsening.

I'm in such bad shape, the mere outline of his arousal has my heart slamming around my chest, and my body primed and screaming for his invasion.

As if giving in at last to its silent pleas, he leans closer, closer, those hands that can sunder mountains flexing and opening, like they're itching to possess and plunder me. A moan of suffering escapes my lips.

Suddenly, the lightning storm skittering in his eyes subsides, and his Glamor is back in full force, hiding the object of my feverish cravings.

Shaking his head as if coming out of a trance, he straightens, taking his temptation out of reach. He completes his reversion to Angelhole mode as he drawls, "As if I need such elaborate maneuvers to toss you around. You did pass three hours. By six minutes, to be exact."

I gape up at him, arousal dwindling as his words sink in.

He means it!

The last time I asked about my progress was three weeks ago. Even with my leaps and bounds of improvement, I had barely passed the one-and-a-half-hour mark.

He has escalated pushing my limits to a killer medley of strength training, cardiovascular endurance, flexibility and agility remolding, precision conditioning and pain tolerance. All disciplines are in the service of that grueling, almost-impossible-to-grasp-and perform angelic martial art technique called *Melek*.

He euphemistically dubbed his torture routine Phase One. Its goal? To make it the whole three hours without reaching failure. Or vomiting. Whichever comes first.

I've done both regularly. Usually simultaneously. Yeah, it's a miracle he doesn't call me Barf or Puke by now.

Besides that, there's the almost as taxing daily battles as disembodied forces in the Mindscape. I still don't fully know what happens after he sucks my consciousness in there, but I'm now aware it's happening, and retain some memories after I exit, especially of that thing inside me.

When I first told him, he called it massive progress. My happy dance was *very* undignified. I've been *yearning* for any at all in that department.

Though I've been getting stronger than I ever thought possible, as he pledged—not during the routine itself, when I feel I'm dying a thousand painful deaths—I thought I would surely die before I completed his impossible three hours in one go.

But I did it! I'm *six minutes* past his target! The girl who just weeks ago couldn't complete one push up. From the knees. Today I gave him the twenty he demanded that first time, in perfect form, plus twenty more. In under a minute.

"You're officially ready for Phase Two," he purrs, sounding too pleased with himself.

I would have loved to smack the smugness off that mouth, by hand, then by lips.

Phase Two. Ugh.

Just the idea that he has worse in store for me makes me flop back in a boneless heap. "Couldn't you let me bask in my achievement for one more minute?"

He consults that Nephilim-grade wearable of his. "You've been basking for four."

"I've been trying not to die," I groan. "And I think I deserve some kind of reward, before you toss me over an even higher cliff."

His lips twitch as if fighting a harder-to-resist smile. "Phase Two *is* your reward."

"With rewards like these, who needs punishment?"

But though I'm whining, I grin up at him like a lunatic. I'm fully recuperated already. Not to mention those amazing endorphins I never thought I could produce are flooding my body. And it's all thanks to that beautiful slave driver.

He stares down at me, at my *lips*, as if transfixed, then his eyes start emitting that hypnotic, heart-stopping emerald. What I've only ever seen in response to me.

Early on, I realized the lava and obsidian lightning are shock and awe techniques, when he wants to scare someone shitless. I now see the difference when they're a spontaneous reaction. They're even scarier then.

But even without those light shows, I've come to decipher the dizzying range of his eyes' expressions, when I first thought they could only spew arrogance and violence.

Now there's something new in them. Not exasperation or resignation or provocation. It's not cold command or searing lust, either. It's more like...

No, I don't want to give it a name. I won't. I'm probably wrong anyway.

When I finally rise to my feet, he documents how I do it, in the no-hands method he taught me through so much sweat, and some literal tears. He says in Phase Two I'll master that elastic-rebound one he does, what should be impossible with his mass and height. The first time he demonstrated it, I burst out that I *hate* him. He shouldn't be this agile, as well as everything else.

At least I learned the handless method. He inclines his head at me in silent approval. The approval I've come to crave. To *need*.

The now-familiar electricity of gratification races through me. It shoots to my fingers, making them ache to stab into the luxury of his mane, drag him down by it, bring those lush lips down to mine, wrap those steel hips in my legs, and grind my aching core against that...

Down, girl.

With a glance that says he realizes my condition, he walks away to the Arena's exit.

As I follow him, I know what he's doing, too. Putting distance between us. So as not to encourage the Abomination-Who-Shouldn't-Exist's intensifying crush.

There. I admitted it. Beyond the mind-scrambling lust, I have a crush on him. As massive and overpowering as he is.

Not that it should be a big deal. I wouldn't be alive if I didn't crush on him. The whole female student body shares my condition, and a percentage of the male one, too. Those who don't swoon at his mention or approach, hero-worship him. It's a unanimous state for any being with brain waves.

All his haughtiness and heartlessness aside—what everyone thinks he has every right to, and worship him more for it—the guy *is* irresistible.

The worst part? This crush isn't hate-fueled anymore.

Though I still loathe him with the old ferocity at times, he's been giving me less reasons to hate his guts. And many reasons to salivate like Pavlov's dog when I even think of him. Since this is almost all the time, we are talking *a lot* of drool.

Problem is, it's not only that he's gorgeous and powerful beyond measure, and his attraction is on par with a planet's gravity. Those things are givens. But I've been discovering other things that appeal to me terribly. Even the terrible parts.

Like he's been probing and investigating me, I've been observing and researching him. The latter by interrogating Lorcan, then expanding on his tidbits at the Metatron Library.

That has been no mean feat, since it sprawls over six buildings, and all volumes are in angelic script. As freshmen, we're now allowed there for only two hours, twice a week. We can't check out books, and that auto-translate feature is unreliable. When it works, context and nuance are mostly jumbled or missing.

I still gleaned some juicy info on Godric. Like that he graduated five years ago. His class was the fifteenth since the Academy reopened after the Accords were signed.

I also learned the first Nephilim cadets after the reopening were born in the decades after the Apocalypse started—*long* before it came to earth. How long ago *that* was, those who know, aren't telling. Which means Godric might or might not be as young as he looks. I choose to believe he's late twenties.

If not, at least he isn't a few thousand years old. I hope. That's how old some of the Nephilim in existence are. They are the ones Celestial Academy was built for millennia ago. But from all I gathered, their relationship to both their parents' races has always been—problematic.

Yet it was when they didn't side with Heaven during the Apocalypse that the angels realized they were a lost cause.

Thinking they've learned their lesson in raising half-angels, they decided to start fresh, and sired a new generation. Their goal: to make their new offspring warriors the likes of which existence has never seen.

From Godric's example, they're succeeding spectacularly.

The story goes that after the Apocalypse fizzled out, and the angels came to Earth to stay, they rounded up their new offspring, and brought them to the Academy to start their training.

Which brings me to some of the terrible things I learned about Godric. Not things he did—though those were many and varied—but what was done to him.

Turns out the Nephilim are taken from their mothers, and raised by the *Cultores*, a sect of angel worshippers. This happens when they are six to ten years of age, when their powers start to manifest. Though their full extent develops later in life like Astaroth explained, what manifests this early is formidable enough, mere humans can't withstand it, let alone help Nephilim children handle it. This still means they have some sort of childhood, before being drafted into the life of a soldier in the Army of Heaven.

Not so Godric.

As the first archangelic Nephilim, Godric's powers manifested at birth. The *Cultores* took him then.

It almost made me hurl, reading about the methods those fanatics use to teach the Nephilim to recognize and control their powers. Some are beyond horrific. And that's when the children have been prepared for them all their lives, and have far lesser powers.

I can't even imagine what they did to Godric to control his superior powers, and what he suffered from infancy until he was old enough to understand why they were torturing him.

This explained a lot of his angelholeness, and how he's become an expert torturer himself.

But what really stirred my empathy was discovering we have far more in common than our leashes. I don't remember my mother, didn't have a childhood, and was as abused.

He is also as unique as I allegedly am. He is the first of his kind, and the most powerful nephilim in history even as a baby. He is what prompted the other archangels to follow Azrael's example and sire more Nephilim. But there hasn't been another like Godric since.

That I can attest to.

Now I fall into step with him, post-exercise, Godric-induced energy and euphoria surging through me.

I whoop and skip.

His sideways glance flash turquoise in the overcast morning light, singeing me. "Glad to see you so enthusiastic about the next phase in your training."

I flail my hands above my head in mock-panic. "Earth is tilting on its axis! It'll spin out of orbit and hurtle into the sun! Godric's *glad!*"

His lips twitch, and his eyes even crinkle. These slips in control—intoxicate me.

"Figure of speech. No real gladness implied or included." As I grin wider at him, he purse-pouts those bitable lips, his way of pretending I don't amuse him. "But the world must be heading for something cataclysmic if you're calling me Godric. What happened to Godawful and Angelhole?"

I snicker. "Oh, they're right here, and bulldozing me into their next torture program, before I catch my breath from their first one."

"If this is you out of breath, if you're ever in it, my ears might fall off."

"Ha-*ha*! Who knew? You rolled off the archangelic assembly line with a humor software installed. But not with a timing one. You should have laid off the announcement until I deal with these Trials. Y'know, one affliction at a time?"

His expression reverts to his default grimness, making me realize how lighthearted it has been. "And now I failed to exempt you, our only hope is the method I taught you in the Mindscape."

He's referring to using that white ring that manifests in response to the encroachment of his power. He has guided me into making it flare with what looks and feels like fire. He hopes it would convince the forces conducting the assessment that my supposed Grace has an Elemental component.

Doubt and worry creep down my spine. I think I've mastered that trick, but... "What if I can't replicate it outside the Mindscape? Can you intervene like you did in the Divining?"

"Not this time."

"What happens if I can't do it?"

"Then that anomaly inside you might be discovered."

"Now it's an anomaly! The Abomination that keeps on giving." I exhale in resignation. "Any idea what happens if it is?"

"Nothing good."

"Yeah, I got that, from the thousand times you told me. But you never really explained why this 'anomaly' is such a terrible thing you have to hide at any cost."

He slows down to brood down at me, and I feel him struggling not to reach for me. As always, my every nerve screams for his touch, and blood rushes to bombard my skin, just to be closer to him. And as always, his hands fist, crushing the urge.

Looking away and ahead, he resumes his speed, voice dipping into gravelly depths. "At first, I thought exposure of your Angel Essence collecting ability would have terrible and widespread repercussions. But this thing inside you—I think it has the potential to tamper with the very balance of existence."

My mouth drops open. "Please—tell me you're being a drama queen again!"

He shrugs. "Better dramatic than sorry at this point."

I guess he's right about that. I'm already a glorified prisoner because I can collect tiny amounts of Angel Essence. I don't want to find out what would happen to me, to Sarah, if it's discovered I can do something else that's unprecedented, and far more catastrophic.

I sigh. "No idea what 'it' is yet?"

His lips thin, yet look so sensuous, so—edible. And what a time to drool over them. Seems not even impending disaster can douse the hormonal wildfire he arouses.

I sigh again as he exhales. "I still only have theories."

"Any of them good? Better than the others, at least?"

"All equally bad."

"Whoa. Way to fill me with optimism as I head into my second potentially fatal probing since you dragged me into your world."

"I'm telling you the truth. I believe this is one thing you appreciate about me."

My hands itch to run over his expansive chest, to bunch in his sweatshirt and jerk him down so I can whisper in his ear, *"Oh, I appreciate loads of things about you. Let me strip you naked and show you how I appreciate the Hell and Heaven out of each and every one..."*

But we aren't at the smutty confessions and demonstrations stage yet. Heh—who am I kidding? We will never be.

Since this will remain a feverish fantasy I'd better keep to myself, out loud I say, "Let's assume I fail to keep it a secret, and the Trials expose me. What then?"

"Only one hope would remain." When he doesn't elaborate, I spin my hands in a hurrying gesture. He exhales again. "That I'd manage to redirect everyone to another conclusion."

"Which is?"

"That you have a rare Grace manifestation, one that hasn't been seen for millennia."

"And that's better than one of your bad theories?"

"Anything is better than those."

"And you still won't share any of them?"

"When I know for sure, you'll be the first to know."

"Will I?"

His fraught silence answers me loud and clear.

This super-secret-agent of Heaven shared what he did with me, because he needed me to understand the gravity of the situation, and to train me into not exposing myself. He won't share anything I don't need to know unless forced to, by some catastrophe of equal weight.

So I ask something else he may answer. "If there's this anomaly inside me, how come I can only sense it in your virtual reality arena? Or when I'm spacing out or hallucinating? Why do I barely hang on to its very memory when I'm in my right mind and in the real world?"

"First, there's nothing virtual about the Mindscape. It's just another plane of existence. Second, whatever this thing is, it eludes your conscious mind because it's still dormant."

"Dormant! You're telling me all these—encounters, not to mention all these efforts and worries, are about something that's actually asleep?"

His jaw muscles bunch as he gives a tight nod. "Yes, and we can only sense and interact with it in the Mindscape or your subconscious, where I believe it's still—dreaming. I have no idea what will happen when it awakens."

I frown, my thought processes tangling. "But isn't that what our Mindscape escapades are all about? You're trying to awaken it?"

He glares at me as if I just told him I killed his pet. Yeah, he has one. And I hear it's a panther. I plan to see it, *and* pet it, if it's the last thing I do.

"Absolutely not," he bites off. "Exactly the opposite. I'm trying to make you recognize it, and gain control of it, *while* it still slumbers."

"But if it's so ultimately dangerous, why are you probing it? Aren't you risking waking it up yourself?"

"I think it will wake up sooner or later, no matter what I do or don't do. If it awakens when you're not ready…"

The helplessness in his shrug, that being of almost unlimited power, makes a shudder rattle through me like a freight train.

I'm sorry I asked. Every time I do, his answers only make things worse.

If he's right, I have a literal sleeping monster inside me that we can poke awake at any moment. One I'm supposed to tame and keep in check.

Hoping it remains slumbering forever, I have to ask something else. "You said you don't know if it's connected to my Angel Essence extraction power, but it has to be, right? There can't be two inexplicable things within the same puny human, can there be?" When he opens his mouth, I know he's going to give me another inconclusive answer, so I rush to add, "Just give me a theory. Your worst one."

He says nothing until we reach Fem's main doors, where he's been leaving me after our sessions for weeks now. He now allows me to shower and dress before heading to breakfast.

As he turns and walks away, I sigh, resigned to another dead end in my understanding of what's going on with me.

Just as I settle for ogling his heavenly behind, he suddenly stops, swings back to me.

"You want my worst theory, White?" he grits, obsidian lightning bleeding from his crimson flaming eyes. The scary, involuntary kind. "It's that yes, your power is connected, is a symptom of that thing's existence within you. And that from the first time you saw and collected Angel Essence, it stirred in its slumber. And that everything I do to guard against it, will only accelerate its awakening. That you might be a cosmic nuclear weapon—and I'll be the one who arms it."

39

This time when Godric turns, he keeps walking. At some point, a flash encompasses him, then he shoots up in the air.

I watch him until he disappears, my mind doing backward somersaults.

Me? A nuclear weapon? And of cosmic proportions, too?

This guy is out of his flipping-through-the-heavens mind!

He has to be. From the beginning. When he said I have the potential of being one of the most dangerous entities in existence. When he claimed I could play a role in ending the Eternal Battle. And now when he thinks that ephemeral thing within me, with its ineffective dreamtime tantrums, could destroy the world, or even the cosmos.

He may look and sound totally put together, but his brain must be completely scrambled. It must be from constantly inhaling the fumes of his greatness and gorgeousness.

Deciding to save my energy and sanity, and dismiss everything he ever said about me, I run inside Fem. I have to join the others for breakfast, but I first need to shower, dress and attempt to tame my rioting hair. The hair they all think I dyed.

I didn't. Of course, I didn't. The most I've ever done with it was bunch or braid it out of my face. But in the times I bothered examining it, I thought I could see bluish/purplish reflections in its darkness. I always thought it was the light.

Turns out it wasn't. I now have nebula-hued low and some highlights that are getting more pronounced after every Mindscape visit. They're the only outward proof that something is changing within me.

But I can't claim it's a manifestation of my Grace. Godric forbade me to, saying the dye explanation is safer. I can't even tell Sarah a more plausible story. Even if I'm no longer afraid of what Godric would do to her.

A couple of weeks ago, after that first time Godric exposed me to an almost-touch, to my hair, he withdrew his hand, his action and grimness leaving my every nerve rioting. He made it worse when he made that shocking announcement. That he exempted Sarah from dying at his hands, under any circumstances.

I had no idea what made him decide that. It sure wasn't my persuasive skills. But he did make it a pledge, so I knew he meant it. Not about to look a gift executioner in the axe, I took the win. I also thought I could finally share some truths with her—for about two minutes.

He brought my new hope crashing down, telling me I can't confide in her, and I'd better pray she never works anything out herself. My life would be in danger if someone suspects what's going on with me, and Sarah, as my best friend, would share my danger. There's no telling who can read her mind or manipulate her into exposing what she knows about me. Like that time the demoness influenced her into exposing personal stuff about me. Keeping her safe meant continuing to hide everything from her.

So I—the girl who used to wash her hair with dishwater, and now considers Academy-issue shampoo and conditioner the ultimate in luxury hair care—let everyone think I dyed it. Such a subtle, spectacular dye, too. How the others believed that, and that I spent any of my meager leisure time at the hair salon in Raziel Complex, I have no idea.

Yeah, the others. I now have to hang out with them. Because of Sarah,

Not only that, but increasing numbers of the Angel-Graced and the minority races now wave and smile and stop to talk with her. A lot of the Nephilim do, too. Those who don't, I have no doubt it's because of my presence by her side.

Even in our forced-proximity quintet, I'm still the odd-girl-out. Cara's resentment has been simmering hotter every time she's seen me with Godric. And since that's at least twice a day, we're talking *a lot* of acrimony. Ms. Archangelspawn—or Aela as those allowed to speak to her call her—ignores me, since I never trespassed on even her shadow.

As for Jinny, she continues to be my vicious rival for Sarah's company. Which is funny, since she gets it all to herself while I'm with Godric. A fact I resent like hell.

But as I delight in how much stronger I feel, how I'm barely breathing fast by the time I reach our room, I have to grudgingly admit it's been worth it. Every hour Godric has taken me away from Sarah and every minute of physical and mental torment he's put me through has been for a great cause. Maybe I should thank him?

Nah.

I burst into the room to an unusual sight. All my roommates are still here.

I rush towards Sarah, suddenly alarmed. "I thought you'd be at breakfast."

Sarah shakes her head with a forlorn expression. "We're not having breakfast today. Azazel's orders.

My heart drops to my left big toe. "But I'm starving!"

Jinny grins at me, the personification of malicious glee. "And if you die of starvation, his plan to weed out the weak and useless would be complete."

Sarah scowls up at her. "Wen is the farthest thing from weak or useless. You know how hard she's been working out."

Surprisingly, Jinny doesn't hand Sarah her head for daring to scold her, or come to my defense. Or maybe not so surprisingly. Jinny seems willing to allow Sarah anything. She really must be desperate for company around here. And who is a more accepting and accommodating company than Sarah?

Color darkening as if with embarrassment, Jinny only mumbles defensively, "We all work out hard. This place is worse than a hard-labor camp."

Sarah tuts. "But Wen is human, and works out twice as hard, once with Godric, then in the regular fitness and combat classes. So she needs food more than any of us."

"I still don't get why Godric is training you privately." Cara grunts, still harping on the one thought she seems to have between her ears.

Sarah transfers her frown to her. "I don't know why you're still asking this, Cara. We all already know it's the archangels' orders."

"Yes, but we still don't know why," Cara says, face reddening with pent-up frustration. She'd trade places with me at any cost. If she thought killing me is the price, I'd be long dead in my sleep.

Sarah shrugs. "You're welcome to ask *them*, Cara."

It's a masterful comeback that stymies Cara. Everyone here seems to consider the archangels gods, and questioning their decrees is akin to blasphemy.

As the only one who doesn't have the least reverence for the archangels, or Godric, it's Jinny who smirks at Cara. "You don't need to ask these feathered blowhards anything. We already heard the truth from the most reliable source. So I don't know why you're still harping on this, angel-crazed. Your pathetic obsession with this Semi-Angel of Death bastard is getting old, so put a sock drawer in it, already."

As Cara glares at her then pretends to resume browsing her tablet, I huff a scoff.

By reliable source, Jinny means Lorcan. He teased Godric about it, with cadets within earshot. On purpose, I'm certain. Said "truth" spread like wildfire on steroids among the student body within minutes.

And that "truth"? It's that the archangels are punishing Godric, assigning him as the private mentor of a cadet. The one they consider their most problematic yet. It's considered the most severe dishonor without straight out demoting him from his position as Prefect Praesidium of the Praetorian Guard and the youngest General in the Army of Heaven.

This scenario has explained away our weird situation to everyone's satisfaction. It allayed any questions about any special treatment I'm receiving, or suspicions about my importance to the archangels, or to Godric.

It's an ingenious lie, if you ask me, playing on everyone's biases and resentments. Where Godric is concerned, it comforts the Nephilim to think that even he isn't immune from the whims of his superiors. While the professors and anyone else who works in this place are *really* smug thinking he's being taken down a peg—or a thousand.

As for me, everyone is reassured I'm not being singled out for a privilege, but a penance, while enjoying the proof that I am what they all think I am. What the archangels consider the worst possible punishment for their supreme nephilim.

But Cara, that jealous bitch, is still unsatisfied with that explanation. She keeps asking and probing every chance she gets, hoping she'd squeeze a different answer out of me. Her fixation on him makes her the only one who smells the Godric-sized rat.

My stomach growls louder than I do as I head back to the doors. "I'll go find something to eat."

Sarah rushes after me. "No food is available anywhere. Azazel made sure no one can eat anything until after the Trials."

I look down at her in horror. With my newly-acquired muscle mass and accelerated metabolism—and the effort it has taken me to pass Godric's Phase One—the idea of not eating for hours makes me go weak in the knees.

"Anyone have anything to eat around here?" I hate to hear my pleading tone, but I'm too hungry to care.

I wince as Sarah does in apology, while the others give me baleful glances.

I should have known it's a pointless question. We are not allowed to have food in our rooms. Any snacks smuggled in are to be treated with the gravity human academies treat the possession of hard drugs. And we are not allowed to ask why. It's in the archangelic handbook of rules. Break them at the risk of the aforementioned blasphemy.

Risks notwithstanding, I was never tempted to break them. We are so well fed, I never get the munchies between meals. I even began to forget what hunger felt like.

Now all the years of deprivation come crashing down on me, and the terribly familiar feeling of my digestive tract feeding on itself twists in my guts.

But if anyone dares to flaunt the Academy's rules, it would be Jinny. And this girl eats like a locust.

Hating to ask her, but desperate enough to, I turn to her. "You got nothing smuggled somewhere?"

Jinny gives me a vicious smile. "You think if I have something, and you're actually starving at my feet, I'd give it to you?"

Sarah gasps, coming between us to scowl up at the demon. "Jinny! That's just too mean!"

Jinny, looking embarrassed of all things, grimaces at Sarah. "I was only joking, Sar."

Sarah's disapproval only deepens. "It wasn't funny, and you know it. Now, do you have something for Wen to eat or not?"

And wonder of wonders, Jinny's lightest mocha complexion reddens as she mumbles like a kid being reprimanded by her teacher. "No, sorry."

Sorry? Did Jinny just say sorry?

Granted, she said it to Sarah, not me. But still! This is weird beyond words.

It's even weirder for Sarah to be my protector, when I'm so used to being hers. I probably wake up every morning in one piece because I'm her friend.

But her popularity's shield can only go so far. Even that of Godric's enforced investment in my one-piece-ness. I always feel I'm one word away from breaking a bone or losing an appendage.

Not that I worry about my roommates or anyone else I've annoyed anymore. Not with Godric's predictions and the looming Trials in my center-stage concerns. And then Azazel manages to make even those pale into insignificance.

I now realize why he's the head of the *Pax Vis*. He *is* a unifying force and a peace-keeping presence. A common threat is the best disciplinary measure after all. His "applied" classes continue to provide sneak peeks into how we might not survive the term's tests. From the bone-chilling glee in his eyes during said classes, I have no doubt some of us won't. And that he's already decided who won't make it. He might now be starving us so we'd be slow and jittery, and the Trials would thin the herd in advance.

Those damn Trials. They've been hanging over my head like another guillotine blade. We've been trying to find out what they really are, but no matter how much we asked or researched, we only got the impression they are some glorified placement test. Even Godric seems only worried about "exposure." But I wouldn't be surprised if they turn out to be eliminations.

They might be that for me, if I attend them this hungry.

"So is this some kind of enforced fast?" I groan as I fetch my uniform and boots. "A ritualistic part of the Trials?"

"They just don't want to clean up human vomit," Jinny snickers.

I turn on her, hunger making me extra snappy. "Since they're not feeding you either, they must know your demon spew would eat through the Academy's foundations."

As Jinny stalks towards me, eyes promising a completion of her previous strangulation, Sarah turns urgently to me. "We were told to leave our rooms only in time to get to the Assembly Hall at Raziel Complex. It's a twenty-minute walk, and we have thirty-five minutes left, so go shower already."

I'm about to obey her until Jinny drawls, "Yeah, unless stinking so bad is your plan to get disqualified from the Trials."

Wishing I could lob a spit like her, I settle for my most inflammatory grin. "You mean a Brimstone Born like you actually has a sense of smell? That must be torture."

Sarah puts up a hand, stopping Jinny from resuming her threatening march, while the other pushes at me, a firm warning in her eyes. "Let's keep all this energy for the Trials, okay?"

Knowing it's stupid to test Jinny's Sarah-induced tolerance, I can't help making a taunting face at her above Sarah's head.

Before I find my neck in her grip again, I bolt to our shared yet magical bathroom.

In under a minute, I'm standing beneath the scalding jets, still unable to credit how Sarah has changed. She's taken to life in this incredible yet treacherous place like a fish to water, has been navigating its turbulent currents with zeal, dexterity and a twinkle in her eyes.

It's as if she were born to it.

Maybe she was. Maybe it's why Lorcan and the archangels feel something inside her that necessitates her being here.

But whatever it is, it can't be as dangerous as what I have, or they would have had Godric on her case, too. At least, Lorcan.

Sarah's urgent knock jerks me out of my musings, making me hurtle out of the shower. I attempt to towel-dry, but end up jumping into my uniform almost dripping wet, before running out of the bathroom—and into Jinny.

Jinny catches me with that effortless strength of hers, stopping me from hurtling to the ground. As she steadies me and before I can pull away, she drops a few words into my ear.

Then she turns to the others with a grin, and a fond gaze pinned on Sarah. "Promise you'll be careful in the Trials, girls. I don't want the hassle of getting used to replacement roommates. Now, off you go."

As Sarah grabs my hand and drags me out of the room after her, I swing one last look over my shoulder at Jinny. Her eyes glow a menacing red, and her smile widens.

Her words—her threat—echo in my mind all the way to Raziel Complex.

She said, "Maybe I can't kill you, Nothing, but my 'corrosive spew' can accidentally melt off a hand, or a leg—or a face. That would be a shame, now, wouldn't it?"

40

"**E**ach dorm room denizens—stand in your own line."

Azazel's snarled order reverberates the air around us, a pressure that barely stops short of rupturing my eardrums. Everyone around seems to suffer the same discomfort.

"*Now!*"

This shakes the ground below us like an earthquake. But at least he didn't blow us off our feet, or our flesh off our bones.

As every five scramble into a line, Azazel roars, "*Horizontally, imbeciles!*"

This time it takes the crowd longer to figure out what he meant, then to form his demanded configuration.

After each quintet is standing close together, shifting on nervous feet, Azazel flicks a hand at Astaroth.

The princely demon, who seems to be his errand boy at times, comes forward to the podium.

Opening a massive ledger, Astaroth starts speaking at once, "Welcome to the Imperium Trials, cadets. Each five of you will..."

"*You*, maggots—explain yourselves."

At Azazel's vicious interruption, a wave of horror sweeps through the hall, as each group fears he's addressing them. Then I realize where he's pointing.

At us.

I instinctively put myself in front of Sarah as he snarls, "Where is your fifth, maggots?"

I feel Sarah move behind me. Unable to let her respond, giving him a bullseye for his displeasure, I step forward.

"Sh-she's not here."

I hate that I stuttered, but only hope it appeases him.

"Is she dead?" Azazel rumbles, looking like the supernatural dictator that he is today, with hair pulled back and his *Pax Vis* boss elaborate costume. "That's the only reason I'll accept for her tardiness."

"I-I don't think she's coming."

"You don't think or you know?"

I cast a frantic glance at Aela, hoping she'd say something. She's staring ahead, as if she doesn't deem to look at me—or at Azazel. She must consider us both beneath her regard.

But there's something else in her vibe. It's—fear?

Fan-fallen-angel-tastic! Azazel scares even our resident archangelspawn, and I went and made myself the center of his attention.

But it was either Sarah or me. And I'm already in it. If I fall silent now, it would incur his wrath. Being inconclusive would also bring it down on me. And anyone standing next to me.

Since I'm already trapped, I shrug. "I just think it makes sense she isn't here. She's a demon, and the Imperium Trials decide what kind of Grace we have and all. She must have thought they have nothing to do with her."

Azazel barrels into Astaroth, shoving him violently away from the podium. He snatches the ledger up, tears through the pages until he stabs a finger down one and roars, "Bring me the demoness Jinnifer, daughter of Lilith—*now*."

A couple of his *Pax Vis* angels shoot into the air at once. They zoom above us, their massive wings creating a powerful draft that knocks us into each other, and dishevels every head on their way out of the Assembly Hall.

As the crowd buzzes and shuffles, one thing percolates in my mind.

Daughter of Lilith? *The* Lilith? Mother of all demons? Now that's a tiny bit of info she left out. It makes it even more amazing that I'm still breathing now.

"*Silence.*"

Azazel's growl plunges the hall into abrupt muteness. Anyone standing outside would think it's empty, not packed with over two thousand newly-adult Nephilim and Angel-Graced.

We stand, barely breathing, until the two angels return with Jinny. Each has an iron grip on an arm as she walks among them, head held high, glaring ahead at the reason she's been dragged in here so unceremoniously.

The angels leave her in front of the stage where Azazel towers, and retreat.

Azazel inclines his head at her. "So you absented yourself from the Trials. Without permission."

"I thought..." Jinny starts.

Azazel cuts her off, voice like a scythe. "For *daring* to think when you were given a directive, I will make an example of you. Come here."

She lowers her gaze to where he points beneath him, then lifts her chin, higher this time. "I won't. And you can't make me. You're an angel, and you're all about free will. So suck it."

"Seems you were never educated in the ways of the Fallen, hellspawn. Let me rectify the gap in your knowledge."

He waves and suddenly Jinny is somersaulting in the air with a yell of shock and rage.

Sarah bolts forward with a whimper of dismay. I shove her behind me again, almost missing the moment Azazel flicks his hands, and slams Jinny down at his feet with a thud that cracks the floor beneath them.

Jinny's cry of pain is brought to an abrupt, wheezing end when Azazel stomps his heavy boot down on her chest. Anyone else would have been a splattered mess of flesh and bones beneath him now.

What follows is a scene right out of a horror movie.

That's where the two creatures who morph right in front of us belong.

Crimson flames burst from Jinny's eyes as her face turns pitch black. Her mouth expands to double its size as she screeches in that nerve-wrenching polyphonic voice, this time an ear-splitting whistle entwined with a bass rumble right from the bottom of Hell.

Her pearly teeth elongate into three-inch fangs and start dripping something like tar. Her red nails turn into finger-long claws as she struggles with the foot crushing her ribcage.

But it's to no avail. Maybe if this were a fair fight, if she's been prepared for the attack, she'd have a chance. But in that disadvantaged position, she's no match for whatever Azazel has turned into. Something that will echo its horror in my every waking and sleeping moment till the day I die.

Quadruple his original size—or maybe this is his original size—his wings are masses of flaming soot that emit billowing clouds of smoke, making us all tear up and choke in hacking coughs. His face has lost its skin, becoming red flesh pocked with fiery black pits. His teeth have also elongated and multiplied inside a mouth that could easily fit a basket-ball, a dozen inches-long, razor-sharp rows, like those of an alien shark.

But it's his eyes that almost make me piss myself in terror. Gaping black voids with horizontal, glowing-white slashes of pure evil in their depths.

Worst of all, he is *laughing*.

The more horrified he feels he makes us, the more she struggles and screeches, the harder he laughs. His guffaws sounds like a thousand serrated knives scraping along a blackboard lined with broken glass and sandpaper. I think it might shred our very souls.

The sickening sound of steel bones fracturing has bile rising to my eyes as he crushes his foot harder down on Jinny's chest. Her writhing form begins to glow, as if she's going to ignite and explode at any moment. Sarah must have suspected the same thing, as her weeping becomes shearing sobs that rattle my own bones. But it is the sight of Jinny's tears turning to steam in her burning eyes that finally shatters my paralysis.

I grab Aela's arm, shaking it with my violent tremors. "Do something! He's killing her."

She glares down at my clawing hands before removing them calmly. "She's a demon. We kill her kind every day."

I pounce on her arm again, when I've so far avoided even breathing in her vicinity. "But she's here as a cadet. She's alone among hundreds of you and she trusted you not to harm her."

She scowls down at me. "And no one tried to do so. She's now paying for her transgression."

"Not showing up for a test, because of a perfectly logical misunderstanding, is now a transgression punishable by agonizing death?"

"Azazel is the Tribune of the *Pax Vis*. It's at his discretion how he chooses to end what he considers disruptive behavior. She flaunted the Academy's rules, and he would never let other cadets think they can survive that."

"She didn't know she was flaunting the Academy's rules!" Though I don't know if she did or not. She just can't be executed for it!

"Again, she's a demon. They exist for corruption and mayhem. They are the scourge of existence. She is the scourge of *your* existence. I heard her threatening you today. Why do you even care if she dies? You should be applauding Azazel for ridding you of her."

"I do want to get rid of her, but *not* this way!"

Aela shakes me off, harder this time. "Well, it's not up to you, is it?"

"But it can be up to *you*. You're an archangel's daughter, you have powers, influence. If you intervene…"

"Why should I intervene on a demon's behalf?"

Her return to calmness makes me see red, and I lose all discretion, slamming my palms into her chest. "Because it's the right thing to do! What he's doing to her—it's—it's just evil. If you go along with it, it makes you party to his vile treachery and cowardice. It makes you worse than the demons you despise so much! *Much worse!*"

A gurgling sound issues from the stage, an unmistakable sound of impending death. Jinny's.

Still cackling, Azazel slashes his hand and a sickle of angelic energy zooms towards her face.

For the suffocating eternity of a heartbeat, I think he'd lop off her head.

What he does feels somehow crueler.

He shears off her horns.

Her blood-curdling scream quakes through me. But it's the sound the severed horns make as they clatter to the stage, even masked by the cacophony of his merriment, that turns my stomach. And that's before I see the stumps that remain.

The moment I realize they're bleeding from their severed ends down her forehead and into her eyes, something snaps inside me.

"Jinny!" Sarah shrieks as she tears out of my restraining grip and explodes into a run.

I pounce on her, rabidly dragging her and tossing her back at the line of cadets who haven't moved an inch since this macabre execution began. I barely see her landing in Aela's startled arms before I run to the stage myself.

Nothing exists in my mind anymore but the horror of watching Jinny's amazing glow sputtering, her immortal life-force leaving her body under that brute's boot. There's no more thought or logic or even self-preservation in my mind as I somehow jump up on stage, and barrel into Azazel's gigantic form.

At the negligible impact of my body, his hellish wings unfold to their full span with a snap that almost breaks me, body and mind. He looks down at me with those pits of horror, and the sound he makes—it's as if the heavens themselves are enraged.

Terror, so vast and primal roars to the forefront of my instincts. It bombards me with the urge to prostrate myself, to await my own execution in abject surrender.

But as I fall off him like a dead bug, something—else, deeper, older, *ancient*—scorches through the terror, surging within me like lava. It sees the fallen angel's Essence storming around him and it knows. It can seize it, use it.

I don't know how, but I'm back on my feet, something bottomless and unstoppable gnawing at me as I raise my hands to that tantalizing energy.

As it funnels toward me, coating not only my hands, or arms, but my whole torso, I barely register Azazel raising a massive hand tipped in blade-like claws. Some awareness screams that when this blow descends, it would do to me what his sickle did to Jinny's horns. It would hack me to pieces, just not as cleanly.

The thing inside me shouts back, silencing it, roaring for me to get all his Essence.

Suddenly, something pulls me back so hard, I fly off the stage, and slam to the ground feet below.

Among the agony and disorientation, I realize many things at once.

The leash saved me from being shredded to gory bits. Godric's brutal tug on it. Around my waist, not neck. A tug like that would have broken it. He lassoed me away at the last moment.

Before I can move even my eyes to look for him, Azazel is descending on me. The beat of his nightmarish wings grinds me into the ground with a body-sized fist of strangulating smoke and fiery ice.

He won't be stopped from ending me. Then he would finish Jinny. I haven't only failed to stop him, I managed to provoke him into killing me along with her.

I turn my head. Not wanting to see the moment he squashes me into a gory puddle. Wanting to get a last glimpse of Sarah.

I only see a heart-stopping sight. Godric shooting toward me, his eyes crackling with blood-red lightning, every inch of him encased in black fire.

Before I can even blink, he's inches above me. Ramming into Azazel in midair.

The collision detonates like a bomb. A burst of blinding fury amalgamating with searing evil, razing out in a shockwave that engulfs me, unravels me.

Everything disappears, ends.

41

I'm suspended in nothingness.

I only know that when something fractures it, starts to exist.

It's an image. Of Godric's murderous face, twisted in loathing and wrath.

Then more images pour through the crack, in rapid-fire sequence. Replaying his clash with Azazel.

The unimaginable violence and brutality of those celestial beings, colliding a hairbreadth above me, razes through me again. There's no way I could have survived their climactic conflict.

So was I collateral damage? Is this nothingness death?

It feels exactly like that thing that exists within me. It *is*.

So maybe it isn't as dangerous as Godric thinks, is just something that activates when I'm in danger? Maybe it always thought Godric wanted to hurt me during our Mindscape sessions? If it works on a physical as well as a metaphysical level, maybe it activated to save me from the fallout of those monsters' fight? If so, does being inside it now means it succeeded? Or is my body destroyed somewhere, and this is only my consciousness floating within it?

To get answers, to see if I'm still alive, I have to exit its confines. Even if I somehow know it wouldn't want to let me go.

It doesn't. I almost tear my mind apart, peeling it away from its greedy grasp—only to find myself plummeting.

I land on something flat and hard with a chest-emptying oomph.

"Wen!"

My eyes open to find Sarah swooping down on me, eyes stricken and streaming tears.

I'm crumpled on pristine marble, beside a bed draped in stark white, in a vast, sterile space. It's a ward, in Raphael Sanatorium, and I'm wearing something like a hospital gown. On a bed to my right, in the same gown, Jinny lies unmoving.

Apart from a slight swelling and her cut off horns, her face looks the same as it always has. She seems so young and innocent.

But she doesn't seem to be breathing!

A burst of alarm has me staggering up to my feet. Sarah almost knocks me off them when she drags me into a fierce hug.

"I was so scared you wouldn't wake up, too!"

"She's...?" A lump rises in my throat, cutting off my question.

Sarah shakes her head, sobbing harder, hugging me tighter. "In a coma. Healer Althea said her injuries are beyond any healer's abilities, might even be beyond Raphael's. She doesn't know if she'll ever wake up."

"That evil turd!" I hiss. "I wish I had time to suck all of his Essence."

Sarah blinks up at me, her tears slowing down. "What do you mean?"

I blink back at her, unable to understand her question for a moment, before I remember.

She doesn't know about the Angel Essence business. All she knows is what we both did before coming here. That my so-called power is akin to soaking up angel lingering sweat.

But whatever it is, Godric's training *has* expanded it, like he predicted. When I saw Azazel's Essence, it was still connected to him. Until that point, I've only seen Essence *after* it was expended. If he wasn't about to fillet me, I felt I would have been able to draw it from him.

Now I wonder what would have happened if I did. Would it have caused him the angelic equivalent of dehydration? I really would have loved to put him in a coma, too.

Before I can think of an answer, Sarah hugs me again, whispering tremulously, "He would have killed her if you didn't intervene."

"Yeah, right." I huff. "After I stood there until he almost did."

She pulls away to gape at me. "No one even *thought* of doing anything, but you put yourself in mortal danger for her—when you don't even like her."

"Don't even like her" is a gross euphemism of how much I dislike and resent, not to mention fear this girl. So why am I so cut up over seeing her this way?

It has to be what I told Aela. About how much I hate treachery and power abuse. This was so unjustified and dishonorable it still makes my blood boil.

"You forget I stopped *you* from running to her rescue," I say, stepping away to approach Jinny's inert form.

Sarah clings to my hand as her tears thicken again. "All *I* was going to do was try to pull her from underneath his foot. *You* attacked him!"

"And a whole lot of good that did. I'm not in the morgue now, in a body bag in several assorted pieces, only because of..." The memory detonates in my mind all over again. "Godric! That bastard!"

Sarah blinks up at me. "You're angry at him? But he saved you!"

"He sure as hell took his sweet time doing it." I stab a finger towards Jinny. "And he didn't save her!"

She shakes her head. "If you saw what happened after he clashed with Azazel, you might understand why he was reluctant to interfere."

A fist suddenly forms over my heart. "What happened?"

Her face crumples, as if remembering it hurts. "It was horrible, Wen. I couldn't bear to look at the nightmarish forms Azazel kept morphing into. Those *Pax Vis* angels who're always trailing after him joined the fight, and it became three to one. Azazel withdrew when Godric drew some kind of flaming sword out of thin air. But more angels kept pouring in, until there were two dozen—or more. The radiation of power bombarding Godric was—unbearable. I felt it would liquefy my insides. Then I saw nothing more as everyone stampeded out of the hall and swept me along. But since they didn't bring him here, I-I don't even know if Godric even survived..."

The fist around my heart convulses, and blood empties from my head. Everything around me swings in a violent vortex. I almost keel over Jinny before Sarah grabs me.

"Lie down, Wen, please!" Sarah sobs as she tries to drag me away to the bed I fell off. "I'll go get Healer Althea!"

Forcing down the nausea until the world stops spinning, I struggle to straighten, to pull myself away from her rabid grasp. "No—no, I'm fine. I have to go."

Then I'm running, blind to everything but finding my way out. Finding Godric.

He *has* to have survived. All this power and uniqueness can't possibly be snuffed. Not in such a pointless flare up of violence. Not over me. Not at all.

He can't be dead.

The very possibility expands inside me with something uncontainable, brimming with rage and desperation. It shrieks for release so it would...

Everything jogs in my brain the moment I run out of the building, the ground quaking beneath my feet. Like it did many time before.

My eyes burn as I raise them, praying to whatever rules this universe that I'm right.

The sight filling my blurred vision has my heart kicking so brutally, I almost bursts.

Godric.

He's landed in front of me, his impact rocking my world, in every way.

The urge to sock him for intervening so late, and the need to make sure he's real, and whole, clash together as powerfully as he did with Azazel.

I end up doing both. I punch him in the abdomen, then throw myself at him.

"You're alive!" I pant, painful moisture blossoming in my eyes as I mash my face into his expansive chest.

He goes rigid under my onslaught, chest heaving under my cheek as erratically as mine. For heart-thundering moments, his hands hover over me, and I think he'll put his arms around me.

He only holds them off me as he steps away, forcing me to relinquish my grip on his jacket.

His gaze crackles with a new deadliness as it sweeps me in my hospital gown. It's as if he, too, is looking for injuries. Was he rushing here to check up on me? And is that relief I see in his eyes, now he saw for himself I'm okay?

Next moment, he brings my wishful thinking crashing on my head.

His gaze falls disgustedly to the stain my tears left over his shirt, before hardening with disdain as they rise to mine. "And you had a suspicion I might not be alive, why?"

I wipe my tears angrily, kicking myself for the uncharacteristic meltdown, and over him of all people. "Because Sarah told me Azazel and the angels ganged up on you, that's why! But you're not even injured!"

"I was."

"How?"

"I healed."

"Yeah, point out the obvious, why don't you? You know that's not what I meant."

He jerks one shoulder dismissively. "You overestimate the eloquence of your single-word question."

"Or your intelligence!"

"I prefer to engage it in more worthwhile endeavors than deciphering your incessant questions. Also, reading minds, especially ones as shifty and mercurial as yours, is not one of my powers."

"Now I wish you were injured bad enough to need a prolonged recovery. A concussion might have made you less of an angelhole for longer!"

"Ah, you're wondering how my injuries were minor enough that I already healed completely."

"You knew this is what I meant. Admit it."

He only relinquishes my incensed gaze to roam my face.

If what I feel is any indication, I must be blotched with emotion, and swollen from the ordeal. And he seems to be examining my every pore, and disapproving of his findings.

Yeah, way to remind me of my flimsy humanity.

I don't know why, but looking disheveled and distorted, when he is so immaculate, hurts. I always knew the unbridgeable gap between us, but now it suddenly makes me want to weep.

I swallow the tears when I notice his gaze fixed on the side of my neck, and his eyes...they're inky and bottomless, a universe of nightmares. If it's ever unleashed, if *he* is...

I can't even finish this thought.

I suddenly realize what he's staring at when I register the sharp pain across my neck. My hand flies to it, only to feel a healing slash across my Mark. It's probably due to my own accelerated healing that I didn't bleed out.

Is this why he's so incensed? That I risked myself and could have died?

But I somehow feel his wrath isn't directed at me. So is it at Azazel, for almost killing me? Himself, for hanging back until he almost did?

His eyes empty of all expression, leaving me wondering if I imagined what I saw there. He's really good at making me suspect my senses and judgement.

"I admit nothing," he finally says.

I throw my hands up in frustration. "Do you have to be the biggest angelhole in the cosmos, *all* the time? Dude, can't you take a day off? So again, how? Sarah said a horde of angels attacked you, or is she wrong?"

"A host."

I blink up at him. "What?"

"It's called a host of angels."

"Thank you for the English language lesson, or is it literature?" I roll my eyes. "That's your takeaway from my question?"

If I can trust my senses where he's concerned, I'd say he's fighting a smile as he sighs. "Do you realize every single thing you said to me was a question? But I have one of my own. Why?"

"Why what?"

"Why are you surprised I didn't sustain worse injuries?"

"Because of the aforementioned *host*? Unless there weren't as many as Sarah thought?"

"There were. The whole *Pax Vis* First Legion, the highest-ranking soldiers in his Fallen Cadre. They're four dozen."

"Then it couldn't have been an all-out fight as she thought."

"Oh, it was. As you Americans say, as all get out." His expression twists in such delicious condescension, his British accent deepening. "But the day these 'chicken wings', as you once so eloquently put it, can best me, is the day I turn in my 'archangelspawn' badge."

"You really beat all of them?" I gape at him. I already knew he's much more powerful than a regular angel. But *all* of them? Could even an archangel hold his own against a battalion of angels?

We're talking immeasurable power here.

He exhales, the sound laden with frustration. "Not as cleanly as I would have liked."

"Meaning?"

"Meaning I had to cut off an angel's wings before his brothers backed off."

I frown. "So what? They will grow back."

"Wings are the only things an angel can't grow back."

Oh. *Oh.*

I have no idea how huge an offense this is in their celestial circles. But since it's irreversible, I suspect it's probably unforgivable.

"But if you had to do it, it means you had no other option?"

From his pitch-black frown, I know I'm right.

"Azazel's Fallen Cadre are fanatics," he finally says. "They would do literally anything at their master's merest whim, let alone to avenge blasphemy against him. Azazel withdrew from the fray and let them gang up on me, not only because he knew I could vanquish him, but because I'd already lost, no matter what I did from that point onward."

"Lost? But you just said you beat them all!"

Volcanic exasperation fills his gaze, as he grips the back of his neck, that move he makes when he'd like to punch a hole in the universe.

"Attacking him to save you, was the highest form of sacrilege to his Cadre. I compounded my unforgivable sin when I shielded you, so our fight wouldn't disintegrate you, then flung you out of our range. I cheated their master, and them, from executing you for daring to lay a hand on him."

So this is how I survived? Not because of whatever is inside me?

That makes far more sense. That he contained me in some forcefield so their clash didn't turn me to ash. And he must have tossed me far enough, still enclosed it in, until the battle was over, and the healers came to collect me.

How did I even think that thing inside me protected me, when it's still sleeping, and in another plane of existence? It couldn't have protected my corporeal body in this one.

I lurch out of my musings to Godric saying, "...and they weren't going to stop until *I* was vanquished, or they were all dead. Since I wasn't going to stand there and let them kill me, and didn't want to kill them all, my only remaining option was something angels consider a fate far worse than death." His scowl suddenly sears me. *This* fury is *all* mine. "Now I have a bigger mess on my hands than that of attacking one of the Elite Fallen. For a human. And depriving him and his Cadre from their rightful retribution. I took an angel's wings, and in our world that is a crime no celestial has ever perpetrated against another, not outside a heavenly court. And it's all because of you. Because you're insane."

Guilt threatens to crumple me—until those last two words. "Me? *I'm* insane? I'm not the one who decided to crush someone to death, while cackling like a maniacal monstrosity from some B-rated horror movie!"

"A demon."

I frown. "What?"

"Not 'someone.' A demon. It would have been good riddance."

This time I punch him in the head. He taught me how not to break my bones punching something as hard as him.

From the way his eyes widen in disbelief, no one has ever dared box his ears before. Probably not even in the heat of battle. Another first for that Divine Dickwad, courtesy of the Abomination-Who-Shouldn't-Exist.

His eyes now narrow, but I'm not intimidated in the least.

I yell at him as I land another punch to his chin. "I knew it! You monster! You didn't intervene earlier because you agreed to what Azazel was doing! You would have stood by as he drove his boot into her chest and pureed her organs!"

This time, I use a *Melek* technique he drove me beyond endurance to perfect, intending to take him down. But I took him by surprise with the first blow. He let me have the second one. This one, he effortlessly parries, making me stumble with the unopposed momentum.

I catch myself and go after him again, and he raises an imperative hand. It makes me angrier that it almost stops me. Almost. I punch him in the other ear.

"I wasn't standing by, since I wasn't even in the Academy," he grits, eyes blazing emerald. "I only came back when I felt *you* in danger."

I pull back from my latest attempt to rearrange his face, hand going to my neck. "How? You didn't have your leash on me."

Something like bewilderment enters his eyes as his hand rises to his chest, where his tattoo is, before it evaporates, to be replaced by suspicion. One that clearly unsettles and enrages him.

Is it true, then? What I've been feeling? That there's some kind of connection between us, independent of the two-way leash? And it has something to do with that rune that appeared within his tattoo? I didn't imagine it? Did it appear because of me? And it now links us?

Was it through this inexplicable, and fiercely unwanted link, that he felt my danger? Did it also compel him to intervene, against his better judgement? Or did he come to my rescue only because he has to preserve his test subject?

Not that it matters. One fact remains. His intervention saved my life—again. And Jinny's. And it came at a steep cost to him.

I hate being this hugely indebted to him, even if he did it for self-serving reasons. This time, it wasn't him who put me in danger, so his motives don't cancel my debt. I have to find some way to repay him.

But until I do, I'll keep telling him what I think of him. "Whatever

310

your reasons for intervening, and whatever it cost you, you're even worse than your cousin. Yeah, Aela expressed the same prejudiced shit as we watched Azazel grind Jinny into mincemeat. You've all been deluding yourselves to what you really are. But never fear, I'm here to tell you the truth. You're all a cowardly, dishonorable lot! You're the bad guys here, God-wretch!"

By now I'm wondering why he's standing there taking my blows and insults and accusations. He's put me "in my place" for far less before.

As I also wonder if I see hesitation or doubt on his face, it becomes as hard as his voice. "We'll see if you'll continue to hold that opinion when the demon you're defending so fiercely eats your organs while you're still alive to repay your kindness."

The horrifying images he paints sound like something the girl who threatened to melt my face off would do. But they still clash with those of her being indulgent and considerate, almost loving, with Sarah.

I shake my head. "She's not all bad. And from what I've seen today, she's probably better than any of you!"

Our gazes clash as we face off in silence that strains and seethes.

He's the one who looks away first. A flash consumes his wings as he turns on his heels. "Follow me. I have to test you, see if I can find something I can report as grounds for exempting you from the Trials."

I rush to catch up with his ridiculously long stride. "The Trials are still on?"

"Of course. They've been rescheduled for tomorrow."

"Tomorrow? But everyone must be too shaken after what they witnessed today, probably injured from the fallout of your fight. Why not give us more time to recover?"

"It's actually inexplicable that they gave you that long. I thought they'd resume the Trials as soon as my showdown with the angels was over. It's why I hoped that your crazy stunt, what ended with you lying unconscious in the Sanatorium, would provide an excuse for you to miss them. But, for some reason I can't fathom, they decided to postpone till tomorrow. I guess it was too much to hope something good would come out of this disaster."

"Apart from being disappointed you couldn't use said disaster to your own ends, you think they shouldn't have postponed at all? That giving us till tomorrow was some kind of extraordinary kindness?"

"*Inexplicable* kindness—*if* it was that."

"You don't consider the cadets' physical and psychological states reason for postponement?"

"Of course not. On one hand, the Trials have never been postponed, and I didn't even think they could be. On the other, if the cadets can't handle sustaining non-lethal injuries, and witnessing a minor conflict…"

"Minor!" I exclaim. "That was a full-blown horror movie come to life."

He flicks me a dismissing glance. "It was indeed minor in this world they now belong to. If they can't handle it, I don't foresee them surviving long in this war."

"What war? You mean the cold Eternal Battle between Heaven and Hell? Or is there something more coming?"

His incredible eyes pan down to me for a moment too long. He seems to be debating his answer, before he nods. My mouth dries to cinders.

Then he makes it even worse when he says, "But because of you, I started an internal war that might consume us all, long before the real one begins. And both of us are at the center of it all."

42

The deja vu is overwhelming as we stand in lines of five in the Assembly Hall of Raziel Complex.

In my group's case, we're only four, again. Jinny won't be joining us any time soon.

She won't die. That is as much as we could get out of Healer Althea. What would happen to her, if she'd wake up, if she'd have permanent damage or be a vegetable if she does, the angel-graced woman couldn't tell us. Or maybe, wouldn't.

So here we are, without her again, waiting for our professors to tell us what the Trials entail.

Yesterday, everyone stood in these same spots, hungry and anxious, but mostly eager to find out the nature of their Grace. Today, we are all subdued and afraid, after another brush with the brutal reality of the beings who hold our fates in their hands. Even with Azazel's pointed absence, his threat is ever-present.

Sarah is desolate over Jinny's condition, and Cara is wary of whatever random cruelties we might be subjected to. Even Aela looks uneasy.

As for me, Godric couldn't find anything to spin into a reason to exempt me from the Trials. Since he already tried, I suspected any new evidence he presented would get rejected. Citing psychological trauma from my almost-fatal run in with Azazel was dismissed out of hand. They used the same reasoning he did when I protested not postponing the Trials longer. If I can't take a near-fajita experience in my stride, I wouldn't survive long in this world.

But according to him, I *have* taken it in stride. He didn't find a trace of psychic damage he could use. Which is a fat silver lining in his opinion. He already knew I have stamina and fortitude, but he now thinks I'm stronger than he imagined. This bodes well for enacting our plan, which depends on my steadiness and clarity.

But though it's strange yet true my clash with Azazel hasn't left me duly rattled, I am beyond agitated. And it's all about my confrontation with Godric. None of his dire predictions have affected me this way before. They've always sounded so far-fetched.

But his latest one *feels* real. It's based on something I did. I antagonized one of the most dangerous entities in the Academy, maybe the world, and my actions have caused horrific consequences.

All I once hoped for was to keep my head down, and escape anyone's notice. Now I've managed to hurl myself into the spotlight, made myself the focus of not only attention, but animosity. Having Azazel and his Cadre as enemies is something I haven't imagined in my worst projections.

But since there's nothing I can do about it, I have to focus on doing what Godric taught me, to project an Elemental Grace. If I fail, I'm to at least contain that thing inside me. He'll deal with interpreting my Trials' results as long as I do.

Astaroth takes the podium, and the already hushed buzz fades away. It's amazing to think I'm bone-meltingly relieved at the sight of the demon. If anyone told me a couple of months ago I'd prefer a demon to a human or an angel, I would have laughed their heads off.

But Astaroth is by far my favorite of all our professors. Of everyone here, actually. Apart from Sarah. And Lorcan. And Godric.

Hey! What am I thinking, putting Godric in the same category as Sarah, or even Lorcan? So I lust after the guy, empathize with his upbringing, and I had a near-breakdown thinking he could have died. But that has nothing to do with liking him, let alone lumping him with my favorite people…

Focus, idiot.

Astaroth is talking, and I've missed at least a few sentences.

I tune in again as he says, "…in all the eons the Imperium Trials have been performed, it has always been when the four celestial Hosts of Aldebaran, Regulus, Antares and Fomalhaut are in alignment. And though we have no way of knowing how this delay will change the

Trials themselves or the results, missing them completely is out of the question. But we are fairly confident we have not missed the alignment altogether, and are still in the allotted cosmic window."

"Fairly confident" huh? In my extensive life experience, this translates to, "We have no fucking clue" and "We're flying blind here, folks."

How very reassuring.

"So, to continue what I was saying before being—interrupted yesterday." Astaroth holds his hand over the open ledger before him, before sweeping it out to encompass us. "The Choosing selected each five of you for a reason. In forming your Unitas, it senses faculties in each of you that complement the others. And this is how you'll go into your Trials."

I exchange baffled glances with my own "Unitas" as everyone around us does the same.

How are we supposed to do this together? And do what exactly? We haven't trained to do anything with each other yet.

Even if we have, I stink at team games. In the few times other kids let me play catch with them, I was always the reason they lost. I dropped every ball tossed at me.

I groan inwardly. That's really all I need. To make the roomies who already hate my guts, flop whatever this test is. I doubt I'd survive *that*.

"Each Unitas will now ascend to the platform, starting by the first row."

Astaroth gestures at the five girls from the room six doors down our corridor. Their self-appointed leader is a nephilim with the trite name of Angela, who might one day bury my body with Cara. Yeah, another Godric cultist.

She moves at once, nose in the air, as if she considers being called first a well-deserved honor. She can have it. I'd rather be last. I'd rather something happens before it's our turn to cancel it. Like a comet destroying the Complex. Or the Apocalypse resuming.

The others scramble to follow Angela, tossing nervous glances at the rest of us.

As soon as they are standing in front of Astaroth, he waves his hand, and in the depth of the stage, a shimmering veil that looks like the roiling waters of mid-ocean forms. It soon parts to reveal a towering gateway.

A gasp tears through the hall. Though it isn't massive like some of the structures around here, it makes everything else look normal, earthly. It feels totally alien. I can't tell what it's made of, or rather, what I'm even looking at. Whatever its material, it seems to warp my senses so I can't see its details.

No—I see them, I just can't retain them. It's as if I register them and forget them, over and over, every single second. All I know is that it looks...as new as an unformed-yet life, but feels as old as time. Or made of time.

Unaware or unconcerned with the collective awe gripping the crowd, Astaroth addresses us again. "Before you pass through the Imperium Gate, each quintet will take an Angel Amulet, where fragments of all the Graces are contained. Once you make it out, each of you will wear the Amulet, and it will light up with your specific Graces."

Without intending to, my hand shoots up in the air, and I hear my voice, loud enough for everyone in the massive hall to hear. "You still didn't tell us about the Trials themselves!"

Every gaze in the hall lands on me, but only Astaroth's makes me wish for that ground-swallowing miracle.

I have managed to avoid any contact with our professors—until I rammed into Azazel yesterday. Now I've forced Astaroth to focus on me. And it feels as if he's probing me. I wouldn't be surprised if he is. Some demons have powerful psychic abilities. Mostly mind-control, but telepathy has to be a part of that. And then he isn't any demon.

He adjusts his monocle in a suave movement that, to me, speaks of uncertainty. As if he's taken my measure—or rather failed to.

"As it has been explained," he says. "They will determine what your specific Graces are, or lean towards."

Without intending to still, I fire back, "Yes, but what do they entail? This hasn't been explained, and we were promised an explanation."

Can you sound more aggressive and accusatory, Wen? Go ahead, provoke yet another all-powerful entity. Don't rest until one melts your head off!

As I wince inwardly, dreading I've incited that demon into showing his true face, too, Astaroth just inclines his head graciously. "There has been no such promise, since no one knows what the Trials are. They are different for each Unitas."

Before he can move on, I blurt again, "So tell us some of the previous cadets' experiences! Y'know, so we'd have a ballpark estimate."

The others shuffle uneasily around me. I know my questions are burning in their minds, but they must be glad I'm the one stupid enough to voice them. Especially now they must think his patience is running out.

Not that it is. He seems the epitome of forbearance as he steeples his fingers over the ledger, and regards me with the calm curiosity of a scientist examining a grotesque specimen.

Or maybe this is the quiet before the storm. Maybe there won't be any outward indication he'd lash out. After all, he is a collected, cultured creature, and his retribution wouldn't involve Azazel's demented theatrics.

Probing the nature of the Imperium Trials openly might be some sacrilege, and he'd be required to dole out proper punishment. Maybe that's specified in the Celestial Codex—the archangel's handbook of rules—too. We just saw him uncover that Imperium Gate with a flick of his hand. Maybe he'd snap my neck with another.

My hands lurch up to clutch it defensively when he brings his down. I feel like a fool when he only answers in his composed manner, his voice almost soothing, "Cadets are not required to relate their experiences after the fact. In fact, it has always been strongly discouraged."

Knowing I'm beyond foolish for persisting, I again stop him from dismissing the subject. "So no one ever told you what happened to them?" His nod is too smooth, his face too expressionless, I know he's lying. A long-practiced lie. It takes a liar to know another, after all. So I push on, "At least you know if they can be dangerous?"

By now the crowd is watching us like a tennis match, gazes swinging back and forth between us. All eyes pan to Astaroth as he simply says, "They can be."

"Does this mean you had incidents when cadets came out injured? Or didn't come out at all?"

Astaroth's gaze finally leaves me, and sweeps over the hall. That's a clearer dismissal than if he shouted for me to shut up already. "What you face inside will be unique to both your personal attributes, and your Unitas's combination of strengths and weaknesses."

"But that's not an answer! And how do you even know that if…"

My latest protest is cut short by a vicious tug on my arm. It's Aela.

She drops a fierce hiss in my ear. "You almost got yourself shredded yesterday. Shut up now, before they have your tongue ripped out."

"Why, Aela, I didn't know you cared," I mumble, the need to interrogate Astaroth further burning in the back of my throat.

She tosses my arm back at me. "I care about completing the Trials. And you're regretfully a key ingredient I've been saddled with."

I snort a huff. "Yeah, it's a common sentiment with your kind. Seems I'm the burden you archangelspawn have to lug around, one way or another."

"Maybe we don't have to." Cara pokes her head between us, glaring icicles at me. "Since we're the only quartet instead of a quintet, our Unitas is irregular already. One less so-called key ingredient shouldn't be a big deal in our case. It's certainly in our best interests that we go in as a trio."

Aela seems to be considering it. And neither girl is thinking of making it a duo or going solo. It's only me they want to get rid of.

While I'm glad Sarah is safe from their nefarious intentions, I don't want her to set foot through that Gate either.

Before this little exchange with Astaroth, I still hoped the Trials were some placement test that only posed the threat of exposure to me. But after he ignored my question about possible injuries or even death, I'm "fairly confident" they will be dangerous to all, and lethal to some.

And even if Sarah is among those who make it out unharmed, I'm as fairly certain she isn't Angel-Graced. There's no telling what would happen when the Trials expose her, too. I have no idea what they do to those who don't belong here.

As my thoughts roil, Aela and Cara continue discussing how to dispose of me.

Sarah interrupts them. "Even if you can get rid of Wen, I'm going nowhere without her. But you can't, since not going isn't an option for any of us. So how about we focus on what's coming?"

It amazes me that this silences them and ends their debate.

Meanwhile, a few dozen quintets have disappeared through the Gate.

The good news is, no one screams in agony or terror as they step through. But maybe they started to the moment that Gate swallowed them. Something we wouldn't find out until it is our turn. Which is quickly approaching.

I have to do something to stop us from going through this Gate!

But what can I do? A fainting spell might work, considering what I went through at Azazel's hands yesterday. But if it does, it would only exempt me. Saving Sarah takes precedence. But if I ask *her* to feign fainting, she won't. She'd consider it abandoning the others, and she's infuriatingly responsible and committed that way.

Shoulders slumping in resignation, I trudge forward with the others. There's no way to get out of this. If there were, Godric would have told me about it. He doesn't want me to go through these Trials even more than I do.

I'm examining my feet fatalistically when another wave of gasps snaps my gaze up and around, hoping for anything that might stop us from reaching our destination. I'd welcome another attack by Azazel right now.

But as the cadets behind us part, I see the cause of the commotion.

Jinny!

Head held high and looking ahead at no one, she is cutting through the lines with purposeful strides. I can still feel her struggling not to limp or stoop. Her rigid face is still swollen from her ordeal, and her fiery hair now has bangs, sloppily cut, hiding her shorn-off horns. I wonder why she didn't Glamor them as she sometimes did when they were still intact.

"Jinny!" Sarah cries as she hurtles toward her.

I feel the stupid urge to follow, but force myself to stay where I am, to watch as Sarah hugs Jinny frantically.

"Order, please," Astaroth calls out. "Return to your lines."

Jinny puts Sarah away with a stiff smile, and walks on.

"You can't be thinking of going through the Trials," Sarah exclaims as they approach. "You almost died! You were in a coma when we last checked on you an hour ago! You should be recuperating!"

"I'm fine, Sarah," Jinny says, though it's clear to me she isn't. She's faking it very well, though. "Archdemons are the most resilient beings in existence."

"But you don't have to!" Sarah persists tearfully.

Jinny shakes her head. "When I woke up, Healer Althea told me no one has ever gone through the Trials in less than a group of five. She spouted some mumbo-jumbo about a cosmic balance in each Unitas that the Trials require. And that they could be extremely dangerous even when all requirements are in place."

I huff. "She sure told you more than our esteemed demonic professor told us."

Jinny ignores me, eyes fixed on Sarah. "Bottom line is, they could be gambling your life away letting only the four of you go in."

"I didn't know you cared, Jinny," Cara repeats what I told Aela minutes ago.

Jinny deadpans at her. "I didn't, until I realized Sarah's fate is tied to yours, and that my presence is vital to this little field trip. So here I am. *You* better not mess up in there." Her glare sweeps over Cara, then rests on me.

I'm the one she singles out as a danger to our combined outcome? Even after yesterday?

You're welcome for your life, Infernal Ingrate! almost slings out of my lips.

Knowing I've caused enough disruption, I clamp them shut. Especially when Jinny's eyebrows jerk together. As if my fury hit her between them.

Which is a stupid idea. Even if she felt I was hopping mad, she'd relish it. This must be a spasm of pain escaping her mask of control.

Tearing my gaze away, I watch the line dwindling, and inwardly call her every filthy name yet to be invented.

Now she dragged herself from her deathbed to complete our Unitas, there's no way we aren't going through this Gate.

Then we are there, and one of the angels flanking it steps forward. He's the one distributing the Angel Amulets.

At the sight of the gleaming gold disc, something tumbles inside me, like a breaker crashing on a shore. I have no idea why, since its rune-dial design resembles the frieze's frame and Godric's tattoo. But it seems its very material is what provokes this swarm of emotions.

I cringe behind Aela and Cara who are leading the way.

But the angel bypasses them and holds the amulet out to me.

I stumble back, bumping into Jinny, almost taking her down in her weakened state, and Sarah with her in a domino effect.

As we all steady ourselves, with assorted grunts and groans, I snatch my hands behind my back before he foists it into them.

"No, thanks," I croak.

The angel scowls. "You have been charged with safekeeping it throughout the Trials."

"That should be a job for the strongest among us." I point at Aela.

"Take it, human," he grits.

My gaze darts around, pleading with Aela and Cara, even Jinny, to step up and take this thing. More responsibility means more ways to mess up. And more reasons to be murdered afterward. If there is an afterward.

The trio only glare back at me impatiently. Cursing them under my breath, I reluctantly bring one hand forward.

"Don't wear it around your neck under any circumstances," the angel says as he shoves the amulet into my palm.

I'm about to argue this is the safest place to keep it when a yelp rips from me.

The moment it touched my skin, a charge of something indescribable coursed through me. Cut through my brain and spine, like a laser made of memories.

Sweaty and shaky, my hand closes around the Amulet, and it chokes me up how familiar it feels. How terrifyingly—right.

What does this mean? When no one else seemed to have any reaction to their Amulets?

Where is Godric when I need to pelt him with a few dozen more questions!

"Lead the way through the Imperium Gate, human," the angel orders.

I start to object, but Jinny shoves me, hissing low in my ear, "Let's get this over with, before I pass out, okay?"

Stuffing the resonating Angel Amulet in my pocket, I put one trembling foot in front of the other.

It's only when I'm about ten feet away from the Gate that I see what's inside. Or maybe it activated or whatever, at my proximity. A hypnotically rotating vortex, like a fiery galaxy with a white-hot center. It looks as if it would incinerate me on contact.

The one thing that makes me venture closer is that I've seen others step through it. Still, as I do, I expect anything. From instant vaporization to a tumble down some cosmic rabbit hole.

What happens is something totally different, of course.

I find myself in a homogenous space that doesn't have hue or dimension or substance. I spin around, not feeling ground beneath my feet, but treading something stable, dreading to find myself alone.

I am. No one else is coming out of the vortex. It looks so far away, yet so close. There's no distance or perspective here, either, it seems.

Before my heart bursts with panic, Aela appears. The moment she materializes out of the vortex that now looks a mile away, she's feet away somehow. She's followed by the others, each treading into our new indeterminate surroundings tentatively.

The moment Sarah crosses over, the vortex blinks out.

43

We stand in a circle, exchanging wary glances, surrounded by this state of nonexistence.

Unable to wait for someone to break the silence, I blurt out, "Now what?"

"Now we wait," says Aela.

"For what?"

She shrugs. "You heard Astaroth. There's no way anyone can predict what happens."

My eyes widen incredulously. "And you believed him?"

Jinny cocks an eyebrow at me. "You're suggesting he was lying?"

"No suggestions here." I scoff at her. "As a fellow demon, you should know how your kind roll."

"Why, what a racist thing to say, Nothing." Jinny's lips twist, but the expression lacks her usual menace. Then she waves her hand, feigning boredom. "But whatever 'my kind' is prone to doing, I myself never bother lying. I neither care about anyone's opinion, nor fear the consequences of telling the truth. That's actually why *your* kind are the best liars. Which sort of makes you the expert here. If you think he was lying, he probably was."

I glare at her, chagrined that she just said what I thought earlier, about one liar recognizing another.

Before I can lob something back, Aela frowns at me. "I have to agree with the demon in this instance, human. It's your kind who sees and spreads lies everywhere. But in this situation, I believe your instinct for catching another liar in the act is off. As much as it pains me to say this about a demon, no matter his position in the Academy, Astaroth has to be telling the truth."

"Think whatever you like, about me or him," I grumble. "My gut is never wrong about stuff like this."

Aela gives a dismissing gesture. "Whatever it's telling you, his words carry more weight. The Trials are sacred, and they've been a fact of the universe since the first Nephilim were born. If there were anything to learn about their specifics, it would have made its way into the Celestial Codex or Angel Lore. It would have at least spread like hellfire through the angelic grapevine."

"Maybe it's you who didn't come across those facts, *Princess*," I sneer, amazed at how I've lost my awe of this beautiful monster since I let loose on her yesterday. "They might be filling volumes not on your 'required'—or 'allowed' reading lists. Or buzzing in circles you never deigned to step one uppity toe into."

Aela scowls. "Are you calling me uninformed and elitist?"

"About the rest of the world, and with anyone you believe is beneath you?" I shoot back at her. "Abso*lutely*!"

"But why would Astaroth lie?" Sarah says, eyes begging me not to antagonize Aela. "When you squeezed him for answers, I got the impression not all cadets survive the Trials. But if we're to eventually join the Army of Heaven, it's in the Academy's best interest to prepare us with any information they have. They would want all of us to make it through if they could help it."

"Or maybe the Trials are how they get rid of the 'weak and the foolish' Azazel said the Archangels don't want in their army. Maybe it's their way of thinning the herd without appearing responsible for anyone's demise. Who knows?" I throw my hands up in frustration. "I only know Astaroth knows more than he let on."

"Yeah, because your Liar Detector Gut said so," Cara mutters.

I swing my gaze between the girls looking at me as if I dropped some mental screws crossing that Gate. "C'mon, guys! Don't you find it suspicious—hell, *unbelievable,* that he knows every Trial is different, when he claims no one ever related their experiences?"

From the way they stare at me, it's clear none of them noticed that inconsistency before. Sarah looks dismayed, and Cara unsettled. Jinny looks focused, on standing steady, and maybe not throwing up.

Aela finally shrugs. "Whatever the truth is, it doesn't make a difference to our situation now. However he came to know this, I believe Astaroth was telling the truth about no two Unitas's experience being the same. Therefore, he could have said nothing to prepare us."

But the calmness in her voice belies the worry in her eyes. Arnchangelspawn Princess here is rattled. And if she is, what hope do the rest of us have?

I exhale heavily. "That brings us full circle to my original 'what now?' But I guess we can't figure it out, whether it's true or not that every Trial is unique to the trialees."

"Trialees is not even a word." Cara scoffs.

I toss her a belligerent glance, my least favorite inferiority complex —of being the least-educated one around—rearing its head. "Then it should be. What else do you call people undergoing a trial?"

Cara's lips curl in disdain. "Are you sure you passed mandatory education?"

I mirror her smirk. "Give me an alternative, O Highly Educated Grammar Guru. Contest? Has contestants. Entry—entrants, competition—competitors...all words have other words. What does trial have?"

Cara's gaze grows mock-pitying. "They're called nouns, not 'words.' Abstract and concrete."

My ears burn, since I've never heard of nouns having types. "You still didn't come up with a—concrete noun for trial, wiseass."

"Trialists," Aela supplies haughtily.

Cara turns her ridicule on Aela. "That's not a word, either."

Aela sweeps her in a fed up glance. "Look it up. When and if we get out of here. Though, if this is the kind of cooperation you're capable of, we might not. So shut up, and let's worry about what these Trials will throw at us. I refuse to fail, or worse, because the Choosing paired me with you lot. Do you understand?"

Mumbles and grumbles answer her. She rolls her eyes and turns away.

When none of us moves to follow her, Aela tosses a glance over her shoulder. "I would say you're welcome to stand there until you desiccate, but I need you alive, for now. It seems the forces that govern these Trials are waiting for us to make the first move. So move your useless arses!"

Then, like the celestial super-model that she is, even in our unflattering Academy-issue uniform, she prowls away as if on some other-dimensional catwalk, wading into the undefinable medium surrounding us.

"Stuck-up harpy!" Cara hisses under her breath as she starts following Aela.

"Yeah," I grunt as I grab Sarah's hand and rush after them, for the first time agreeing with Cara. "If a pretty spectacular one."

Jinny, limping openly now there aren't hundreds of fellow cadets watching her, still manages to fall into step with us, mainly because Sarah slows me down so she can catch up.

We walk in Aela's wake in silence for a long stretch, seeing nothing new in this nowhere.

At one point, I begin to wonder if the Trials are about finding our way out, which might prove impossible in this blank canvas of a place. Then something darts in the corner of my eye.

I whip my head around, barely in time to see it disappear.

I tug Sarah to a halt. "Guys, did you see that?"

"See what?" Jinny asks as she almost bumps into me.

"If you're asking, then you didn't see it. It was right there." I point to our left.

Cara looks around nervously. "What was *it*?"

"I don't know. It was very fast. But I think it was something elongated and—jagged. And dark. Or maybe it looked dark because of the distance, and shadows. Though I don't see how there are shadows, when there are no light sources. But since there aren't, how can we see…"

"Breathe, human," Aela commands. "Maybe you imagined it."

I scowl up the three inches between us. "Listen, Chicken Wings, I've seen and done and been through stuff your posh ass can't even imagine. I'm not some nervous kid with a hyperactive imagination. Who needs one in a world where you and your likes exist, anyway?"

Aela levels me with a glance, and I expect her to level *me*, at least verbally. She only ends up nodding.

She's taken my word for it? Wonders will never cease.

Aela looks around then back at us. "We need to cover our bases. Each one of you, look in a direction. I'll look ahead. You, demon, look back. The rest of you to the sides."

Then she turns and continues walking.

With none of us contesting her leadership, since I feel we're all glad she assumed it, and with each assigned a direction, we follow her.

I'm looking where I first saw the moving object when I suddenly jump.

Sarah jerks, too. "Did you see it again, Wen?"

I tear my eyes back to Jinny, who's two steps behind us, looking back.

But I *heard* her voice. It felt as if it had poured right into my ear.

She said, *"Why did you do it?"*

I shake my head at Sarah, resume my surveillance. Maybe I *am* starting to see, and now hear things.

"Well?"

There it is again. Jinny's voice. But not really Jinny's voice. It's not a voice at all. It's like she's in my head.

"Yes, I'm talking in your head. I can do that sometimes."

"Sometimes how? You have part-time telepathy?"

I blink in surprise. I answered her, and not in the way I "hear" my own thoughts. I am actually talking, but in a soundless voice.

"I do have low-level telepathy—or more like empathy. It's why I liked Sarah on sight."

*"*Now *I've heard it all. Jinny, The Empathic Imp."*

I did it again. And I know I'm doing it. She's not putting words in my head.

"You got that right. Your head is like a steel vault. It's partially why I loathed you the moment I laid eyes on you, because I couldn't get a read on you."

"And it's because I could read you loud and clear that I despised the hell out of you *on sight. But you seem to have an all-access key to my mind now!"*

Okay. This is officially creepy. What *is* this?

"This is some sort of connection we share, since I tasted your blood. It's why I did. I wanted to get a read on you, when I couldn't any other way."

"Ew, Jinny. Gross."

"Yeah, tell me about it. But even after tasting that weird blood of yours, I couldn't read you, let alone communicate with you. Not that I wanted *to communicate. All that taste did was make me feel—things within you. Things that made me want to tear you open and stomp on your every organ."*

That's close enough to what Godric said she'd do to me if given the chance. And to think I risked everything to stop her from getting *her* organs stomped.

"Yeah, that's ironic for sure."

Ugh. She got that, too?

Peachy.

"So what happened to suddenly make you jump in my head so easily?"

"I don't know. But since waking up in that hospital bed, I found the connection intensified. Your worry for Sarah practically dragged me out of my near-deathbed. It was probably what woke me up."

If this so-called connection involves blood, I think I know how it happened.

In the tussle with Azazel, I sustained the wound that so incensed Godric to see, right over my Mark. I think I know which serrated part of him sliced my neck and almost killed me then and there. It would have really been a cosmic ick if I died by his chainsaw dick.

My hand shoots up to examine the injury, and I find no trace of it.

But what matters here is that I bled. Over Jinny. When his boot was deep in her cracked-open chest. He has probably ruptured her organs, and my blood must have mingled with hers directly—maybe even with her very heart's blood—and in a copious amount. That clearly had a far more intense effect than the smear she tasted after almost poking a claw into my brain.

"Yeah, that sure as hell explains it."

I jerk again at the way her thoughts shift so smoothly, so effortlessly between my mind's pressed pages. The idea that she now has access to my every thought, my every secret infuriates me, terrifies me. Until an even worse thought hits me.

"But this will fade when my blood is out of your system, right?" I hear my mental voice choking. *"You demons renew your blood like we do, don't you?"*

"I guess. But it doesn't work that way. It's blood tasting that fades. Blood mixing is forever."

"You're saying this connection is here to stay?" My disembodied voice rises four mental octaves. *"You can jump into my mind any time you like?"*

"It's clearly a two-way thing."

"As if I want to be in your mind. And I'd rather be a vegetable than have you in my head any time you like!"

"I don't like! And I don't know if I can do it any time or not. This is as new to me as it is to you. Maybe we can communicate only because we're in Nowhere Land." `

"I sure hope so. All the more reason to get the hell out of here."

"Agreed. But first, answer my question."

"What question?"

I swear I hear her huffing in aggravation, even in this soundless medium. I do see her look Hell-ward.

"I asked why you did it."

"Why I tried to stop Azazel from killing you, you mean?"

"Yes. You're literally the last person I expected to intervene."

"Yeah, I'm crazy like that—a-surprise-a-minute."

"Answer me!"

"Hey, if you're angry I intervened, I'm sorry I did, okay?"

"I'm—I'm not angry."

Is that hesitation I hear in her "voice"? Confusion? The archedemon daughter of Lilith hesitant and confused? Nah. Her transmission must be getting spotty or something.

"I am confused. And I must understand. Everyone else was either happy or indifferent to seeing this insane angel squishing me to death. Yet, you tried to stop him. You attacked him, for Hell's sake. He would have killed you, too, if Godric didn't save us both."

"Oh, don't flatter yourself that he meant to save you. It was just an unintentional side effect of saving me."

"That's where you're wrong. After he enveloped your puny human ass in some forcefield and tossed you out of range, he turned and did the same for me."

That he neglected to mention. But come to think of it, I didn't even wonder how she survived, when she was at ground-zero of their annihilating battle.

So he actually saved her, on purpose. When he made it sound like he didn't care if she died, would have even preferred it.

"Yeah, I don't understand it either. With our history, I thought fucking Heaven's Sword would take the chance to chop my head off, and mount it in his trophy room."

Curiouser and curiouser. I already have about a thousand new questions to rain on his semi-celestial head. About their history, why he saved her, said trophy room—and that title! I'll pester him for answers for the rest of my life if need be. *If* we get out of here alive.

"Let me know the answer, if you get one. Owing him a life debt is terrible enough, not knowing why makes it unbearable. So what about you? After I almost killed you once, and after I just threatened to maim you, why did you try to save me?"

"Because I hate bullies, okay? And even if you are one to me, you're nice to Sarah. And she likes you."

"Who can't be nice to Sarah? And then, she likes everyone."

Is that insecurity I hear, too? If it is, I should let it eat her alive. Or she can extract the truth from my mind. I won't be the one to say it "out loud."

But for some reason I find myself correcting her. *"Sarah doesn't like everyone like that. The way she treats you isn't part of her amazing, and amazingly frustrating inbuilt kindness. You're special to her."* As much as it pains and outrages me to know and admit it. *"She hasn't had much special in her life."*

I feel her digesting my declaration, before her mental voice, still tinged with incomprehension, expands in my awareness again.

"So you think I contribute to Sarah's wellbeing, and you were basically trying to protect her quality of life?"

"Yeah, along with hating bullies."

I can feel her shaking her proverbial head, not convinced. *"Was that really what went through your mind in the moments before you hurled yourself at a fallen angel? Who's morphed into a five-ton monstrosity that almost broke my mind with terror? You decided to risk your life for a girl you hate, for some lame moral principle, and to preserve your best friend's newly-acquired social life?"*

"Why else do you think?"

"I'm the one asking here. You tell me."

I throw up my mental hands in exasperation at her persistence. *"Because you're alone here, okay? You've been abandoned by your kind, and forced to attend this angelbrat-infested Academy, just like I was. And this slime-ball Elite Fallen took you by surprise, and would have mashed you into demon puree, just because he wanted to. And no one else thought this was wrong. No one would do anything. No one but Sarah, and I wouldn't let her near that monster. It had to be me who tried to stop him. So even when I knew I couldn't, I just had to try."*

In the wake of my outburst, there's total silence inside my head. For long, long moments.

Just as I think our connection has been terminated, and start to breathe a sigh of relief, I "hear" her voice again, ragged with oppressive frequencies this time.

"I hate being indebted to you."

A dozen abusive retorts flare in my mind. But it seems she doesn't hear them, or she would have hurled something back at me.

Good to know I may have control over what to transmit and what not to. Especially in case this is actually permanent. I wouldn't want Jinny as a mental albatross around my frontal lobes.

Though we need to exit this place first before this can become a problem to worry about.

On our shared channel, I sneer, *"Well, suck it up, Demon Douche, and live with it. At least thanks to me, you will live. But if it'll make you feel better, I promise not to try to save you next time."*

"There won't be a next time!"

"There better not be!"

I can just "see" us both, two girls who are like gasoline and fire, each flouncing away from the mental confrontation. The images strike me as so funny in our current situation, I huff a laugh.

"Glad to see one of us is enjoying herself."

Aela's voice makes me jump. It blares as if from a sound system after the strange soundlessness of my dialogue with Jinny.

So I laughed out loud. Great. They must really think I'm crazy now.

"Yeah, that is a better explanation why you did what you did!"

Jinny. Again.

Every hair on my body bristles at her intrusion. *"Get. Out. Of. My. Mind!"*

"As if I'd want to be in your mess of a mind!"

"And stay out, Demonspawn!"

"My absolute pleasure, Abomination!"

My head almost bursts with alarm. She read the memory when Godric called me that?

What else did she see in my mind?

"I can only see your immediate or superficial thoughts, and they are such a grimy disaster zone. Just like your corner of our dorm."

"Excuse me if I don't have time, or energy to clean up!"

"Sarah would do it for you, if the rules didn't forbid her. I hate to think she spent her life cleaning after you."

"She didn't! I did my part, and anything else she wanted!"

"I bet she never told you what she wanted, so she wouldn't impose on you. I really hate to think she had no one but you. With your mess of a mind and that—thing deep inside you, Abomination is right. I bet it's Godric's favorite endearment for you."

Feeling somewhat reassured, I hit back at her, *"At least he doesn't want my head in a jar or on his wall!"*

"Yeah, I'm special. But heads always roll anyway, when Heaven's Sword is involved. Yours probably will, once his assignment with you is done."

Finding no appropriate comeback, I wrench on the connection. She yanks on her side, and between us, it snaps with a recoil that sends us both stumbling.

Though there are no footfalls in this ground-free place, we both stomp our aggravation for a while.

Somehow, all through this telepathic interrogation/confrontation, my vigilance hasn't wavered. I'm certain nothing has moved again, until I'm forced to question if I actually saw anything.

I don't know how much longer we continue walking in silence. No, absence of sound. I can't even hear my breathing. I hear nothing until someone speaks. It's some noise-cancelling feature, like those earbuds Godric is so fond of. This nullifying place is starting to feel like those sensory deprivation experiments I once read about.

I'm starting to think maybe this is part of the Trials, to take away all orientation, all stimuli, and see how we fare—when it happens.

One second, there's nothing as far as I can see in this weird distance-deficient place, the next, that thing I saw before appears again. It coalesces out of the nothingness surrounding us in between blinks.

A shout bursts from my lips as I swing around to warn the others, only for it to choke to a wheeze in my throat.

It's no longer *a* thing. There are many now. Too many to count. And they are converging on us from every direction.

44

The creatures are dark, serrated shapes that look like congealed nightmares.

And they are getting closer with every heartbeat

But they're not streaking like before. They're oozing towards us in slow-motion, giving us every chance to see their details. It's actually far scarier this way.

They're a cross between man-sized, bloated-with-blood leeches, and those acid-dripping monsters that lay eggs inside people's chests. I've seen so many ugly supernatural critters in my life, but these are in a class of their own. Their revulsion factor alone is overwhelming.

Along with the talons of terror sinking into me, something else gnaws at me. Though they don't resemble anything I've seen in the Supernatural World, I feel as if I've seen them before. Where, I can't remember. Maybe in a comic book? A dream?

Not that it matters. Only that they will soon surround us. And we have no weapons to fight them off with.

Is this the test then? We are supposed to manifest our Angel-Graced powers under duress? That doesn't bode well for Sarah and me, since we have none. Jinny, too, since whatever demonic powers she has, she's half-dead on her feet. Cara may or may not be able to access any powers.

That leaves us with the nephilim who can already use some of her powers. If she's a thousandth as powerful as Godric or even Lorcan now, we may make it out of this alive, after all.

"Hey, Aela..." I whirl around, in time to see her snapping out her wings.

It's the first time I've seen them. They're nothing like any of the other Nephilim's. As unique and spectacular as Godric's and Lorcan's, but in the palette of golds and silvers, and seem to be spun of heavenly fire. As my heart trips on its next boom, she beats them once and shoots up.

Before I can yell if she has a plan, and how we can help—Aela disappears. Right before my eyes.

Does she have cloaking powers? Or is that a Glamor? Or did this air that isn't air somehow shroud her, as soon as she put some distance between us? Is she going to fly over the monsters and pick them off?

This must be why she took off. She couldn't have left us to face them alone, could she? Not when she's our best—our *only* weapon against them.

But the monsters are still advancing. She isn't doing anything yet. Is she waiting to see if they'll attack?

Of course they'll attack! These horrors aren't converging on us to drool over us and wag their tails in welcome!

So is she debating how to round them all up? Or—has she already gauged she can't take them all on? And that we'd be no help? Has she decided it's every woman for herself? Will she just hover above us until this is over? With all of us dead?

Maybe that is part of the Trials. To see who can make cruelly pragmatic decisions to survive in the face of overwhelming odds.

This is what happens in war.

But why would they get us here, only to have us killed, in the very first test? It doesn't make any sense.

Unless it isn't supposed to. Just like war itself, like life and death never make any sense. Unless this is an elimination like I feared.

Yelling curses, at Aela for abandoning us, and at our so-called professors—who should be renamed our ring-masters—for tossing us like unarmed gladiators to these supernatural maggots, I whirl around to Sarah, and blood freezes in my arteries.

Sarah isn't there!

Screaming her name frantically, my gaze slams around.

Where is she? She was behind me seconds ago! But I can only see Jinny and Cara, standing almost back to back feet away, stances defensive as they gape at the approaching horde of horrors. I forget them even as I look at them, every sense funneling into searching for Sarah.

Then I see her. Dozens of feet away. How did she get so far? But what almost makes my heart burst is that she's coiled in a fetal position on the ground that isn't ground. And one of the creatures is almost on top of her!

There's no premeditation as I explode into a sprint that ends in a flying leap. All of Godric's training takes hold of my every muscle and nerve as, while still in the air, I swing my leg in an arc. My heavy boot thwacks into that terror's dripping-in-inky-slime snout, the full force of my dread and disgust packing the *Melek* roundhouse.

I feel my hip almost dislocate at the impact. The nauseating sensation of hitting its mass—what felt like a shark and scorpion hybrid, both rotting judging by its stench—almost makes me hurl. At least the kick has been as brutal to the creature. It falls beside Sarah, writhing and chittering in a high-pitched, insectoid frequency.

Landing in a crouch, whole being rioting with violent revulsion and aggression, I kick its head with my other foot, even harder. This time, it goes still. Whether it's dead or just knocked out, I can drag Sarah away now.

I turn to her, only for another breaker of horror to drench me. Four more creatures are converging on her!

Shredding my throat on a roar, I launch myself at them, and into a frenzied series of kicks and blows. As each fells a creature, more keep coming, all undulating towards Sarah. She remains curled on the ground, arms over her face and head, shaking like a leaf in a storm.

She has never been one for physical confrontations, but she's always been brave. Too brave. Like when she jumped into a nephilim's arms, hurling herself into the unknown to be with me. Her condition isn't normal. Neither is their targeting her in specific. It's as if she's become a monster magnet. Are they attracted to her terror?

It doesn't matter why, and I can do nothing but keep kicking and punching, warding the monsters off her.

Then I discover their slime burns, like the acid of those creatures from that horror movie. It's the burning-skin reek that alerts me. I know it's mine, from experience, since I can't feel anything in my frenzy. All of Kondar's Circadan cigars have been put out in my back and legs.

Since our uniforms provide full coverage, it's my hands burning, or my face, or both. Maybe my spotty healing will kick in, or not.

I won't stop defending Sarah until my hands burn right off. Not even then. Godric has taught me to fight with hands tied behind my back. I'll fight as long as I have feet. So until I lose those, too, I won't surrender to exhaustion. If I stop, even for seconds, we will be swarmed.

Not that I'm exhausted. Adrenaline is roaring in my system, and my movements are getting more fluid, more explosive. With each blow that takes down one of those horrors, I can only send a fervent thank you Godric's way. I wouldn't have been able to defend Sarah if not for those supernaturally effective moves he's engrained in me, through so much sweat and tears.

Suddenly, my back bumps into something. I whirl around with a war cry, only to realize Cara has slammed into me. Because a creature has slammed into *her*. No, two. Three!

So it isn't only Sarah they are drawn to like flies to a lollipop? Or were they just going through Cara, on their way to her?

Whichever, she *has* been fighting them off. It's clear from her disheveled appearance, and the black goo covering her hands and top. But since she's in one piece, she's been holding her own. She may not have had Godric for a mentor like she yearned to, but she's been getting adequate training.

Now three creatures are ganging up on her, and I can't afford to help her, can't let even one escape me and get to Sarah. I suspect these creatures liquefy their prey before feasting on them.

But if Cara can't hold them off, they will do this to her. And once she falls, no matter how successful I've been in knocking these things out so far, there are too many of them. I will tire out eventually. Then I'll be overwhelmed. Once I am, it will be over for both Sarah and me. I have no idea if Jinny is even still alive or not.

As for Aela, that treacherous bitch might be back through the Imperium Gate by now. Even if it's a total breach of the Trials rules, not even attempting to save her Unitas, I'd bet Raphael's daughter will get a mere rap on the knuckles for it.

Cara screams with rage and disgust, terror a mere tinge, as she knocks down two creatures with impressive kicks. But she only stuns them, and the third is undeterred, with five more closing in.

She's good, but nowhere as well trained as I am, can't hope to ward them off for long. And I can't do anything for her. My hands, and feet are tied fighting those who keep coming after Sarah.

This is it then. Cara will be the first to fall.

I can't even feel sorry for her. Not because I dislike the hell out of her, and she would probably love to see me dead. It's because I won't last much longer after she goes down.

As I dispose of four more of Sarah's attackers, Cara shoves her hands out to ward her closest one off, and suddenly they're glowing bluish green. Next second, the glow leaps, covering her whole body like wildfire.

The moment the creature touches it, it lets out a horrific screech as it joins its fellow writhing monstrosities on the ground.

But this one doesn't move at all. It curls on itself and shrinks like burning paper, as the terrible stench of its charring flesh sears my lungs.

Cara fried it. Just by touching it.

Her Grace power has manifested!

Now *that's* some handy power. Why can't I have something that flashy and useful?

But she doesn't seem to be handling her power's discovery well. While she has faced the creatures with steady vehemence, she now staggers, mouth and eyes round with shock as she holds up arms that look engulfed in blue-hot fire.

A plan bursts in my mind. To see if it can be put into action, I need her to snap out of it.

"Cara!" I shout as I continue to punch and kick the horrors vying for Sarah. Yet another one rams Cara, only to meet the same fate. "Quit standing there playing mosquito zapper. I need you to flare this frying field covering you out, take them all out at once."

It seems I manage to aggravate her out of her stupor as she shouts back, "What makes you think I can do that?"

"Just try, dammit! And by try I mean, *do it!*" I scream as another half a dozen nightmares worm their way toward Sarah, appallingly silent and inexorable. She's now almost buried in the bodies of the fallen ones.

"What if I fry you along with them?" Cara screams back as another one zaps itself against the energy field surrounding her.

"They'll overwhelm me by sheer numbers sooner rather than later, and we'll be dead anyway," I pant as I kick another one in the head. "I'll take our chances with your zapping powers!"

"If I burn you to a crisp, just remember it was your fault!" Cara gives a straining shriek just before a shockwave of magnificent teal and azure flames burst out of her.

Before I can draw my next breath, the blaze engulfs me, razes through me as I watch dozens of monsters spasm all around us, their jagged, slippery hide distorting as it combusts.

But as they shrivel up on the ground in these supernatural flames, I don't feel anything. Maybe that initial burn before every sensation ceased means Cara has seared off my every nerve-ending. I may already be dead, and I don't know it yet.

But I can still see and think, and Sarah is still quaking on the ground, which could mean Cara's flames have passed harmlessly through us. To test my theory, I turn, find I can move. This proves I'm alive and in one functioning piece, right?

The monsters continue to shrivel at my feet, including the ones I struck down, disintegrating around Sarah, freeing her from being slowly entombed by their accumulating corpses.

It worked! Cara did it!

But as soon as I see her, all elation is snuffed. Just like her flames have been. She's now kneeling on the ground, retching. This stunt seems to have depleted her completely. And the manifestations of horror that haven't been caught in her blast's radius, are still oozing from all around us.

As soon as one gets close enough, I swirl around with another roundhouse, taking it down as I shout to Cara, "Come over here beside Sarah, so I can protect you until you recharge!"

If she recharges.

She can't even push herself to her feet, hobbles awkwardly toward us on her knees. As she approaches, something red flares at the edge of my vision.

I snap around, only to see Jinny for the first time since the mayhem started.

She's firing what looks like lava from crimson-glowing hands. The scorching streams arc in the non-air, hitting the two creatures floating above her on their way to us, melting their heads right off!

A "yes" explodes from me, as if my favorite soccer player has just scored an impossible goal.

The glow of her hands flickers and flares, as if revving for another blast. Before she can unleash it, the rest of the creatures' twitching bodies crash into her.

Jinny yells as she collapses beneath their literally dead weight.

In the moment of distraction, another one rams into me. Before I fall, too, I catch myself on one extended arm, and perform the two-legged kick Godric almost killed me before I got right. One boot tears through the monstrosity's wide-open maw, and gets stuck there as it crumples, dragging me down with it.

I tear my foot out of its now-flaccid jaws, squelching in its inky, stinky slime, and scrape against its rows of jagged teeth. My yell echoes Jinny's as she shoves the carcasses off of her. I stagger up to my feet as she hauls herself up, and limps towards us.

As soon as she stumbles into our circle, I snarl at her, "You left me fighting for Sarah alone, the only one who cares for you, when you can fire lava lasers? That's a new low, Evilspawn!"

"I couldn't 'fire lava lasers' until I absorbed enough of their dark energy, Nobrain," Jinny snarls back.

"You mean you can *feed* off them?" I shout as I ram a creature in the midsection, making it spew a gallon of rotten slime down my front. I'm past shuddering in revulsion. "Guess it takes a bigger monster, huh?"

"I didn't know if I could 'feed off them,'" she grunts as she blasts another lava laser, punching a hole through a creature before it poured that burning gunk over Sarah's head. "And when I first tried, it literally knocked me out. I'm not firing on all cylinders, what with having a fallen angel's footprint all over my vital organs."

Though I hate to give her that, it's a miracle she's up and running at all in her condition. But she's doing far more than that. She's using her power, one of them, at least. Another cool, or should I say, red-hot one. I can't even use mine, as lame as it is, since those things don't emit any energy I can detect, let alone harvest. Jinny clearly does.

At least, I have the skills Godric ingrained in me.

I grab one by what passes for a tail, what feels like dipping my hands into a thousand worms and cockroaches. I swing it with all my newly-minted strength into its twin. Or its clone? They all look identical, which is more gruesome somehow.

"When I came to, I didn't know how long I was crumpled like a used hanky," Jinny pants as she strains, and blasts another two. Her hellish beams slice one in half, and drills the other a fist-sized hole where its eyes should have been.

The stench of their fetid flesh burning is almost enough to make me black out. For once I'm thankful for something Azazel did. Sending us here on empty stomachs. Unless they knew they were sending us to our deaths, then it becomes evil beyond measure. We didn't even get a last meal!

But it's weird that Jinny is bothering to explain herself to me. Or is it to Sarah? Letting her know why she hasn't come to her rescue sooner?

Not that Sarah can grasp anything in her condition, or is aware of anything going on around her. She's shut down with panic.

"You were out for the time it took me to knock out dozens of those uglies," I gasp. "And for Cara to manifest her Grace power and fry them. Though her batteries are depleted for now."

I kick another one away from Sarah, only for Jinny to laser it.

And for a while, we play clay pigeon shooting with them. I'd knock one to her, and she would blast it.

Then her crimson energy starts to sputter. Cara's blue-spectrum one isn't coming back online, but she keeps her end of the fight. If only with her feet, burned hands curled close to her chest.

I still can't feel my own burns, or other injuries, when I'm certain I have many. Nothing too serious, I hope, since I've been running on adrenaline and my new-found stamina.

At one point, what feels like forever later, depletion starts to sink its claws into me.

Every breath feels as if I'm inhaling that slimy acid into lungs filled with razor-sharp debris. Every muscle feels made of barbed wire, and trembles as if about to snap. My mind keeps phasing in and out as if to escape the endlessness of this struggle. And those gigantic maggots keep coming. It's only a matter of time before they overwhelm us. Then it will be all over.

There's nothing more I can do. There's nothing to *be* done. We can only keep fighting. Until the end.

What feels like an hour later, I stumble around as another creature closes in on Sarah. But I know I won't be able to stop it this time. I can barely move. Can barely breathe.

Then my legs twist over each other, and I crash to the bizarre medium beneath, knowing I won't get up again. Jinny and Cara have already given up.

Now I'll watch as these things swarm Sarah. Then it will be our turn. Only Aela has gotten away.

It *has* been an elimination. She'll be the only one to exit the Imperium Gate, the only one worthy of serving in the Army of Heaven.

I could have told those angelic monsters *that* without any of this.

They didn't need to send us all to our gruesome deaths, to find out that the daughter of an archangel is superior to any of us.

Not that she is. That cowardly bitch is the least worthy of us. Even Jinny fought for her friend with everything in her. Those creatures wouldn't have targeted her otherwise. Jinny will now die along with us because she didn't abandon Sarah.

But I can't see Sarah die. I can't watch them drench her in that hideous slime, can't watch her flesh melt for them to consume. Even if it would make dying myself easier, knowing she's already gone.

I still can't let her die without knowing I'm there.

As I start crawling toward her, Jinny drags herself limply from the other side.

We meet over Sarah, Jinny covering her legs with her body, while I protect her back with mine.

Together till the end, my darling Sarah.

But I can't even say this out loud.

All I can do is close my eyes, and wait for the end.

45

The eerie absence of sound envelops me.

I wish it will spare me hearing Sarah's agony as she dies. That I'll remain in the darkness behind my closed lids until I follow. For I do know she'll die first.

Though Jinny and I are shielding her, those monstrosities will target her first. She's been the one they wanted from the start. We're extra food. She's the main course.

Even now, with death oozing toward us, my mind races with questions.

Why? Why Sarah? What is it about her they crave? It can't be only fear, since I was terrified at the start, and they didn't target me.

Theories rattle in my mind, even when they're futile, even as my last wish is thwarted. The selective sound transmission of this place means I continue to hear Sarah's sobs of terror, and the others' moans of pain and depletion.

Suddenly, I want to hear something else. Godric's voice. Just one last time. Saying my name. What he never said.

But I'd take anything. Even a *"Move your scrawny arse, White"* will do.

What I hear is a mighty whoosh, and my lids light up with crimson.

Can it be? He's come to save me, again?

Jerking with insane hope, my eyes snap open, my heart almost uprooting itself—only to plummet with crushing disappointment.

Not him. *Not him.*

It's Aela, her golden wings ablaze. She looks more like a phoenix than a nephilim.

But—what is she doing back here? Come to watch us die?

I raise my head, gulping down a tearing breath. When I release it, I'll scream all the filth in existence at her. I'll roar her pathetic, low-life truth. I need to incense this arrogant bitch so she'll come closer. Then I'll yank the fucking Essence out of her...

I choke on my breath. Sh-she is coming closer. Swooping down towards me, feet first, fast as a missile. She's going to...to...

A horrifying, gelatinous crack reverberates like a gunshot in the stillness. The sound slices through my spine. I can't move, can't breathe...

Did-did she just...

A creature slams on top of me. From its angle, it's been looming over Sarah. Its maw is open, pouring liquefying goo over her arms-covered head.

Screeching, I explode up to catch the nightmare-hued sludge before it hits her. This much will eat through my hands. I don't care. Those things, and Aela, won't get to her until I'm dead.

But I can't catch it all. Or any of it. It's spilling like water through my fingers and drenching Sarah.

Shrieks of rage and futility shred my throat, until I realize—the gunk isn't burning me. Or Sarah. And that monster—it's dead. In two pieces. That must be Aela's doing, the crack I heard. She literally snapped it in half.

I swing my head around, looking for her—and see two dozen more creatures converging on us from every side. Before I can shout a warning, Aela flings out her arms, hurling jagged bolts of golden light.

The creatures explode, pelting us with cold slabs of fetid flesh.

Jinny and Cara echo my nauseated cry. Sarah remains cowering on the ground beneath us, shaking apart with silent sobs.

Aela flies up again, her wings spread wide and emitting a blinding radiance that conquers the pervasive gloom. All the creatures that have been oozing in the distance in their hundreds, or thousands, start shrieking. I barely see their retreat as they clot back into the fabric of this nebulous place.

Then they're gone. Just like that.

Aela lands soundlessly, folding her wings. With another flash, they're gone.

I scramble off Sarah just as Jinny does, and Cara sits up. We exchange depleted, wary looks before panning dazedly around. We're half buried in the carcasses, body parts and ashes of the horrific creatures we've killed, each in her own way. Though I mostly knocked out mine, before the others finished them off.

As if we agreed, me and Jinny crawl to drag Sarah into a monster-mess-free spot.

Her arms are still covering her head, so spastically, I have to apply force to remove them. Her eyes are squeezed shut, her lips quaking on fractured breaths. The creature's postmortem goo—which doesn't burn like its feeding one—is covering her head and arms and back. Apart from that, she looks unharmed.

I stroke her hair, removing as much tar-like slime as I can. "It's all right, Sarah. They're gone. You're okay."

"We killed them all." Jinny runs a soothing hand down her sticky back as she, too, scoops gunk off her.

Sarah's lashes flutter, then her eyes open, reddened, their azure too bright as she looks brokenly up at me.

I force a trembling smile as we help her sit up. "You're fine. It's over."

"You!" Aela's furious hiss makes us all jerk.

It takes a moment to realize she's stabbing a finger at Sarah, not me.

"You pull your weight around here, human," Aela growls. "You don't get to cower and indulge in a panic attack when things get nasty. I'm not playing guardian to your damsel in distress again."

Still shaking, Sarah only nods and hangs her head.

I don't think she's ever directed a word at Aela. Even when she said she wasn't going without me, she wasn't addressing her, just stating her decision. She talks a mile-a-minute with Lorcan, doesn't find any difficulty talking to our professors. Or even Godric, who stares down at her as if she's some sort of talking pet. Hell, I heard she even dared talk in class to Azazel.

But for some reason, Aela has always struck her dumb.

I heave up to my feet, shielding Sarah as I glare at Aela. "Sarah isn't a pampered-from-birth, supremely-trained archangelspawn with powers at her literal fingertips like you."

Aela swings her volcanic ire to me. "You're not, either, and I saw you fighting. To my shock, you far more than held your own."

"Thanks to Godric's training," I grit. "And then she's always been the brains in our outfit."

Aela flings a contemptuous glance between me and Sarah. "Unless she wants those brains splattered all over this—nothingness, she better put the training the Academy has been affording her to use in situations that need brawn."

"It's not like you put yourself in danger or even broke a sweat to help her out," I snap. "You just landed on this thing, then crackled and glowed like some on-the-fritz celestial lightbulb for a minute. So stop your whining, you spoilt, heavenly brat!"

Aela's jaw muscles bunch and her eyes start to emit that amazing, scary golden light. "You will watch how you speak to me, human."

"Or what, archangelspawn?" I square off with her, then another thought strikes me. I can't *believe* it wasn't the first thing that did. "And how dare you complain at all, you—*deserter*!"

Her eyes round, turning a glowing purple. "*What*?"

I limp to crowd her personal space, poke a finger into her ample chest. "You took off as soon as those things showed up! You left us fighting them alone for what must have been three hours!" Judging by the state of my exhaustion, the same as at the end of Godric's Phase One. "We could have all been long dead by the time you deemed to come back! Whatever the reason you decided to come back. So don't you dare behave as if you rode to our rescue!"

"I hate to say this, but I'm with Wen on this." Cara rises to stand beside me, voice and face racked with pain, hands still curled at her chest. "You're the only one who had access to some of her powers already, and could have done what you just did from the start. I might end up l-losing my hands—and it's all because *you* left us!"

"What those two said, archangelspawn," Jinny drawls, her usually coppery complexion ashen, as if her hellfire is depleted. It probably is, after firing it nonstop for a couple of hours. Apart from that, she seems back to normal. Her regenerative powers must rival Godric's. She now completes our trio of accusation around Aela, even using my name for her and her cousins. "These things weren't targeting me, but I made myself a target standing between them and the others, because *I* take this Unitas business seriously. But because *you* weren't here to 'pull your weight,' as you just accused Sarah, I got depleted. A minute more, and you would have gotten rid of me like you wanted to yesterday."

"I didn't want to get rid of you!" Aela exclaims.

Jinny waves a bored hand. "Oh, you did. I would want to get rid of you, too, so don't sweat it. You just got cold feet about being the direct cause for my death, and theirs, too. So don't expect thanks because you worried about your own test results and standing within the Academy, and decided to save us at the last moment."

Aela's frown deepens as she glares from one to the other. "Have you all gone insane with fear, or is this place warping your minds? I was gone for mere minutes. I had to see what we were up against from an altitude, and where these things were coming from."

"*That's* the story you'll tell back at the Academy?" Jinny scoffs. "That you flew up to assess the situation, like the good little general that you are, and we all lost our minds in your absence, and imagined everything?"

"Oh, yeah?" That's Cara, any remaining awe she had of Aela evaporating under the brunt of anger and dread over her hands. "How are you going to explain all those creatures we killed? We killed *hundreds* while you hid away. Or are you going to say you killed them all?"

I smirk at them. "She probably counted on not saying anything, since the Academy discourages cadets from recounting their Trials." I swing my venomous glare at her. "But you miscalculated, Princess. *We're* telling them everything."

Aela growls. *Actually* growls. Like a lioness about to lash out.

From the way Cara and Jinny take a step back, they must have felt my same surge of fright. We're enraging a nephilim who can cut us all in half. And we just gave her reason to do it, to silence us.

The one thing that makes me stand my ground is sensing Aela's confusion. She's more bewildered and frustrated than incensed and cornered.

Her next words prove she isn't on the same page as the rest of us at all. "What the Inferno are you all talking about? I *was* gone only a few minutes! Three or four at most. And I know you fought these creatures, I saw it from above. Though…" She stops, stares at us, eyes glazing. "…it was a—very long fight, I remember now. But how…?"

She falls silent, frowning again, but this time it seems as if her vision is turning inward. She looks as if she's afraid *she's* going insane.

As the other two girls glare up at her, thinking she's pretending, my mind races.

A whole scenario forms as I step between them. "Hey, guys, I think I know what happened here. This place is messing with us. It must have identified Aela as the strongest of us, the one capable of ending this test prematurely. So it trapped her in a different level or whatever, where she couldn't judge the passage of time. What felt like minutes to her, was hours for us."

"That's a cute theory," Jinny says, sounding bored. "What's with taking the archangelspawn's side all of a sudden, Nothing?"

"I'm not taking anyone's side, Demonspawn. That's the one thing that makes sense."

Jinny gets in my face lazily. "What I said makes the *most* sense. She left us to die, then got cold feet, probably because she realized she might need us if there are other tests. She might have also feared they were observing all this somehow. I did keep feeling a presence watching us every now and then."

Now that she mentioned it, I did feet the brush of some awareness. Vast and timeless. Like what I've been feeling surveilling me for the past two months. But I was too busy fighting for our lives to fully register it. But something *was* there. Maybe still is.

"Bottom line is," Jinny says, like an attorney summing up a murderer's motives. "She worried there'd be evidence of her crime, and probably feared it could deprive her of joining their blasted Army. So she cooked up this alternate timeline story to absolve herself of any nefarious intentions, and put on the last-minute light show to look like a hero."

I twist my lips at her. "Seems you missed your vocation as a writer, O Daughter of Lilith." Jinny's eyes flare lava. But I feel more acrimony directed at her mother than me for mentioning her. Yeah, more Supernatural family strife for me to use, if I ever get the chance to. I scoff. "Never too late, though. If you survive this Academy, get this attempted-murder mystery published in *your* nefarious Court. It would break the Infernal Charts. But, while the angel-hating denizens of Hell would eat it up, there's one major plot hole in your story. Aela is telling the truth. As she believes it. So my 'theory' is a way better explanation."

Jinny scoffs. "*You're* telepathic now, White?"

I smirk at her. "Just a human who lied all my life to survive. We established I know a liar when I see one. This here Princess of Feathers? She can't lie to save her life."

Another growl issues from Aela. "Say one more word about me as if I'm not here, and I will knock you both out. It will rid me of your incessant bickering."

We snap our gazes to Aela. She means it.

As if agreeing we'd rather remain conscious, we hobble away from each other.

Aela exhales. "I now realize how dangerous this place is, if it can mess with my mind."

"*That's* why it's dangerous?" Cara whimpers. "Not because it spewed a million giant, acid-vomiting worms that m-mutilated us, before almost making us their next meal?"

Aela blinks at Cara, as if seeing her for the first time since she returned. Then she flicks a gesture at her hands. "Let me see those." Cara gapes at her. "I'm Raphael's daughter." Cara still looks uncomprehending. Aela exhales her impatience. "*The* Healer? Ring any bells?"

Cara's eyes widen with such vulnerability. "Y-You mean you have healing powers like his?"

"Oh, nowhere as powerful. At least for now. But I can heal the worst of the damage."

"So I'll still have scarred, useless hands," Cara moans.

Unmoved by Cara's pain and desperation, Aela shrugs. "Possibly. I won't know until I examine you. Now, your hands?"

With a sob, Cara stumbles closer. Her face twists in agony as she lowers her burnt-raw hands, forcing them open with a cry.

Aela holds her own hands over them, and they start glowing. The glow looks like her destructive energies and what fuels her amazing wings. All the range of silvers and golds, but entwining with the purple/violet hues of her flaring eyes.

"Those creatures' secretions are more corrosive than napalm," Aela murmurs. "It's proof that you are already way beyond human that your hands didn't melt right off. You only have second and third degree burns, and muscle damage. But your nerves and tendons are intact."

This was her diagnosing Cara's condition? Holy CAT scan! Literally.

I look down at my own hands, find remnants of the same feeding slime that burned Cara's hands. It did burn mine, too, but they're almost healed now.

Sticking them behind my back, I wipe them on my butt. I don't want them to wonder why I didn't suffer the same injuries. I can pretend it's my Grace powers kicking in, but I'd rather hide my vacillating healing feature for now. Now it has activated in Godric's absence, I no longer understand how it works myself.

As for the gallons they belched all over me, I have the same alibi as the others, our weapon-proof uniforms. They're made to withstand anything from human bullets to demon fire and Fae blasts. They did protect our bodies, but at the cost of severe damage. Mine looks like it's fresh out of an incinerator.

Cara's shriek makes me and Jinny jump.

"W-What are you *doing*?" Cara struggles to pull her hands away. But though Aela isn't holding them, they're trapped within her light.

Totally unfazed by the other girl's agony, Aela frowns at her. "Stop squirming, angel-graced, or I will put you out during the treatment."

"J-just tell me what's happening," Cara sobs raggedly.

Aela exhales, as if it's such an imposition to explain herself to others. "You do have supernatural healing abilities, but left to their own devices, at this level of damage, they're already taking shortcuts in their effort to restore you quickly. Such hastiness has a haphazard component, one that I'm stopping, otherwise, it will leave you with scarring, and loss of function. I'm arresting your own abilities until I supply them with order and a perfect pattern to follow, along with the correct healing spark, so they can complete the process properly. Satisfied?"

Cara nods shakily, tears streaming down her trembling face.

There's total silence from then on, apart from Cara's agonized moans.

I bet even Jinny breathes again when Aela's light goes out, and she steps away from Cara with a nod. "It's done. You should be fine soon."

"Th-thank you," Cara chokes as she stares down at her half-healed hands, her shuddering cheeks drenched. "Oh, Aela, you're amazing!"

Something flits in Aela's eyes. Embarrassment, discomfort, even a little shyness? This paragon of perfection isn't used to receiving thanks? Or praise?

Nah.

"Aela was right."

I whirl around at Sarah's rasp. Finding her struggling to her feet, I race Jinny to her side. As we support her, our gazes meet above her head, and I bet she sees my guilt as I see hers.

After we made sure she was okay, we confronted Aela and all but forgot about her.

She sways between us, and I squeeze her hand. "Take it easy, sweetheart."

She shakes her head. "Aela was right to be angry at me."

"Oh, no she wasn't!" Jinny growls.

As we both visually dagger the nephilim for making Sarah feel guilty about having a panic attack, Sarah insists, "No, no, she was. Just not the way she thought. I think I figured out what this test was all about. And maybe what to expect next."

46

I stare at Sarah, her last statement ringing in my ears.

I bet everyone is bating their breath like me as she continues, "I-I never told you about it, Wen, because you hate my parents too much already. I didn't want you to dwell on such terrible emotions. They-they're not worth poisoning yourself over."

My hatred of the so-called parents who sold her mushroom like a nuclear explosion all over again. "It's not over them! It's over what they did to you..."

Aela interrupts me with a scowl directed at Sarah. "Why are you telling us this sob story, human? Do you think this excuses your—"

Both me and Jinny yell at her in unison, "Shut *up!*"

"Guys, please...just listen." Sarah's hands tighten on our forearms, bringing our attention back to her. "My parents once brought home what they called Hiruda..."

"Aren't these magical leeches that...?" Cara pipes up before our glares silence her.

Sarah nods. "Yes. But those didn't only leach blood from one person, they transfused it into another."

"Does this revolting tale have a point?"

Before we could blast Aela again, Sarah tugs on our arms. "My parents said I have a rare blood type they would sell to covens and vampires at any price they set..."

Jinny makes that terrifying polyphonic sound in the back of her throat as her nails elongate and curve into claws. "You *will* give me your parents' names, Sarah. I will send them to my very own brand of Hell."

"I'm with Demonspawn for once, Sarah," I hiss, my blood already boiling. "I was helpless to find and punish them before. But once we're out of here, I'll find a way to track them down. Thanks to Godric's training, I can now break every bone in their bodies!"

"Guys, please, this isn't about them. Just let me finish." We both nod reluctantly, and she goes on, "Each Hiruda was as big as my finger, but I was six and very little with it. My parents stripped me naked, tied me down, and connected my arm to an intravenous solution. They placed them on my legs, arms and chest, and they kept growing. The ones on my inner thighs grew to the size of my hands..."

"I'll drag them back to the Academy and give them to Godric to torture!" I seethe. "No, to Azazel to eat!"

Before Jinny can add her own pledge of torture and mayhem, Sarah pushes at me and stands without support. "This isn't the point, guys, please." We both lapse into fuming silence and Sarah exhales. "This became a regular thing until nothing they did between sessions worked to replenish my blood—and this is when they sold me."

"And if you say they had to, to feed the rest of the family, one more time..."

This time, her pleading glance is what stops me. But nothing will stop me from exacting a vengeance as depraved as they are on these inhuman pieces of human shit. I really need to survive these Trials so I'd get back to Godric, and have him teach me his torture techniques.

"Somehow, I don't remember being too bothered by this procedure," Sarah says. "Until one time, the TV was on. It was that movie Alien...and suddenly, that monster and the leeches became one in my mind. I screamed until I lost consciousness. And every time after that, and every night in between. I guess it's one of the reasons they sold me."

"Because they couldn't get a good night's sleep after they traumatized you?" Jinny actually grins. "Oh, this is going to be the most delicious damnation I ever performed!"

Sarah gives her a pained glance that makes her manic smile wobble. "The point I was getting to is, when I was sold to Zeral, she bought me a Quelling, so I wouldn't keep *her* awake every night. I still remembered the incident, but the spell suppressed my phobia. In time it became a very distant memory." A pause to draw in a shaky

351

breath. "But I think this place must have dug up both memory, and phobia—and amplified them a hundredfold. At my worst times, I woke up screaming and sobbed for a while before I went back to sleep. This time I was totally paralyzed, and the hybrid leeches from my nightmares manifested into those monsters, who only want to feed on me."

"*That's* why you were their target," I shout, jumping with excitement at having an answer at last. "*Now* it makes sense. You're a *genius*, Sarah."

Sarah hangs her head. "Not really. I'm the one who knows about my monster leech phobia. I just put two and two together."

"Genius, I tell you!" I turn to the others, feeling very smug. "See, the brains of this outfit."

"I still don't get why you thought Aela is right to be angry at you?" Jinny snaps, glaring at Aela again.

"Because I'm the reason all this happened."

"Oh, that's not why Ms. Angelass here was angry at you." I scoff.

Aela growls again, but Sarah is shaking her head. "Maybe it was. She has uncanny senses, and she might have felt I was at the center of all this. Since she didn't know how, she thought her anger was about me not participating in the fight."

"Well, she had no right to be angry, either way," I hiss, fighting the urge to break my fist against the nephilim's perfect nose. "None of it was your fault!"

Sarah shakes her head again. "I could have fought the terror…and maybe the monsters would have disappeared."

"That's not how phobias work, Sar," Jinny exclaims.

"Yeah," I second Jinny, really hating how we're uniting over Sarah. "If people can fight them or control them, they wouldn't be called phobias."

Sarah exhales, and looks at Cara. "I'm-I'm sorry about your hands."

"What these two said. Not your fault." Cara holds out her hands for us to see. "And thanks to Aela, they're almost healed."

Sarah deflates with a tremulous exhalation. "Thank Heaven."

After a long beat of silence, when we all take stock of the situation, Aela looks at Sarah, with that same unrelenting displeasure. "You said you have an idea what the coming tests would be."

Before Sarah can answer, I step in front of her, shielding her until she gets herself together. "It stands to reason they will target the rest of us."

Aela shakes her head, and even her golden ponytail looks disapproving. "I can't understand how this place chose *her* as our first test."

I crack a nasty laugh. "Oh, you poor princess! You're put out because it didn't start with you?"

Aela looks down her nose at me. "It stands to reason, as you said. I'm the superior one here."

Jinny joins my snickering. "This place clearly doesn't agree. It put your deluded ass where it belongs, beneath the one you consider the weakest of us. Doesn't that just ruffle your stuck-up feathers—Ruffle-Aela?"

My laugh becomes a snort as I fight the urge to high-five Jinny. "Yeah. How pathetic is it, to be snubbed by nothingness, Nephi-lame?"

Jinny bursts out laughing at my newest addition to Aela's nicknames.

Aela sniffs haughtily at us. "Vulgarity and name calling are to be expected from both of your species."

My laughter ends abruptly on an exclamation. "You call us names all the time!"

"I do not. I call you human or angle-graced, and demon. That's what you are."

"It's the way you say them, then," I mumble, unable to believe she's right. I could have sworn she insults us all the time.

Jinny puts what I'm thinking into words. "You make them sound worse than insults."

Aela shrugs. "You must be hearing your own inferiority complexes concerning your respective species. I would never engage in your juvenile games of insolence."

"You *should* engage us," Jinny taunts. "It might loosen the stick you have up your celestial butt."

Cara steps between us. "Guys, we need to strategize for our coming tests."

"Who says we have more tests?" Aela says.

I hold up one finger. "First, they're called Trials, plural."

Aela pouts dismissively. "That can mean all of the cadets' trials."

I unfold another finger. "Second, we're still here."

Aela doesn't have an answer to that. She lowers her gaze for a second before exhaling. "Fine. How do you suggest we strategize?"

Unable to believe she gave an inch, I rush to offer my opinion. "Let's assume more tests may target each of us. So, out with it, guys—what's your phobia?"

Aela waves a nonchalant hand. "I have nothing to contribute. I'm not afraid of anything."

"Hah, a likely story." Jinny scoffs. "Every sentient being is afraid of something. *Many* things. Pick the worst one you can think of."

"I have nothing to tell you, demon."

"C'mon guys, we don't know when the next test will start," I urge. "We need to be prepared. I'll start. I discovered I'm terrified of suffocation. So anything that includes that is my phobia. Like being buried alive, drowning, stuff like that. Just in case we fall into an ocean or a crypt or something and I go catatonic."

"I'm afraid of fire," Cara chokes. "It's why I almost died of fright when I thought I burst into flames."

I raise my eyebrows at her. "You sure recovered fast when I yelled at you."

Cara twists her lips at me. "You have that effect on me."

That's the first time she says something to me without a "drop dead" undertone. It does still say "aggravating bitch." But it's progress.

I grin at her. "Fire, check."

Jinny shakes her head. "That's ridiculous. Fearing fire is not a phobia. Every sentient being is afraid of it. It's why Hell was created."

I gape at her in dismay. "Ugh, you have a point there. Anything else, Cara?"

"Uh, I'm terrified of injury, of losing body function, that's why when I thought I lost my hands…"

Aela takes an exasperated step forward. "Quit with the generic fears. It has to be an irrational fear, something specific to you that others will not be afraid of. Like those monster leeches."

"I can't think of anything else, okay?" Cara mumbles.

Flicking her a glance that proclaims her useless, Aela turns her gaze to Jinny. "What is your phobia, demon? Azazel?"

Jinny's eyes crackle with the hellfire I thought exhausted. That was actually too unfeeling of Aela. "Your morning breath, nephilim."

I rush to come between them. "Guys, guys, we don't know how much time we have before the next feature movie starts. So put a sock in it, both of you. Spill!"

Jinny glares at me with those terrifying hell-pits. "You didn't spill *your* phobias. Suffocation is like fire and losing body parts. Everyone is afraid of that. What are you hiding?"

"I'm not hiding anything!"

"Stop it!" We both jerk around to Sarah, shocked at how sharp she sounded. We find her standing steadily, scowling at us all. "Stop bickering, all of you, and remember we're a team, a Unitas—please." I'm almost sorry she added that to soften her reprimand. I like this assertive side of her. "I think you're going about this the wrong way. I didn't mean that any coming tests will be about more phobias. I doubt it can be this predictable."

I gape at her. How didn't I think of that? How did none of us?

I throw my hands toward her. "See that? *That's* brains." I rush to her side. "What do *you* think it will be?"

Sarah's eyes fill with the eagerness that always accompanied a good idea. Which used to be regularly. "Let me explain my thought process first. The first trial proved this place has—logic. It can read us, then exploit our weaknesses, test our strengths, and force our development—along with necessitating teamwork. It boiled down to exploiting my weakness, using it to test Wen's and Jinny's strengths, to force Cara's development, and to necessitate relying on each other."

"What about me?" Aela asks. "What did it do with me?"

Sarah lowers her gaze. "Uh...it's only my interpretation..."

"Out with it." Aela bites off. "What do you think it did to me?"

"It sidelined you!" Sarah blurts, still unable to look at Aela. "It—it..."

"Quit stuttering, human." Aela scowls at her bent head. "What are you saying the purpose of that was? The lesson learned?"

I get in her face, taking her disconcerting focus away from Sarah. "Not only are you a winged bully, you're a dim one, too. Sarah provided all the dots, and you still can't connect them, featherbrain? Let me explain in simple terms even you can understand. When you left us, left the *Unitas*, without consulting us, and took it upon yourself as the "superior one" to resolve the issue singlehandedly, this place showed you that you're *not* all that. It did whatever it wanted to you, kept you prisoner without you even realizing it, and let you go only when it saw fit."

"Yeah, it did to you the opposite of what it did to us," Jinny puts in, grinning from ear to ear. "While it unleashed us, it reined you in. It took away the one thing you value most, control. And it hit you where it really hurts a being like you, in your confidence, your pride. You came out of its grip unable to trust your own mind and senses. That should have made you realize it's not all about power, that you're not the leading lady here, and we're not your extras. *That* should have been the lesson *you* learned."

An exquisite color creeps over Aela's chiseled cheekbones. Man, if she isn't Godric-level magnificent!

She finally nods. "Fine. Lesson learned. Apologies, Sarah. What else do you think?"

We all gape at her.

She can do that? Admit she was wrong, can learn from her mistakes, apologize, and respect "lesser" beings' opinions? She even called Sarah by name. Miracles *do* happen.

Encouraged, Sarah raises her gaze to her. "Keep in mind my deductions are built on the first trial. The next one might be totally random."

Aela inclines her head at her. "And if it isn't? If it still follows the logic of the first one?"

"I might be wrong, but I can't find many other possibilities, since really, sentient beings are not that complex, even the immortal variety. We all play by a limited set of universal rules."

"What are you suggesting?" Aela asks, seeming genuinely intrigued.

Sarah blushes under her attention and interest. "If the first test was about fear, what other emotions are as powerful?"

"Love?" I suggest at once. That's certainly the most powerful emotion and motive I ever had.

"Hate," Jinny adds, predictably. Yet, not so predictably, I'm not her target. Her eyes are jeweled amber again, focused somewhere— beyond. Who does she reserve her true hatred for?

"Jealousy," Cara mumbles, looking at me. Ugh, I was premature thinking things might be improving between us.

"Vengeance," Aela intones solemnly, as if pledging it.

"Trust."

We all swing our gazes back to Sarah.

Aela frowns. "Trust isn't a primal emotion. In fact, it's the antithesis of one. You need to go against your survival instincts and gamble with your best interests to have trust."

Sarah shrugs uneasily. "It's what came to my mind."

"It's a brilliant idea, Sar." Jinny rushes to assure her, before I can. That *bitch*. "Trust is powerful enough to suppress the most narcissistic emotions. And…"

"And from my experience," I interrupt her. "What comes to your mind is always right. I'll go with your gut any day."

Cara raises both healing hands. "Okay, okay—we get it. Sarah's the brains. So, now we have a list of possibilities, what do we do with them?"

"We make sure to consider anything that happens from now on with those possibilities in mind," I say.

"Also, always remember this place can be messing with your mind," Aela says, angry again that it has messed with hers.

"*And* remember that in this Unitas, we're equals. We take decisions together, and no one thinks they're superior, or knows better than the others." Jinny glares challengingly at Aela. "And by no one I mean you, Nephi-lame."

Aela glowers back. "Don't harp, demon."

Jinny wiggles her brows at her. "Just saying, since heavenly bodies like you have brains with equivalent density."

"Maybe it would have been better if you remained in a coma," Aela grits out.

"Guys!" Sarah's sharp cry yanks us from this latest confrontation. As we turn to her, I realize she's not reprimanding us again. She's pointing a shaky finger into the distance. "Look!"

We swing around as one, and we see it.

A vortex.

The hope that it's the Imperium Gate, opening again to take us back flares.

But this appears to be the same size, when it's at least a hundred miles away. And while the Gate's depths looked like a roiling galaxy with a white-hot center, this thing feels like a window into the abyss of eternity.

But it's worse than that. In the distance, this non-existence seems to be tearing apart at the edges, its components streaming in spirals, revolving helplessly towards its center.

I try to avoid making the deduction, admitting the realization. But there's only one thing I know of that looks like this, that has this effect.

A black hole.

47

"**Y**ou've *got* to be kidding me! This can't be a..."

The rest of Jinny's shout gets swallowed by the sudden roar of wind.

I haven't felt any air before. I knew it exists, since we're breathing, but that's been the only indication it does. Now, between one breath and the next, it has become a storm. One that's getting worse by the second. It reminds me of Azazel's sigh.

"It does look like a black hole," Aela shouts, voice raised an octave against the wind. "And it's sucking the air into it. That's why it's suddenly raging."

I feel nothing as I stare at that new horror. It's probably shock. While Aela looks unruffled. And I mean literally. She has sprouted her wings, and they're arched behind her in serene stillness. This must be some sort of celestial forcefield. Either she always had it, like her cousins, or she manifested it here. Whichever, it's really neat. And it will come in handy.

Seems it will be Aela to the rescue again.

I grab Sarah as she sways with the force of the wind and shout, "So why isn't it sucking *us* in too...?"

No sooner have the words left my mouth than we start stumbling toward it, as if pulled by an inexorable gravity. Which, if this really is a black hole, is exactly what's happening.

"You just had to open your big mouth," Cara yells as she clings to Aela's legs as she rises in the air, her feathers now rioting.

So, no celestial forcefield? Or is it simply no match for that thing's gravity?

I cling to Sarah tighter and yell back at Cara, "Yeah, the black hole decided to work only because I reminded it!"

Our spat is cut short when Jinny barrels into us. She's almost swept away before Sarah and I each catch a hand and pull her back.

"Wen," Sarah shouts over the howling wind. "I think the pull isn't the same on all of us. It seems most powerful on Jinny, and least on Aela."

It's only then that I notice it. Clever Sarah.

So is the pull directly proportional to Angel Grace concentration? With the one who doesn't have it most affected, and vice versa?

Then I notice something else.

I don't feel the pull. At all. I'm stumbling only because I'm holding onto Sarah. She's the one being dragged.

So what does this mean?

If I have no Grace, like Jinny, shouldn't it be strongest on me, too? Or is it that thing inside me? Is it neutralizing the black hole's effect on me?

It seems so. But how can I use that to help the others? My strength and weight are not enough to hold them back. Even if I do manage it, for how long?

"I'll try to break free," Aela shouts. "If it works, you hold onto me and each other, and I'll fly us away until we're out of this thing's range."

"Thanks for including us in your decision making, nephilim," Jinny shouts back. "When we don't need you to!"

"I don't even know if it's possible to escape a black hole's gravity well, no matter how far I fly, but considering it must have a supernatural component..."

"Stop explaining, Aela!" Cara yells. "Just do it!"

Clamping her lips in a thin line, Aela beats her wings powerfully. But the best she can do is fly for a few dozen feet before being dragged back.

As for me, holding on to Jinny is becoming harder by the second. And is this thing getting larger? Or have we been dragged that much nearer?

"Let me go," Jinny hisses. "You said you won't do it again."

"I won't—after this time," I hiss back.

Sarah's frantic gaze darts between us in confusion, before she yells, "Everyone, lie flat on the ground, or whatever we're standing on. This'll give that thing less surface area to work on!"

I immediately do it, dragging her with me, and forcing Jinny's body beneath me. The other two follow, Aela retracting her now useless wings. Good thing they didn't argue.

Once we're lying as flat as we can, Cara's voice trembles against the wind. "What do you think this is? What is this testing us for?"

"Maybe it's about how we deal with the problem, until we get sucked in," Sarah pants. "Since there's no way we won't eventually be."

"You're suggesting that once we are, we won't find ourselves in another realm, or even in outer space?" Aela's voice betrays a crack in her immaculate facade. Seems she's uncertain if she would survive either scenario. It's also amazing she's referring to Sarah for answers. "You think there's no real danger here?"

"I didn't say that, since Astaroth said the Trials can be dangerous, but..." Sarah yelps as she wrenches away, as if the tug on her has suddenly intensified.

I almost lose my grip on her before I snatch her back. This time I maneuver her beside Jinny and throw myself diagonally over both.

I'm still swallowing down my heart when Jinny starts fidgeting beneath me. "Stop wriggling, Lizard Brain! I'm the only thing stopping you from hurtling into that cosmic sinkhole!"

"That's it!" Sarah exclaims, jerking beneath me. I pin her down more securely before pulling back to blink my surprise at her. Her eyes are round with fear—and a tinge of excitement. "You're not being pulled! You only were when you held on to me." So she noticed what I did. She isn't the brains for nothing. "You're only being dragged now because *we* are being dragged. This must be your power manifesting! Some gravity Grace, maybe?"

Since I haven't told her about that thing inside me, that's a very good explanation for what's happening here. It may even turn out to be the truth. For what if I don't have to pretend to have some elemental Grace? What if I *do* have one, just nothing Godric has ever encountered before, and it would explain everything?

"Now that you mention it, I always sensed something about you. Something totally—*still*," Aela shouts, barely raising her head as we inexorably slide closer toward the vortex. "Even your hair is not moving in the wind. Maybe this is *your* test. If this is your Grace, and it activated to protect you, if you manage to cast it around us, you'd ground us all. Until this passes."

"Assuming this passes!" Cara chokes in pain, grabbing onto my legs with her still healing hands.

"Try, Wen," Sarah urges.

Godric's ominous warning, about how dangerous whatever I have inside me can be, slams into me like a stinging slap.

What if I do try, only to rouse it, and worse, release it? What if it's even more terrible than this thing that wants to swallow us?

I shake my head, desperate for an alternative. "What if you were right, Sar? That the first trial prepared us for this one, for trusting each other, and sticking together till the end, when this thing pulls us in? Maybe it'll only spit us back into the Academy!"

"We can't assume that, Wen," Sarah gasps beneath me, my now-considerable weight, after Godric's intensive nutritional bootcamp, hindering her breathing. "Astaroth avoided answering you when you asked if sometimes cadets didn't make it out. This was as good as admitting some never did. If you don't try, we might be among those who get lost forever!"

"What-what if I do..." I swallow the jagged lump of dread in my throat. "...and cause something even worse? If I have some kind of gravity powers, what if I end up crushing you instead?"

"We know one thing for certain, Wen," Cara grunts as her weakened fingers begin to slip off my legs. "We're going to be sucked in. Based on what happened before, it will prove fatal, if we don't do something to stop it. Only your gravity powers have a shot at that now!"

"We don't even know they're anything like that!" I protest.

"You know how it pains me to say this..." Jinny cries out as she flips on her face, the vortex seemingly bent on snatching her from underneath me. "...but whatever your powers are, they're our only hope now!"

I snatch a frantic look at the black hole. It's bigger than ever. We're getting closer to its event horizon or whatever. There's no more than a few dozen miles between us and being siphoned into the unknown.

And as some cruel cosmic joke, only I can do something about it. It doesn't matter to them what kind of worse evil I may unleash. They'd rather take their chances with me.

But I can't risk it. *I can't.*

If only Godric were here! Though he's unsure how that thing inside me is related to my power, he's been able to—touch it, to wrestle it into submission, to make me aware of it. If he were here, he might have guided me in accessing it, using it, without waking it.

Only he can help me navigate my way out of this fatal situation!

But it shouldn't be fatal! The archangels seem to *really* need me. Why would they let me participate in these Trials, if there's a danger I'd never return?

But right now, *I'm* not in danger. Only the others. If I let go of them, I'll stand right here and watch them get swept into oblivion.

Yet, I'll still be lost. I'll remain here, staring at that black hole, or roaming this nothingness, till some new horror kills me. If not, till I die of dehydration.

There's one last possibility. That once they're gone, as the one left standing, literally, I'll be transported back to the Academy. Maybe not all Unitas return together, and it would be an elimination after all.

It still doesn't make sense. Why pair me with these girls, only to deprive me of their "complementing" influence? Before we really did anything together, or became a functional team? And if I don't blink back into the Academy once they're gone, why leave me stranded until I follow them in death, in a far slower, more agonizing way?

Unless there's no sense here, and the archangels really have no jurisdiction or control whatsoever over the Trials.

But I can't believe these trials are just random, as Astatroth implied. They have logic, purpose, like Sarah said. And like Jinny and I sensed, there's some presence presiding over this realm. This indicates a sentient will, a premeditated intellect.

But if it's not the archangels orchestrating them, then who? Who else could have designed those Trials for eons, and dictated their timing and inevitability? What entities could be so much more powerful than they are? And what else, besides Grace powers activation, are these calculating, ruthless Trials after? What are they really testing us for?

But none of this matters now. Only reaching Godric does. Through the connection between us. It does exist. It's how he sensed Azazel about to squish me. I only hope it's strong enough I can reach him through it now.

I scream for him, inside my mind.

Godric! Please, please...pick up!

Nothing happens. His presence is nowhere.

Of course it isn't. It's a crazy hope, thinking he can sense me across realms. If he could, he would have when I was about to be liquefied by alien maggots.

No. I didn't reach out to him then. But our connection is real, and realms apart or not, if I call urgently enough, he *will* hear me.

I pour all my desperation into my voiceless screams.

Godawful—answer me, damn you!

Again, nothing. And something occurs to me. Why he might not be tuning in.

This time, when I scream, it's fueled with more rage than despair.

If you can feel I'm not in danger, Angelhole, so you don't have to intervene, I'm telling you now—if anything happens to Sarah, you lose the one thing you really have over me! The one person I value far more than life! If you let her, and the others, go down this cosmic drain, like the nothing you once claimed I am, you'll get nothing from me. Do you hear me? Nothing!

Our connection remains dead silent. Or maybe it's nonexistent and I imagined it all.

No. No, no, *no.* It exists. I feel it deep within the fibers of my being.

But maybe it cannot traverse the realms between us. I can't waste more time on wishful thinking. I must do something—*now.*

I focus inward, probing the force neutralizing the black hole's unstoppable might. I can see it, coiled over its own endlessness.

Before I attempt to unfurl it, something moves. Between my sealed concealments. A code to my destiny, a conflagration of my voracity, a cautery for my soul. It's vast and ancient. It's addictive and enslaving. It's an eternity of torment and ecstasy, of ruin and rebirth.

It's Godric.

Then he's there. Standing in the middle of the still maelstrom within me.

He feels like the best thing to have ever existed. And he burns me to my recesses with the inferno of his beauty, his hunger.

What do you need?

He doesn't move his lips, but I hear him. Not like I heard Jinny in my mind. His presence, his voice—*that* voice, fills my every cell, abrades my very essence.

I almost sob with relief.

Almost.

His infinite calm lights the fuse of my explosive resentment and despair.

I shriek at him at the top of my being

What do you think I fucking *need? To petition for the removal of fucking kale from your fucking dietary dictates? I need to get the fucking hell out of this fucking nowhere we've been shoved into by your fucking Sinister Academy!*

Where are you?

Argh. You see *where I am, you fucking archangelspawn!*

I can only see nothingness.

That's exactly where we are—and we're being sucked into some kind of black hole!

I don't feel anything pulling at you.

It's the others, okay? They think I have some gravity Grace. They want me to extend my ability to neutralize this thing's pull to them. I don't know how.

You know how.

Not the time to be cryptic, Godwretch!

Always the charmer, even while facing a black hole.

And I roar loud enough his image wavers like a TV about to blip out.

Just. Tell. Me. How!

You know how to access your—void in the Mindscape. That's how.

We're calling it a void now?

Whatever it is, I taught you to navigate it already. Now focus, and cast it over them.

That's all?

Yes.

What if I can't?

You must, White. I can't afford for you to lose them, either.

Really?

Yes. If you lose your Unitas, you will be lost, too.

So it's an all or none rule?

I suddenly wonder who Godric's other quartet are. Come to think of it, he never said anything about undergoing these Trials.

Cast your void, White.

What if this void, that terrible slumbering thing you keep talking about, swallows them instead? Or worse? Can you rein it in if necessary?

You won't make it necessary.

I don't have time for your reverse coaching strategies, Godawful!

Then it's fortunate that I stopped time since we connected.

You can do that?

Not for long. Time always slows down for us in the Mindscape anyway, but I put my back into it and halted it completely, while we figure this out.

I feel my proverbial knees going weak with reprieve.

That's good. Great. Phew. Okay, I like you again.

You never liked me, White. And I never want you to like me.

What does he mean by that? What does he want me to feel about him? Is it what I think, or at least hope?

I can assure him I certainly don't like him, or anything else that's tame or sane. I lust after him with a violent passion to fill even that void inside me. I would swallow him whole if I could.

On our channel, I only say, *Yeah, you're right. You're impossible to like. So—we have time.*

I already explained, there's no time right now. Literally.

Don't you be a literal Angelhole. You know what I meant.

Do I ever know what you mean, you confounding creature? Now— enough. Let me feel and see what you feel and see. All of it.

I open myself to him, like he taught me. And I see him frown.

What?

Even though we're not wasting time, I can see you're almost out of it in the realm where your friends are. This black hole is so close it will soon start tearing them apart.

Oh, hell no, no!

The only reason they're not already scattered cells is because of you. You have been *accessing that void unconsciously, and it's been protecting them. But that won't be enough for much longer. You need to do it consciously, to lash it into doing your bidding, and holding its reins. I suggest you get on with it.*

Yeah, sure. Get on with harnessing a bottomless void, to take on a black hole, and snatch its meal from the maw that eats stars. Easy peasy.

Focus, human.

Human again, huh?

Or whatever you are. Now, like I showed you when you're fighting me in there. Let it out, let it expand, blanket them in it. Get it done.

And I try. I can feel that—void clearer than ever now, with him nudging it and provoking it into unfurling. But no matter what I do, or what he does, it doesn't do what I want it to do.

It's resisting me, Godric. It doesn't want *to cast its protection over them!*

I can sense that. Odd. I thought it would be eager to...

Not *the time to ponder the whims of whatever this thing inside me is. How do I get it to cooperate? Quick, spout something wise—and useful.*

I'm on it. Keep your hair, your masses of it, on.

What the fuck! Was that a joke? Now? I swear, if I get back, I'll find a way to kill you!

Such a violent creature.

That's it! You're dead, Godawful! Dead!

Shut up, White. I'm trying to lend you Grace Energy.

Huh? How? Why?

Bloody Hell, there's no end to your questions, even now. Fine, just so you'll let me focus on what I'm trying to do. Using my power from this plane didn't work, so I'm trying to transfuse it into you through our connection. It should bolster your ability to control that thing.

That shuts me up as I struggle to grasp what he's trying to do. I wait, certain my heart is no longer beating, until he nods.

I try again—and nothing. He shakes his head in resignation.

As I feared. There's no other way then. Brace yourself. I'll buffer it as much as I can, but the transfer will be a terrible shock this time, since I'm giving it all to you.

All your Grace Energy? Godric, you're practically a god!

The magnificent bastard has the nerve to flash me a dimple.

Indeed. Good to see you finally made peace with the fact.

That's it. When and if I'm back, I'm petitioning the archangels to take you off my case.

There's no getting rid of me, White.

I thought you can't wait to shake me off your hands!

It's amazing you've survived that long, being this oblivious.

You mean you don't want to anymore? Because you're now invested in fulfilling your mission of weaponizing me? Or whatever it is you want to do with me?

He doesn't respond for a while, then he shakes his head.

You're never escaping me, White. That's another fact. Live with it.

We'll see about that. I bet the archangels value me more than you, at least for now. I bet I can make them transfer me to Lorcan. Or better still, Gideon.

I didn't know you hated these two.

I don't hate them. I hate you.

Try to transfer to either of them, and he dies.

You—bastard!

If you mean that my parents never married, or had any form of holy union, then yes, I am a literal bastard. I'm also one in every other sense.

Seriously? Now you tell me stuff about yourself? When I'm about to get sucked into space, or lost in another realm?

You never asked. And you're going nowhere but back to the Academy.

I do nothing but ask, dickwad. And you don't know that.

You don't ask the right questions. And I do know. I'm not losing you. Now shut your foul mouth. Divesting myself of all my Energy isn't something I've ever done. You'll understand if it's tricky.

Just give me some of it, that should be enough.

I already tried that. By the time it reached you, it was too weak to force that void into submitting to you. Actually, the texture of my power only managed to enrage it, and made it retract farther. Now it needs a major blow to shock it into letting you harness it.

Surely giving it a kick in the pants doesn't require all your Energy!

You forget I've been dealing with it on a regular basis. It takes a considerable portion of my Grace Energy to control it in the Mindscape. With you on a different plane of existence, I estimate said kick in the pants needs either the shockwave of a few nuclear warheads—or all my power. Guess which I have access to.

You really think you can transfuse it all into me?

I don't think. I will.

Then you must be out of your fucking birdbrain! I can't handle all your power! Just give me a little more and let's see.

We can't afford experiments. I'm not giving you too little again, and risking it imploding on itself altogether. If it does, you won't be able to access any of it to shield your friends. You're protected by default by its very existence within you. But they will disintegrate in seconds.

The horror of that vision makes me almost shudder apart.

But if he gives me that much power and I explode, I will still fail them.

White, you can handle all my power. You can handle anything.

He really thinks so? Or is this a coach's pep talk to his underdog fighter? What he hopes will incite a miracle a la Rocky?

But just what is Grace Energy? Is it like Essence? If so, I have to tell him about my previous experience with his. If his expended Essence zapped me, the whole unadulterated reservoir *will* detonate me.

Listen, Godric, if your Energy and your Essence are alike...

They're not. Energy is the fount of powers in any supernatural being, while Essence is their life force itself. The younger and weaker the being is, the more connected they are. They become more separate as a being ages or their power grows. Mine are completely separate.

Whoa. Why am I hearing about this for the first time?

I didn't find a reason to inform you before. Even more so lately, when you started tapping into Energy.

What the hell? How do you know that?

His sigh of exasperation fills non-existence around me.

Because some of the samples you collected recently were Essence tinged with Energy, and far more potent for it.

But isn't that what you want? Why didn't you train me to recognize it? Why keep me in the dark, when it doesn't serve your purpose of strengthening my power?

I 'kept you in the dark' because I didn't want to strengthen your Energy siphoning. I wanted it to remain at that minor, accidental level until I knew how to regulate it, or eliminate it. It's far more dangerous than Essence harvesting since Energy rarely regenerates, and reports of Energy loss would have no doubt ensued. I had enough you-originated conflicts on my hands.

Sounds fair, I guess. But was this Energy what I saw around Azazel? Did I actually see the fount of his power? Hell, I now wish I'd sunk my talons into it. I would have loved to bring that monster's power-level down a peg or two.

What matters here is that you can handle everything I give you, White. You're the only one who can withstand me. You always did. And always will.

Suddenly, something devouring lashes out of him. That hunger I can swear he can't contain at times. I freeze under its onslaught, as it besieges me in a cage of obsidian craving, tears the rage of my own desire from my probably endless depths.

He's no longer thinking of giving me only his Energy. Neither am I. I've been craving it all from him, since that first day.

But in all my feverish scenarios, I certainly never dreamed he'd give me the fucking fount of his power. It's something I *can't* take.

What will happen to you—without all your Energy?

Why, White, I didn't know you cared.

Answer me, you infuriating lout!

Hmm, lout. I didn't realize you knew such words.

Godric!

Icy reluctance douses the inferno in his eyes. My mind almost fractures with alarm. It's that bad.

A full drain will leave me comatose. Until my Energy returns to me.

H-how do you know it will return?

I know.

He sounds so certain. But that doesn't reassure me in the least.

How long will that take?

I only have estimates from somewhat similar precedents. Maybe a year.

A year!

That's the most optimistic outcome.

Everything inside me collides in dread. But I still have to ask.

A-and the worst case scenario?

A hundred years.

Do you mean I—I might never see you again?

Yes.

The very idea feels like an end to everything. A plummet into that void, for eternity.

Not see him again? I can't even imagine it. I won't.

Wouldn't you just love that? You'll be rid of me, after all.

I gape at him.

No, I won't let him joke about *that*. I want to hurt the hell out of him for even suggesting it.

Yeah. I'll throw a parade. And get assigned to Lorcan or Gideon asap.

Do that, and I will kill them, painfully, whenever I awaken. Now, shut the bloody hell up. I'm trying to focus.

On what? Planning your coma for the next century, followed by your only friend's and brother's murder?

I swear by all that's unholy, White, I will find a way to strangle you into silence across the realms.

But it's not his fury that finally shuts me up. It's the reality of what he's doing sinking in.

He's tearing his Energy, which fuels his endless powers, and his very consciousness along with it, from his body and being, and giving them to me.

How will it feel to him? Will it hurt? Of course it will! It might be like tearing off his own skin, or scouring his every cell! And what if it leaves him comatose, forever? What if it kills him? It *will* leave him vulnerable, helpless. I bet to him *that's* even worse than death.

I can't even wrap my mind around such a concept. A powerless Godric. The universe would tilt on its axis in mourning.

I can't let him do that. *I can't.*

But what if this is the only way to save the others? Save Sarah?

No. I thought I'd do anything, sacrifice anything for her, but now I know.

I can't sacrifice *him*. For her, or for anything else.

My only currency here is my own life. I would gamble it in heartbeat for theirs.

Godric, don't do it. *I'll do it on my own. Whatever the cost.*

369

You can't, White. The only way for you to use that void now, while keeping it slumbering, is an energy injection of celestial magnitude.

Even so, half of your Energy is certainly that. And it will keep you awake!

You need it all because you're in another realm. From what happened the first time, by the time it reaches you, it'll be a mere fraction. But it should be enough.

Oh!

This is even worse! Most of his Energy will dissipate in the transfer. Even if it returns to him as he insisted, it might only be that fraction. And the unique force of nature that he is will be no more. That's an outrageous waste of cosmic proportions.

That's it, Godric. I forbid you to do it! I'll deal with it. You just keep your back to time's door as long as you can until I figure it out!

He doesn't answer my frantic yelling for long moments. When his voice fills my being again, it almost ruptures my heart.

Make good use of my Energy, White. Save yourself and your Unitas. And whatever you do, don't get transferred to Gideon, unless you want him dead, in a year, or a century.

Don't—don't say that. Don't make it sound like goodbye.

There's another long silence before he shakes his head.

It doesn't sound like goodbye, White. It is.

Then his image disappears.

48

G odric!
   My scream tears through the fabric of my sanity. Of the realms. Of anything and everything.

But he doesn't come back.

He said it's goodbye. He'll transfer his Energy to me, then fall into a coma. Even if I use his mind-boggling gift right and manage to return, I'm no Princess Charming. I won't be able to wake him up, with a kiss, or anything else.

Can I even live in a world where he doesn't exist? Where he isn't filling mine with his challenge and exasperation? Igniting me with his mixed signals and temptation? Fueling me with his ruthlessness and inspiration?

Can I go on without seeing his viridian eyes bleeding the lightning of wrath and desire? Without hearing his voice biting off orders or crooning provocation? Without his scent enveloping me in bliss, and his presence in unbridled life?

Can I bear knowing for certain I'll never feel his touch?

No, to everything. No, I can't. I can't lose him. I can't be without him.

And I start screaming my dread and despair again.

Don't do it, don't do it, don't do it. Don't you dare make it goodbye. There's another way. I will find it, you mule-headed madman! Come back here! Come back—please. Godric.

Suddenly I hear his voice again, but I can no longer see him.

You're waking up every slumbering entity in existence, White.

I only shriek, loud enough to wake up even the dead stars.

Godric, you insane bastard! You scared the eternal shit *out of me. Show yourself. Did you hear what I said?*

I always hear you, White.

No, you don't. You have noise-cancelling earbuds shoved in your ears half the time we're together, so you won't *hear me.*

I still hear you. I heard you across realms. I will always hear you.

You won't if you're in a hundred-year coma!

Even then, or even across the veil of death. Nothing will ever stop your voice from filling my mind.

He tells me this now? When he intends to deprive me of him for the rest of my life?

I sweep around, rabidly looking for his image, every spark of awareness inside me rioting with rage and fright.

Then hear this, you lunatic. I'm doing this. You keep your Energy inside that godly bod of yours, or I swear, I'm dragging your celestial butt into my void. Then we can be lost in there together.

You can't do it, not alone, White. I made certain with a thousand computations. But you got your wish, after all. I can't do it, either. I tried to transfer my Energy to you every way it has ever been done, and every way it has never been done—and nothing.

See? Even the multiverse agrees with me. It won't let you do something that crazy.

Actually, you're right, something is banning me, but it's not the multiverse. It's whatever controls the Trials, and the realm you're in. After I managed to send you some Energy initially, it now knows my intention, and won't let me help you. I tried every work-around, and failed.

This makes me more certain these Trials aren't some cosmic dice being thrown at every Unitas. There's a calculating, and malevolent, sentience controlling the whole thing. It plots and maneuvers, blocks and manipulates.

And because of my capricious void, we don't have time to learn its complex chess game.

Now we're both useless.

On our channel, I yell desperately.

What do we do now?

There's only one thing left to do.

What?

You have to draw on your Unitas's Energy.

No!

Either that, or watch the black hole take them.

If it does, I'll go with them.

You won't. You will remain.

First you said I'll be lost with them, now that I'll remain. Why don't I wait a bit more? You might change your mind again.

I didn't change my mind. All those who got lost with their Unitas were nothing compared to you. There's never *been anyone like you, White. Only they will die.*

But I can't take their Energy, Godric. You said it's connected to their Essence, their life force. I'll kill them!

Do it, or lose your Sarah.

Low blow, Godawful. Your lowest yet. For the record, you're a loathsome creature, and a lousy mentor.

I am indeed an abhorrent entity. But I'm not your mentor, White. I'm your molder, your keeper. Now do as I say.

What if...?

If you end up killing them, at least you tried. They'll die anyway if you don't try.

You can't know that! Maybe this Trial is just testing our resourcefulness and cooperation. Maybe this is my test like Aela said, and if I don't do something insane, like what you're asking me to do, it will be over. Maybe this isn't really a black hole, just something that will siphon us back into that Assembly Hall.

Are you willing to take a chance on that? When you and I feel this thing is real? The dangers of the Trials are always *real, White. Cadets died by the thousands throughout the ages*

Now *you tell me that?*

Why do you think I tried everything to exempt you?

You said it's because you didn't want the Trials to reveal what I really am!

Yes, this is a trial by fire to force your mettle to emerge. But it's also a simulation of what the cadets will face, once they become Heaven's soldiers. It's an existence of a terrible scope. One without safety nets. Or happy endings.

Then why put them through it when they're just starting their training? Why not after they graduate?

Because they can't train without activating their Grace Powers. It always seemed like a Catch-22 to me, too.

But how do you know all that, when everyone insists they don't know what happens in the Trials?

Your professors might not know specifics, but they know enough from the amount of mutilated and lost cadets throughout history.

Then they're even more evil than I thought! They should have prepared us better for this.

There's no preparing for the Trials. They're never what you prepare for.

Yeah, cause it's the perfect time to be vague. You should have at least told me everything you know before we were shoved in here.

I—couldn't.

Why couldn't you?

There's silence for what feels like an eternity. In this halted-time zone, it might as well be.

But I know he won't answer that question. Maybe even can't, like he just said. So I ask more.

Does part of your knowledge come from going through the Trials yourself? And what happened to the rest of your Unitas? Aren't these supposed to stay together, one way or another?

Another silence stretches, until I think he won't answer again. I'm about to say something when he does.

I lost my Unitas.

The way he said that feels like a direct punch to my heart. I have a zillion questions about this momentous confession. But they all have to wait, since I need to know more pressing details.

But you said teams are lost whole, that I'm different, cause there's never been anyone like me.

No one else. *We're both anomalies. That's why there's no one else in this universe who can handle you. That's why the bucket stops with me.*

That's a revelation of Godric proportions. And the bastard tells me that now.

Well, I'm not losing my Unitas!

You will if you don't do as I told you. Take their Energy and save their lives.

But their Energy can't be as powerful as yours, even the fraction that would have reached me. I won't risk killing them for nothing!

They were picked for you by the Choosing, because, while not on par with you, they're powerful enough to complement you, to withstand you. Their Energy will *be enough.*

I have nothing more to counter with.

Even if the endless moment we've been stretching between doesn't snap, my void will not protect them for much longer. I feel it. It has already resisted me, might be punishing me for keeping it suppressed, for wanting to harness it against its will. Even if time doesn't resume for me, I feel it running out for them.

I have to act. Or everything will be lost. All of them will be.

Reaching a decision, I start to leave the Mindscape, under my own power for the first time.

Godric's voice bellows in every fiber of my being. Then he's back before me, his image gigantic, his wings black and blazing, like rivers of magma.

Don't you dare *exit the Mindscape!*

I have to return to them.

No you don't. You can sense their Energy and draw it inside you while you're here.

Even if I can, I have to ask their permission.

A rumble of volcanic frustration shakes the non-existence cocooning us.

If you exit now, I won't be able to reach you again. Or to guide you. Or to save you if things go wrong.

You said no matter what, I won't die.

You won't. If things go wrong, you'll worse than die. You will remain where you are and be lost. *You will be lost to me. And I will go insane for real, knowing I can't reach you.* Forever.

That's one of the options I thought of before. But…

It won't be forever. I'm still human. I'll die within a week, tops.

If I can freeze time, I bet your void can, too. Once you're weak enough, it might awaken. Then it will never let you die. It will preserve you in stasis, aware and at its service for as long as it exists. I think it has always existed, and always will.

Now you're just pulling nightmarish scenarios out of your ass! You can't know any of that. You don't even know what this so called void is.

Maybe not. But I have touched it. I know what a malevolent bitch it is.

Are you sure you weren't sensing me?

You're not malevolent, you fool. You're the very opposite of malevolent. Why do you think it chose you to house it?

Okay, stop! Stop! You'll say anything to get your way, won't you?

To save you? Of course, I would. I won't let you get lost because you're too stupid to disregard some pathetic human ethics.

Ethics are not pathetic. And you *didn't get lost when you lost your Unitas.*

375

Who says I didn't?

A universe-full of desolation permeates his voice, and an eternity of loneliness stains his image.

But it isn't time to dwell on that now.

Time is running out for them, Godric. I feel it. I have to get out. I will not gamble with their lives without their consent.

They won't mind once you save them. And if you do what I tell you, you will.

You don't know that. Not in absolute certainty. Because nothing in existence is certain.

There is *one certainty, White. That you were* made *to torment me.*

The way he said that...

Later, Wen. Later.

Now make sure there's a later.

Back at you, pal. But it's their lives, and only they can decide to risk them. I won't play god. I'm not you, Godric.

There's a silence as absolute as the vastness of the realms I see him across, surrounded by a lightning storm of obsidian fury and frustration.

If he could stop me, he would. He would leash the hell out of me and yank me to his side. He wouldn't care about my consent.

But he knows he can't force me this time.

When I hear him again, his voice is a tumult of emotions that unravels my very essence.

Do it then, my Hell-sent bane. Follow your moronic code. But do one thing for me.

What?

Come back to me.

Before his words sink in, he fades.

I snap back into my conscious mind, to the feel of Sarah sobbing beneath me, shaking me. And we're almost at the vortex, only a few thousand feet left. At least my void is still protecting them.

"I tried, guys," I yell over the deafening wind. "There's only one way this might work. You have to give me your Energy so I can snare it, and you, into whatever's holding me back. Or use it to amplify my power. Whichever works best to stop the black hole from sucking you in!"

"What's that energy?" Sarah asks raggedly.

"Grace Energy, the fount of our powers," Aela rasps.

"I need your consent to this plan," I yell.

"You have it, dammit!" Aela growls.

"How do we give it to you?" Cara pants, barely clinging to my legs by her fingertips.

I feel I can take it, as Godric wanted me to. But I don't know how they can give it to me of their own free will.

But whatever's inside me knows. It whispers the answer in my head, using me as a mouthpiece to repeat the coaxing of its sinister seduction.

"Just open yourselves to the idea, to me. Don't resist. I'll do the rest."

To my surprise, the first one whose Energy flows into me is Aela. I know because it—tastes of her, like a spicy chai latte with a spoonful of the heart of a star. Even though she already consented, I thought she'd be the one to hold off till last.

"Hurry up, will you?" Aela yells. "I'm not ready to die this pointlessly!"

Sarah grabs my hand tighter. "Take what you need, Wen. Always."

My eyes burn and my chest tightens. She's everything to me, my whole family. I have to do this for her. So she can continue living in this new world she loves so much.

Her Energy flares inside me. This proves that she has a Supernatural component to her. What it is, we need to survive to find out. It's bright and breathtaking, and completely untamed. It's totally unlike Aela's, which was scorching, devastating even, yet fully leashed. It swirls around me like a hug, permeating me with all the colors and scents of her generosity and trust.

Trust. Seems she was right, and this test really is about trust. Me, trusting Godric. And them, trusting me.

"I don't know what you can take from me," Jinny pants beneath me, her face mashed into the nebulous medium below. "I've been told I have no soul, and my powers come from unadulterated evil—but help yourself."

I have no time to tell her what Godric told me about Energy being universal to Supernaturals, before hers passes through me.

It shocks me to my very core, like touching a high-voltage wire with wet, bare hands. It veers away into the void inside me, as if from a like charge it cannot approach, before settling in an orbit around it's non-existent heart, like an asteroid belt made of blazing sin.

I feel we're almost there, but not yet. Something's still missing.

"Cara?" I look down at the girl digging her fingers like talons in my calves.

"What-what if we can't get our Energy back?" she whimpers.

Before I can say anything, not that I have the words to reassure her, Aela slaps her upside the head. "Do it, or I'll kick you into the black hole myself!"

Cara squeezes her eyes and her Energy surges inside me, a braided rope of hues, and I can *hear* each and every fiber. Like a serpent, it winds itself tight around the others' Energy, gathering them, binding them.

And it's done. It's complete. We are.

The void inside me sniffs all around the amalgamated Energy before it shudders in appreciation. Then, it rises from one edge of forever, crests like an existence-sized tidal wave. Its hunger spans eternity before it crashes, obliterating everything.

49

T he absence is entombing. But it's also insulating, concealing.
For beyond its abyss, worse things are watching. Waiting.
Waiting for me. Have always been waiting for me.

I remain buried in my nonexistence as I have done for eternities. I've evaded their greed, escaped their grasp, for eons.

But I know. My refuge will disintegrate soon. And they will see me. They will recognize me. And they will want me. They will destroy everything in their path until I'm theirs.

I can't let them have me. Can't let them use me.

But hiding in cessation is no longer an option. I have to face them. I have to exist again.

I have to be reborn.

I come to with a cry, vivid terror overflowing from my eyes.

A kaleidoscope of images splinters into a billion shards, gouging my mind with memories. Of how the void stirred, yawned, stretched, and consumed everything.

Including the black hole.

But these aren't my memories. It's the void's. I'm feeling what it felt as it delighted in the delicious Energy feeding it, that of the others and the black hole's, after eons of starvation. The alien, endless gluttony as it feasted. Gorged itself until it was glutted.

More sensations deluge me. Of the absence. The burial. The ancient terror and despair. Someone else's. Yet mine.

More follows. Sensory snapshots of every moment since I was pulled out of the burning rubble, clutching that antique locket with its glowing gem, its shape branded in my flesh. Then the reel spools backward, rewinding to earlier and earlier times, times I shouldn't remember, couldn't have lived through.

Details flood me, drown me, mind and soul.

I cry out again, press my fists to my head, begging for the stampede of memories to stop.

Too much. *Too much.*

Then suddenly, it ends. The recollections evaporate as fast as they accumulated, like rain on scorching asphalt. My mind resets to its usual state of spotty memory and blank early years.

Relief trembles in a hot gust over my parched lips.

It lasts only seconds before a new distress crests.

I'm floating. In static vastness. My hair is undulating above me, the only thing free of the stillness. I should be able to move, too. I shouldn't be alone.

Before panic sinks into me, the others' forms jut out of the murkiness, one after the other, a few dozen feet away from me, and from each other.

I got them out of the black hole!

Any excitement dies when I notice they're in my same, unmoving state, but their eyes are closed. I can't tell if they're breathing.

No. They have to be. Their faces are peaceful, and they look asleep.

But are they? Or did I put them in a coma? And if I did, when will they wake up? Will they? Where is their Energy now? I can't feel it anymore. Did it return to them? Will it?

Suddenly, everything falls silent in my mind as I realize where we are. I don't know how I know, but I do. At the center of the void. Or I am. The others are orbiting me like planets around the sun.

Are we really here, physically? Or are these our avatars? Did the void manifest outside me, and expanded to cocoon us? Or are these only our consciousnesses?

Either way, I feel the void wants to keep me here, and them with me. It wants us to keep it company, to join it in its slumber.

I need to be careful not to rouse it, let alone its temper or hunger, or it might not let us go.

But first, I need to check Sarah. She has to be okay. Once I make sure she and the others are, I'll figure out how to exit the void. Now I got us out of the Trials' realm, I can contact Godric again. He'll guide me out.

But before I can test my mobility, tentacles of compulsion sink in my every cell. Before alarm even registers, I'm enveloped in tangible energy. No—I'm *dissolving* in it, mingling with its particles.

As I shoot up into infinity, I'm broken down to nothing and everything, scattering across every atom filling the cosmos.

I feel it all, everything that has ever happened, or will happen, from inception to ending.

I relive Essence forming, existence unfurling.

I witness the genesis of awareness, of discontent. Of inspiration and conflict. Of order and destruction.

And of hunger.

When the endlessness ends, downloading into material again, into a single entity, destroys me. Until all I absorbed of knowing dissipates, and I reform. Speck-narrow awareness, and weakness-filled flesh.

As the last of the transcendence ebbs, I crash back into my mind, and realize what happened.

I was freaking beamed up!

I weep again, with the loss of what I no longer remember. I sob and retch, and pat myself everywhere. I'm still me, still in one, unaltered piece.

Then stimuli start seeping in again, and I register my surroundings. They're no longer formless, the ominous cavernous structure solid. Yet I know. I'm back in the Trials' Realm.

The cavern reminds me of the one Fem led me to. But this one is easily triple its dimensions, with every surface simmering like burning coals, as if in the wake of a firestorm.

I've been re-formed in its center, and the chiseled-by-time walls feel a mile away on all sides, so does the stalactite-weeping ceiling. The ground beneath my boots looks battle-scarred, feels death-soaked. I only hope the ashes I'm sinking in up to my ankles aren't burnt corpses...

My morbid musings come to a stuttering halt as fiery light and heat floods the cavern.

Then I hear clapping.

It's coming from everywhere, its echoes multiplying, merging, until they become a cacophony that can sunder sanities. The overlapping rhythm warps to a crescendo of wails, those of a million damned souls.

But among the overlapping distortion, I can still tell. It's one pair of hands, powerful enough to shatter worlds, lazily, teasingly applauding.

"Brava, my dear. You eclipsed my hopes, and leaped over my expectations."

I stagger around, looking for the owner of the voice that feels made of the substance of my being, of this realm's, and almost keel over.

I do crash to my knees.

It's *him*.

The burning angel.

Just as I remember him, with only one difference. He's no longer a statue.

But he's still a giant, maybe a hundred-feet tall. His wings are gathered high as he approaches with the slow-motion horror of a tsunami. My neck almost snaps as I gape up at his terrible, transcendent form.

Each step is a shockwave that gnarls me within a maze of primeval emotions. But I recognize none of them is terror. Terror is a protective mechanism, what lashes survival into action. It has no place here. Once a threat becomes too overwhelming, too inescapable, resignation is the only response left.

And this guy is the definition of overwhelming and inescapable. His impact equals that of the archangels' collective, a dozen times over.

But—am I imagining it, or is he shrinking?

His steps continue reverberating within me like a knell of doom, until he stops only thirty feet away. Thankfully, he *did* shrink. A lot. So did his flames.

Their heat is still flaying, but like that time in the cavern, I somehow feel they won't burn me. Not unless he wants them to. Since I didn't join the ashes at my feet already, he doesn't want to incinerate me. Yet.

He raises his hands, in that same gesture of his statue. A leader rousing fanatic crowds, a maestro conducting an enslaved orchestra. He wants me on my feet.

They're numb, like every inch of me, but I find myself rising. Then he beckons me closer.

Resignation evaporates in blast of mind-tearing panic. I feel the moment I obey, my fate will be sealed.

But what else can I do?

Heart booming so hard it shakes me, I put one wobbling foot in front of the other. He gets smaller with every step. I'm about ten feet away when he stops shrinking. He still dwarfs me. And I still can't see his features or details within his personal inferno, beyond the outline of a Roman emperor/alien warrior outfit.

Within my roiling thoughts, I wonder again about the flames. A strange choice for an angel. Though this guy is no mere angel. He's probably one of those higher celestial beings we hear about, but never witnessed on earth. A seraphim maybe?

"At last, Uri. I have waited eons for you."

I almost shudder apart. His voice. It could shatter me if he wished. It only cascades over me.

And it's exquisite. Like a cosmic cello played by a lonely god.

It strums an answering chord of violent longing and pervasive melancholy within me. And that maddening elusiveness I've been suffering since I set foot in the Celestial Court.

"Uh, name's Wen, actually. Quite an entrance, by the way." I clear my throat of what feels like the cobwebs of millennia. I'm flabbergasted I can talk at all. Seems my smart-mouth auto function will only expire with my very life. "And you are?"

His flames diminish a little more as he places an immaculate hand over an expansive chest in mock hurt. "You do not know me?"

"Does meeting your statue count?" I rasp.

He inclines a majestic head. "It matters not. Memory is unreliable, therefore inconsequential."

"It's a good thing you think that, since mine is—problematic."

"You will remember what you need to, when you need to. What matters now is that I finally found you."

I swallow around the heart now blocking my throat. "Why did you need to find me? What did you mean by eons? How did you bring me here? Where is here?"

He goes still under my barrage of questions.

But I get the impression he welcomes them, is pleased I'm engaging him. He must have expected I'd writhe at his feet, tearing my flesh out in abject terror. I should be. I want to. If this was about only me, I'd give in to the brutal urge that demands a quick, gory death.

But it's not. It's about Sarah, and the others. So even when every flimsy human component of me is begging for a swift end, questioning him takes precedence.

Like Godric, when he responds, he doesn't answer. "The temptation to give up overwhelmed me every few centuries. Only the

Prophetia kept me going. And I kept the Trials going, in hope of one day finding you."

Prophetia? Is this Latin, or rather Angelic for Prophecy?

Then his meaning hits me, so hard it's like a slap of icy water, rousing me from my fugue of dread. "I knew it! I knew the Trials weren't random, that someone orchestrated them. It was you! But... wait...you can't mean..."

"That the Trials were created to find you?" he completes for me, placid, overpowering. "Indeed." He shakes his head, and I make out vital locks cascading past his shoulders, the color overlaid with the hues of fire. "I endured it all for you. Interminable waiting, millennia of false hope, and thousands upon thousands of failures and dead ends."

My logic circuits blip and whirr with the enormity of what he just revealed, until they snag on one detail. "But thousands of cadets passed your tests throughout history."

"Not the test designed to find you."

"W-what do you mean?"

He falls silent, as if debating telling me anymore. Then he exhales. "For thousands of years, the Academy drafted every nephilim and angel-graced in existence. That is, apart from the last millennium when it was closed, before reopening only after...only two decades ago. And every cycle my acolytes determined my candidates. Only these faced that specific test, my unbeatable *Cavum Nigrum*, the one only the *Renatus* can pass."

I raise staying hands. "Wait...wait...*Cavum Nigrum* is literally Black Hole, right? And *Renatus* is—what? Reborn?"

"They've been teaching you well." He nods, and I see hints of perfection and a smile of approval. "But for millennia, every single candidate failed, miserably. Until you."

"So...so all those who were lost during the Trials, died in this test? You killed thousands of cadets trying to find—me?"

"I would have killed millions more to find you."

I shake my head, shake all over, the serenity of his declaration making it even more horrifying. "But you could have killed us all, killed *me*, too. Isn't that counterproductive to your—purposes for finding me, whatever those are?"

He makes a nonchalant gesture. "Absolutely not. There were only two outcomes. Either my acolytes were wrong about you, as they have been about thousands before you, and you were just another useless cadet, and I couldn't have cared less if you died. Or—you would survive, and I become certain they were right this time, and you're the one I've been waiting for. And here you are. My *Renatus*, my Reborn. At last."

I shake my head again, the logic not computing. "But before I passed the black hole test, I could have died during that first test. What was that for?"

He continues as if he hasn't heard me. "But on top of conquering the *Cavum Nigrum*, you did what I would have never expected. What not even the *Caeli Gladius* did."

This time my Latin fails me. "Who's that *Caeli…*?"

"You preserved your Unitas." He bulldozes over my question in the same tranquility. "When it should have been impossible. It is. You truly decimated my expectations."

I gape at him, shudders intensifying. He sounds high on the triumph of ending a seemingly eternal quest. Finding the *Renatus*—the Reborn. Whatever *that* is.

But he thinks it's me, and that terrifies me more than anything ever has. If he went to all this trouble to find me, he might not kill me, but might do far worse.

This could be the worse-than-death fate I've been dreading all along.

Even if it is, I can only dig for more information. He seems chatty, and anything he tells me, I might be able to use to save Sarah and the others.

I can barely stand anymore, but I force myself to straighten, to raise my voice. "Let's say I believe I'm the one you've been looking for. Now, I'm here, what do you want from me?"

A shadow of that smile again. "All in good time, my dear. When you can take your place in my plans, and by my side. I didn't even intend to reveal myself to you now. I wouldn't have if you only resisted the vortex, let your Unitas get swept away, and returned through the Imperium Gate. But you insisted on saving them, and in such a novel and wholly—unholy way. Even I was impressed."

"You saw what I did?" I choke, breath strangling with a new kind of fright.

He inclines his head. "Once my acolytes determine my candidates, I watch them through the *Regnum Speculi*, from the moment they're identified, until they brave the *Cavum Nigrum*."

Fury is sudden and violent, blowing up my fear, and erupting within my laboring chest with an insane urge to jump up and punch him. "It was you! That presence I felt watching me!"

His head jerks, as if in surprise. "Not even my pompous brethren can detect my surveillance. More expectation decimated, Uri."

"Can you please quit calling me that?"

I'm not the one you're looking for, you delusional, mass-murdering angelhole.

Thankfully, I only scream this inside my head. Even in the throes of hysterical anger, I know it's not wise to antagonize an all-powerful entity when I'm in his realm, and at his mercy.

I need to suppress all my emotions, like Godric taught me in the Mindscape, play along. So he'd let Sarah and the others go.

I have no illusions about my own fate. I'm cut off from Godric, the only one who can help me. I can't even connect with the void. I'm stranded here with this mad god. This...*inevitable* entity.

I know I can never escape him. Maybe not even in death.

Whatever he wants with me, or will do to me, this is it for me.

50

Oblivious to my state, or uncaring, the burning angel starts circling me.

Even in his reduced size, and his tranquil pace, his footfalls reverberate in my marrow. I swear I hear the ashes wailing under his every step.

"I will never call you anything else, Uri." His flames flicker higher as he stops at my back. I can feel his breath, a different kind of fire, caressing my hair and nape. My every instinct shrieks. His ponderous timbre abrades my every organ, scrapes my every bone. "And to think I almost didn't watch you during the Trials. Even though you were the only one who intrigued me among the candidates this cycle."

"Do-Do you mean…there are others?" I wheeze, almost at the point of begging him to face me again. Not seeing him, but feeling him bearing down on me is a new kind of horror.

"There *were*. They are gone now."

My heart kicks so hard, I'm the one who stumbles around to face him.

Knowing thousands were led to their death in this monster's quest to find me is one thing. It's another that they might be people I know.

Bile fills me up to my eyes as he continues his musing. "I no longer wanted to waste a moment of my eternity on this futility. But watching you fight, and interact with your Unitas, especially how you came up with that ingenious solution to preserve them in mere seconds—that was more than worth the millennia of disappointment."

Mere seconds? This means he couldn't detect the halted-time ages I spent debating and strategizing with Godric in our Mindscape. I have that precious encounter, and my connection with Godric itself, to myself.

He's not omniscient. Not even in his realm.

I still watch him closely, but his stance and vibe don't change. He's not reading my mind. And I'm certain he would if he could. Which means he's also not all-powerful.

The relief, that he can't invade my mind, that I'm not fully vulnerable and exposed to him, is knee-melting.

"Yeah, well, glad I entertained you," I choke. "On that note, it was really, uh—something, meeting you in the—fiery flesh. But I'm really wiped out after surviving your *Cavum*—something, and I need to get back to my friends…"

"Ah, your Unitas. I thought them disposable once you entered my realm. But then that first test…" He stops, shakes his head, as if deciding not to say anything that would answer my earlier question about it. "They proved useful then. But after they played their part, and tided you over to the *Cavum Nigrum,* your surprises began. The moment I manifested it, it should have torn them apart like wrapping paper…" His nails elongate and curve like a great feline's as he mimes a shredding movement. "…exposing the incomparable gift that you are. But when you preserved them, and I saw your unique amalgam, I subjected them to a closer examination. My findings made me view the *Prophetia* in a new light. They may prove worthy of being the satellites of the *Renatus.* As such, I will have use for them, after all."

Protectiveness hurtles within me like a meteor shower, its white-hot shrapnel lodging in my fingertips. My mind blanks with the same viciousness that assailed me when I attacked Azazel.

And I see it, even through his senses-numbing blaze. His Angel Essence. And his Energy.

My palms itch and burn as my power rushes to the surface, howling for them, demanding I feed it, that I eviscerate him and bathe in his ichor…

What am I thinking? Feeling? That appalling hunger, that maniacal savagery—they're not mine. I hope. And even if they are, I can't take on that—that deity.

You just took on a black hole.

That voice has a point, wherever it's coming from. But he's more than an inexorable phenomenon. It sounds like he's the guy who created it. And he's cunning, and obsessed with it. No matter how powerful I may be, even without the void, I'm flesh and blood. One swipe of these talons, or a flare of that fire, and I'm a mangled, smoldering corpse.

Even if he seems to need me, and wouldn't hurt me unless forced to, and I can use any initial reluctance to incapacitate him, I can't do it. I need him intact and cooperative so I can get to Sarah and the others, to free them and send them back.

I struggle to suppress my aggression, to sound neutral. "You do send those who pass your Trials back through the Imperium Gate, right?"

He nods. "I automated the process for those who don't concern me."

"So you'll send us back now?"

I said us, even knowing he's not letting me go. No harm in haggling, even if it's pointless.

He shakes his fiery head with an exhalation. "I already tried, and it's why you're here. I could teleport only you, and only back here."

My heart stops—then it bursts out clanging like a tower bell. "Y-you meant to send me back with them?"

He nods, and my every conviction shatter, my mind scrabbling to construct new ones.

So he's been looking for me for thousands of years, and now he's found me, he's letting me go? What does this mean? I misread the situation? I'm not damned to an eternity in this realm?

Shut up, Wen. He meant to send you back. Don't wonder why. Take the win.

I try, until the rest of his words hit me, and I exclaim, "You're telling me you can't end the test you created?"

"I created it, but in all the millennia, it never played out. There's no precedent here."

"Yeah, I'm unprecedented this way," I mumble, fresh dread creeping up my nerves. "But this might explain why your usual way didn't work. If you try another..."

"There is no other way."

"I can't accept that! I won't. If you can create a black hole, you can find some other transportation method. I can't remain trapped here with you!"

"It would destroy my plans if you do."

Okay. Now I know why he doesn't want to keep me. He has plans for me elsewhere. Which somehow sounds more ominous than a worse-than-death fate.

Out loud, I say, "Glad we're on the same page. So keep trying, will you?"

His talons retract as he fists his hands, as if in equal frustration. "I always surmised that once the *Renatus* came through the *Cavum Nigrum*, the automation would take hold, would send them back. But you have more surprises within you that nullified the Gate's function. It's why I had to reveal myself to you prematurely. You needed to know the situation, so you can help me send you back to the Academy, where I need you to be."

My galloping heart hiccups. "If you mean me alone, forget it. I'm going nowhere without my Unitas."

"I indicated keeping your Unitas intact is to my advantage. But whatever you have preserving them will surrender them to only you. So, retrieving them, restoring them to life, and to their destined path— is all up to you."

"How the *hell* do I do that?"

That smile is back, and more detectable. This time, it's one of —delight?

Then he simply says, "You must trust me."

What I do is burst out in braying cackles.

Tears of hysteria and helplessness run down my trembling face as I snort and splutter. "Trust you? The celestial voyeur who's been stalking me? The boogeyman in a realm of nightmares of his own making? Who feeds pet black holes thousands of lives, in search of a— what? A PA? A spy?"

"A soulmate."

The word penetrates my chest like an armor-piercing bullet.

The way he said it, that it was him who said it—it unearthed a yearning I didn't know I had, in the same moment it tarnished it, destroyed it.

I feel robbed, violated. I want to weep with the loss, rage at the defilement. I want to inflict an equal and permanent damage on him.

This time when I see myself eviscerating him, it's all me.

"How dare you!" I screech so violently I feel my vocal cords tear- ing. "You insane piece of celestial shit! I don't care who you think I am, or who the hell you think you are..."

The rest of my tirade is smothered in a hacking fit.

Blazing brighter, he finally says, "I am Samael."

Smothering my coughing, before I start spraying out bits of bloody lung, I rasp, "As if that means anything."

"It will. Mean everything. Eventually. Until then, I forgive your overwrought outbursts. I understand I am too much for you to bear at the moment. Mortality is a truly unfortunate state."

"You think that's why I almost burst a cerebral vessel yelling at you? Dude, you're out of touch. No surprise, with you living like a hermit crab in this macabre wasteland."

His flames burst higher, making me jump back with a yelp.

He could have reduced me to ashes, like the remains beneath his statue's feet. And those I'm ankle-deep in. But he only singed me, showing me he'd resort to corporeal reprimands to keep me in line if need be.

I maddened him enough to overcome his indulgence. Great strategy.

Too late to take it back, though. He'll know I'm placating him.

Not that I want to take it back. I'm barely suppressing the suicidal urge to attack him.

His flames diminish again as he sighs. "Enough of this nonsense, Uri. We must get you back as swiftly as possible."

I narrow my eyes at him. "I know why I'm in a hurry. Why are you?"

He ignores me as he intones, "Visualize your Unitas, and the plane where you preserve them. Once you do, contain them. Then visualize a place to return to. Unlike the Imperium Gate that returns cadets where they entered it, you will determine your destination. Pick it carefully, lock on it utterly, so it would become a magnet that would draw you in across the realms. Otherwise, you risk being lost in between."

I skewer him with a scowl. "Be more ominous, why don't you?"

"I am merely stressing the importance of visualizing a place with the utmost emotional resonance to you. It needs to be where you found contentment, worth, purpose. Where the aches of your soul abated."

"Such common criteria." I cough a mirthless laugh. "I just need to pick a place from the dozens that answer them. Easy peasy."

A hint of a smile peeks through the flames again. It only stokes my banked terror. "The choice *is* the hard part. The execution *will* be easy. You'll have access to the greatest fount of power in existence. My own Energy."

"Such modesty."

"That was certainly never one of my vices. Neither was it yours. Not with powers on par with mine. Together we can do anything."

A burst of recollection chokes me again. What Godric said to me, what he tried to do, and failed. Because of *him*. *He* foiled Godric's efforts to transfer his Energy to me.

He must have been able to, only because Godric's Energy was diluted by the barrier of realms. I *refuse* to believe this Samael is more powerful that he is.

But what if he is? What if he knows it was him trying to help me? I don't want Godric on his radar…

No. He doesn't know, like he couldn't detect our Mindscape interlude. He was only stopping me from drawing on any outside power. He couldn't pollute the results of his precious test. I had to survive it on my own.

But I would have anyway. Stopping Godric's Energy transfer would have only killed the others, if I hadn't drawn on theirs. I still don't know if *that* saved them, or doomed them to a coma for the rest of their lives.

And it's all because of him!

Now he seems eager for me to release them from the void, what he failed to do.

What if I only hand him our whole Unitas to enslave? I know a slave master when I see one. And this guy? I can see him presiding over realms-full of thralls…

Suddenly, I can no longer see him, or this cavern, and everything blinks out…

51

I'm looking at the black hole again.

But this time, I'm alone. And I want to find out what it is, what it contains, where it leads.

It rages as I approach it, as if unable to accept that my power is nullifying its pull, its greed. What should be the one un-opposable force in existence.

Then I reach the edge of its eternity, and look inside.

He's there. As far away as the moon is from the earth, and almost as big. He's being swarmed by countless, blazing comets. No, not swarmed. They're revolving in his orbit. And they're screaming, the unimaginable collective suffering tearing the very fabric of reality, funneling all its goodness and light.

Souls. Damned souls. They're what fuels his black hole...

I blink back into my conscious mind, find myself looking up into the flame-swathed face of my new captor. Seems he didn't notice my mental detour. It must have been one of those halted-time moments.

But I'm already forgetting it, only remembering that I mustn't. That it's too crucial.

I try to hang on to it, to tie it to another memory like Godric taught me, so I can later use it as a fishing line, dragging it back to the surface. I want to shriek my lungs out when I fail.

"You can trust me, Uri." That voice that can make mountains kneel, sluices over me, attempting to wash away my agitation and resistance. "I would never hurt you. I would burn down worlds for you."

I cough an appalled scoff. "Just what every girl wants to hear from her celestial stalker."

And the insane bastard has the gall to chuckle!

"More surprises, Uri. Our destiny will not only be glorious, but... entertaining, too." I glare a thousand agonizing deaths at him, and he croons—*croons*, "You have no choice. It has been foretold, and so it will come to pass. As for you and your precious Unitas, only our powers together can send you where you belong. For now."

There's that "for now" I so hate. And it's always some all-powerful monster saying it.

But he's right. If I don't work with him, the others will remain captives to my void. And without me, it won't preserve them for long. Like Godric said, if I don't act, they will die anyway.

I have no choice. I never had any.

Closing my eyes, I do as he told me, focus on Sarah, see her sleeping in my void.

I draw her gently into the universe of emotions I have for her. Once she's floating peacefully in its center, I turn to the others, and pull them around her, cocooning them within her orbit, where she wants them to be. Then I visualize the destination he described, the only place where I want to be. Then I nod.

He holds out a blazing hand to me. "Now we mingle our powers, and it will be done."

With one last ragged breath, I place a sweaty, trembling hand in his.

It feels as if I just placed my fate, all our fates, there.

As his flames engulf my hand, there's only his surprisingly soft touch. There's no burning, no shock, nothing.

Then without warning, a force of indescribable magnitude razes through me. I would have fallen to my knees if he weren't holding me up.

That force—it feels as old as time, *made* of time, of the texture of existence. Unending, unraveling, uncontainable. It dissects through my tissues, besieging every cell. It wants to invade me to my essence, and beyond.

Godric said I can handle anything. I *can't* handle this. Once it pummels through my defenses, it will end me. Then it will be all over for Sarah and the others. Because I was stupid enough to make a bargain with that devil...

Everything inside me ceases as I stare at his shape through the inferno, the realization a supernova.

I am Samael.

"Lucifer…"

My rasp jolts through him. Not with surprise, but with gratification so vicious, it sears me until I'm thrashing in his hold.

He tugs me closer, pressing me into his chest. "Yes, my light. You remember."

I shove at him with hands that feel like shriveling straw. *"I don't."*

He draws away, yet tightens his massive vise on my hand. "Yes, of course. You wouldn't yet. But you worked it out. My clever, Uri." He immobilizes me as I writhe and convulse and keen like a skinned lamb. "Let my Energy in, let it join with yours."

I shake my head, shake apart. "You'll…kill…me…"

"Never! The pain is unavoidable, but it will go away as soon as you let my Energy in. The union will soothe you. And it will bring the barriers of existence down, will return you where you need to be. Only then can our destiny resume."

I want to rave and rant that he's a textbook, megalomaniac villain, and there's nothing in said existence that will ever be called "ours."

But I am no match for him. And he remains my one way out of this hell. His hell.

I let go, let him in.

The dam of my resistance shatters, and his power explodes inside me.

The weight of millennia tears through my soul. The anguish of billions roil in my arteries.

It's a hundred times worse than the Divining. A thousand.

I begged for death then, when it wouldn't have damned Sarah. Wouldn't have hurt Godric. This time I don't have the luxury of giving up.

Withstanding this invasion, this desecration, no matter the agony and the damage, is a small price to pay. For getting Sarah the hell out of here. For getting back to Godric.

You pathetic fool, you don't deserve either of them.

That voice within. Its fury and scorn shoot like acid in my blood, ratcheting the torture. I scream for it to shut up. It doesn't.

You had a chance to protect them, protect everything, from him. Now he's consuming you, because you fell for it. Because you gave him your hand, mingled your power with his. Of your own free will!

The realization is like an axe lodging in my brain.

He needed me to give him access. He couldn't take it. So he coaxed and cajoled, and I fell for it...

Now you'll dissolve in him, and doom them all with you. But I can save them all, if you let me out.

The voice, the void is right. I should let it out. Once he consumes me, it's the only thing powerful enough to stand in his way...

Yes, yes. He's a prisoner here. He needs your power to escape. Let me out and I'll save you, and keep him here, forever.

Let it out? Out of where? Where is it? What is it? And why do I hate it so much? Why can I no longer think? Am I dying?

Yes, you are! If you don't let me out, you'll destroy yourself and everyone. You'll set the Devil free!

And I start laughing, weeping, shrieking as my mind splinters. From the fragments blowing out in slow-motion, one last thought flutters out like an expiring butterfly.

Better the devil you know.

The void roars. But I can no longer hear or feel anything beyond the power punching through the last barrier within me, colliding with mine, decimating existence.

My scream traverses the realms, snuffs out his eternal flames.

And I glimpse him, as he was when it all started, as he will be when it all ends.

As it all ends.

52

Waking up not knowing where I am feels familiar. And irritating as hell. I only know each time involved an impossibly beautiful semi-celestial who has turned my universe inside out.

My eyes are open, but my brain can't translate what they see. It can't do anything else.

Good. I can slide back into oblivion...

"White."

That voice. His.

Godric.

Is he still communicating from the Mindscape?

"Look at me!"

This doesn't sound like soulspeak, or whatever it is we do on our frequency. It's his actual voice.

But I've fallen from another realm, and was smashed into a million fragments. If only he'd let them drift away in peace...

"Bloody Hell, White. You *will* look at me."

It's no use. This demigod won't let me rest. He never did, never will. He's forcing my mind to reconnect with my senses.

I'm flat on my back. It's dim, or maybe it's my vision. The world is filled with Godric, hanging over me like a dark fate. The only fate I yearn for.

His face is gripped in such ferociousness, I know something is wrong. Terribly so. Something I did? To Sarah? And the others?

Dread drenches me, dragging me back into darkness…

"Look. At. Me. *See* me."

His growl compels me to focus on him again. He's looking at me as if he's barely hanging on to his sanity.

A sob chokes on my lips. "Wh-what did I do?"

He goes rock still, feverishly scanning my face, then his chest empties. "You came back to me."

His ragged words spark a memory. Of the last thing he said to me. *Come back to me.*

I could be wrong about how he meant it. I probably am. Even if not, it means nothing now. Memories are seeping back. Of when I took everyone's Energy, used it to harness the void, what it did…

Tears burn my eyes. "I saw it, Godric, *felt* it…the void…decimating and consuming—everything…"

He nods, grimness deepening, gaze cooling. "It is a horrific manifestation indeed, and far more dangerous than I even thought."

More dangerous than having the potential to mess up the balance of existence?

But I can't dwell on that as more images sear away more cobwebs. Sarah and the others, floating inert, captives of the void…

I heave up to my elbows, panic uprooting my heart. "It has them, Godric. It wants to keep them. Because I fed it their Energy…"

He shakes his head. "It doesn't have them. You saved them all. And you fed it nothing. You used their Energy as bait to madden it into consuming the black hole. You held its reins all through."

"H-how do you know that? How did I do that?"

"I don't have solid answers as to how."

"What kind do you have then? Liquid ones? Gaseous?" I mumble, vaguely realizing he didn't answer the first question. "Theorize, then. You're good at that."

"Not that it matters now, but fine. I stipulate that our Mindscape sessions, and clashing with my Energy regularly, honed your instincts more than I hoped. I also think it was love…of your Sarah. And determination, to return to…this world." His eyes grow heavier with unspoken things, before he exhales. "All the void's unending hunger was clearly no match for that. For you."

That sounds good. Too good. But there are other memories, flitting just out of range, telling me there's more to the story. Way more.

"If…if I saved Sarah and the others, where are they?"

His weight shifts, dipping me sideways. I belatedly realize we're on my bed as he makes a sweeping gesture. "Sleeping peacefully."

My heart jackknifes as my eyes fall on Sarah, the force spilling me out of bed. My legs buckle, then I'm clinging to the barricade of Godric's body.

Breath stuttering, I expect him to step back from my touch.

He only stands there, gaze ravaging my face, infusing me with his stability. Like he intended to give me all his power. At the cost of his consciousness, and maybe more.

Unable to withstand the memory, I push away from his support, stagger to Sarah's side, reach a trembling hand to her face. It's warm and her breathing is even. She doesn't have a hair out of place.

I pan my gaze around, find the other girls seemingly as untouched in their beds.

I really did it? I didn't eat their Energy or souls, or whatever else they willingly offered me?

I stagger around to Godric. "Are you sure they're okay? I didn't put them in that hundred-year coma?"

"They actually awakened when you returned."

"They did? When did we return? Where?"

"Yes. Ten hours ago. And right there." His eyes crinkle as he answers in order, pointing to the space that acts as a distributing hall to our sections of the room.

"I brought us back here?"

"All cadets exit the Imperium Gate where they entered it, in the Assembly Hall. But, of course, you had to be different."

Another memory tries to form, fails, but I still know why I brought us here. "The Assembly Hall doesn't hold emotional resonance for me. Or it holds the negative kind."

His eyebrows rise. "Emotional resonance, eh? Interesting that you thought of that concept, too. But it stands to reason. Something as powerful as the Gate's pull had to guide you back. With that detour through the void, I feared you might not be able to…" He stops, jaw muscles bunching. Then he exhales. "If it was emotional resonance that you locked onto, it's strange you didn't go back to your apartment."

"I could have done that?"

"White, you traversed realms without an Imperium Gate, with four passengers. You could have done anything you wanted, gone anywhere."

Something tells me that's not an accurate explanation of what happened. But another confusion takes precedence. "Why do you think I would have gone there?"

"Because you consider it home." I blink at him in surprise. I have considered it home. Because I shared it with Sarah. "But you came here instead."

So do I now consider this place home? Because Sarah is also here?

But she was with me when I "locked" onto this place. I don't remember how it happened, but I know one thing. This place has emotional resonance because it's where I lived two lifetimes' worth of unimaginable experiences and emotions. With him, because of him.

I came back here for him.

None of that passes my numb lips until he looks away, shaking his head.

The searching intensity is gone from his gaze when it swings back to me. "I expect the Trials' Committee will question you about the method of your return. I need you to corroborate my explanation. I cited the seven Unitas who didn't return to make it incontestable."

Blood stops in my veins. Thirty-five cadets. Lost. Dead. And I know something about them. Something important. The vagueness screams at me to remember. I can't.

"Wh-what did you tell them?"

"That I sensed you the moment the Gate opened, before it did in this realm. But it started closing prematurely, and wouldn't have given you a chance to step through. So I cast the leash to guide you back, circumventing its programmed destination, since it has already malfunctioned. I used your quarters, which is full of your collective 'resonance,' as a beacon, and a return location."

My mouth drops open. "And they believed you?"

"I am very convincing."

"Tell me about it. They must have also preferred to preserve the arrangement of their organs."

A vicious twist to his lips agrees with my assessment of his reputation. "My bloody history wasn't a factor in swaying them—this time. Contrary to what happened in the Divining, I was there 'confessing' what I did. Suspecting my story was not the issue. Taking matters into my own hands was."

"So, what did they say about that?"

"They took me to task, said I tampered with the Trials' results. I maintained that you already finished your tests, and I only guided you back. They still spouted the rules to me, so I counterattacked with a knowledge they thought I wasn't privy to."

"What's that?"

"That throughout history, they would have intervened to save the cadets, if they knew how. But no one who isn't slotted for the Trials' can cross the Imperium Gate, so rescue missions have always been out of the question. That's why they have no knowledge of what happened to the cadets who didn't return. But *I* was in the unique position to connect with you across the Gate as my charge. I knew what was happening to you, and how to help you. I took *them* to task for suggesting I should have let you die to preserve rules that stem from ignorance and helplessness."

It never ceases to amaze me how he comes up with elaborate yet seamless stories on the fly. "Wow, that sure put them in their place. I just hope I remember all that."

"I did mix fiction with truth, though, since I did connect with you across the realms. Also, the moment I felt your return, you could have been anywhere on earth. I had to cast the leash to find you."

I glower at him, feeling its phantom imprint around my neck. "At least it had one good use."

His lips twitch. "It has nothing but good uses."

"Sheesh, Godjerk, you missed your calling as a slaver."

His shrug is virile nonchalance itself. "I wouldn't want any other slaves."

The way he said that. The way he's looking at me. The same way he did when he pretended I was his at the Divining. Multiplied into infinity.

My knees knock and my heart somersaults into my gut.

I'm imagining things. I'm probably outright hallucinating by now.

But he did look at me like that before. Many times.

No, not like this. This is new. This makes me wish he'd take everything his eyes are saying he wants to take, to rip from me. My consent, my virginity, my sanity. I want him to destroy me with pleasure, and enslave me with the need for more. And more.

That's my insane lust talking, what he's been stoking since that first day, most of it unintentionally. And he more or less said he considers me his one and only slave, for Kondar's sake. I shouldn't be melting at *that*.

But I am. If he were to push me back on my bed right now, I'd beg him to take me. With the others within sight and earshot.

"Glad to see the world is as I left it," I croak. "With you as Godawful as always."

He inclines his head in calm consent.

To escape his inflaming gaze and my runaway reactions, I turn back to Sarah, stroke her cheek.

She stirs. I almost collapse when her eyes slit open and she slurs, "Wen—you're awake…"

My heart almost ruptures. She's awake. She knows me. I didn't put her in a coma—or worse!

"You scared us to death—when you wouldn't wake up." A dreamy smile touches her lips. "But you're awake now."

Everything in me wobbles and spills over in sheets of tears. "Yeah, I am. How are you feeling?"

"Great. Really great. I just want to sleep for a few weeks. Sleep never felt so goo…" She turns on her side mid-word, and starts snoring softly.

Relief is so acute it hurts. Her mind is intact. She's still my Sarah.

But I still need reassurance, that the worst I did was knock her out, that the most she needs is a long, recharging sleep.

Wiping at my tears, I turn to Godric. "Tell me everything that happened since we returned."

"What happened, if you didn't surmise from your friend's statements, is that you were the one who wouldn't wake up." His eyes darken to a terrifying black-forest storm. "I found your mind inert, floating amidst the void. I kept trying to leash you back, but I couldn't. It kept disintegrating everything I threw at it, until I feared it would keep you in there forever."

"You thought I would never wake up?"

He grinds his teeth. That could probably powder steel. "It was a possibility."

Not knowing how to deal with this new brand of intensity, I resort to teasing. "Of course it wasn't. Godric the Great ordered me to come back."

His fierceness only goes supernova. "And you did."

Before I can recover from this latest heart attack, he looks away to the girls' sleeping figures. "The others gave the same report. That you amalgamated their Energy to bolster what they think is a gravity Grace, went head to head with that black hole, with them clinging to you—and won. They don't remember anything after that, before waking up here. I found you all on the floor, with you prostrated in the middle, and them lying on their sides, forming an uninterrupted circle around you. They all seemed asleep, while you had your eyes open, but were unresponsive."

He stops, his gaze growing vehement. Unable to withstand his focus, I make a hurrying motion.

He sighs, the harsh sound making my unsteady legs tremble. "They woke up shortly, but were so tired, they climbed in bed and went to sleep. And before you ask again, Raphael himself checked them, and there's nothing wrong with any of them. He checked you, too, but found nothing to heal. I wouldn't let them take you to his Sanatorium, insisted on keeping you here. I hoped my—their proximity would help bring you back."

And it probably did. "So I didn't eat their Energy or Graces or souls or anything else? Not even bits of them?"

His lips tug at my persistence. "They actually feel far stronger than ever."

"Feel? Your diagnosis is based on 'feelings'? I'll need something more 'solid' than that."

"How about this?" He whips out an Angel Amulet from his pocket. "Solid enough for you?"

Jerking in alarm, I shove my hand in my own pocket. Or I try to, before I realize that, like Sarah, I'm in one of our Academy-issue pajamas. Which means they changed us.

I have no idea who did, only hope it wasn't with Godric around. This sure isn't how I want him to see me undressed for the first time. And then, even if my "scrawny arse" has been coated in fifteen pounds of muscles and fat, thanks to his physical and dietary torture, what if glimpsing my nakedness *still* made him want to barf?

But—if they got me out of my uniform, that also means...

"That's our Amulet!" I exclaim. "You took it!"

"You're not meant to keep it."

"You're not meant to take it! I'm supposed to guard it, and give it back myself!"

"You did bring it back. Consider your mission accomplished."

For some reason, I feel cheated out of something important. And I'm also afraid. Of what this Amulet will reveal about Sarah. And me.

"Why didn't the Professors take it? And how exactly is it solid proof that the others are stronger than ever? Did they wear it and it revealed the nature and extent of their Grace powers? What are those? What is Sarah's? Does she even have any?"

He shakes his head with a mocking huff. "You really are back, aren't you?"

"I'll sic the void on you if you don't answer me!"

His lips spread. In a full-fledged, all-out smile. Full of perfect teeth, laughter lines and dimples. It's realms-shattering.

And he calls *me* the most dangerous entity in existence?

"Hold your void, White." A short, rough chuckle abrades my inflamed nerves and desires wholesale. "The professors think you still have the Amulet. I took it as per the Archangels' order—after I convinced them it's prudent to examine its contents before the ceremony."

"Why? What do you think it contains?"

"A secondary functionality of the Amulets is recording the events in the Imperium Realm. The Trials Committee long vowed not to peruse those records. But with the irregular method of your return, no matter what I told them, I know they will take a look this time."

"Did you?"

The last trace of his smile disappears. "You didn't tell me about that first test."

Goosebumps storm over me as I stare into eyes turning bottomless. "Uh, yeah? I had other pressing issues at the time."

He suddenly looks drop-to-your-knees-groveling-for-your-life scary. The carnage-hued cracks that shatter across his irises are even worse than those emerald-laced bolts. Because it's a glimpse into what he's capable of in full premeditation. Cold-blooded wrath to burn down worlds.

A memory flashes at this thought. It's gone before I can grasp it.

"You almost died."

At a loss at how to deal with his new level of blood-curdling, I shrug. "You told me that's what the Trials are all about. 'A simulation of a terrible existence without safety nets. Or happy endings.'"

We stare at each other for long, oppressive moments as the storm rages higher in his eyes, and then there's another first. The blood-tinged lightning crackles around me, cocooning me in a cage of destruction. Of anything that would come near me.

"I should have felt your danger," he rasps.

That's what's bothering him? "How could you? You were in another realm, so cut yourself some slack. And you came to the rescue when it really mattered."

"I *failed* to come to your rescue."

404

"No you didn't!" I stumble to grab him by the arms. The feel of his steel flesh beneath my fingers, hot and inexorable even through thick fabric, makes my head spin. Blinking away the swooning sensations, I focus on what he must hear. "You wanted to transfuse me with your Energy..."

"And I couldn't."

The gory cage snaps to envelop us both. It's not hurting me, but it's hurting him. It's an extension of his upheaval.

Godric doesn't understand failure, can't imagine helplessness. And he suffered both on my account.

I dig my fingers into his muscles, at least try to, needing to snap him out of it. "You knew what to do, knew how to push me to do it, and that's the only reason we're back here. No matter what you say you are, you *are* my mentor. If not for your guidance, and for every-thing you taught me, we would have all died."

The storm dies down. The cage dissipates and his eyes glow viridian again. But the room darkens along with his frown. It's clear he's not buying it. And that all this rage is directed at himself.

I see a long argument in our future, to disabuse him of his macho misconceptions.

For now, I need to distract him. "So the Amulet recorded every-thing that happened there?"

I'm wishing he'd tell me whatever it is I can't remember.

"Yes, both tests."

"Nothing else?"

"You mean what happened between then and your return? No."

Damn. Guess I'll have to remember on my own. Or not.

"I'm working on deleting the black hole incident."

"What would that serve?" I ask. "If the Committee investigates our 'irregular return,' at least two of the girls will report everything that happened."

His frown deepens as he shakes his head. "I believe they won't. Then there would be no record in the Amulet either. If I'm wrong about them, and they do, it would only be their report. That will have a far lesser impact than actually witnessing the whole thing."

"Won't the Committee be more suspicious if the records are deleted?"

He shrugs. "They can assume it's another glitch."

I sigh. "Too many glitches surrounding me."

"As long as they remain inexplicable, they can think whatever the bloody hell they like. Suspicions are easier to dispute than hard facts. I'll do whatever it takes so the black hole incident goes undiscovered. But we'll work with whatever develops."

"Yeah. What you said." I stare at the Amulet in his perfect, power-laden hand for a moment, then frown. "That still didn't answer my question. How did the Amulet tell you the girls are stronger than ever, if they didn't wear it yet?"

Silently, theatrically, he holds it up.

I almost jump out of my skin when laser-like bolts shoot from every bed, from every girl, to strike the Amulet, setting every rune on celestial fire.

Lowering the Amulet, he engulfs it in his hand again, cutting off the transmission.

He broods down at me as he puts it back in his pocket. "When I got here, the Amulet was on your chest, with your Unitas caught in that energy web. It connected all of them to the Amulet and to each other. But like now, the bolts didn't hit you, just crisscrossed over you, making you the center of an arcane symbol. One I've never seen before."

My every hair stands on end as a nebulous shape forms in my mind. I've never seen it, but I somehow know it. And it fills me with a crazy mixture of anxiety and…elation?

I should be used to these contrary feelings by now. These in specific must be a side-effect of the ordeal. I'll examine them later. Now I have an archangelspawn to berate.

"Why didn't you tell me that before? Will I discover more momentous tidbits each time you tell this story? Isn't it in your best interest *not* to keep me in the dark this time? So I don't contradict you, and mess up your elaborate fictionalization of events?"

His lips spread again. I have no idea how I don't pounce on him and sink my teeth into them. "Amazing. Not even battling a black hole, and a void, slowed down your avalanche of questions."

"Godawful!" My exasperation is directed at both of us equally.

He quirks a challenging pout, like he's daring me to do what I'm a hairbreadth from doing.

I manage to hold back, and he exhales, as if in disappointment. "That energy show isn't supposed to happen. *That's* how I know how strong they are now. Probably stronger than anyone who's ever passed the Trials."

"Stronger than you?" I gape at him.

"I thought we established I'm in a class of my own."

And how!

"I could have thought those bolts are an outcome of you connecting their Energy, but the Grace Runes only illuminate once the Amulet is around a cadet's neck and settled over their heart. That they do remotely is another—glitch I have to deal with before the ceremony. Your situation is already irregular enough."

I gulp as I stare at the girls. My gaze snags on Jinny's fiery hair. "How is this happening with Jinny, when she's a demon?"

"This I have yet to discover."

My eyes move to Sarah before returning to his. "So Sarah *is* Angel-Graced?"

He shakes his head. "Sarah is—something else."

"What? What is she?"

"I'm not at liberty to divulge that."

I take a threatening step towards him. "May I remind you of my void? Answer me or get swallowed whole!"

His eyes fall to my lips. And if I ever suspected I imagined it before, the blast of hunger that microwaves me to my DNA is unmistakable. Then I realize what I said.

Yeah, I put him and swallowing whole in the same sentence.

Before I burn to ashes of mortification, he tosses his head back and treats me to a sight I never thought I'd witness. His laughter.

Growly, fathomless, ovaries-combusting laughter.

Maybe I *should* have that void swallow him. He's too dangerous to exist.

That tormentor actually wipes away tears, rumbling deep in that acres-wide chest. "If you 'swallow' me, you'll never know. So it's in your best interests to swallow your curiosity instead, and get back into bed."

I almost thank him for not taking advantage of my unintentional innuendo.

I want to mean it when I say dirty stuff like that to him.

But I need answers, dammit!

Standing my ground, I face off with him, trying to bend him to my will. He only raises an eyebrow that all but says, dream on.

I throw my hands in the air and stalk away. "Fine, you slippery, aggravating, Godawful being." At my bed, I turn and smirk over my shoulder. "Come tell me when you get Daddy's permission."

That hormone-scrambling mirth only flares in his eyes.

What the Hell, Heaven and everything in between happened to him while I was at the Imperium Realm?

Now anything I say seems to tickle him. And to my immense regret, Bedeviling Godric is more irresistible than any other version of him.

As if he heard me, he prowls toward me. His slow approach almost buckles my knees.

I mentally smack myself up the head. I'm *not* swooning at his feet. Even if I can blame it on the ordeal.

That's easier said than done when, instead of stopping at his usual arm's length, he keeps going. Until there's less than a foot between us and his heat drenches me, inside and out. Then his eyes sober, becoming more distressing for it. Anything he does yanks extremes of reaction from my depths. And now I know these are literally fathomless.

"The window is that way," I croak, barely breathing. "Flap along before someone catches you in the girls' dorm, and reports you to your prudish family."

"In a minute," he murmurs, deep, deep and devastating.

"Want to hang around longer? What with all those nubile bodies around?"

His expression takes on such feline wickedness, taunting loud and clear: *Jealous?*

Am I? I haven't been so far, because the old Godric was so general-like, all scowls and growls, and looking through everybody. Even then, almost every female in the Academy would have prostrated herself for a look from him. If they're ever exposed to this side of him, they'd hurl themselves against his lightning, even if it zapped them to death. And such a paragon of masculinity must have appetites as powerful as he is. I've heard whispers that his sexual exploits are as legendary as he is. No one has any details, though, since it's said he considers anyone in the Academy off-limits.

But though I'm already at the top of his Will-Never-Touch list, and he's the last male in existence to ogle sleeping girls, this room is studded with the epitome of femininity, with me nowhere in their leagues. The comparison is just—ugh, painful.

So, jealous? I probably am.

No. I definitely am. Gnawingly, ridiculously, pointlessly jealous.

But since it is pointless, I ignore his unspoken taunt, and say something that needs to be said instead. "Before you take a literal flying leap, I have to tell you something. Actually, elaborate on something I already said."

He inclines his head. "As long as it's not in the form of more questions."

"As if you ever answer me."

"In the last couple of months, I answered two-centuries' worth of questions. I should get an award. You should make me a statue."

Instead of smacking him, then climbing him and losing my mind all over him, I nod. "I'll see about making you that statue. You deserve it."

He huffs derisively, before he goes still. "You mean that."

"When have I ever said anything I don't mean?"

"Indeed. You're the only one I can count on to always flay me with the truth of your thoughts and feelings. It makes dealing with others —problematic."

That sounds…better than anything I hoped I would make him feel.

Better say what I need to, before I show him how *he* makes me feel.

I clear my throat. "Here are more truths to add to your collection. Your torture bootcamp turned me from a weakling who couldn't do a single push-up, to a fighter who held her own against a swarm of acid-puking, man-sized nightmares-come-to-life, for hours. And your mental molding in the Mindscape, and everything you told me in the Trials' Realm—when you were willing to give me all your Energy, at the expense of your consciousness, and maybe your powers and life, you madman—are the only reason I could take on that black hole, keep that void contained, and get everyone back here. As Godawful as you are, I couldn't have dreamed of a better mentor. I couldn't have done any of this without you."

And I don't want to ever find out what I'd do without you.

I go rigid as the words echo, until I realize I didn't say them out loud. But did that thought originate from only me? Or him, too?

And is his head getting nearer, or is my vision distorting?

The world does tilt and veer around me as he eliminates the last breath between us, and seals his lips over mine.

Everything stops. Disappears. Not even the void remains. Only his taste and scent and feel. Only the possession of his lips and the necessity of his breath. Only the scorch of his tongue at the seam of my lips, and its brand on mine. Only the sharpness of his teeth sinking in my flesh, hard enough to curb my tremors, and his savagery. Only the inundation of agitation and delight.

This monster capable of leveling cities—worlds—is devouring me. As if he's been starving for me all his life. As if he'd never have enough. He's destroying any fantasies I had of my first kiss. Our first kiss. The only kiss I ever craved. The kiss I despaired I'd ever have.

If I could, I would throw my arms around him, drag him down to me, deepen our fusion, devour him back. But I'm paralyzed. With too much emotion, too much hunger. But mainly with fear. That this is my one and only chance, that it's a mistake he won't repeat, and I won't have this again. And with disbelief. That even with such a leashed touch, he ignites me, enslaves me. Nothing should feel this ferocious, this total.

Even though I should be depleted after what I've been through, my core is already molten and begging for his invasion. My heart is attempting to ram out of my ribcage, to toss itself at his feet. My paralysis will shatter any moment now, and I'll...

He tears his lips away. A keen of shock escapes mine. It feels as if he's torn off a layer of my skin, of my heart. Before I can clutch him back, demand he finish what he's started, he withdraws.

I keep my eyes closed. If I open them and find his knowing, teasing, I *will* murder him. I will find out what his kryptonite is, then pluck and boil...

"White."

His voice is the deepest I've ever heard it, a bass thrum that almost shatters me with longing. It forces me to look up at him. He's at arm's length, again.

His gaze is not teasing. It's not smug. It's not even aroused. It's solemn. Almost anguished.

Then he says, "Come back to me—always."

Before another thought fires in my liquified brain, he walks away to the window.

I gape after him as a flash encompasses him, then his wings are out. Did he just make sure I don't see how it happens?

I hear my voice, barely recognizable in my swollen throat. "You said you'd never touch me, Godawful."

Turning around as he levitates to the sill, he sweeps me in a glance that scalds me inside and out. "And I didn't, White. I just kissed you."

Then with one effortless beat of his great wings, he shoots up into the air.

I stare into the darkness where he disappeared.

I just kissed you.

He just kissed me.

He just kissed me.

And he did more than that. What he said, and the way he said it…

Come back to me—always.

This is more momentous than taking on a black hole.

Collapsing on bed, a heap of hot, wet tremors and gnawing arousal, I touch my stinging, swollen lips, still feeling his there, still unable to believe it.

Godric *kissed* me. When, not so long ago, he wanted nothing more than to kill me. I am the relentless water drip to his indestructible rock after all. I broke through control and aversion as powerful as he is.

So it was fleeting, and that massive pain still didn't touch me. But I can build on that. I can wear him down until…

Something bursts inside my head.

The pain is paralyzing, dread even more so. That this might be an aneurysm rupturing. That I would be dead before I could reach out to Godric. When I didn't tell him how I feel, didn't even kiss him back. That Sarah will wake up to find me gone, when I promised to always be there for her and…

Another comet of agony crashes in my head. This time I know what it is. An explosion of memories. Searing through the vagueness with the blast of flames that almost consumed me. Those of the burning angel. Samael.

Lucifer.

I remember now. What my mind tried to protect me from, what it tried to erase.

I met the fucking Devil.

I wait for the memory to strike me with terror. It doesn't. Or it does to the point where it numbs me. I remember the similar reaction when I first saw him. When he was sky-scraper-sized.

According to him, ours was a prophesied reunion. The culmination of a millennia-long search. And he created the Trials and killed thousands of cadets to find me. They were an elimination after all, just not in the way I thought.

I'm still drawing a blank on many details. Like the names he kept calling me, and most of what he said. Not to mention how he helped me get us all home. I only remember that he did, because he needs me here. Needs me, period.

Yeah, him, too.

But how much of my memories can I trust? When I'm certain I've forgotten more than I remember? When I'm having fuzzy flashbacks to events I haven't lived?

This whole Lucifer scenario could have been a hallucination. Like those I've been having since Godric leashed me into his world.

Apart from that one where he drove his sword into my heart, I've been considering them subconscious coping mechanisms. It stands to reason the Lucifer episode was one.

I had just snatched Sarah and the others from the grasp of the black hole, only for them to fall into the void's. I must have thought I needed something equal to Godric's Energy or the others' to force it to release us. So I conjured up an imaginary, all-powerful ally. I must have picked Lucifer because I've been wondering about him a lot, and tied him to the burning angel statue. After all, who better than his diabolical self to help me wrestle that equally malevolent thing inside me?

I like that theory. Even if it means my mind is unreliable, or even disintegrating. The alternative is that Lucifer is real, and he considers me a vital part of his plans. Plans that must be as heinous as he is.

Two problems with that theory, though. It assumes I managed to deal with the void, and returned us here, on my own. I doubt I'm anywhere near that powerful, yet. Even if I am, it discounts my luck. Knowing how terrible it is, Lucifer probably is real, and is after me.

But if he is, how can I tell Godric? That his infamous uncle helped send us home, succeeding where he failed? Compounding his turmoil, and tossing another major conflict and mystery on his plate? He already has enough of both on my account.

No, I don't need to tell him. Not until I make sure it was real, anyway. Maybe not even then. Even if Lucifer exists, he isn't going anywhere anytime soon. According to what I remember, he might rule the Imperium Realm, but it's also his exile.

For now, only one thing matters. That we faced unbeatable odds, and returned unharmed. The others seem even more powerful than anyone who ever survived the Trials.

But—what if that's not a good thing? What if it's a "glitch" I caused them? And it would have unpredictable, and terrible consequences?

Even if not, what about Sarah? What can be so unsettling about her that Godric can't reveal it? When he's already shared world-shaking theories and secrets with me?

My gaze clings to her peacefully sleeping form, and a chill of foreboding tumbles through me like a breaker.

Shuddering uncontrollably, I scramble beneath my magic-imbued comforter. As it wraps its warmth around me, I try to empty my mind of the worst-case-scenarios that come as easily as breathing to me. Instead, everything that happened since that fateful night Godric crash-landed in my path comes back to flood it.

In the violent current, I feel the new memories being swept away. Whether for good, or until I can handle them, I'm thankful for the break. I can use one after everything I've been through.

And to think the most I worried about a couple of months ago was my next *Angelescence* transaction, and our lives.

Then Godric dragged me here, and I thought all I had to contend with was the archangels' interest in my inexplicable power, Azazel's threat of dismemberment, my roommates and other undisclosed enemies, and Godric. Then came the Trials and that "horrific manifestation" within me, and I thought things couldn't get any worse.

I should have known that in my world, worse always comes. And if what I remember is true, it just got infinitely more complicated.

The Devil himself has come into play.

Strangely, I'm not afraid. Okay, so I am, but nothing like when I was facing this Afterworld, and trying to shield Sarah from its brutalities, on my own. Whatever new disasters are heading my way, I feel I will no longer face them alone.

Beyond my wildest expectations, I have Godric, that every-shade-of-grey powerhouse. My enemy and captor, my mentor and protector, and my one overriding desire. I have Sarah, my soul sister, as more than my unwavering emotional support now she's unearthing her true potential—whatever that is. After these two, the ones my world revolves around, I have Lorcan, that open-hearted enigma. I may have Gideon, Tory and the other archangelspawn, too.

Hell, I may even have my Unitas, that disparate and dangerous trio who hate me. No matter how reluctant we all are in this enforced alliance, I suspect our fates are now entwined forever.

And then, I'm no longer that helpless hustler struggling to survive at the bottom of the Afterworld's food chain. I still can't wrap my head around it, but I'm becoming the warrior Godric has pledged to forge, the one who took on a black hole and won. I may even become the weapon he thinks he can wield in a war to end all wars.

According to him, there's an apocalyptic showdown in the making, maybe the final one this time. With the Devil in the equation, what's coming may be worse than he thinks, or my worst-case-scenario mind can imagine.

Knowing I can theorize until the celestial cows come home, I close my eyes, and let everything go, one last thought echoing in my drifting mind.

Even if I am in the eye of the impending cosmic storm, I say bring it.

Just not today.

EPILOGUE

GODRIC

Beyond a roiling cloud cover, a full moon struggles to illuminate the bitterly cold night. It only races turbulent shadows over me, echoing those slithering within my mind as I hover outside her window.

I'm watching her sleep. When I scoffed at the very idea on her first day at the Academy.

It's beyond ridiculous, yet I can't move. Like I couldn't that fateful night when I first heard her voice.

"Are you my birthday surprise?"

These preposterous words, spoken in her soft, scalding tones, hit me worse than my father's paralyzing Grace ever did. Totally unexpected and confounding. Just like every word out of her mouth ever since.

From that moment forward, it has all been—inconceivable. Everything I've felt, and done.

All through the past two months, I've rationalized risking all I did for her. First because the archangels demanded it, then because I recognized her power's cataclysmic potential, and my need for it.

But how can I explain what I did when she was at the Trials?

If that bloody realm hasn't stopped me, I would have transferred all my Energy to her. At the unspeakable cost of vulnerability. When I have too many enemies who would have pounced on the opportunity. They wouldn't have been able to kill me still, but they could have done worse, even thrown me in the deepest pit of *Carcerem*. I would have had no use for her power then. I would have forfeited my lifelong plans.

I can't even imagine the consequences.

Yet I was still willing to do it.

Fool.

I snarl at that maddening inner voice and its favorite name for me of late.

No. Not a fool. A madman. Only one would think of such a catastrophic gamble, let alone enact it.

And I believed not touching her was the best resolution I ever made, and almost killed myself to keep to it. But abstaining from ravishing her has only messed with my mind, and shredded my control. *She* has.

And that was before I made my worst mistake yet. Before I kissed her.

Now, they're almost upon me. I felt them coming from miles away, but had no intention of evading them, or even hiding what I'm doing. I actually welcome their intrusion. If it weren't for their approach, I would have stormed back into that room, and taken her right there and then, whether she wanted me to or not.

But she wants me to. The prod of her desire has been like barbed wires wrapping tighter around my every nerve. Even in sleep, I feel her reaching out with the tendrils of her bottomless greed, tearing at my own inexorable hunger.

So let them come. Let their conflict distract me from her consuming compulsion.

Turning with a tranquility I've left far behind, I watch them exchange a tense glance. It's good to see them uneasy in my presence. And that's when they know nothing of my truth.

If they did, they'd do everything in their collective power to end me.

I feel the agreement passing between them a moment before the breaker of teleportation crashes over me. My wrath towers at their presumption, then higher when I realize the destination they picked. My private quarters, where I never allow anyone.

For moments, a fraction of what I feel escapes my compromised control. Before they can register discomfort, let alone pain, I clamp down over the tide of my power. They should never suspect what I'm capable of.

"You should have let her die."

The words feel like that spiked whip that once flayed my flesh off my bones.

For I know they're true. I should have ended her life that first night.

What her very power did to me, even before I laid eyes on her, have been grounds for execution in my book. Then I saw her, and with that first lash of her challenge, something unknown and unstoppable lurched within me, came into being. It unfurled and grew with every second near her. I knew it would continue to invade me as long as she breathed.

That night, I wanted to unleash myself on her, glut myself with her, before snuffing out the impossible flame of her existence. I told myself only the archangels' interest in her stayed my hand.

I've long admitted that was a lie. I wanted her alive. I wanted her, period. When I never wanted anyone before. I now crave her, far more than I do vengeance and annihilation.

"What do you have to say for yourself?"

I watch them, invading my sanctum, and add it to their offenses. "You must be mistaking me for some subordinate. I tolerate you at my discretion. I have none right now."

Their stances and gazes harden. Wisely, they don't act on their affront.

"The malfunctioning Gate was the perfect opportunity."

"This is the second one you actively wasted to be rid of her."

"If you want to so much, why don't *you* do it?" I interrupt. "You killed countless humans, after all, for far less reasons."

And that's when they want her dead only as a precaution. They know nothing of her truth, either.

Not that I know everything myself. I am still putting the pieces of her puzzle together. I suspect it's far bigger than even I can imagine. If *they* suspect any of it, they would do anything to end her.

I'd stop them, even at the cost of killing them all. The consequences of that would make the brewing internal war I started on her account seem like a children's spat.

I still can't believe what she's done to me.

But from that first night, she's been mine. Mine to torment, to

417

temper. Mine to control and covet. When I fully lose my mind, she'll be mine to possess and plunder.

"We would have gotten rid of her, if it were possible. But we cannot be connected to her—demise."

"Of course." I scoff. "Now that taking a human life would cause you trouble, you want her blood on someone else's hands, either be commission or omission. Such nobility and courage."

"You forget your place, Godric."

"I forget *nothing*."

The silence that follows my bark makes me fear they realized a truth I never intended to reveal. I'm in even worse condition than I thought if I let that slip.

"Then remember your place in all this. It was you who put the wheels in motion."

"I'm merely trying to finish what you started."

"Because it serves the only purpose you have; your revenge."

I don't answer at once, my gaze sliding between them, trying to gauge if they did understand. There's no indication of the wariness that should be the only sane response if they did.

Knowing I can do nothing about it now either way, I exhale. "My motives are none of your concern. I will do what I need to do, the way I need to do it. You do your part the way you see fit. But you will not question me again, or infringe on my...turf."

They exchange another glance. This time I know they heard my threat. Loud and clear. But they need me too much now to antagonize me any further.

Without another word, a flash fills my quarters, and they're gone. Just seconds before I brought the whole tower down on everyone in it.

I need to vent the violence of my emotions far from here. Emotions I'm not supposed to have. I was not made to feel what others are allowed to. I should never risk losing control.

But I fear it's too late.

Flames are already consuming me.

It takes me moments to realize they're real. And that I've burned off my sweatshirt.

No, not me. Her rune has. What has appeared within my seal. Over my very heart.

I stare at the fiery mark. She has somehow carved herself into my flesh, by what has felt like the hand of fate itself.

After what I was willing to do to have her back, I can no longer deny what it means.

I am hers, too.

I can't think of a bigger disaster.

I have killed everyone who came close to me. Before this war is over, I will most probably kill the rest. And If I succeed in making her my ultimate weapon, I will kill her, too.

I no longer want to. I never wanted to. But I may have no choice.

I have always been, and will always be, a destroyer.

And since I am hers, when it finally comes down to it, she'll be mine to end.

Thank you for reading my debut book, CELESTIAL ACADEMY: Essence!

If you enjoyed the journey with Wen, Godric and the rest of their reluctant team so far, their trials are just beginning.
To continue their epic adventures Pre-Order CELESTIAL ACADEMY: NEXUS, book 2 of 5 in the Afterworld series today!

To support my own journey in bringing you more Afterworld tales, your word of mouth and reviews are *vital* to me as a debut indie author! Even a couple of lines or a rating can lead new readers to my work and help make it a success!

I would truly appreciate you posting a review on: Amazon, Goodreads, Bookbub and any of your social platforms.
Thank you so much in advance for every word you volunteer!
Also come join the discussion of everything CELESTIAL ACADEMY and AFTERWORLD in my Private Facebook Private Reader Group, Pharos Phanatics!

Thank you again for reading, and see you in the next book!
Olivia

Would you like a FREE prequel starring Godric?
Get OMEN (available soon), when you sign up to my
VIP Newsletter at www.oliviapharos.com.

About the Author

Olivia revels in creating addictive tales in richly-imagined worlds, each heavily-spiced with complex characters, unpredictable relationships, realms-shaking twists—and soul-searing passion.

She lives in Florida with her family, both human and feline. When not writing, Olivia can be found cooking, painting, exercising, watching paranormal/fantasy series (she insists it's research!) and chatting with readers on social media. But mostly, she's eavesdropping on her characters, and planning ever more heart-wrenching crusades and conflicts for them.

Currently, she is hard at work expanding the AFTERWORLD universe, and mercilessly complicating the lives and relationship of her hero and heroine.

You can continue their adventures in the next books, COMING SOON!
    CELESTIAL ACADEMY: Nexus
    CELESTIAL ACADEMY: Schism
    CELESTIAL ACADEMY: Oblivion
    CELESTIAL ACADEMY: Apocalypse

For first-look updates, exclusive content and giveaways, and a chance to join her ARC/Street Team, please sign up to her VIP Newsletter, and join her Private Reader Group. and follow her on her social media here:

GLOSSARY

Celestial Hierarchy (so far…)

Seraphim:
   Metatron: Seraph of life and knowledge

Archangels:
   Ariel: Archangel of nature and nourishment
   Azrael: Archangel of Death
   Gabriel: Archangel of messagings and the word
   Jegudiel: Archangel of leadership
   Jeremiel: Archangel of dreams and visions
   Jophiel: Archangel of inspiration and enlightenment
   Lycurgus:: Archangel of sportsmanship
   Michael: Archangel of warfare
   Oriphiel: Archangel of wilderness
   Raguel: Archangel of justice
   Raphael: Archangel of healing
   Raziel: Archangel of secrets and mysticism
   Uriel: Archangel of portals and seers

Designated Celestials:
   Cherubim
   Thrones

Dominions
Virtues
Principalities
Powers

Non-Designated Celestials
Angels

Semi-celestials
Nephilim

Hosts of Celestial Academy:

After the Imperium Trials, according to their category and level of powers, the cadets are assigned to one of the four hosts:

Regulus Host: named after the fixed star of Archangel Raphael, the watcher of the North.

Fomalhaut Host: Archangel Gabriel's, the watcher of the South.

Aldebaran Host: Archangel Michael's, the watcher of the East.

Antares Host: Archangel Uriel's, the watcher of the West.

Printed in Great Britain
by Amazon